WEM-BER-LEE WARRIORS

DEDICATION

This book is dedicated to my wife Sonya,
and my children Yasmin and William
Also to the rest of my family,
especially my parents Dave and Kath.

RIVERHEAD

A CIP catalogue record for this book is
available from the British Library

ISBN 978-0-9567782-1-5

Design and Production by Riverhead, Hull
44-46 High Street, Hull, East Yorkshire. HU1 1PS
Telephone: 01482 318218
email: mike@riverheadbooks.karoo.co.uk

Printed by: John Boland Print, Hull

FOREWORD

The Challenge Cup Final is a special time in the Rugby League calendar. I was lucky enough to have played in it on many occasions and played in the 1992 Final and was honoured to lead Castleford out at the Old Wembley Stadium.

Unfortunately the result didn't go our way that day.

But the Challenge Cup Final is more than just the 80 minutes on the pitch it's about the Event that is the Rugby League Challenge Cup and all its tradition. It's about the fans from all the clubs coming together to celebrate one of the sporting events of the year.

I can still remember going down Wembley Way and seeing all the colours of the fans from all the clubs integrating and sharing the moment, because whether you are a player, coach, referee or fan, Wembley is a special place and scenes like this will stay with me forever.

In fact if I hadn't been playing that day I would have been there as a fan on a local Wembley trip to watch the greatest sport of all, Rugby League. I guess you could say I would have been one of the thousands of Wem-ber-lee Warriors

LEE CROOKS

ACKNOWLEDGEMENTS

I would like to thank all the people I have had the pleasure of playing with or against and the friends I have made through the great game of Rugby League.
Also, all the people that are involved in this great sport and the great characters that make it so special.
A special mention goes to two friends George Youngs and Paul 'Curly' Quinney who are no longer with us but are in our thoughts constantly when remembering the good times we had.

Thanks also to:
Cooper Construction at
cooperservices@cooperservices.karoo.co.uk
for all your building needs.
LeeCrooks
Mike Sterriker at Riverhead Publishing
JM Sports
Kev and Sally Farnhill at Barkers Newsagents Cottingham.

CONTENTS

Wembley captured my imagination and has always been a special place to me ever since the first time I saw that bright green turf as a young boy on my first trip in 1978 with Kinloss School.

The first adult Wembley trip I went on was in 1983 and was a real eye-opener to the magical world that is the Wembley trip and the fantastic three days of mixing and having a laugh with the best people, Rugby League people.

The Wembley trip is a tradition that should continue forever as it still is THE Rugby League event in my eyes and I will forever be a Wem-ber-lee Warrior.

DAVE ROE

INTRO

The annual pilgrimage to 'that there London'.

Every year thousands of rugby league fans converge on London for the Challenge Cup Final, which is held at the famous Wembley stadium.

For months pubs and clubs collect money from the people who go on the trips so that they can put a little away and not get the full impact of having to pay it all at once. This is a time when people young and old go on the same trips and mix with rugby fans from other teams and towns and drink like there's no tomorrow without any sign of violence or trouble, just good-natured, harmless banter. Club colours are worn and everyone mixes.

This is the story of one of those trips, which if you've never been lucky enough to go on one will give you a little insight into what it's like.

Before you know it you'll find yourself wanting to go on one of these trips. For those privileged enough to go on them every year, they provide a couple of days of relaxation in London, maybe a little bit of mayhem, and the chance of going back to the days when they were single and carefree.

So sit back and enjoy this little insight into a world of chaos and discover what goes on in the mind of a fully-grown man's head, when he is let off the leash with his mates for a weekend...

DAVE ROE

CHAPTER 1
WHAT'S SO GOOD ABOUT SATURDAYS?

It was another cold and rainy Saturday afternoon and in the park thirty players were going at it hammer and tongs.

This is amateur Rugby League and sport in its rawest form. The players train twice a week in less than adequate conditions and turn up on a Saturday to knock eight bells out of each other.

They work all week and this is their leisure time. And despite the cuts and bruises and sometimes broken bones, they all love it. They love everything about it, the banter, the camaraderie and at the end of the match, a well-earned beer. But undoubtedly the thing they all love most is the annual Wembley trip.

There was a buzz in the dressing room before the game, but not about the game, the excitement was about the forthcoming Wembley trip.

They go out and play and forget about pleasure for 80 minutes. They take their sport seriously and the only thing on their minds is winning. An hour and a half later, the final whistle sounds and it's another impressive win for Dockers.

The players shake hands and walk to the dressing rooms chatting about where to go after a few drinks in the clubhouse and already rallying the troops for a big night out.

Jonno has cut his eye and will need stitches, so he arranges to meet everyone later after a visit to the local hospital. As for the rest of the boys it's a quick shower and then into the bar for a well-earned beer and to organise the night ahead and the meeting for the Wembley trip.

The boys who are going on the trip sort out the meeting for 12 o'clock the next day so that the ones with families don't have the full day wasted. Eddie gets the senior players together to see what is planned and what kind of coach is required.

'What kind of bus do you want lads?' asks Eddie.

'Don't care but it has to have a fucking bog on it - no way are we going to London without a bog,' shouts Skip the club captain and leader of virtually everything.

'Aye, do you remember last year? We ended up pissing in empty cans and I'll be fucked if I'm doing that again. I cut me foreskin and was in agony every time I went for a piss,' said Tosser who is Skip's right hand man and best mate.

'Another thing,' interrupted Skip, 'Some silly bastard started offering luke warm cans about, didn't they Thommo?'

'I know and some daft twats couldn't tell the difference, I mean I like a laugh but I can't stand watching blokes having boat races with bottles of piss, it turns my stomach.'

'Okay then lets move on to the hotel, it's a 4 star hotel but it's a bit out of the way,' said Eddie trying to stop the debate raging on about the disadvantages of not having a toilet on a bus.

'4 star! 4 star! Fucking hell, it'll be a 2 star when we've been there, hey Thommo?' said Tosser.

'As long as its got a bar and no cockroaches it'll do me and of course a pool, a Jacuzzi, naked maidens to pamper my every whim and decent towels that I can take our lass home for a present I'll be happy. I've nicked her towels from all over the country, she's got a great collection, her favourite one is the....'

'Alright, alright, enough of the trip down memory lane with Ronnie Biggs here, let's sort out the trip,' said Eddie trying to cut it short as he'd promised to be home early and he still had to clean out the changing rooms.

'As I was saying the hotel is a bit out of the way so you've been told so you know what to expect.'

'How far is out of the way? We're not staying in Leeds are we?'

'No, it's about a couple of miles out from London, near the Isle of Dogs. But we got it cheap as it's not as busy at weekends.'

'Alright, we'll get thinking and plotting what the theme will be, the debate can start tonight, 7 o'clock in Shoey's pub.'

'Right you lot I'm going to clean your mess up, have a good night, I'll see you tomorrow at 12 and don't be late.'

Eddie departed and Artie the club chairman came round with the raffle.

'Come on lads get your tickets, 1st prize is a joint.'

'What a spliff? Things are looking up,' Thommo chirped up.

'No a beef joint, mind you, you could do with all the drugs you can get your hands on the way you played today'

'15 love to Artie,' this was Skip stirring it as he knew that Artie and Thommo didn't like each other much, Artie thought that Thommo was a waste of space and a twat and Thommo thought Artie was the same.

'Fuck off Artie, I scored didn't I?'

'I could have scored that and I'm waiting for me hip to be done.'

'Artie you couldn't score in a brothel with a £50 note sticking out of your ear, that's if they could spot the £50, you've got a fair bit of growth in those ears, is that why they call you Spud?' Thommo retorted like lightening.

'It's a two-man job them ears - you'd have to get an estimate on clearing them out.' Thommo was now in full flow.

'Last year they refused to syringe your ears as they didn't want a hosepipe ban bringing in.'

'Look, do you want a ticket or not?' Artie said losing his cool.

'Go on then £2 worth. I said £2 pound worth,' Thommo shouted at the top of his voice. 'Did you get that through the undergrowth?'

'I'll swing for you, you shithouse.'

'Not fast enough Artie.'

'Anybody else for this raffle? I'm drawing it at 5,' said Artie, whose ears were ringing by now. Artie had grabbed Thommo's money but hadn't given him his ticket.

'Woo! woo! woo! Where's me ticket you dick?' shouted Thommo.

'Here twat.' Artie just threw his tickets in the general direction the noise was coming from.

'Charming, I love winding that old get up,' said Thommo.

Artie carried on selling the tickets and the rest of the lads bought more beer and waited for the draw to take place.

'Now has everyone got tickets? Because I'm going to draw the winning ticket out,' Artie shouted, trying to get everyone's attention but no one was taking much notice.

'Right then, here goes,' Artie continued.

'Just draw the ticket for god sake,' shouted Tosser.

'We'll have less of that, I'm doing my best.'

'We know but just draw the bloody thing, no one wants any more tickets,' said Skip.

'Okay, here we go - and the winner is 254 on the blue ticket,' announced Artie after he had managed to get the ticket out. After about five minutes of everyone checking their tickets, Thommo who'd just got back from the toilet came running in to hear the last call for the 1st prize.

'Last call for blue 254 or I'll have to re-draw it.'

'254 blue? That's me, I've won, I've won, come here Artie give us a kiss,' and Thommo jumps on Artie's back and tries to kiss him which really pisses him off.

'That's half me board this week I'll tell me mam I've treat her,' said a rather pleased Thommo. As Artie reluctantly handed over the meat, Thommo saw that he wasn't pleased he'd won it.

'Cheer up Artie, might never happen. But it already has, this really sticks in your throat me winning this, well I'll be thinking of you Artie when I sink my teeth into it, oh yes Artie, roasties and a big Yorkshire pudding.'

'You got the bloody pudding bit right, you are a pudding. Hope it bloody chokes yer, you cheeky little sod.'

'No, it'll go down nicely. You couldn't recommend a nice wine to go with it could you Artie?'

'Piss off,' came the reply.

The bar slowly emptied as Dave the miserable barman started to turn the lights on and off as he called last orders.

'Come on time on your glasses now, it's 10 past 5,' Dave announced in his usual, customer-friendly style.

'It's not a fucking disco Dave, leave the lights on, we'll only be a few more minutes you miserably old get.'

'I've got things to do before we open again at 7.'

'Like what? Don't pull it too much, it'll fall off,' chipped in Tag, the team's 'Jack the lad'.

'Ho, ho, come on before me sides split. It's not easy this job you know.'

'He wants to get his head down, he's got a nice warm coffin waiting for him, or is it hanging upside down in the wardrobe?' quipped Skip.

'Has anyone ever told you, you could get work as a Ray Reardon look alike, or as the Count from Sesame Street?' he continued.

'You should be on stage you should, you funny sod, come on time at the bar.'

'We've all finished anyway and we're going.'

'Alright we're going, I'd ask for me money back though if I were you,' said Tag.

'Money back for what?' asked Dave.

'From that school of charm you went to, oh! wes, full refund I'd say.'

'Piss off, see you Tuesday,' said Dave.

'No you won't, we're all back tomorrow to see your happy smiling face and to sample your witty repartee, so see ya tomorrow, missing you already,' said Tag.

'I didn't know you lot would be in tomorrow, I'd better warn the regulars, they won't be pleased,' said Dave shaking his head.

'Who are you trying to kid, you'll triple your takings and the place will be livelier and not one step up from the funeral parlour as it normally is,' Tag answered him back.

Dave wanted to lock up as everyone had gone, but had to have the last word. 'Are you still here?'

'Well I'm waiting for a lift,' replied Tag.

'Not in here you're not.'

'Why?'

'Because I want my tea and I'm locking the doors.'

'So you mean to tell me you expect me to wait outside in the cold and dark?'

'Got it in one. You're not scared are you? See yer.'

'You really are a miserable old bastard aren't you?'

'Yeah I suppose I am, now piss off,' and Dave shuffled Tag out of the club and locked the doors.

Tag went outside just as his lift turned up. He had to rush to get home as he was due out in an hour and a half's time. Actually Tag wasn't going home. He already had his gear on and had decided not to go home for the earache he'd get from his now live in girlfriend Fay. So he went straight to the pub that they were meeting in. All the others who were going out were well on the way to getting ready.

At 7 o'clock, the boys began to arrive one by one full of cuts and bruises from the day's game. They started to drink the first of many beers that would be consumed that night.

'Is Jonesy coming?' asked Trev.

'He's supposed to be, if the dragon lets him out,' replied Tag, who hadn't had any problem getting past his missus as he hadn't bothered to go home, that had been an easy way to avoid any conflict.

'He wants to tell her straight, show her who's boss, who wears the trousers and all that,' he continued.

'Oh yeah! Like you do you windy bastard, you haven't been home yet 'ave yer?' quizzed Skip.

'Well you see it's like this, she can't keep her hands off me especially when I've played, she loves all the scratches and bruises and all that you know it drives her wild see, plus the fact that I'm irresistible and great in bed.'

'Fuck off dreamer,' replied the full pub.

'Is that why she told our lass that you were having problems getting it hard?' scoffed Skip.

'The big-mouthed bitch, wait while I see her, what did she say to your lass?'

'She said fuck all to our lass. So having trouble getting it up are we?'

'Bastard caught me out. Well you know just a couple of times it's just laid there looking up at me, all pathetic like with its one eye but that was a bit ago now last month.'

'Have you tried scaffolding or a splint?'

'Oh very fucking funny, it's not a laughing matter, wait till it happens to you.'

'Me, no way, my soldier stands to attention at the drop of a bra strap, anyway your secret's safe with me, I won't tell anyone'

'Cheers Skip, you're a mate, what do you want to drink?'

'Guinness please.'

The door opened and in walked the last four lads.

'You took your time didn't you, get one in quick and then we'll have to get off, I told the others we'd meet them at half past and we haven't got a taxi yet,' said Skip.

'So then, what's new?' said Jonesy

'What's new, well you being allowed out is for a start. What's new we only saw you two hours ago you soft twat,' said Tag.

'I'm off to drain me spuds,' he continued and then Tag went to the toilet.

'Nothing new except Tag was telling us how he's been having trouble getting it up,' laughed Skip. Tag came out of the toilet just as the laughter stopped.

'Are we ready yet,' said Tag impatiently, as he couldn't wait to get into town to meet the rest of the boys and hit the livelier pubs.

'What's the rush floppy?' sneered Jonesy.

'Yeah, keep your hard on floppy, we're going as fast as we can,' Trev chipped in.

Tag turned to Skip who was by now holding his sides with tears running down his face and shouted, 'You lousy bastard, you fucking lousy bastard, that's the last time I tell you anything - and I bought you a beer.'

'And very tasty it was too,' said Skip as he finished it off.

Then the whole party of lads went outside to the taxi rank. Within minutes they were in taxis and on their way to town. Inside the taxi, Tag started his usual taxi patter. He did this without fail to every taxi driver he met.

'Alright driver, been busy?'

'Yes all night. You out all night then?' answered the driver.

'Yeah, ready for a big one. Can I ask you driver, are you divorced?'

If the driver answers 'yes' then Tag starts his usual line of questioning.

'Yeah mate, I'm divorced, why?'

'I told you didn't I lads they're all divorced or single these taxi drivers, it's the hours see, am I right mate? Course I am. I mean you go for a last minute kebab before going home the old Stavros is a bit slow with the chilli sauce you're 10 minutes late and the missus thinks you've got a bird. Then it's the divorce courts due to adultery and all because Stav was too slow.'

'I don't eat kebabs' the driver said as he finally gets to answer.

'Well that brings me onto my next question you must get some offers eh! You know 'I've not got enough how about I give you a quick 'BJ' and we call it quits' '

'Why are you offering' replies the driver stopping Tag in his tracks.

'No, no you know what I mean some bit of skirt, your wife finds out and that's it, Tammy Wynette time - D.I.V.O.R.C.E. - it's tragic.'

'It might be that he couldn't get it up any more eh driver 'cos Tag's having trouble in that department aren't you Tag?' said Skip trying to give the driver a bit of peace.

'I've fucking told you about that in confidence you twat,' said Tag.

'Listen if you must know although its none of your fucking business it was a bit of skirt actually,' said the driver.

'Told you didn't I, the old 'Tagmeister' knows you see, was she worth it?'

'I don't know you'd have to ask my wife she was the one with the bit of skirt not me,' said the driver. 'This is your stop here.' the driver pulled over for them to get out.

'Fuck it, take us around the block one more time, we can't leave it at that, finish the story.' Tag couldn't have gone all night not knowing what had happened. So the driver carried on with the story as he drove them around the block.

'Well I just called in to my house for a leak and there they were at it in the fucking living room, her and the young babysitter, a student with big tits she was.'

The car was silent until Tag interrupted, 'What did you do? Did you join in?'

'Well at first no but we came to some arrangement and I ended up videoing them and selling about a thousand copies and that's why we got divorced.'

'Fucking hell driver you're a dark one, a threesome and a porn baron.'

'Right, that's the story and we've been around the block that'll be £10.'

'£10? It's normally only £6,' said Tag.

'I know but we went around the block three times didn't we.'

'It's fucking daylight robbery,' said Tag

'Just pay him,' shouted Skip who was already at the door of the pub.

Tag paid for the taxi and as he was about to go into the pub the driver shouted from the window of his cab, 'By the way 'floppy', if you believe all that bullshit I told you, I've got loads more where that came from! Have a good night you gullible bastard.'

The driver then sped off and Tag was left fuming.

'Can you believe that cheeky twat?' said Tag.

'Jesus Tag, don't you remember him? He brought us home last week and you gave him a really hard time, so looks like he's got his own back,' said Skip.

'Anyway what do you want? It's my round.'

'Oh I'll have a Babycham,' said Tag sarcastically.

With that the door opened and the rest of the boys came in ready for the night out.

'Fuck me it's Tosser, how did you get out?' said Pete, the club wind up merchant and Tosser's other best mate.

'Don't ask, just don't ask, but all I'll say is this, it's not looking good for the trip to London. I've promised to take her away that weekend,' said Tosser.

'You've done what? You prick you won't get out of that one,' laughed Pete.

'I know she was going on about, you never take me anywhere and I thought to myself play it cool, and then I heard myself saying well, where do you want to go? And she said, I wouldn't mind going to Wembley to see what all the fuss is about.'

'No, no, no you must be joking, she doesn't even like rugby and acting daft and getting pissed, I hope you told her to piss off,' said Pete.

Tosser looked down at the ground.

'You weak bastard, you weak, selfish bastard – you were my roomy, now I'll end up with God knows who,' blasted Pete.

'Thanks for thinking of me and my marriage, anyway I never said yes, well at first I did, that was yesterday and I went to work and thought she'd forget about it. But tonight she mentioned it again and then she accused us of going on one long 'shag-a-thon' for the weekend, so I told her that I had to go as the taxi was waiting and just left it really,' said Tosser.

'That's it then, you've no chance now have yer? You'll go home tonight, she'll start playing with your cock and then get you to sign the contract she's typing up right now for you to take her to London,' said Pete. But he then thought for a minute and came up with a great idea.

'Yes, that's it,' he shouted

'What's it?'

'We'll get all the disgruntled women to have their own night out on the weekend we're away. Am I a genius or what?'

'Well I could try, see if she goes for it,' smiled Tosser.

'Here lads, how about getting the girls to organise their own night out while we're away,' announced Pete.

'What about baby sitters and all that?' asked Trev.

'Look, don't worry about the women, they can sort themselves out. It's ages away yet, Toss your lass will have forgotten by next week.'

'I don't think so, she seems pretty determined.'

Skip came back from the bar and handed everyone their drinks but left Tag until the end.

'What the fucking hell is that?' shouted Tag.

'A Babycham, that's what you asked for. Take out the umbrella and cherry if you want Tag,' laughed Skip.

'Funny, funny, you know what I drink.'

'And that's why I bought you a lager as well so put your dummy back in and drink up,' said Skip.

'Is everyone here?' enquired Skip.

'No, Jonno isn't. He rang to say he'll meet us in The Bush at half eight,' said Trev. 'He's had twelve stitches and can't see out of his eye.'

'Well look on the bright side, he'll only be able to see half their lass which is a blessing. I mean between me and you, she's no oil painting is she? They have a picture of her above the fire to scare the kids away,' said Jonesy.

'Do you mind, he's my mate but I see what you mean, Christ knows what she looks like with no make-up on,' said Trev

'Like a bulldog licking piss off a nettle,' Gaz the 'posty' chipped in.

'How do you know? said Jonesy.

'Well I was doing some overtime on her round and I had a packet for her and she answered the door without any make-up on,' said Gaz.

'Was you sick?'

'I'll tell you what though, she's got a great pair of tits, I didn't take much notice of the face, she just looked the same to me.'

'I can vouch for her tits, we went away for a weekend and went swimming she's very fit if you know what I mean and I don't mean she can do loads of press-ups,' said Trev in a trance.

'Trev snap out of it, you didn't did you?'

'Didn't what?'

'You know, have a feel after a couple of drinks?'

'No I fucking didn't. He's a mate and you don't shit on your own patch,' said Trev. 'Wouldn't mind though if I had a bag to put over her face. I mean she's no Linda Lusardi is she now?' he continued.

'You're right there Trev. Bella Emberg maybe but certainly no Linda Lusardi,' agreed Gaz.

Meanwhile across town at Tosser's house, the girls were already more than one step ahead of Pete. They were organising not just a night out but a weekend away in Blackpool. The trip was to be top secret and they were all sworn to secrecy. They had all just popped in for a quick meeting but the real meeting, which was 'disguised' as a clothes party, was to take place the following night.

'Right girls we'll meet here tomorrow for the clothes party and I'll be able to go through it with you then. But up to now we're having a weekend in Blackpool while the blokes are in London,' announced Skip's wife Mandy.

'So is this trip a secret then?' asked Jonesy's wife Sue.

'Too bloody right it is don't even think of telling them,' replied Mandy.

'So then, what we'll do is act normally all week and on the Friday they go at 8.30 in the morning, which gives us plenty of time. Our bus leaves in town at five so that all those with kids or work can get sorted and then it's Blackpool here we come, are there any questions?' asked Tosser's wife Clare.

The room went silent for a second then Trev's wife Cary said, 'Can't we just tell them and have done with it, I hate lying to Trevor. I mean he's great really and he wouldn't stop me going.'

'Yeah but you tell your Trev and they'll all find out and they all aren't as understanding as your Trev believe me,' said Tag's girlfriend Fay.

Tosser's wife Clare intervened, 'We can't tell them, it's got to be a secret, just do what I've done, ask to go to London with them to see what all the fuss is about. I'll tell you what Tosser nearly had a heart attack when I brought that one up.'

'You did what? What did he say?' said Fay.

'Alright, we'll see - and then he left for work. That was yesterday and I asked again tonight but he hasn't said anything about booking anything. But I could see his little brain ticking over, thinking how the fuck am I going to get out of this one?' said Clare.

'You see he's that worried about what he's going to tell his mates he's not going to give a shit in the end what I do as long as it's not going on his trip with him and his mates. And he'll even pay for me to go and buy me a new outfit because he'll be that relieved that I no longer want to go to London, he'll virtually give me his wallet'.

'Jesus! do you think it'll work? Shall we all do the same?' said the girls.

'I'm not sure,' said Trev's wife, Cary. 'I don't like lying to Trevor.' 'Well just bring the subject up tomorrow and see what he does to get out of it and I can guarantee he'll shit himself,' laughed Fay. She was all for it and slightly annoyed in a strange way that it hadn't been her who had thought of the idea, as she liked to think that she was quite the devious one.

'No it has to be a secret. Because what if they all said yeah come along? So, just keep quiet about it. Is that okay Cary?'

'Alright I'm in,' said Cary, knowing full well that she would tell Trev the situation but swear him to secrecy.

They all agreed that it had to be a secret and that it would be fun and exciting to keep it that way.

'Right, see you all tomorrow night for the clothes party at seven,' said Clare winking. They all started to leave, already starting to look forward to the trip.

Back in town with the boys, Tag was about to tell Skip and Gaz a secret.

'I'm not going to London lads,' announced Tag.

'Fuck off,' said Skip after spitting his beer out and nearly choking.

'No really, I'm not, I'm going to Blackpool with Suki.'

'You're going to Blackpool on a Suzuki?' said Gaz.

'No, I'm being serious, we're going on a weekend of passion and filth, the likes of which you've never even seen or heard of. So please don't tell anyone else, there's only you two who I've told.'

'And what does Fay think about all this then?' enquired Skip.

'Fucking hell, she doesn't know, she'd kill me or should I say her huge brothers would, they can't stand me anyway.'

'One question,' said Gaz, 'Who is Suki?'

'She's the receptionist at work and she's fucking lovely. I saw her out a couple of months back when you bastards abandoned me in La La's. She said 'Hiya' and we got talking.'

'Hello - is it me you're looking for?' sang Gaz.

'Very funny, but really it's a big secret, don't tell anyone.'

'What you gonna do about the trip? Someone is bound to say you didn't go and where does that leave yer?'

'I've only paid a deposit and I'll explain to Eddie the day before.'

'How long has this been going on then? You know shagging and that?' asked Gaz.

'I've been seeing her about twice a week for 6 to 7 weeks, but the problem is she doesn't know about Fay.'

'Jesus! you don't do things by half do you? How the fucking hell are you going to keep this one going? If your dick doesn't fall off, you'll die of exhaustion. Hang on a minute is this where the hard on problems have come from?' said Skip

'You want to give Pete a ring he can help you out with that one,' quipped Gaz.

'Well I'm only human and this Suki well she goes like a Suzuki and I've nothing left for Fay.'

That boast was bullshit on Tag's part as Suki had only kissed him and sex hadn't even been approached. That was the reason for the 'dirty weekend' but he thought he would look stupid if he told his mates - so he put on a macho front - but in fact he couldn't get it up because he'd gone off Fay.

'Hang on a minute that's why you're always late for training and don't go home after a game, you lousy bastard Tag. Come clean and finish it one way or another,' fumed Skip who liked Fay and could see what Tag couldn't, all the hurt and anguish it would cause to everyone involved.

'I'm going to after this weekend in Blackpool.'

'Was this weekend your idea?' said Gaz

'No, it was hers and she's promised me if I show her a good time then she'll show me one.'

'You want to watch it, she could be a nutter. I mean she's got all your details at work, what's to stop her ringing you up at home and your lass answering it?' said Gaz who had encountered this kind of situation many times before.

'All the details I have at work are for me mam's house and she hardly speaks to Fay.'

'Got it all sorted out haven't we?'

'Well I hope so,' said Tag.

'This Suki then, she doesn't know about Fay and Fay doesn't know about her, if they both catch you it'll be curtains son for you,' warned Skip.

'I know but I'll see what happens and take my chances.'

Across town Grant the student was on his first night as a delivery boy for the local Indian 'Curries 'R' Us' where Mr. Khan and his brother are the proprietors.

'Hello Mr Grant, good to see you and on time to, I hope you're not a work shy lazy bastard like the last one we had,' Mr Khan said.

'No, I love graft me, can't get enough of it,' replied Grant who thought he would get all the free curry he wanted and get paid for the privilege.

'Good, this is how it works, all you do is go out with the orders and deliver them and collect the money and then you come back for more orders. If you get any tips, you can keep them. Any questions?'

'No, it all seems straight forward.'

'Right do you know where you are going, do you know the area?' asked Mr Khan.

'Yeah, I've lived here all my life,' said Grant enthusiastically

'Right, here are your orders. Take them, then come back as soon as you've delivered the last one and there will be some more to take out.'

'What now?' said a shocked Grant who thought he could have had something to eat and then start work, he was starving.

'Yes now, it's your job. That's what you're here for, to deliver food. Now on your way and don't take any shit from anyone. They'll try every trick in the book to get something off - tell them to G.F. - which means Get Fucked.'

So Grant took the orders and got into his dad's old car, as he didn't have one of his own and his dad had two. His dad had leant him the car, but in fact he would have probably bought him one, as he was so pleased to see his couch empty again. He'd almost forgotten what colour it was, as all Grant seemed to do was lay on it and watch telly. Grant drove off with the orders.

'Shall we put another advert in the window, 'cos he won't last long,' asked Mr. Khan's brother, Imrie.

'No, we'll give him a go, I know his dad, he is a good man and he'll make sure he doesn't let us down. Besides we haven't had many takers have we? And we advertised for a month and I'm not delivering it myself, fuck that. You don't have a dog and wag your own tail do you?' said Mr Khan.

The owner had helped Grant by sorting out the orders in the best way of delivering them and had given him a float, which was his own money for the night's work. If he made a mess and gave out the wrong change it was his money he was losing. The thought had crossed Grant's mind to dump the curries or eat them and take the money and join the lads for a night out. But two things stopped him. Firstly he wanted to get on the London trip and secondly he didn't want his dad to go to prison for murder - his murder! So he carried on to his first call because if he made a mess of this job his dad would kill him.

He didn't need to knock at the first house, the people were waiting at the door for him. It was a big, burly bloke with arms like railway sleepers. He was huge.

'Where the fuck have you been?' said the big, burly bloke.

Grant looked worried as it looked as if the man was going to kick off.

'Do we get discount for cash then?' the bloke asked.

Grant still looked worried and didn't dare say anything.

'Only joking son, keep the change,' said the man laughing as Grant's face went from despair to joy and relief at the fact he wasn't going to get filled in over a cold korma. The man took the food and Grant was on his way to his next call.

This is alright, thought Grant. I'll pretend I've hardly got any change and they'll probably tip me. This thought soon went out of his head when on his next call they had the correct change. The next house claimed not to have ordered anything at all, then tried to get the food for half price but Grant kept his cool and said he would take it back. The owner of the house suddenly remembered that his wife had ordered it and out of embarrassment gave him a £2 tip.

There was only one more call left and then back for more, but by this time Grant was starving and the smell of the food was driving him crazy. He got to the last call, which was a block of flats and the flat was on the top floor so he pressed the buzzer and the voice told him to come in.

He got into the lift, pressed the floor number and was on his way but by that time the smell of the food was unbearable. Fuck it thought Grant, I'll have a couple of chips, no one will be any the wiser. So he carefully opened the bag containing the chips and got a handful out and ate them and then wrapped them up again. Boy, did they taste good. The lift arrived on the top floor and Grant got out. He knocked on the door of the flat but got the surprise of his life as the door flung open and a very irate woman started to shout at him.

'Enjoy my fucking chips did yer? You greedy little bastard, give me that here,' she said grabbing the food.

'Can you whistle? Well you can whistle for your money, you thieving twat! I watched you on the CCTV in the lift eating my chips, now fuck off!' And she slammed the door. Grant tried to think quickly and opened the letterbox to protest that he'd only had a few.

'Come on Mrs. Taylor, it's my first night and I've had no tea and if you don't pay me, that's my wages up the spout. I'll give you discount for the chips,' pleaded Grant remembering it was his money it would come out of.

'Fuck off. I'm ringing that place and telling them what's happened, you had me bhaji as well you thieving little shit,' continued the lady.

'Fucking bhaji? Now you're trying it on you stupid cow, I haven't touched your bhaji,' shouted Grant, remembering the customer is always right.

'I'm going to call security if you don't fuck off this minute,' shouted Mrs Taylor.

So Grant went back to the curry house to collect more deliveries thinking that he was now well down on his wages and that he would have to try and get some more tips to make his money up. And hoping that Mrs. Taylor, the silly bitch, hadn't rung up and complained.

'How did that go young Grant?' enquired Mr Khan.

'Great, not a problem, you were right though, they do try it on but I handled it pretty well,' replied Grant with a certain amount of confidence that he hadn't been rumbled.

'Right, there are your orders for your next trip. Be quick, as we will have more for you when you get back. They are all in order for you so you can get back quickly.'

'Great,' said Grant thinking it had all blown over

'Hungry are we?' said Imrie

'Err, well yes, now you come to mention it, yes very hungry,' said Grant thinking a free curry was on its way.

'Well have your bloody tea before you come here and don't start nicking the fucking customer's food you dozy twat. You are a student yes? You are clever yes? Well give me one good reason why I don't sack you right now?' shouted Mr Khan.

'Because you can't get anyone else to do this,' replied Grant thinking that if Mr. Khan was going to sack him, he would anyway.

'Good point,' said Mr. Khan stumped for an answer.

'Well, don't go eating the customer's food. We don't have many rules but that is one of them, alright? And you won't be very pleased about one of these next deliveries. Mrs Taylor rang again to say that if you deliver her a bag of chips and a bhaji, which she never ordered in the first place and pay for it, she will give you the money for the other food. So come on, pay for the chips and bhaji and we'll say no more about it,' said Mr. Khan holding his hand out for the money.

Grant handed the money over which meant that all his tips had gone and went on his way.

'Another lamb to the slaughter poor lad. Tarty Taylor the temptress is at it again, we'd better give him an extra half an hour to get back,' said Mr Khan laughing as he said it.

'Why?' said Imrie

'That women, it's her who is the man-eater. She goes through delivery boys like tissues and I think she has taken a fancy to young Grant. He'll be getting more than a couple of chips. I think she asked for extra hot sauce on the chips if you know what I mean?'

'The one that lives in the flats?' asked Imrie

'Yes Imrie, I thought you delivered to her two weeks ago, she is a regular and a good customer. I myself have delivered there and she was very 'forthcoming'. I could have had a bit of fun there but no I am a man of integrity, besides I had to get back. She walks about with hardly anything on it's a wonder she doesn't catch her death by cold'

'I know,' replied Imrie sheepishly and looking away.

'No, no, no, no, no I don't believe it, my brother doing the do with Tarty Taylor,' said Mr Khan

'What, you must be joking,' said Imrie trying to sound convincing.

'You are the worse liar in the world Imrie Khan. You told me that you were stuck in traffic, you dirty randy little bastard. One question Imrie, you never committed the cardinal sin did you?'

'What adultery?'

'No, not adultery, discount. You never gave her discount did you?'

'No,' replied Imrie not too convincingly.

'Are you sure you didn't say you would give her 20% off when she had your cock in her hand. We are trying to run a business here. It's all well and good you wasting time being abused but we are trying to run a business. You dirty little Indian.'

'I had no choice, she answered the door with no clothes on and then bent down to pick her bag up. I didn't stand a chance but she never asked for discount, you won't tell Isha will you?' pleaded Imrie.

'Oh yes, when I come around tomorrow the first thing I'm going to say to your wife is, 'Hey Isha, guess what, Imrie was up to his nuts in guts the other week with a customer who is the one who eats delivery boys for breakfast. What do you take me for now I think it's time you made me a cup of tea don't you?' said Mr Khan.

'Yeah I suppose so but let's hear no more of it please,' said Imrie.

'Just one more thing, did you use protection?' enquired Mr Khan.

'Oh yes, she got out this big box of 'jonnies'. She must do it for a hobby,' said Imrie.

'Fucking hell, would you believe it, my brother and Tarty Taylor, is nothing sacred?' Mr Khan said with his mouth wide open.

Meanwhile Grant was on his way to the flats, shitting himself and thinking what he was going to say to this woman. He had decided on,

'I'm very sorry and it won't happen again'.

He got to the flats and buzzed up to be let in and was very surprised when a very welcoming voice greeted him. He didn't think this was odd and proceeded to the lifts, this time checking out where the cameras where and not daring to do anything but stare at the floor. To his surprise as he approached the flat the door was open and he heard a voice say, 'Come in. I'll be there in a minute just shut the door behind you.'

So he did as he was told and was rehearsing his lines in his head when from out of the bedroom came Tarty Taylor, the black widow. She had set her trap and was now going to devour her pray to satisfy her sexual needs. Grant tried to get the words out of his carefully prepared apology but the words wouldn't come out. Before he knew what was going on she started to kiss him and feel his cock. She grabbed his hand and placed it on her breast and Grant thought, actually she's not too bad for her age. This continued for a few minutes and then Grant tried to speak.

'I, I'm...' tried Grant.

'Come with me,' demanded Tarty, taking him by the hand and then ripping at his clothing whilst leading him to the bedroom.

Grant tried to resist but once she had put his aroused cock in her mouth he thought fuck it, enjoy it and he began to join in. He parted her legs and began to lick her very hairy box whilst trying hard not to shoot his load too soon . He at least wanted to look like he had some experience, even though he didn't except for a couple of 'knee-tremblers' after the college disco.

Tarty looked like she had Don King in a headlock down there. Then she did something that he never expected and put her index finger right up his arse. Instead of letting out a scream he ejaculated but this was no ordinary coming, he thought he'd blown the woman's head off, it was like a volcano erupting. She carried on sucking whilst he was trying to pull away, the only time a man doesn't want his cock sucking is a minute after he's just come, it was like a bruised peach.

'Like that did you?' she asked. '

Stay there, we'll have the chips and you can shag me,' she continued, she had a way with words.

'I've got to get back to work,' protested Grant realising what had just happened.

'I'll ring and say you've got a puncture,' said Tarty.

'Err, okay then,' said Grant, frightened what might happen if he said he was going.

So she rang Mr. Khan with the excuse and then they ate the chips. Mr Khan smiled as he put the phone down as he of course knew exactly what had gone on.

Back at the flat Tarty had noticed Grant had some scars from the day's game. This turned her on even more and she proceeded to play with him again and then while he lay there she began to ride him like a bucking bronco. Grant didn't mind too much as she was fit for her age and knew exactly what she was doing. He had never experienced anything like it in his life. When she had finished they said their goodbyes and Grant went back to work with his cock throbbing and his head in a spin. Could that have really just happened, he thought. He couldn't wait to tell everyone about it.

When he got back to the Indian, Mr. Khan had made him a cup of tea and he then told Grant to have a quick break. Just as he sat down Mr. Khan piped up,

'Terrible those estates for glass and things aren't they?'

'Err, yeah terrible,' said Grant trying not to talk about what had gone on, as what had happened had finally started to hit him.

'Good of the lady to ring and tell us about it, I mean she wanted your cock and bollocks on a plate earlier on,' Mr. Khan added staring at Grant.

'Yeah, she was pretty good about it, even gave me a tip,' Grant replied, trying to cover up what had really happened.

'Come off it you randy little bastard, she got your cock and bollocks didn't she? You've been shagging haven't you?' scoffed Mr. Khan

'No,' retorted Grant.

'Yes you have, Tarty Taylor has claimed another victim, another delivery boy has bit the dust.'

'You mean she does it to all the delivery boys?' asked Grant

'Ah! So you were shagging, you mucking dirty stinky little student, so tell us all about it.'

'Yeah, come on split the peas,' said Imrie.

'Spill the beans you mean,' said Mr Khan. So Grant started to tell the tale.

'Well, you know, she just kissed me and tried it on but I said that I couldn't and I had to get back to work.'

'Bullshit, bullshit, we both know there is nothing to be ashamed of, it's only natural, let's hope her husband doesn't find out with him being a bouncer and all, he goes out on a Saturday and she has her fun with the take away delivery boy.'

'A bouncer, where?' asked Grant, now really shitting himself and panicking.

'That club in town, he's the big bastard with the bald head, a real nasty piece, he comes in here later on I'll introduce you, tell him you've been keeping his missus warm and supplied with gratis chips and bhajis.'

Mr Khan was now in his element, he didn't actually know if Tarty was married or not.

'Fuck off, I don't want to meet him. I'm only a fucking student and I've just turned 18, he'll fucking kill me. I know the one you mean, big scar down his face, he's as big as the flats,' said Grant now getting even more nervous.

'Don't worry, he's only pulling your pisser, she isn't married, she's divorced. Her ex comes in here for a korma every Sunday, he's a nice man,' said Imrie putting Grant out of his misery.

'Thank fuck for that, I thought I was going to have to get a posse together,' said Grant as though he hadn't really been bothered at all.

'There is nothing wrong with being a yellow bastard Grant. Now, tea break is over, I've got a few more deliveries for you and the last one is for a Mrs Taylor at the flats. She wants some more chips, you must have given her an appetite,' laughed Mr Khan handing over the orders.

'You lying bastard,' said Grant checking the orders.

'The old ones are the best, you stupid little twat, got you there. Did you hear that Imrie? I got him there.' The two brothers laughed and even Grant had a little smile on his face at the humour of them both.

'I like you Grant, you'll do alright here as long as you keep your cock in your trousers.'

'Good one Mr Khan, good one,' said Grant as he left with his next lot of deliveries.

CHAPTER 2
GRANT'S
SECRET

Back in town, the boys had just walked into the local 'slapper's bar' where all the pulling goes on. Tag was in his element.

'Look at the tits on that,' said Tag

'She is a cock teaser,' replied Gaz.

'How do you know?'

'She's renowned for it at work answering the door with virtually fuck all on when someone delivers there. A couple of the fellas have asked her out and she's just laughed at them,' said Gaz

'Bet she wouldn't turn me down,' said Tag confident he could pull anything.

'How much?' said Gaz.

'£10,' replied Tag.

'Shake,' said Gaz with a very assured manner and holding his hand out.

'I'll have £10 too,' chipped in Skip.

'Alright boys watch and learn, watch and learn,' Tag said with all the confidence in the world. Tag walked over to where the girl was stood with his usual swagger.

Now Tag was wearing light grey trousers and he walked up to the girl and tried to chat her up. Little did he realise that he had sprayed his trousers with water when he had washed his hands and wearing grey trousers, there was only one assumption that could be made.

'Look darlin,' I've been watching you and I like what I see. What do you say, can you and me go out sometime?'

The girl looked him up and down, pointed at his crotch and simply said, 'I think you need a plumber, you've either got a leak or you've left the tap running.'

All the girl's friends burst out laughing and one shouted at the top of her voice, 'He's pissed himself.'

Tag wanted the ground to open up and swallow him and he rushed back to the boys saying, 'Drink up we're going.'

'No we fucking aren't and you owe me a tenner,' replied Skip.

Tag then ran to the gents to dry his trousers.

'He's a fucking prick isn't he?' said Gaz to Skip

'Yeah, he is but I'll tell you this he'll come a cropper if Fay's brothers find out he's fucking her about, they'll kill him,' answered Skip.

'Well maybe it'll teach him a lesson,' said Gaz.

'Doubt it, people like Tag never learn, even when they lose everything,' said Skip.

After a few minutes Tag returned from the toilet.

'Well what did she say then Tag, or should I say pissy-pants?' laughed Gaz.

'Nothing really, she's a bit rough isn't she? And her breath stinks,' said Tag trying to put a brave face on it.

Unfortunately for Tag the girl heard his comments and slapped him on the back of the head just as he was about to take a drink and the beer went all over his suit. He turned around to see the full pub laughing at him. Then, in a flash, Tag poured the half a pint of beer that he had left in his glass over the girl's head and quickly left the pub before he got collared.

The girl's friends immediately converged on Gaz and Skip to find out who Tag was and where he'd gone. The two of them replied that they don't really know Tag that well and that he only 'tagged' onto them. But they do know that he would be in the La La's nightclub later as he always went in there on a Saturday. This calmed the girls down and they started to plot their revenge for when they see him again.

After Tag had gone and they had finished their drinks they decided that it was take away time and a taxi. As they came out of the pub the taxi queues were enormous and neither of them fancied waiting but then Skip had a good idea.

'Tell you what we'll do, we'll go to the Indian for a take away but ask for it delivering. Then when Grant, who's working there, sets off to deliver it, we'll get him to pick us up around the corner and take us home, genius eh?' said Skip.

'Too right, fucking genius you are Skip.'

They got to the take away and went in to order.

'I'll have two onion bhajis, a garlic nan and a chicken bunha with pilau rice and can you deliver that?' said Skip.

'Deliver it? But why not take it with you?' replied Mr Khan confused.

'You see it's not for us, we're going clubbing. It's for the missus a sort of peace offering so we can go clubbing and that,' said Skip thinking on his feet.

'Very well it'll be half an hour, the delivery boy isn't back yet,' said Mr Khan.

'Maybe he's shagging again,' shouted Imrie from the back, thinking the lads hadn't heard him.

'Shagging, who would that be, your one and only delivery boy

Grant?' Skip enquired.

'Yes, young Grant, he had a bit of a learning curve at the flats with a client,' said Mr Khan

'Not Tarty Taylor the temptress?' said Gaz.

'Yes do you know her? She likes delivery boy doesn't she Imrie?'

'Yes,' Imrie replied very quietly.

'Likes delivery men too, everyone is shit scared of her in my office, she has postmen for breakfast,' said Gaz, knowing full well that once in her lair there was no way out. He had been there himself many years previously when new to the job and there had been many a 'postie' who had emptied his sack in that flat.

With that Grant came back in to pick up the deliveries for his last round.

'Now then shaggy,' said Skip and Gaz simultaneously.

'Oh! fuck off you two,' shouted Grant, forgetting he was at work.

'Jesus Grant, you're at work,' said an outraged Mr Khan.

'Sorry Mr Khan but how did these two find out? You should have put it in the local paper, these two twats will tell everyone.'

'Your secret is safe with us young Grant as long as you get this take away to my house safely and without trying to shaft my missus. That alas is my duty, I know I'm brave but someone has to do it,' said Skip winking at Grant.

'Got something in your eye Skip?' asked Grant.

'Yes young Grant, I have as I am going nightclubbing and you are delivering curry will you be setting off now?' asked Skip.

'Yes he will with another three orders, here they are Grant.'

'In that case give us a bhaji to eat on the way to the club,' said Skip and he and Gaz walked out of the door.

'Farewell Grant, see you tomorrow.'

They both walked out of the shop and Grant picked up his order and went to his car. Now Grant had left the door to the car open, as he knew he would only be a minute and there was nothing worth nicking anyway. He then started the engine and set off. He had been going about two minutes and stopped at the lights and then he got the fright of his life. Skip and Gaz had climbed into the back of the car just before Grant left the shop with his orders and when the car stopped Gaz got Grant in a head lock.

'Don't hurt me. I've got nothing but curry on me, all the money's back at the shop,' cried Grant nearly in tears.

'Just give us a lift home then you prick and we'll say no more about it,' said Skip.

'You, you fucking bastards, you could have given me a heart attack. What are you doing here? I thought you were going to La La's,' said Grant.

'Two birds with one stone Grant my boy, a taxi and a take away 'all in one.'

'But I'm not a taxi.'

'You are tonight. You're taking the food to my house and I'm coming with you to make sure you don't try to snake my wife, you randy little student you,' said Skip.

'Cheeky bastards.'

'So what was she like?' asked Gaz.

'Who?' replied Grant pretending, unsuccessfully, not to understand who they were talking about.

'Tarty Taylor, I'm telling yer, you wanna get yourself checked out, she likes cock that one,' said Gaz.

'How do you know?' asked Grant

'I just do that's all. But your secret's safe with us if you take us home,' said Gaz.

'A couple of the lads at work have been there, well she gets lonely you know what with her husband being in prison for G.B.H., a woman has needs, that's her usual line.'

'You are fucking joking aren't you? Mr Khan said her ex-husband was alright, he gets a curry from there every week.'

'Wish I was joking but I tell you this if he goes in there for a curry every week first of all he'd have to escape and then travel 150 miles. Look he doesn't mind her high sex drive, in fact he used to video them and sell them on until he got done for blackmailing somebody with the tape. Now carry on driving the car and I'll tell you all about it,' laughed Gaz.

So Skip and Gaz stayed in the car while Grant made his deliveries and Gaz told him all about his new love.

'Go on then tell us or is it a wind up?' asked Grant.

'Not a wind up Grant, oh no this is no wind up my friend. About three years ago a few of the delivery boys from work were getting invited in. I mean she's not bad now but she was even better then and she used to answer the door with fuck all on and ask if they'd like a coffee. Well a couple went in, heard a noise and shit themselves thinking it was a set up. Then a few weeks later it was all over the papers about illegal porn videos and her husband blackmailing this fella who had read the gas meter,' Gaz continued.

'I remember that, she's the one who tried to blackmail the copper,' interrupted Skip.

'Who's telling this fucking story me or you?' said Gaz rather pissed off that Skip was trying to steal his thunder.

'I shall continue. This copper had gone to investigate something or other and they tried it on him, but he was having none of it and reported them to his superior and the case went to court and the fella got six months.'

'What's he inside for now?' asked Grant.

'He tried to kill an Indian delivery boy who was playing with his missus's onion bhaji,' laughed Gaz.

'Really you're kidding, he'll kill me,' said a worried Grant.

'No, he had a fight in a club where he worked and went over the top. Don't worry he's got six months before his parole.'

'How the fuck do you know all this stuff?' asked Grant.

'When you deliver the mail it's not hard to know who's getting what, all the information is there. You can spot jail mail a mile off, it has all the bullshit about how good it is in prison and doing it easy. You know the usual shit about how much they love the person who they are writing to. But instead of getting a real job when they get out they end up back inside again. I mean your mam gets her sex toys through the post and your dad's into S and M, it all comes through my hands. I can tell what's in every package.'

'Fucking hell Gaz, get off your soapbox. Anyway, drop off time Granty boy, just here will do and we'll see you tomorrow at the club.'

'Yeah tomorrow, here Gaz is that true about my mam and dad?'

'No - it's the other way around. See ya Grant and thanks for the lift.'

The two friends then went off to their homes for the night, leaving Grant shitting himself for the rest of his shift and wondering about what his parents were up to. No wonder his dad was so keen that he took this job, they were probably swinging right now.

He managed to get through the night without any mishaps and ended up with £20 worth of tips, his wages and a free Indian banquet. He could get used to perks like that every week, Grant thought to himself...

The Willows Club was fairly quiet on the Sunday with just a few volunteers making tea for the people watching the youth teams. Miserable Dave had just opened the bar and gradually the boys were filtering in for the meeting. Eddie had been there with all the information they needed for the trip and was expecting them to all pay their deposits so that he could actually make the booking. This was Eddie's forte he was great at organising things and collecting fees from the boys, who took great delight in trying to con him but no one ever conned eagle-eyed Eddie.

Six players had congregated around the bar and were chatting about the night before and what had happened.

'What happened to you last night Thommo, you pissed off at 10, where did yer go?' asked Skip.

'You won't believe this I was talking to that bird who works in my office about nowt really and she starts to come on to me really strong like, telling me how she's always fancied me. She saw that I had a shiner and she said she loved it when I had a black eye and that she got all moist thinking about it,' replied Thommo.

'So what did you do, get her some toilet roll?' quipped Jonesy.

'No, I said I'd love to shag her and she insisted that she wanted me there and then. Well, after trying to sneak her into the toilets and being chucked out by the bouncer I had a fucking brain wave, the bus station.'

'Am I being slow or just plain fucking stupid, the bus station, how's that a brain wave,' asked Skip looking puzzled.

'What do you get at a bus station?' asked Thommo.

'You catch a plane there don't you?' said Skip.

'I know but you also get the buses that are parked up for the night and if you pull that leaver on the door, hey presto the door opens and you have privacy to shaft the bird from work,' said Thommo with a smirk.

'Well tell us did you then, shag her?' asked all the other five in anticipation.

'Let me set the scene, we went upstairs and straight away she's got me trousers off and I'm fingering her then she starts to blow me off so I counter her and I'm muffing her very well cropped bush. Well I'm that excited I'm having to think of horrible things to stop myself from blowing me dust.'

'What kind of horrible things?' interrupts Greg.

'Fuck off Greg, let him finish,' said Jonesy who was getting quite aroused.

'Yeah horrible things like you on the job Greg, with your come face all distorted.'

'Cheeky fucker,' said Greg.

'Anyway I shot my load and she couldn't get enough, she swallowed it all and then said she wanted me to fuck her,' Thommo carried on.

'Did you straight away?' asked Jonesy

'Well my knob was like a bruised peach, so I made an excuse to go for a piss to give me more time for it to recover. In the meantime she's flicking herself off while I'm away, she was really horny.'

'Sounds like she's a sex maniac to me,' said Jonesy rather jealously.

'So did you leave her?' asked Greg.

'Did I fuckers like. I went back upstairs and she had fuck all on, and she wanted it doggy so I bent her over the seat and started pumping away, it was great until something unexpected happened.'

Thommo went quiet and there was a pause, which seemed like an eternity. Skip broke the silence, 'Well what happened?'

'I'm going for a piss I'll tell you when I get back,' said Thommo laughing.

'Shithouse!' said Jonesy. 'I don't believe him do you? I bet he got some chips and went home.'

'Well he was talking to a bird when I last saw him so he might be telling the truth. You know what he's like, all dramatic. Anyway he's back now he can tell us,' said Daz.

'Where was I? Oh yeah just as I'm banging away we heard a noise but I just carried on. Anyhow the fucking bus only started to move,' continued Thommo.

'Fuck off 'Jackanory' – you're making this up,' said Jonesy.

'Straight up, the bus is moving, I'm banging away - then I looked out of the window and we're going down Hessle road.'

'What did you do?' asked Greg.

'Well we both started to shit ourselves thinking what's it gonna look like if he starts picking up passengers? So we put our clothes on and then the daft cow only goes and rings the fucking bell to get off! I said, 'What you doing?' and she comes out with that's what you do when you want to get off a bus. So I said to her, yeah but not when you've been trespassing and using it as a shagging wagon.'

'Then what happened?' asked Jonesy, knowing that no one would make up such a story.

'Well the bus stopped at the next stop and we got off, me with me shirt on the wrong way around and her with her skirt inside out. And do you know what the cheeky bastard of a driver did? He asked for £5 to keep his mouth shut.'

'You never paid did you?' asked Greg.

'Course I fucking paid. I felt about as big as Tom Thumb's dick.'

'So what happened then?' asked Skip.

'We got a taxi and I dropped her off.'

'Didn't you finish the job?'

'No, she blamed me and said that it was a stupid fucking idea to get on a bus. I don't think she'll be fantasising about me anymore. Besides she was in a state of shock. Can't wait for work on Monday.'

'You don't half get into some scrapes don't yer, you jammy bastard,' said Jonesy.

'Well you know me?'

'Yeah and your cock will drop off,' said Jonesy jealously.

'You'll never guess what Grant was up to last night?' said Skip.

'What, homework or buying a Mars bar with a cheque, the student faced bastard,' said Thommo, who didn't like students much and was not keen on Grant.

'No, he was only shagging in the flats with a customer.'

'What, he's on the game?' Thommo replied looking puzzled.

'No, he's got a job delivering Indians for Khan's.'

'Well that's me with a new best friend, I think I might have underestimated Granty boy. I love curry, especially when it's free,' said Thommo.

'Fuck off, you only want a freebee. Anyway how do you know he was shagging, you were out with us,' said Tag who had finally perked up after two beers to cure his hangover.

'We went for a take away and the owner spilled the beans and then we got the full S.P. out of the randy little bastard ourselves on the way home,' said Skip.

'What was it some dog?' said Tag.

'Better than that it was some old slapper who apparently eats delivery boys for breakfast, isn't that right Gaz?' laughed Skip.

'Fuck off, not this delivery boy, some have been there but not I. Not my type she's got mild tattooed on one nipple and bitter on the other and another one which is an arrow pointing to her fanny saying

'Get it here,' said Gaz.

'Never wait while I see the little bastard,' said Thommo.

'No don't we're sworn to secrecy leave the lad alone' said Gaz.
With that the doors open and in walks Grant with Mike, his mate from Uni, and the whole club falls silent. Grant walks to the bar and orders two drinks the club is still silent until it is Grant himself who breaks the silence.

'Somebody died or what?'

'Yeah some old women in the flats apparently, she'd been shagged to death by some Indian delivery boy, they thought she was in a korma but she later pssed away at the local hospital,' said Dave the barman.

'You big mouthed bastards I told you that in confidence you twats' said Grant.

'They call him mister lover lover, mister lover love, they call him mister bombastic, fucking fantastic, tickle on the box, they call him mister ro romantic,' the full bar started to sing, then came the barrage of abuse started coming from every corner of the room.

'Was she good? Was there sawdust coming out? Help the aged shag a granny, fancy a bit of granny fanny?' until Thommo shouted

'Leave him alone, so was she your first Granty? Did she deflower you, I bet you didn't last long?'

'Fuck off Thommo, you can talk, that elephant I saw you with last week with the leather trousers on, her arse looked like two hippos having a fight in a black binliner. A full herd of cows must have died just so she could have those trousers,' replied Grant quick as a flash.

'You cheeky little twat, I'll flatten you.'

'I think Grant won that one by a knockout,' intervened Skip.

'Were you really shagging,' asked Mike who Grant had forgotten was there.

'Eh up, the boyfriend's jealous?' Tosser chipped in.

'Oh for fuck sake, yes, but don't tell anyone at Uni, I'll be the laughing stock. What do you mean boyfriend?' panicked Grant.

'A joke Grant, a joke.'

'What was the number of that flat again?' asked Thommo.

'Fuck off Thommo.'

'It wasn't old Tarty was it?' enquired Thommo. Grant went red.

'Jesus not old Tarty, when she opens her legs there's an echo. I'm surprised you didn't fall in, a couple of years back the moorland rescue had to be called in to rescue two milkmen and a coal man. Fuck knows why she wanted coal in a high rise maybe to get the full set,' continued Thommo.

'Leave it,' said Gaz, 'He's had enough.'

There was a loud noise at the bar, Eddie was ready to start the meeting.

'Can I have your attention lads,' shouted Eddie.

'Yes Eddie, you've got it. Listen up lads,' shouted Skip.

'Right then the trip is for two nights. We set off Friday morning at 9 and get back Sunday night. It's a 5 star hotel and we're going by bus the full price is £125, deposits by the end of this month of £50, the £125 includes match ticket any questions?' Eddie rattled this off at lightening speed as to have no interruptions. He was a master at this and knew if he stopped for breath someone would interrupt and try and be a smart arse.

'5 star pull the other one, it was 4 star the other day,' said Tosser.

'I'm telling you it's 5 star, I checked last night and it's a 5 star rated hotel. It's a bit out of the way that's why it's cheap.'

'Where is it, Grimsby? I'm not spending a weekend in Grimsby,' said Tosser.

'Your name really suits you Tosser, someone already cracked that one yesterday. The hotel is in Canary Wharf and has no tube station, so the hotel is virtually empty on a weekend as you have to get cabs everywhere, that's why it's cheap.'

'Sounds alright to me lads what about you Tag?' said Skip on purpose as he knew Tag wasn't going.

'Fine,' replied Tag thinking you shithouse.

'You're not going though are you Tag?' chipped in Gaz.

'What you doing here then?' asked Eddie.

'Look this goes no further. I am going officially but I'm not going if you get me drift,' said Tag.

'Yeah that's made it a lot clearer, what are you talking about?' said Eddie, puzzled.

'Well I'm going to Blackpool.'

'He's going to Blackpool for a dirty weekend and he's that piss weak, Fay thinks he's in London, so he's going to get away with it the prick, and we'll all have to lie to cover his sorry arse, isn't that right Tag?' interrupted Skip.

'You rotten bastard Tag,' piped up one of the boys.

'Yeah, yeah, please just tell Fay I'm going if she asks,' said Tag and he left the bar and his drink behind.

'He's got troubles that boy,' said Eddie.

'Too right he has. Listen whatever he's doing no one say anything, It'll only cause trouble, let him look after it himself,' said Skip.

'Right, any other questions? Because I'm in a rush. I'm going to the flats to shag a granny. No I'm going home, remember, deposits and I'll see you losers on Tuesday,' said Eddie, winking at Grant as he left the meeting and went home.

Skip then stood up and took the meeting over.

'Right are we having a theme? Fancy dress? Or any suggestions?' The room fell silent.

'Why don't you go as rugby players and dress up like them because it's the only time any of you will be one,' came the call from the bar.

'You can fuck off and get back in your coffin Dracula. You could come as a barman in your dreams because you're a shite one,' shouted Tosser back at Dave who for once was in a good mood.

'You're in a good mood get your end away last night did yer, hope she only charged you the going rate,' continued Tosser.

'Fuck off,' shouted Dave, which put him in a bad mood again.

'Come on any real suggestions?'

'Knights, cartoon characters, or what about just general fancy dress,' a few people shouted out.

'Why don't we all dress as women, you could go as that pensioner you shagged last night, she'll lend you a dress won't she Grant?' laughed Thommo.

'Piss off Thommo you twat,' Grant shouted giving Thommo the finger. To which Thommo gave Grant the 'V' sign and said wittily,

'Double your money'.

'We could go as 'The Bay City Rollers', Greg announced proudly.

'That's easy for you Greg, you still dress like one. No it can't be that, we wouldn't be able to get the tartan,' said Tosser shooting Greg down in flames.

'What about Cowboys and Indians,' Mike, Grant's mate blurted out to defuse the situation.

'Great idea, I fancy that with me six shooter and me Sheriff's badge,' said Tosser.

'Is everyone agreed then cowboys and Indians will be the theme. Any more for any more? Right, show of hands, sorted,' said Skip. All hands went up.

'Right we all get dressed up, no exceptions, or fines and forfeits will be imposed. Do we all agree?' said Gaz.

'What about a song each? That's what we do in Oz,' chipped in Damo the Aussie.

'Great idea, listen everyone. Another thing, we can all bring a cowboy song on song sheets for us all to sing on the way down. Do we all agree? Sorted then,' announced Skip.

'I can't fucking wait can you Grant?' said Mike.

'No, I can't but if you tell anyone about me with that woman at Uni you're off the trip. I would be the laughing stock of the Union Bar.'

'I won't honest, but how come you ended up, you know?'

'I don't want to talk about it. It's been a fucking nightmare all because I nicked a couple of chips out of her food.'

'Well that's it then, anyone got anything else?'
Skip looked around but no one seemed interested in making any other suggestions.

'No other ideas? right then, meeting over, see you Tuesday. Good suggestion mate, what's your name?'

'Mike, I go to Uni with Grant.'

'Not another student, well we know whose room to terrorise don't we?' said Thommo as he left.

'You and whose army, you prick. You better watch your back, that's all I'm saying,' replied Grant who didn't like Thommo much either.

'Toys 'R' Us will do well. The gun aisle will be sold out so you better get in quick partners, yee-haa,' shouted Gaz.

'We've got ages yet it'll be the songs that take all the organising. Anyway I'm going, taking the kids in park, I'll see you later,' said Skip as he got to leave at the third attempt.

The meeting ended with everyone excited about the trip. The few that remained were chatting about their outfits and were all shitting themselves about the songs they would bring. They all eventually dispersed. Some went home while others went for a Sunday dinner session...

That Sunday night at Tosser's house all the girls were meeting to have a few drinks and a clothes party. Well that is what they'd told the men, they were really sorting out who was going on the Blackpool trip, what time they were going and which hotel they would be staying in.

Tosser was duly sent to the pub, which he didn't object to and the meeting began.

'Where are the clothes?' said Trev's wife Cary.

'There are no clothes it's to sort out the Blackpool trip,' replied Tosser's wife Clare.

'Oh, I thought we were having a clothes party as well.'

'No Cary, just a few drinks and sort out the trip.'

When all the girls had arrived, all eleven of them, they started opening the wine and chatting. Most of them didn't see each other from one month to the next but they usually got together if there was a Cup Final to show support for the lads. They all enjoyed each other's company and that's why they thought of the trip.

'Right before we all get pissed, let's sort out what's going on,' said Clare who was the main organiser of the trip.

'We've got a B&B to stay in, four twins and one triple. The hotels were taking the piss so this is the only other option it is clean and breakfast is full English and it's right near the town centre. It's also only half the price of the hotel. The price is £10.00 each and I'll get a cheque off if we all agree, any questions?'

'What's the triple room like?' asked Cary

'Apparently it's a single with a bunk bed so I'll have the top bunk and for the price we're only there to drop our bags off and sleep so it won't really matter. So are we all agreed then let's have a show of hands' said Clare trying to get it sorted before anyone got cold feet.

'Yes fine' they all said at once.

'Good I'll need the tenner as soon as possible. Tonight if you've got it. Next thing is we set off from here at 5 o'clock on the Friday night and the bus is £10 each, we can pay on the day, and we set off to come back at 4.30 on Saturday afternoon. We get back Saturday night so no one is any the wiser. Well, if they are they can't do anything about it,' said Clare

'Oh! and for Christ sake don't let on because if they find out, you know what they're like, they can go away but we can't.'

'Here, here,' agreed Fay. 'My Tag is so jealous if I go anywhere. I suppose it's because he loves me so much.'

Clare glanced over to Mandy, Skip's wife, who has her mouth wide open in amazement at the last statement as she knows that Tag will shag anything that breathes.

'How's he been your Tag? enquired Clare.

'Skip was saying he was a bit down in himself and didn't like to ask him if anything was wrong,' continued Clare. She knew that Tag was carrying on with Suki as she knew Suki's mother who kept telling her about this fantastic new man in her daughter's life and how they were going to get married.

Fay hesitated and then began to cry.

'What's wrong lovey?' said Clare expecting her to come out with the fact that she knew about him and Suki, but instead she told them it all.

'Well you see we've been having a few problems, well Tim has.

(Tim is Tag's real name and part of the reason he likes to be called Tag)

'He can't get excited when we, you know, do what couples do?'

'What do you mean?' said Cary.

'Fucking hell Cary give the girl a break he can't get wood, it won't stand to attention, Mr Floppy doesn't want to play,' blurted out Mandy.

At this point Fay is now in floods of tears and inconsolable.

'More wine anyone?' asks Clare as Mandy hugs Fay to stop her crying.

'Don't worry love, all men go through this stage at one time or another they all get stage fright, it'll pass.'

'My Tom's hasn't ever had stage fright, I have to beat it with a stick. It's always standing to attention,' said Steph quietly to Daz's wife, Tracey.

'I know Daz is always up for it. I don't know any bloke that isn't unless he's getting it elsewhere,' replied Tracey.

The two of them looked that knowing look as if to say, he's shagging around.

Fay finally calmed down and more wine is drunk and lips get a little looser, this is why men don't like the women getting together they let all their secrets out.

'Them bastards don't like us lot getting together you know. They shit themselves because they go to that club and act like they're tough and take no shit from anyone. Well my Skip is a great big soft shite at home, he does exactly what I tell him. He comes in when I tell him, he doesn't know it but I wear the trousers in our house. I sometimes tell him not to be late or to wash the pots before he goes out just to test him and he always does as he's told,' said Mandy.

'I agree they'll all be at home thinking we're talking about the size of their dicks and how good they are in bed or not as is Fay's case,' chipped in Jonno's wife, Chris. This nearly set Fay off again but she just laughed.

'Pete thinks he's great in bed but half the time I fake it,' said Sally who was usually very quiet and prim and proper.

'Just for once I'd like missionary Pete to take me roughly from behind and shag my brains out but all he ever manages is a quick shuffle. I'm sure he thinks he's in the 100 metres and has to finish as quickly as possible.'

'Sally, well I wouldn't have thought you'd have liked it like that. Tracey maybe,' said Clare.

'Cheeky bitch,' replied Tracey.

'I've got a solution for you. If he comes too quick then an hour before you fancy it toss him off and that'll stop him being quick on the draw the second time. Then later he'll last miles longer,' said Steph.

'Why has that worked for you then Steph? Has Tom had

problems?' asked Tracey.

Steph hesitated and then laughed and confessed.

'Problems, he only had to see me naked and it went off, before he could get his undies off. But we're alright now and he lasts up to three minutes if I'm lucky, no longer, I'm only joking.'

'What a bunch of imperfect pricks our men really are, aren't they? Some can't get it up, some can't control it when it's up and some don't know what to do with it when it is up,' said Jonesy's wife, Sue.

'Do tell Mrs Jones,' laughed Clare.

'Well it's all, 'Do you like that when I touch you there?' 'What about this, is that good?' You'd think he'd know by now after being married five years but he hasn't got a clue. I love him like but he plays me like he plays bloody rugby, lots of effort but no expertise. He gives 100% but he wouldn't win anything.'

'Has he ever worn his kit for you?' asked Mandy.

'No, I don't think I could kiss him with his gum-shield in and all that grease on his legs,' came the reply.

'No I mean just the shirt and shorts. Skip has tackled me on to the bed and shagged me, it was great, try it next time you're doing some role play.'

They all started laughing uncontrollably then suddenly the door opened. It was Tosser who looked shocked to see them all still there.

'Are you lot still here? How did it go then?' asked Tosser to which there was no reply, only continued laughter.

'What's so funny then? Come on, let us in on the joke,' asked Tosser thinking they were laughing at him.

'Nothing's wrong, we've had a great time darling? Have you got your kit upstairs?' said Clare.

That started the girls off again and this time Tosser clicked what their conversation had probably been about.

'You've been talking about Skip shagging in his kit haven't you?' Mandy's face changed immediately.

'Has that twat been talking about that to you lot? The bastard, wait while I get home.'

'You're talking about it so you're just as bad,' replied Tosser.

'I suppose so, any way we better be off,' said Mandy trying to get out as quickly as possible.

'Yeah, see you Mandy, hope you score a trrrrrry!!! when you get home,' said Tosser with a smile on his face.

'Cheeky get,' said Mandy.

All the other girls looked puzzled until Tosser explained, 'That's what she shouts out when she comes.'

Everyone burst out laughing again except Mandy who was going to kill Skip when she got home.

After training the following week, the boys had a night out at the local and having downed a couple of pints, Grant stopped Skip for a 'private word' in the pub toilets.

'Skip, can I ask you something?' Grant asked sheepishly.

'Yeah what is it?'

'Well it's about that thing that happened on Saturday.'

'Don't worry, I'm sure that she won't bother you again, said Skip.'

'It's not that - look.'

At this point Grant showed Skip his penis – there was puss coming out of the end.

'Fucking hell, you've got a dose there lad, you better get to the clinic in the morning with that,' advised Skip.

'I won't die will I? I mean are you sure it's that?' asked Grant nervously.

'Fucking hell don't worry, all they'll do is take a sample, pop a cocktail umbrella up it and give you some tablets to clear it up. And tell that slapper that she gave you it, if she tries it on again. I presume it is her?'

'Yeah, but don't tell the lads, she's the only bird I've had really, except for a couple of birds at 6th form but I don't think they count,' replied Grant.

'Fucking hell lost your cherry to a slag eh, never mind.'

Skip had a way with words and an even better bedside manner, he should have been a doctor with his sympathetic manner.

'Don't tell anyone will you?' pleaded Grant.

'Your secret is safe with me sunshine. And don't worry.'

With that they both left the toilets and rejoined the others. Two minutes later though, Tag, who, unbeknown to the others had been in the toilet cubical, walked back into the bar shouting, 'Unclean, unclean, Grant's got a dose lads.'

Grant's face went purple and steam was coming out of his ears, luckily Skip got in between him and Tag.

'You fucking twat Tag, I'll kill you, that was private what you heard,' shouted Grant.

'Was the bit about losing your virginity to the slag, private as well? Will I die Skip? Don't let me die, I'm too young, I only shagged a slapper the once, I don't deserve to die,' continued Tag.

'You're fucking dead Tag, I'll kill you,' shouted Grant.

'Ooh! I'm frightened, you'll probably be dead by then, died of cock rot.'

'I'll get you back Tag you prick. What about Blackpool Tag, what if someone told someone about Blackpool?'

'You little shit, I'd kill you.'

'If there was anything left of you that is. But you know what, I wouldn't because I'm not a little turd like you are. I'm going to see you lot Thursday,' said Grant as he was leaving and he said his goodbyes.

'Here Grant,' said Skip 'don't forget, get to clinic tomorrow and it'll be cleared up in no time. Don't take any notice of daft twat, he's a prick.'

'Thanks Skip, you're a mate,' said Grant as he left.

Tag was still going on when Skip returned.

'Sorted the baby out have you?' said Tag sarcastically.

'If you don't shut your fucking big mouth I'll fill it. You are a twat at times Tag, leave the lad alone,' said Skip.

'I'm only having a bit of fun.'

'No it's not funny that lad is shitting himself, he's only 18 and needs a bit of looking after. What if he told Fay's brothers eh, what would happen then? And if he did I wouldn't blame him. Remember when you were 18 and I got you out of the shit and never told anyone, what if I'd have opened my mouth about that how would you have felt?'

'Don't bring that up' said Tag thinking he'd have forgotten it.

'I won't tell anyone and you know it but how would you have felt?'

'What's all this then?' enquired Jonesy

'Nothing it happened ages ago and that's where it will stay,' said Skip.

The next day Grant caught the bus to the local clap clinic, but unfortunately on the same bus was his mate Mike.

'Where ya going Grant?' enquired Mike.

'Town to the library,' replied Grant, hoping that Mike would be put off as he hated libraries.

'I'll come if that's okay, I've got nowt to do and I'll read the papers, anyway what you going to the library for?'

'Just to get some peace and quiet, anyway what's it got to do with you?' snapped Grant.

'Don't snap, I only asked. Is there something wrong? You haven't lost your job have you? Did that woman complain? You know the one who wanted your body.'

Everyone on the crowded bus turned and looked at the two of them.

'Why don't you shout it a bit louder, there's a fella in the Outer Hebrides didn't quite catch it,' said a very angry Grant as he got up from his seat to get off the bus.

'Where you going? This isn't the stop for the library,' shouted Mike as he followed Grant to get off the bus.

'Fuck off Mike and leave me alone.'

With that an old lady turned to her friend and said, 'Looks like a lovers' tiff to me, the one doing all the chasing fancies the other one who has lost his job because of the woman who wants his body,' she said this and both of them heard her, with that Grant turned on his heels and confronted the old lady and said.

'I am not losing my job because of some old tart and...'

Before he could get the words out Mike butted in, 'And I don't fancy him.'

'Not your type?' replied the old lady to everyone's amusement.

'Not my type? of course he's not,' replied Mike.

'Like 'em a bit bigger and more hairy?'

The old lady was razor sharp and was quite enjoying the attention as the bus was in uproar.

'No, he hasn't got tits and a fanny you stupid woman, I'm not a puff,' shouted Mike.

'Are you sure? There's nothing wrong with it you know there's plenty of you about now coming out of the wardrobe.' This time she was laughing when she said it which annoyed Mike even more.

To defuse the situation and Mike's obvious defeat to an old lady someone stood up and shouted, 'Game set and match to the lady, now shake hands.'

Luckily for Mike the bus was about to stop and he could get off. As soon as he did the lady turned to her friend and said in a loud voice so that everyone could hear, 'Couple of nancy boys them if ever I've seen them, those two are as bent as nine-bob notes.'

When the bus had gone and Mike was chasing Grant down the street as everyone on the bus was waving to them and banging on the window.

'Grant wait, what the fuck's wrong with you?'

'Nothing, I've told you I'm going to the library.'

'Fuck you then, I thought I was your mate, if you can't tell me then who can you tell?'

Grant stopped and told Mike to follow him until they found a quiet spot where they could sit and talk. Mike was getting a little worried and confronted Grant.

'You're not... are you?' he asked.

'Not what?' came Grant's replied with a puzzled look.

'Bent, the old codger wasn't right was she, you don't like blokes do you? You're not in love with me are you?'

'Fuck off you stupid bastard, your cock's not big enough anyway and you've got a shit body,' said Grant as he finally saw the humour of the situation and decided to tell Mike the truth.

'Well it's like this, yes I am bent and it's one of the lads at rugby but I don't know how to approach the subject with him. I mean seeing him in the showers I don't know what to do I have to stop myself getting hard.'

Mike's jaw hit the floor, 'You're bent then, fucking hell, does your mam and dad know?'

'No, nobody knows apart from you.'

'Who is it that you fancy?' enquired Mike.

'It's Skip,' Grant replied, trying to keep a straight face.

'Skip, but he's married and has got kids.'

'I know, that's the problem but I can't wait to have him, just like I'm having you on you silly twat! Me bent? you fucking gullible stupid bastard.'

'So, you're not then?'

'Of course I'm not, I'm going to the clinic.'

'What for, a check up?'

'You really are stupid at times, do I have to spell it out for you?' asked Grant.

'Yes, I don't know what you're talking about.'

'Clap clinic, that old bag has given me a dose of something, I've got loads of stuff coming out of my knob end.' There was silence.

'So now you see why I wouldn't tell you on the bus. With fucking bat ears behind us, I didn't want the full bus knowing I had a dose.'

'Do you want me to come with you to the clinic?' asked Mike

'I fucking don't. Thanks for the offer but I've been accused of being Wayne Sleep once today and what will it look like, two gay lovers getting checked out for aids? I'll meet you at the Union bar this afternoon and tell you all about it.'

The two of then went their separate ways and Grant went to the clinic. When he got in there he took a number and waited. He was quite relieved that no one was in the waiting room and he started to read a magazine.

He was painfully unaware that the receptionist had recognised him and knew his mother. As he was called in to the examination room the receptionist enquired how his mum was because she hadn't seen her at the bingo for a couple of weeks. At this point Grant was shitting himself. His mam would kill him if she found out and the embarrassment factor would be on a par with the most embarrassing moment he had ever encountered in his life. That unforgettable incident suddenly flashed into his head.

The single most embarrassing moment in his life had been the year before when only him and his mother were in the house. Grant was in his bedroom listening to his music with his headphones on, blissfully unaware of the world around him and knowing that the door to his bedroom was tightly shut, he decided to have a wank. After a few minutes he finished and opened his eyes to see a red hot, steaming cup of tea at the side of the bed. He put two and two together and surmised that either his mother had walked in on him having a wank or that the tea fairy had made it – and unfortunately Grant knew the tea fairy didn't exist. He avoided his mum for at least a week then. He tried his best not to make eye contact with her and she never said anything to him. And now if she found out about this he'd have to move out, or else avoid her for the rest of his life.

The receptionist could see his shock and calmed him down by pointing out that patient confidentiality meant that his mum wouldn't find out from her, which eased his worry a little. That was until his examination when he had to explain what had happened and to have all kinds of things stuck up his Jap's eye. He had every test possible and what seemed like an age ended with the instruction that he should go and see the person who he thought he had caught it off and tell them to consult a doctor.

He got a prescription and was about to set off straight to the woman's house but there was still one more final humiliation for him. As he stepped out of the room he saw two people who had been on the bus that morning. He recognised them as they had turned around from the seat in front.

'No, my boyfriend hasn't come with me, in case you were wondering you nosey twats,' said Grant quickly. He was feeling pleased with himself until he saw the receptionist look across in astonishment. Grant reacted very quickly again.

'No, I'm not bent if that's what you're thinking, I caught the clap from a woman, so there,' and he left the building as quick as he could hoping that no one else saw him.

Grant then made his way to the woman's flat, pressed the entry button and she buzzed him up. He thought that he should play it cool and explain what had happened and that she should go and get checked out. But when she answered the door and asked what he wanted all his 'cool' went out of the window.

'I hope you know what you've done you silly cow, you've given me a dose! My dick's got all kinds of multi-coloured slime coming out of it and you've given me it.'

'Calm down, I'll make you a drink,' and she walked off into the kitchen as if it wasn't the first time that it had happened.

'Do you take milk and sugar?' she shouted through.

'Just milk thanks,' Grant replied in a daze thinking about what had happened to him and what he was going to do next. She brought the tea through and sat opposite him. She had no make up on and looked older than she had on the Saturday night. Grant thought she also appeared quite sad in a way, just a lonely woman who wanted a bit of fun.

'I like sex you see and as much as I can get,' said the woman. Grant nearly choked on his tea.

'I get it when I can and getting them up to the flat and seducing people and offering it to them, there aren't many who refuse me. I didn't hear you complaining.'

'You could have told me and I could have worn a johnny,' said Grant.

'It was just a spare of the moment thing with you. I liked the look of you and thought what the hell. Don't worry, the tablets will take no time to kick in and you'll be alright. You'll learn from this son, that you have to be responsible for your own actions. Anyway you don't want to worry, I won't be trying it on with you again unless you want me to?'

'No thanks, I think I've learned my lesson,' said Grant rather embarrassed as he finished his tea and got up to leave.

'Well, I'll see you Saturday and this time keep your thieving hands off my chips and I'll keep mine off your dick, is that a deal?'

'Yeah!' said Grant trying to get out of the door as quickly as he could.

Meanwhile back at the clinic Imrie was getting himself checked out as he had delivered to Tarty on the Sunday night and she had got him too. He had worn a condom going in but it must have dissolved on impact.

The weeks went past and the trip was looming large. The lads were all still playing rugby every week but there was nothing else they could talk about except the trip. They were like little kids waiting for Christmas.

The girls had to be a bit more sneaky. Some of them had started to watch most of the games as this was the only time they could get together without looking too suspicious. They had all the money in and the B&B was booked. The ones who needed babysitters had got that sorted out. And the ones who didn't have kids didn't need a babysitter, as their 'kids' would be in London playing cowboys and Indians.

The week of the trip finally arrived and on the Tuesday night at training everyone was very excited. They had a light training session and Skip had called a meeting to see if everyone was ready with their costume and song. Skip already had his stuff ready and he was head of the 'punishment committee' if people didn't comply. He loved his Wembley trips. Three days away from the wife and kids to be able to act like a teenager again was pure magic for him. He loved the silly games, the stupid dressing up and most of all the endless drinking. The actual match came in at about 10th compared to the other things he enjoyed.

He swore blind to his wife Mandy that it was the game that they all went for, but she wasn't stupid, she knew why they all went and didn't mind really.

Her dad had done the same when she was a kid and it was all harmless fun. Besides she had a trip of her own to worry about and she had to confirm that the kids would be alright at her mother's for the weekend.

At the meeting everyone confirmed that they had got an outfit and a song but in reality only three of the twenty had got them. But so as not to seem like they weren't organised, they all drank up and went their separate ways. The three however, wondered what the hell they were going to do because they knew some of the punishments could be quite severe.

No one wanted to have to do 'the dance of the flaming arseholes' in a packed London pub for instance. This is when two 'players' stick a rolled-up newspaper up their backside and on the word 'go' someone lights the end. The winner is the one who lasts the longest, which can lead to third degree burns and a very uncomfortable weekend. The naked 400-metre dash around the service station can also be a tremendous embarrassment, especially if the person looking after your clothes misplaces them and you have to travel naked everywhere for the day.

No one wanted to get a forfeit so nearly all of them came up with the same idea of going to a fancy dress shop the very next day. That plan proved rather stupid however as there are only two fancy dress shops in Hull and they only stocked three cowboy and two Indian outfits between them. And one of the Indian ones wasn't a red Indian, but that of an Indian waiter.

So from 6 o'clock onwards on the Wednesday the dressing-up aisle in 'Toys 'R' Us' was full of rugby players buying guns, hats and anything else that remotely looked like it had anything to do with the wild west. Come Friday morning there would be 20 sheriffs and one hobbyhorse, Jonesy couldn't resist it. He promptly called it 'Silver' and told everyone that he was 'The Lone Ranger' because of the fact that he'd bought the last mask.

Three times the manager had to go down the aisle as there was such a commotion, with guns going off and grown men rolling around the floor pretending to be dying. After the third time he lost his temper and threatened to bar all of them and refuse to sell them the gear, which soon quietened them down. They all picked up the stuff they wanted and went to the checkout. Then they all dispersed and went off to try and complete the task of producing a song for the trip.

While all the blokes were running around like headless chickens the women were on the phone sorting out where to meet and what they would be wearing. Mandy had sorted t-shirts out for them all to wear. She had giggled at the thought of them when she bought them and now when it was crunch time to wear them, she wondered whether she may have gone too far. The t-shirt had a hand pointing to the right with the immortal words 'She Likes Cock' emblazoned across the chest. This insinuated that the girl stood next to the wearer, loved to be shagged - which in some cases was true but in other cases i.e. being married, they only wanted to be shagged by their husbands. When they all stood in line the girls would look like a bunch of nymphomaniacs, and with the t-shirts being bright orange with black writing you'd be able to see them from space.

They all agreed on a meeting time and again swore each other to secrecy. They were all really excited partly about the trip but also because it was a secret and they thought they were getting one over on the men.

CHAPTER 3
TIMOTHY
THE BOUNDER

The fact that all the boys on the trip were busy trying to sort out their fancy dress and songs, gave Tag an opportunity to take Suki out to a quiet country pub. He arranged for her to pick him up at 5pm and then away they'd go for their weekend in Blackpool. He wanted to say 'dirty weekend' but up until then he'd only kissed Suki. And although he'd boasted that 'she went like a Suzuki' to the lads, the fact was the furthest he'd got was a feel of her breasts, only to be told 'not yet'.

He was hoping that after a couple of drinks tonight she would at least give him a wank. Well he had been patient, this was their twelfth date, which was something of a record for him. He knew that she was a bit special and not the usual easy slapper he was used to. Tag actually loved her. Fay was great but they argued a lot mainly due to him, but Suki was different, she was classy and lovely and he so hoped that when he got her to Blackpool that she'd let him have his way with her. It was like being a kid in a sweetshop but you couldn't have anything. He had a master plan, he'd even been down to the department store and bought some proper cologne, none of your Blue Stratos or Denim, he'd gone for Aramis.

He'd tried to crack a joke to the assistant at the counter, 'Is this what the cowboys used to wear when fighting the Indians? You know… arrow miss.'

But it didn't even raise a smile from the orange-faced, miserable cow. However, at £30 a bottle, he thought that along with the chocolates, the champagne, the flowers and the 3 star rated B&B he'd booked, that it would be enough to charm the knickers off Suki...

Tag was ready and serious. He'd spent all his spare cash and had even had to get his deposit straight back from Eddie who wasn't very pleased as Eddie loved to take money but hated giving it back. Eddie actually liked Tag and swore he wouldn't say anything but left him with a bit of advice, to do the right thing and have the balls to tell one of the girl that he didn't really want her. His parting words were, 'You can't have your cake and eat it . You'll get found out Tag, someone will know someone else and let the cat out of the bag'.

How true those words might prove to be because although Tag didn't know it yet his master plan was nothing short of a suicide mission. That was because he wasn't too bright and he'd only booked Hull's most popular B&B in Blackpool, used predominantly by people from Hull and owned by people from Hull. And what he didn't know was that for one of the two nights he'd planned to stay there, a party of rugby wives and girlfriends from Hull had also booked in at the same B&B...

A potential ticking time bomb was would erupt if the two parties met. Tag had only told a handful of people about his plan and although it was mentioned at the Wembley meeting not everyone took a lot of notice and they knew nothing about the girls' weekend plans.

Trev, who didn't know about Tag's planned trip to Blackpool, soon became the only one who to know about the girls' weekend as when he got home with Stetson and six shooter and of course Sheriff badge, Cary told him, just as he was writing the words to 'Rhinestone Cowboy'.

'Trevor, I've got something to tell you and I hope you won't mind or be mad.'

'What is it?' asked Trev with a bit of apprehension. Was Cary having an affair - had she burnt his tracksuit - or had she crashed the car? he wondered.

'You know you're going away on Friday. Well all the girls are going to Blackpool for a 'jolly' you know a 'girls night out' and a stop over in a B&B,' said Cary nervously. 'I just had to tell you. You know how I feel about secrets.'

'How long has this been planned? Wait while I tell the lads.'

'You can't, you've got to be sworn to secrecy. I'm the only one telling you, all the other girls are going to let it ride and deal with the situation when it hits the fan.'

'I wish you hadn't told me, I'm shit at secrets,' said Trev.
The room fell silent.

'Are you mad about it? Because if you are I won't go, I knew it was a bad idea,' said Cary fretting.

'No I'm not mad, I don't see why you all shouldn't go and have a great time, but why the secrecy? I don't understand, and now I'm going to know all about it and I can't say a word.'

The room went silent again this time it was Trev who broke the silence.

'Don't worry, I won't say anything, what time are you going anyway?'

'Meeting 4.30, setting off at 5.'

'How are the other girls hoping to keep this a secret?'

'I don't think they're bothered, after it's happened there's nothing that can be done about it.'

'You sly twat, this means you owe me,' said Trev with a stern look on his face.

'What do you mean? I won't go I'll make an excuse.' Cary was panicking.

'Ever had sex with a cowboy before? My six shooter's loaded and ready to go,' Trev smiled and winked at Cary.

'Don't be too trigger happy,' said Cary as she lead Trev to the bedroom...

Dawn finally broke on the day of the trip. Eddie had been busy the day before organising the beer, tickets and hotel. Although he enjoyed doing the trips he was a bag of nerves from start to finish. Eddie liked the banter and the laughs. He'd been a player once and still missed the 'mickey taking' and fun of the dressing room. Now, with the trips to London, he could re-live those days and always enjoyed everything about them, except perhaps for one thing. At the back of his mind he knew that it was his name that the trip was booked in and whatever went wrong, which it invariably did, it would be him who would take the blame. The lads all knew this and although they all thought the world of Eddie, it didn't stop them winding him up no end.

He arrived at the car park of the Willows club at 7.30am, dressed in his Stetson to get everything ready for lift off. This would be about the tenth trip he'd organised and he was extremely proud of the fact that they had all gone exceptionally well with everyone asking to book again for the following year. The trip was setting off at 9.00 to avoid the rush hour traffic.

First he went to the changing rooms to get all the bin liners ready for the rubbish. Then he proceeded to the cellar where the all important alcohol for the trip was stored because you can't go on the five-hour trip with nothing to drink.

Whilst getting the beer from the cellar Eddie dropped his Stetson, which he picked up hastily, as it wasn't his hat. It was his brother in law's and it was the real deal. So were the cowboy boots and the spurs. His brother in law was a real collector of cowboy gear. And although Eddie thought he was a twat and called him 'Bonanza Bill' behind his back, he came in handy on occasions such as this.

The bus rolled up at 8.00 and the driver introduced himself.

'Albert's the name and I'm your driver,' he said as he put out his hand.

'Eddie,' came the reply as the two shook hands.

'All that's not for this trip is it?' said Albert pointing to the beer.

'Yes, this is all we've got, I hope there's enough. These lads like to keep occupied or they get bored and start pissing about,' said Eddie, winding the driver up. He could see that Albert was shocked at the volume of alcohol they were taking.

'Well, we've got a problem then,' said the driver.

'We fucking haven't,' retorted Eddie as quick as a flash. 'We always take beer on the bus, in fact your boss okayed it months ago.'

'It's not the beer, it's that, how can I put it, there's no toilet on this bus,' said the driver nervously.

'No fucking toilet, you have got to be joking, we want another bus then.'

'There are no buses left, the one you should have had went to Blackpool yesterday, so it's this or nowt, don't worry though, you'll get some money back,' Albert assured him.

'You're the one who needs to worry Albert me old son, we'll be stopping every twenty miles for a piss.'

Then Eddie had an idea. There was a dustbin in the dressing room that could be used as a toilet but it meant finding somewhere for it to go, so he got on the bus and had a look.

'This'll do here,' said Eddie.

'But that's the emergency exit,' replied the driver.

'I couldn't give a shit, I'll take responsibility if we all die. But I'm not going to London with this lot and no flaming toilet. Now give me a hand getting it on board.'

The driver did as he was told and then they waited for everyone to arrive.

The boys all started to arrive one by one, some dropped off by their girlfriends or wives, others shared taxis, all equipped with their songs and in their cowboy outfits. Although the theme was Cowboys and Indians no one had turned up as an Indian. The only exception to the rule of dressing up were the 'old fellows'. They didn't have to dress up if they didn't want to, as someone had pointed out that as most of them lived through the wild west it would be cruel to make them dress up and bring back all those memories of General Custer. They all posed for the annual trip photo all with their six-shooters and sheriff badges. Some had cap guns and gun shots could be heard all around, then the piss-taking started.

'Jesus Eddie, you look like Clint Eastwood. Nice duds, are the guns real,' asked Skip feeling inadequate with his shabby outfit.

'More like Cunt Eastwood, hey Eddie? If you can't fight - wear a big hat,' laughed Jonesy.

'Yours should be the size of a marquee then you big windy bastard,' replied Eddie as quick as a flash.

'Who's going to help me put the beer on the bus? It's going to have to go on the back seat,' pleaded Eddie.

'Come on lads get moving,' said Skip.

They all helped and the beer was on in no time.

'Eddie, why is there a dustbin at the back of the bus, can't we just use bin liners?' enquired Skip.

'What, to piss in Skip, no we can't. Right lads, due to unforeseen circumstances we've no toilet. So we'll have to make do with the bin,' announced Eddie.

The replies of protest came thick and fast.

'You've got to be joking! All the way to London with a bin full of piss, it'll stink. You've fucked up big style this time Eddie.'

'Whoah, whoah, it's not my fault, ask Albert?' Eddie laughed.

'Who the fuck's Albert?'

'The driver, go and ask him,' said Eddie pointing to the front of the coach.

Skip ran forward and confronted the driver.

'What's the score driver with this bus having no toilet?'

'Listen boys it's this or nothing they've made a fuck up at the office and this is the only bus left, but don't worry I'll stop regularly so you can empty it.'

'Us empty it? Fuck that driver, you'll have to empty it.'

'Well, I'll go without the bin boys, so it'll take about seven hours to get to London, it's up to you. Look, I'm as pissed off as you are.'

'Fair enough, we'll do it. It can be a forfeit,' said Skip

'I didn't think for one minute we'd be cleaning bogs out. This is supposed to be a relaxing trip, we're not camping.'

'By the way no shitting in it,' shouted Eddie looking in Thommo's direction.

'Right, who's missing?' asked Eddie.

'The fucking students, Grant and Mike. Grant's probably got another rash and Mike's putting cream on it. Couple of bummers I reckon,' said Jonesy.

'Takes one to know one,' shouted Gaz.

'Shut up Gaz or I'll shoot, I've got a gun and I'm not afraid to use it.'

With that a taxi turned the corner and Mike and Grant got out.

'Been cuddling in bed together?' asked Jonesy.

'Fuck off Jonesy you twat, I've been on the phone.'

'Who with, Tarty Taylor?'

'No with Pete, he can't come, he's got chicken pox. Sally just rang my house and me mam got me out of the taxi to take the call,' said Grant.

'Shit, I forgot about Pete,' said Eddie.

'I'm off to ring him. Is the club open Eddie?' asked Skip. Eddie gave Skip the nod and he and a few others went to ring Pete.

'Is Pete there Sally?'

'Hiya Pete, sorry to hear about your pox, looks like we'll have to drink your share. You want to see the beer Pete, loads of it and there's a buffet and we're picking up a topless barmaid to serve us the drinks.'

Skip was in his element giving Pete all the details, he didn't realise that he'd already hung up.

Skip went back to the coach and told them about the situation. Everyone started laughing at Pete's misfortune and decided they would just have to 'make the best of their friend's agony'.

Meanwhile Pete was at home calling them all the names under the sun and wondering if was true about the topless barmaids...

'All here and ready to go,' shouted Eddie.

'No, there's no Tag,' somebody replied.

'I thought you all knew he's not coming, he let it out at the meeting,' said Eddie.

'Why the little shit, he never said anything to me,' said Jonno.

'Well he wouldn't would he? He's taking a bird from his work to Blackpool for the weekend behind Fay's back,' said Gaz who was quite proud of himself as he'd never kept a secret that long before.

'Yeah he told us ages ago, poor Fay. He mentioned it at the meeting, I thought we all knew,' said Skip.

'Well, are we going to discuss that little twat all morning or are we going to have a drink?' said Eddie impatiently waiting to start off the trip he'd been planning all year.

'Where's the beer?' a few shouted.

'At the back next to the en-suite facilities, help yourself,' said Skip.

'Right then are we all ready? Strap yourselves in because we're off,' announced Eddie ignoring the sarcastic comments.

The coach pulled out of the car park and made its way towards the motorway through Hull's rush hour traffic. All the lads were banging on the windows and attracting lots of attention as it wasn't every day that you saw a bus full of Cowboys going along the high street.

'Woah! woah! woah! Where's Matt?' shouted Tosser.

'We're picking him up at Ferriby,' came Eddie's reply and he added to himself, 'I wonder what the fucking hell he's come as, the head case?'

'Knowing Matt he'll have hired a horse,' said Tosser.

'Yeah, he said he was doing something special but wouldn't say what,' said Skip.

'Probably got some cattle for us all to round up.'

The beers were flowing and it was only 9 o'clock in the morning and no one, but no one wanted to piss in the bin at the back.

'Now then lads, pace yourselves, it's a marathon not a sprint, besides if you fall asleep you're fare game, those are the rules,' announced Jonesy.

'What rules? You won't get me,' piped up Mike, Grant's mate from Uni who was usually quiet but had already had a couple of liveners for breakfast.

'Fucking hell, it's barely gone nine and I think we have our first favourite for the treatment and it's the student. He's had a sniff of the barmaid's apron and he wants to fight the world,' shouted Jonesy.

'Don't peak too early son you might regret it,' warned Thommo.

'Who's going to stop us getting you if you're asleep?'

'For fuck sake sit down,' said Grant to his friend, 'You'll have no fucking eyebrows by the time we get to Goole if you're not careful, these lot won't piss about.'

'What are the rules?' said Gaz

'Don't fall asleep unless in bed of course is the first rule and the second one is obey all the rules,' said Skip.

'Don't shit in Dusty bin at the back, Ted Rogers wants him back for 3-2-1,' shouted Colin who had only just joined the club and was at the veteran stage of his career. This comment had everyone in stitches, with the two students asking who Ted Rogers was.

When they arrived at Ferriby there was no sign of Matt.

'Where the fuck is he?' said Gaz.

'He said he'd be here by ten past and it's 25 past now, I'll go see if he's in the paper shop,' said Eddie.

Eddie stepped down off the bus but no sooner had he taken a few steps, an arrow flew passed his head and hit the window of the coach and stuck. Then, before Eddie could speak Matt jumped down from a nearby tree with his bow and arrow and tomahawk and started dancing around Eddie doing a rain dance. He had a full chief's outfit on with a headdress and the coach nearly tipped over as everyone rushed to the same side to catch a glimpse of the mad Indian.

'Fucking priceless,' said Tosser crying with laughter.

Matt got on the bus to rapturous applause. He had a big bag of stuff he'd got from the joke shop and was ready to go mad for the weekend.

'Where did you get that get-up from?' asked Eddie

'Big chief Matt, he go to the fancy dress shop and hire it for himself. Now big chief Matt is going to sit down and have um drink.'

'Absolute class Matt. Brilliant,' shouted Jonesy from the back.

'Are we all here now?' interrupted the driver, trying to get the big red Indian to sit down.

'That's it driver we're on our way, all present and correct. Sit down Matt. London here we come,' said Eddie still getting over the shock of being ambushed. The bus then set off along the couple of hundred yards of road and onto the motorway…

'Where's the beer then?' enquired Matt.

'Here, get stuck in chief,' said Gaz throwing Matt a can.

'Hold it, I need a piss first. Where's the toilet?' asked Matt.

His question was met by complete silence.

'Don't say there's no fucking toilet? Anybody, answer me.'

Gaz pointed to the back of the bus.

'Oh! for fuck's sake, not a bin Eddie, I want a refund,' shouted Matt.

'Shut up you tart and have a piss, it's not like we haven't seen it before,' was Eddie's reply.

Matt did as Eddie suggested, then when he'd finished his leak he sat down next to Trev and began to enjoy his first beer.

'When bus stops, chief Matt will scalp paleface Eddie for um balls up,' shouted Matt.

'It's the bus company's fault, they sent the wrong bus,' explained Skip.

'Where's Tag?' Matt asked as he took his first sip and looked around the bus.

'Hasn't come, he's gone to Blackpool with the receptionist from his work behind Fay's back, the little shit. Don't you remember he swore us all to secrecy?' said Gaz.

That was the first Trev had heard about Tag and the receptionist going to Blackpool. He nearly choked on his drink as he knew that all the girls were also going to Blackpool for the weekend and that he couldn't say anything because he was sworn to secrecy.

'What the fuck's up with you Trev, are you alright?'

'I'm fine, beer just went down the wrong way that's all,' said Trev thinking he'd got away with it but just in case there was any doubt he added, 'I wouldn't like to be him if her brothers find out.'

'No, the little bastard has gone too far this time. He borrowed £100 off me last week and said he would bring it today. It's a good job I know what a little shit he is and I got extra money out to bring with me. I'll fucking kill him when I see him,' ranted Matt.

'So you've paid for his dirty weekend then Matt,' chipped in Grant shit-stirring, as he hated Tag.

'Listen student boy, when we get to the service station I'm going to ring Fay and tell her what the little twat's up to, see how she likes them eggs,' said Matt.

'Now then, you can't do that Matt,' said Trev knowing that the shit would hit the fan if they all found out about the Blackpool trip.

'Can't I Trevor? You just watch me.'

'Listen, he's not here and he's still causing trouble. Let's just forget the little bastard for the weekend and enjoy ourselves,' said Skip trying to diffuse the situation as he knew that Matt was true to his word and he would ring Fay up and drop him in it.

'Let them sort it out themselves Matt, we'll just have a good time eh?'

'Alright, but the next time I see him you better get in between us because I won't be responsible for my actions.'

'Yeah, yeah, what's in the carrier bag then?' asked Eddie and Gaz trying to change the subject.

'Oh yeah, I went to joke shop yesterday and got all this for a tenner. There's fart spray, stink bombs, silly string and this, one can of green spray paint and one can of orange, so that we can get anyone who breaks the rules. Also I've brought some sellotape and some electrical tape you never know, it might come in handy later on.'

'What for?' asked Mike the student, looking totally puzzled.

'You never know, for a laugh we might stick you two bummers together naked,' shouted Jonesy.

Mike didn't reply. He just looked out of the window and whispered under his breath to Grant, 'What the fuck have you brought me on here?'

'Where's Pete?' asked Matt.

'Chickenpox,' came the reply.

'I bet he's gutted. Sally was telling Anna that he wouldn't stop talking about it and that he had all his gear, the lot.'

(Sally is Pete's partner and Anna is Matt's wife)

'We'll have to ring him all weekend and take the piss,' continued Matt.

'Already started. Rang him from club and told him we had topless waitresses,' said Skip laughing.

'We'll ring him from the service station next and then when we get there,' chipped in Jonesy.

The boys continued in this vain and more beer was consumed as they sped down the motorway.

Meanwhile back in Hull, Tag was lying low. He hadn't turned in for work as he'd booked the day off and was planning to spend most of the morning in bed. That was until he thought of a potential problem that could ruin everything. What if Fay came back home from work?

So he had to get all his gear ready to make it look as if he was going to London. He would then spend the day dodging people he knew and more importantly people who knew Fay and her large family. He decided to set off at 5pm as Suki was driving and she had to work. They should get there in plenty of time for the fun and games to start, or so he hoped. He and Suki hadn't actually had sex yet, in fact they had only kissed on the dates they'd been on, which came to the grand total of twelve. Strangely for Tag this added extra excitement. The fact that he would have to work at getting into her knickers as she was not easy. But he felt it would be worth it if he succeeded. And it looked like this weekend would be the time.

Tag was used to women who would drop their knickers after a couple of drinks and a crappy chat up line. Fay had been the same as Suki, really not easy. Everything was great but things had taken a down turn in their relationship as soon as they moved in together. At first it was good sex every night and then the drudgery of real life set in. Cooking, cleaning, her using his razors, it had all built up and Tag could no longer wait to get out of the house to go to the pub or to training, in fact he'd never been so fit. And he'd even been picked for the local 'rep' side, which meant more training, which meant less time in the house and more chances to see Suki after training for the odd hour.

It wasn't the fact that he didn't love Fay, he did. It was just the fact that her family was always asking when the wedding was going to be and Tag hated being pressured into things and always laughed it off. Then there was the situation with her brothers who didn't like Tag and were always calling him and saying he wasn't good enough for their sister. Then that fateful night in LA LA's when Suki introduced herself and they arranged a date, which Tag thought in his 'caveman' mind would be a few drinks and a shag. The fact that Suki drove was an extra bonus as he could have a drink, she could drive and he'd get his end away. Perfect! Apart from the fact that he soon found out she was no slapper and he would have to work very hard to bed this one, which he didn't mind. The dates they'd gone on were usually out of town to a village pub away from prying eyes or to a restaurant, which Tag thought was going a bit far as he wasn't on the biggest wages. But he couldn't believe it when on the second date Suki took him out. This was totally foreign to Tag, a women who paid her own way. And now, in a few hours, they were going away for the weekend together.

She had even sorted out the hotel - well B&B - and Tag thought this was fantastic, she was not only driving them there but had arranged everything. All he had to do was turn up.

To help him lie low Tag had a key for his mother's house and he knew no one would be in until six so he could doss there and then Suki would pick him up and no one would be any the wiser.

So instead of the taxi taking him to the club to catch the bus for the trip he got the taxi to take him to his mother's. What a great plan and as soon as he was on the motorway no one would be any the wiser. Tag had gone through this in his mind over and over again and thought it was near perfect. So all he had to do now was sit and wait bored shitless at his mother's house...

The bus was now well on its way, the beer had been flowing quite freely and the usual antics had started, They'd even forgotten about the bin they had to wee in and had started making jokes about it. Eddie hadn't had a drink yet and wouldn't really be able to relax until they were at the hotel and even then he knew he would still be a bag of nerves. In fact Eddie wouldn't settle until he was home again in his own house and sat looking back on it and planning next year's trip. The whole weekend was a nightmare for Eddie really.

He was always worried that some idiot would do something wrong, and his anxiety would double when he looked around the coach and saw who he was travelling with. Then the advice started to come out for Grant and his mate.

'Oi! Granty boy don't be going down to Soho tonight and getting all horny and excited about seeing naked girls. You'll lose all your money and get ripped off,' shouted Thommo.

'He prefers pensioners don't you Grant?' laughed Gaz.

'Yeah, yeah fuck off you two I'm not daft, but it sounds like you've had some experience Thommo?' replied Grant.

Thommo went quiet and then told Grant about what had happened to him on his first trip.

'You're right Grant, it happened to me a few years ago. I went there to see a strip show, went down three flights of stairs with me mate from work and ordered two halves of lager and sat at a table.'

'So how is that getting ripped off?' interrupted Grant.

'That's not the story. Here's the bit where they get you. A bird comes over and asks if she can sit at the spare chair on your table, so obviously you say yes. And there is the sting in the tail, they then bill you for your drinks and charge you for the escort, who is this bird who is sitting at your table. The lagers were £5 each and it was £50 for her just to sit there. We were the only tits in that place, I can tell you.'

'So you just refuse to pay,' said Grant innocently.

'We did and then these meatheads appeared from nowhere and said we had to pay as we were in a private club and they can charge what they like. Besides we were three flights of stairs underground and trying to do a runner was impossible. So we paid and ended up back at the hotel borrowing money for the weekend. So be warned, stay well away from those places.'

'So where are we heading tonight Skip,' asked Grant.

'Probably Covent Garden and then the Hippodrome for some dancing. I've always wanted to go there and tonight might just be the night.'

'Oh yes, I definitely want to get in there, the Hippodrome. It's been my ambition to get in and I'm focused to do it,' shouted Daz.

'Don't forget we're meeting Damo the Aussie. He's had to work and is getting a train down and he said he'd be in the hotel at about 7.30. So we'll leave him directions from there about where to meet us if he doesn't arrive on time,' chipped in Butty the other Aussie on the trip.

Just as they were talking a bus went past full of people going to London for Wembley and they started waving at the coach and pointing at Trev.

'Hey Trev, those geriatrics are waving at you,' said Gaz.

'They work with me Gaz, you cheeky bastard. They asked me on their trip. They said they have a wild time,' said Trev waving back.

'Looks like they're having a ball. Do they all take flasks and sandwiches or is it just the coffin dodgers on the first nine rows?' Skip remarked.

'Looks like a fucking wake Trev and you work with that lot? I bet you're the youngster and the only one who hasn't lived through a world war,' shouted Thommo.

'Driver catch them up. I've got a present for them to spice up their trip,' shouted Matt.

'What are you going to do you mad bastard? I have to go to work with these on Tuesday,' said Trev shitting himself as his boss was on the bus and he might have some explaining to do on Tuesday.

'Keep your fucking hair on. I'm only going to show them me song sheet. Driver catch them up and drive alongside please,' persisted Matt.

As the bus pulled up alongside the coach with Trev's boss and work colleagues on it, Matt got out his song sheet showed it to the other bus and they all laughed and started to sing along, much to Trev's relief. But then it all turned sour. Some of the women on the bus started to point at the back few seats of Trev's bus. They all looked both shocked and horrified. Trev turned to see what they were all staring at and could hardly believe his eyes.

At the back of the coach the two students had started to 'moon' out of the window but worse was to come. Thommo had shoved a bottle of beer up his backside and was displaying it for all to see. It took a few minutes for it to register what was going on but it soon became apparent that Trev's boss' wife and daughter had already seen the bottle incident and when Trev tried to sort it out by grappling with Thommo and trying to get the bottle out, he ended up looking like Trev was trying to molest Thommo.

The other bus had at this point sped away with half of them in shock but secretly the other half including Trev's boss finding it absolutely hilarious.

'You fucking idiot Thommo, you've gone too far this time.'

'I know that bottle really hurt and you nearly shoved it right up.'

'I will next time you stupid bastard, how am I going to explain that away and I bet they're at the next service station.'

'Chill out Trev, it's not your fault, he did it, surely your boss will see that,' said Jonesy.

'It's not that, it's fucking embarrassing.'

'Never mind Trev it'll be something for them to talk about, looks like it's livened up their weekend,' said Thommo as he went to the back of the bus for a pee.

'I'll liven his fucking weekend up, I'll get him for this.'

'I might be able to help you there Trev,' said Mike as he produced a bottle of laxatives.

'Stick this in his drink and he'll be shitting through the eye of a needle.'

'What is it?' asked Grant.

'Got it out of the medicine cabinet and reading the label his arse will fall out completely in about four hours, just as we get there.'

'Good lad, I'll give it a few minutes and then I'll slip it in,' said Trev chuckling to himself.

Just then Thommo came back and sat down next to Skip and tried to explain himself.

'I only did it for a laugh Trev, look no hard feelings.'

'I know and it was hilarious, you're a legend Thommo, that'll go down in folklore. Thommo and his bottle up the arse routine. But it is a bit harsh on Trev.'

'Well I can't help that now can I?'

'Anyone want a beer while I'm up?' shouted Trev, knowing full well that Thommo needed a refill.

'Go on then Trev, I'll have one and no hard feelings eh mate?' said Thommo.

'No, none you little shit,' said a smiling Trev as he slipped the laxative into Thommo's beer and gave him double the dosage for good measure and then handed him his drink.

'Bottoms up Thommo?' laughed Trev and clinked bottles with Thommo.

'Good one Trev, I knew you'd see the funny side of it.'

'Oh, I'll see the funny side when you're shitting your pants every five minutes, you'll wish you had that bottle permanently up there,' Trev whispered under his breath and winked at Mike who had to bite his lip to stop himself from laughing.

'Cheers Trev,' Thommo said as he clinked bottles with him and took a big gulp of the beer. 'By that tastes good, it's getting better all the time.'

Mike was nearly choking at this point with beer coming out of his nostrils as he was trying not to laugh, but Trev kept a straight face as Thommo devoured his drink.

'Another one Thommo?' enquired Trev.

'Go on then might as well,' said Thommo, oblivious to what Trev had done to his drink.

Trev went through the same procedure and gave him a good measure of laxative, this would be it, he daren't give him any more. As Mike had gone to the back of the bus Grant had followed him to see what was wrong and to see if he was alright.

'Are you okay?'

'Yeah' spluttered Mike as he struggled to get his words out.

'Did it go down the wrong way?'

'Listen, those laxatives I gave Trev, he's put it in Thommo's last two beers, that's what's wrong with me. I didn't want to give the game away, the poor bastard's arse'll blow off, he'll have an arse like a blood orange,' explained Mike trying not to be too loud.

'So don't say anything or he'll find out it was me.'

'Your secret's safe with me, besides he'll kill you if he finds out.' And then the two of them rejoined the rest of the party, where Thommo was getting well stuck in to his beer.

Then Grant asked Mike how long did the laxative take to work as there was no toilet on the bus. They looked at the bottle and it said 'four hours or more' to take hold. They worked out that they would be in London in three hours, so everything would be alright.

Matt was getting a bit restless and started looking in his bag of tricks, with that he pulled out his coloured spray, one orange can of party spray paint and one green can.

'Let's have some fun boys, watch this.' Matt proceeded to the front of the bus and started to talk to Eddie who was near the driver, then as he was talking to Eddie he started spraying the back of the bus drivers head orange and then with a bit of green.

'What the fucking hell you doing,' protested the bus driver.

'Nothing, sorry it's just a can of hairspray, you know for your hair.'

'Well fuck off with your can of hairspray, I'm trying to drive a bus here,' said the driver who couldn't see the back of his head. Everyone was in fits of laughter as Matt carried on talking to Eddie who dared not laugh as that would have given the game away. Matt then went back to his seat and told everyone to casually go to the front and see his handy work. This they all did and the full bus was in fits. Then the word was sent around that nobody should tell the driver and he should be allowed to go into the service station like it, besides it washed out anyway.

The driver then pulled off the motorway to the service station and told Eddie that they had 30 minutes to get whatever they wanted and not to be late as the quicker they got back the quicker they would get to London.

'Right lads you've got half an hour here then it's back on the bus. And don't be late, we want to avoid the rush hour traffic in London, and for fuck's sake don't get up to anything in here.'

'No sir we won't,' came the sarcastic answer from half the coach.

The driver got off and went for something to eat totally oblivious of the state that the back of his head was in. People just stood opened-mouthed when they saw him in the packed service station. They must have thought he'd been tango'd. How the checkout girl at the till kept a straight face when he had a green salad and an orange for afters. The full services were laughing at him, people were going out of their way to get a glimpse, but no one uttered a word to him.

When the boys all hit the services, the first thing Skip and Jonesy did was to go straight to the telephone to ring up Pete to see how he was and to take the piss out of him. They dialled his number, then waited and after a few rings Sally answered.

'Hello, is that Sally? It's Skip just ringing to speak to Pete.'

'Pete it's for you it's Skip.'

Pete got out of bed and went to the phone still half asleep.

'Hello Skip, what is it?'

'Woooah! Pete we're having a great time you're missing it, we're all pissed and it's great, here's Jonesy.'

'Hey Pete, we've picked up three hitch-hikers and they're all gorgeous and gagging for it. We're not missing you because there's more beer for the rest of us.'

'You set of bastards is that all you wanted?' said a tired Pete.

'Yeah, just to tell you what a great time we're having, we'll keep you posted.' But by this time Pete had already hung up and was fuming at home while the two of them had gone to tell everyone of their exploits. Pete knew that there was a funny side to it and if it had happened to anyone else he would have been the first on the phone gloating. And as he itched his way back to bed he realised he might see the funny side... in two or three years time.

Sally decided to cheer him up by telling him that the lads were in for a shock as all the wives and girlfriends had arranged to go on a trip to Blackpool. It was all a big secret and had been booked for months, the only down side to it was that she couldn't go now because Pete was ill.

Pete told her to go and he'd be alright but Sally said she'd stay at home with him. This bit of news had cheered Pete up and he thought he would wait until the next time they rang to drop the bomb shell. Or he might wait until the next day when they were in Blackpool, then no one could ring and have a go at their other halves as it would be too late by then...

Meanwhile back in the queue at the services the lads were sorting out who would be the next to ring Pete in 20 minutes time. They would all take it in turns throughout the weekend to inform Pete of the great time he was missing out on.

The people at the services couldn't believe their eyes when 40-odd cowboys and one Indian walked in firing guns and yee-haaing. The majority were amused but a few children burst into tears and some of the staff looked like they would burst into tears when the orders came.

'Yes sir and what can I get you?' asked the assistant who was only two months into the job and had never served a 'posse' before.

'Well Missy, I'd like some coffee and beans, but they've got to be cowboy beans,' said Skip trying to sound like a cowboy but failing miserably.

'I can do you beans on toast,' replied the assistant getting rather flustered as her till didn't say just beans and the queue was mounting up with cowboys and they sure looked hungry.

'Looky here, me darlin' I've been riding all morning and all I want is some coffee and beans, cowboy beans mind and if I have to have toast then so be it. And can I have a bucket of water for my horse 'Lightening' he's outside?'

This totally made the girl panic, she didn't have any buckets, but remembering her training that the customer was always right she said she could get him a large cup of water. And if he needed any more then if he could take his horse to the garage and could use the water there.

'If you say it's fine to do that then that's alright by me, ma'am. You're one fine looking woman.'

'Thank you and here is your order, one beans on toast and two cups. You fill them up yourself over there, that'll be £3.50,' said the girl calmly thinking her ordeal was over.

'£3.50! How much is that in dollars?'

'Er, I don't know, we only take pounds.'

'Them is cowboy beans ain't they?' Skip pointed at the plate.

'I think they're Heinz,' the assistant replied.

'Well if Heinz doesn't object I'll take them then, what's he going to have?'

'Who?' said the girl who was getting more confused by the minute.

'Heinz? If I've got his beans then what is he going to have to eat?' Finally the girl was saved when Eddie came to the front of the queue to see what the delay was.

'Stop pissing around Skip, we've only got half an hour.'

'Who's next please,' said the girl dreading the reply.

'Well howdee, my name's Clint and I'd like...'

With that Skip interrupted Jonesy by shouting, 'Stop pissing the girl about, we've only got half an hour.'

After everyone had ordered their coffee and beans, cowboy beans, and some display stands had taken a tumble in the newsagency part of the services where you needed a mortgage for a Mars bar and a can of coke, the cowboys then boarded their coach again, ready for the last leg of their journey to the bright lights of London.

Back on the bus Thommo had bought the latest 'Razzle' and was showing it to the old blokes at the front.

'Remember one of those you old twats? And look at those, they're called tits.'

'Oh we know what tits and fannies look like, we watch you every week trying to play rugby. Now fuck off to the back of the bus Thommo and drink your shandy before some real men show you how to drink. You'll end up all over the place sitting up here with us drinkers, so run along there's a good boy,' replied Bert who had played for Great Britain and was well respected by everybody at the club. He had been a great player in his time and went on all the trips. Thommo turned on his heels and went to the back of the bus to read his magazine.

'That told you Thommo,' shouted Gaz.

'Fuck off,' muttered Thommo.

'He's just told you to fuck off Bert,' stirred Gaz.

'No I haven't Bert it's this lot pissing around,' said Thommo quickly, as everyone knew that if you got on the wrong side of Bert you were treading on thin ice. He was as tough as nails and he could go with the best of them,

even though he was in his late fifties.

'Right then it's cabaret time. I'll go first to get the ball rolling,' said Jonesy, handing out sheets of paper with the handwritten words to the song 'High Noon'.

He had only managed to get ten sheets done so everyone had to share.

'I haven't got one, you haven't done enough,' shouted Thommo.

'Knob off Thommo, you'll have to share like everybody else.'

'Who wrote these out?' asked Gaz.

'Me and Sue we only got ten done as she got writer's cramp and I fell asleep.'

'Why didn't you just write it out once on a big piece of cardboard like we all did?' said Gaz.

'I didn't, I did sheets, forty of them,' said Tom.

'You mean Steph did them at work on the typewriter?' Gaz answered back.

'Well yeah, she did but then she'd do anything for me,' said Tom quietly.

'Anyway does anyone want to hear this or not?' shouted Skip.

'Go on Jonesy get on with it.'

The whole bus was awash with bad voices singing cowboy songs as one after the other got up and did their stuff with everyone joining in. It nearly brought a tear to the eye to see and hear all these tough hard men singing and enjoying themselves dressed as cowboys (twats). This is what it was all about, mates taking the piss out of each other. But deep down being with your mates on a tatty bus with no toilet, loads of beer and no women to interfere. This is what these trips were all about and had been since 1923, the first Wembley and probably before that to some other destination. This is why these trips are unique.

For two nights they could forget the wife, kids, mortgage, bills and the responsibility of day to day living and go mad like they used to before they were adults. Back to their youth when life was one long laugh. They were on a three-day tour. They were rock stars living in hotels, going to bed when they wanted and drinking till they dropped and no one was going to nag or moan about them doing so. Everyone on the bus had joined in and the finale came with 'Rhinestone Cowboy' performed by Gaz. He was brilliant as he had been used to being on the stage when he won the under 14's talent contest at Butlins in Skegness singing the very same song. As he lapped up the audience's applause the clapping was replaced by gasps of amazement as Matt started to fire his arrows from his bow at the driver who was doing 70 mph down the motorway. One by one they hit the windscreen. Credit the driver he didn't flinch once but told Eddie in no uncertain terms to tell the idiot to stop or the trip was off. He saw the joke and didn't mind his hair being sprayed, a fact that he only found out about when every other coach driver ended up laughing at him at the service station. But getting killed by an arrow fired by an over-excited Indian was not on. Eddie shot to the back of the bus where even the rest of the blokes couldn't believe it either.

'Matt you fucking idiot, we could have crashed. The driver's on about turning back and calling the trip off. You've gone too far this time. You'd better go and apologise to him,' shouted Eddie who hardly ever raised his voice, let alone swore.

'Alright, alright, it was only a joke,' protested Matt.

'Not a very good one, now go and say you're sorry, you prick,' said Eddie pointing to the front where the driver was. Matt got up and went to the front to say he was sorry like a naughty schoolboy. As he was approaching the front he said to the driver, 'Sorry mate just a bit of fun and all that.'

The driver just nodded in acknowledgement and Matt took his arrows from the windscreen. He thought about saying '180' but thought better of it, as he nearly never got back to his seat.

Bert and all the coffin dodgers at the front started giving him loads of abuse, telling him to grow up and hoping he realised that he could have killed them all. Matt began to realise what he'd done and said he was sorry. It was one of those 'sobering-up moments' when you've been drinking and something happens and your head becomes clear straight away with the seriousness of the situation. The final humiliation came as he got to the back of the bus and Eddie confiscated his bow and arrow and told him he could only have it back if he behaved.

The bus was quiet for about ten minutes and then as per usual Skip got the fun going again.

'Right, listen up, from now on, for half an hour, no one can speak in their normal voices. We all have to speak like Bruce Forsythe and then after that like Rigsby and then to finish off as Jimmy Saville. No matter what you say, you have to say it in a Brucey accent. 'Alright my love'. 'Nice to see you, to see you nice'. 'You get nothing for a pair, not in this game, starting now.'

The coach was deadly silent for about five minutes and then the silence was broken by Jonesy who asked how long it was before they got there, but didn't put the accent on. As quick as a flash Skip was onto him.

'Gotcha, come on drink up my love you've got to do it like me.'

'Fucking hell, you're more like someone having a fit,' Matt chipped in but in a Brucey accent of course. Matt loved these stupid games and had come around after realising he'd been a twat.

This went on for the allotted half an hour and then Rigsby came into play - with lots of 'My God Miss Jones's'. In fact this phrase could be heard at the end of every sentence, just as the words 'Alright my love' had been heard for the previous half-hour.

They were approaching London and Jimmy Saville was just about to kick in when Thommo let out a groan.

'Now then, now then, I need a shit,' Thommo shouted as he proceeded to the back of the bus.

'Now then, now then, fuck off, you're not shitting on here. Not a fucking chance, you'll have to hold it in,' said Skip blocking his way.

'I can't, I'm going to explode, driver stop the bus, I need a shit right away.'

'Now then, now then, you didn't do it like Jimmy so a forfeit,' laughed Gaz.

'Fuck you Gaz, I'm in agony here, stop the bus,' shouted Thommo.

'Now then, now then, two forfeits,' Gaz answered back as the driver, realising the situation, pulled over.

'I have a letter here that says 'Dear Jim can you fix it for me to have a big shit on a grass verge whilst dressed as a cowboy just outside London,' said Gaz to everyone's delight.

The bus pulled over and off raced Thommo into the undergrowth moaning as he went. The rest of the bus got off to have a pee so as not to fill up the bin as it was nearly to the top. And although Thommo didn't know it, that was to be his double forfeit - empty the piss bin. They could hear him straining and moaning.

'My god, my god it won't stop,' moaned Thommo.

'Now then, now then, it's Jimmy here what are you doing in there jingly jangly,' laughed Jonesy.

'Fucking dying, it won't stop coming,' said Thommo as he let another ripper of a fart go.

'It's now then, now then, I'm fucking dying. Come on Thommo join in and at least try,' mocked Skip.

'Skip fuck off, this isn't funny, it won't stop coming.'

Trev and the two students were pissing themselves and made a pact that under no circumstances could they let it out what had gone on and who was responsible.

Ten minutes past and there was still no sign of Thommo returning so Eddie went looking for him. He smelt him before he saw him.

'Jesus what have you been eating Thommo, camel shit?'

'It must have been that curry last night, I'll be with you in a minute.'

The others sorted out the bin and emptied it as Thommo came out of the bushes looking drained and worse for wear. All the bus was in shock not least Trev and his two accomplices. Thommo looked like a corpse, he was as white as a sheet and didn't look good.

The bus carried on into London with the beer running out just as they reached the hotel. It was 2.30pm and they couldn't believe their eyes when they arrived...

CHAPTER 4
LUXURY HERE
WE COME

The hotel was in Canary Wharf and was 5-star and virtually new. That new in fact, that there was no underground link yet. The reason they had got it so cheap was because it was so far out of London, plus there were also special rates for weekends.

'Fucking hell Eddie, are we staying here?'

'Piss off, he's taking the piss, come on take us to our proper hotel and then we can get out.'

'Get out of the way I need a shit and that's where I'm going in that hotel so wait while I've finished,' shouted a desperate Thommo. Eddie checked his paperwork and the driver assured him this was the hotel, but to make sure Eddie got off and went in to check anyway.

'You lot stay here, I'll go and check if this is the right place,' said Eddie not really believing that it could be a 5-star gaff with this rabble, he was in for a nightmare weekend trying to keep these in order. After a couple of minutes he came back out smiling a nervous smile.

'Right can I have your attention? This is our hotel and believe me it's too good for us. Look you're representing the club here, please don't let us down. I mean there are chandeliers and paintings on the walls,' said Eddie nervously.

'Fucking hell Eddie we aren't cave men, don't worry we'll behave. Now can we get off this fucking bus? That piss bin is starting to hum,' said Skip rather pissed off at being treated like a schoolkid.

They all entered the hotel foyer and all the hotel staff started to laugh as they were used to dealing with stuffy businessmen and these cowboys looked like they could be fun. Eddie sorted the rooms out while Skip and the others headed for the bar to arrange what was going on and what the plan would be for the coming day and night.

'Hey it's got a leisure centre and a swimming pool' interrupted Jonesy as he read a brochure about the hotel facilities.

'Go away Jonesy,' said Gaz.

'Look for yourself, and if you stay here you can use it FREE!'

'He's right so let's have a couple here and then a swim and then something to eat and then out,' said Skip all excited

'We'll have one in here the lagers nearly £2.50 you can stick that up your arse we'll be spent up in no time,' moaned Jonno.

'Okay then, we'll have one in here and then we'll go to our rooms and then go for a swim. I'll make some enquiries and see if there's anywhere to go around here,' said Skip. 'I'll stay in the bar I can't swim,' announced Greg.

Eddie came back with the keys and gave them out and then sat and had a drink with Greg, his roommate for the weekend. Now for Eddie this had been a tricky choice as he liked things just so and Greg had just joined the club and seemed pretty quiet, so Eddie thought he'll do. Eddie went to the room leaving Greg drinking in the bar in his spurs with his two six shooters.

Skip was at the bar with Tosser and he'd got his hands on everyone's room number so that he could ring them and tell them the arrangements but mainly so that he could terrorise them later with random phone calls and bogus room service. He asked the barman if there was anywhere cheaper to drink and the barman said there was a pub about 200 yards away through a park and they did food as well. Skip and Tosser finished their drinks and left Greg still nursing his brandy and coke on ice. Just before they went to their room they had to ring Pete to tell him that the hotel was great and what a great time they were having so that's what they did.

'Hello Sally is Pete there?' said Skip.

'Pete, he doesn't want to talk to you.'

'But I've got some news for him, trust me he'll want to hear this,' persisted Skip.

Sally passed the phone onto Pete who was watching some old film on Channel 4 and waiting for Countdown to come on.

'What do you want then? Don't tell me it's great.'

'Better than that it's unreal the hotel is 5-star and there's a couple of hen parties here and they're all gagging for it. There's a swimming pool and Jacuzzi and room service and it's a shame you weren't here because you'd love it.'

'You're really enjoying this you bastard well I've got some news for you' Pete was just about to tell them about the Blackpool trip but Sally kicked him and he held back.

'What? You're talking shit, anyway enjoy your countdown, have a wank over Carol.'

Pete could hear Skip and Tosser laughing as they put the phone down. The two of them then made their way to their room, as they did they met up with Thommo who looked like death warmed up after his marathon shit. He'd been on toilet for the best part of three-quarters of an hour and was the worse for wear. Skip told him he was with Gaz and told him his room number.

Now the thing about the hotel was that it was huge and had five sections to it and all the party had been spread out so as they tried to find their rooms everyone was continually bumping into each other all the time. This was the first time any of them had stayed in a hotel that used cards to get into the rooms they were all used to keys. They'd all had success except Skip and Tosser who were right at the far end of the hotel a long way from the front of the hotel.

'What's the number Skip?' asked Tosser.

'345 blue it should be around here somewhere.'

'Found it,' said Tosser trying his key in 354 by mistake, but the door actually opened and the two of them bundled in, to be met by the worse sight any man could be faced with - one double bed!

'I knew this was too good to be true, you don't wake up with a morning glory do you Skip?'

'Fuck off, if I do I'll spoon you, this must be why it's been cheap,' said a deflated Skip.

Just then Skip looked at his key.

'Hang on we're in the wrong room you plantpot, this is 354 and we want 345. We're not supposed to be in here, come on get your gear.'

'Hang on a minute let's think about this. You go find 345 and see if your key works and then we can have two rooms, one each. What room number are we on the hotel records?' asked Tosser.

'345 why?' asked Skip looking puzzled.

'Because we can clear out the mini-bar from here and who's to know? - we're in room 345 and not 354.'

'You're a fucking genius Tosser, I'll go check the other room.'

Skip went to check the other room and returned a minute later with a broad smile on his face.

'Well the other room opens to. So what are we going to do?'

'What's it like?'

'Well it's got two double beds.'

'That's it then, we'll clear the mini-bar out in this room and then go to the other room,' said Tosser.

They left the room with all the contents of the mini-bar safely tucked in their bags, they shut the door behind them and then tried the door of 354 again, only this time they couldn't get in.

'Fucking hell we were lucky there, Skip.'

'Too right but we've got plenty of booze for a party if we want one. You get a shower and I'll ring around everyone to tell them to meet in the bar and we'll go swimming from there,' said Skip.

Skip rang around everyone and gave them all half an hour to meet near the bar.

Eddie was having a quiet drink in the hotel foyer when he was met by a sight for sore eyes, around twenty semi-naked men all going for a swim. This was while the hotel was at one of its busiest times.

'Cover yourselves up, why haven't you brought your going out gear to get changed into?' asked Eddie who felt like a headmaster that had been let down by his pupils, as most of them had just come down with shorts on and a towel.

'This is a swanky leisure club not a paddling pool or Lido in park.'

'Coming in for a dip Eddie? Or scared you'll get your hair wet?' said Gaz.

'I just hope you lot behave.'

'Look Eddie we're going in tell anyone who wants to join us where we are,' said Gaz.

'Will do' replied Eddie shaking his head.

They all ran in like kids that have been let out for the day and had never seen water before. They were diving, bombing and splashing about. Which cleared the place, but to be fair the people were leaving anyway and the one rather glamourous lady who was in the steam room soon left. The security attendant told them to stop diving and bombing, which when they were told they did just like school kids.

They were having a great time and when they were all there they started to plan for the night ahead. Skip was centre stage as per usual which was good because that way they would all stick together.

'Right then are we all here?' said Skip addressing everyone whilst in the Jacuzzi. The fact that the Jacuzzi was only supposed to have a maximum of 8 people there were 12 in it and the rest gathered around as the water overflowed.

'Right I've asked the fella at the bar if there's anywhere that's cheaper to drink than here, and he said that there's a pub about 200 yards away that does food. So I think if we meet at 5.00 ready to go out for the night then we can have a few drinks in the pub and something to eat and then head into London whenever, are we all agreed?'

'Yeah sounds fine' was the unanimous verdict.

'What about Damo?' asked Gaz.

'If he gets here he'll come with us otherwise we'll leave a trail and he can find us that way, anyhow he's supposed to be here for 7.30 isn't he?'

'That's if his train is on time.'

'We'll worry about that later. So the time now is 4.00 so we meet in an hour at reception tell anyone who isn't here and I'll tell Eddie and the codgers and they can come if they want. Is anyone not coming with us? What about you two queer students you coming or still getting used to the room and the luxury of mummy not wiping your arse' said Tosser.

'Fuck off Tosser' Grant was quick to answer back.

'Or maybe you'll be going to a museum to further your mind?'

'Ho, ho you could do to expand your brain the size of your head, there's got to be loads of room in there.'

'Nice one Grant' laughed Daz.

'Thommo probably won't make it he's on and off the toilet like I don't know what. He looks like shit,' said Gaz trying not to laugh.

'That's a shame' said Trev sarcastically 'maybe it the fact he's shoved that bottle up his arse.'

'I doubt it surely that wouldn't make him shit for England.'

'It would when he did it in front of my boss and I gave him the amount of stuff I gave him it would have unblocked a herd of elephants,' said Trev in a low voice.

'What Trev?'

'Nothing I thought there couldn't be any more shit in him he's shat an elephant hasn't he?'

'You're not kidding there.'

With that while everyone was just chilling out talking and getting ready to leave in five minutes the doors burst open and guns started firing. It was Greg who hadn't been to his room but had been in the bar and was the worse for wear. He strode in with his six shooter cocked and his Stetson still on with his sheriff badge on upside down. Everyone stared at him as he entered the pool area. This was Greg's first trip with them and although he was new everyone thought he was just shy and quiet.

'Greg what are you doing you can't come in here like that you need to get changed into your swimming stuff,' shouted Trev.

'Anyway watch yourself I thought you couldn't swim and this waters deep' said Jonesy trying to put him off.

'I don't need to be able to swim because I've got these.' With that Greg held up his six shooters and ran and dived in the deep end over the heads of all the lads in the Jacuzzi. There was a big splash and then everyone fell silent as everyone hoped he came back to the surface. It felt like an eternity but was in fact about ten seconds but time seem to stand still as first of all the Stetson appeared then the spurs and finally Greg still brandishing his guns.

'Yee haa!' shouted Greg as he struggled to the side of the pool.

'Is he with you lot?' asked the attendant.

'Unfortunately yes,' came the reply.

'Right all out then, come on,' said the attendant.

So Wyatt Earp and the posse got out and into the changing rooms to get dried, they would have protested but they were going anyway. As all the lads got dried and went to get changed. Greg was still there trying to dry his money under the hand-drying machine. They told him where to meet but thought it had fallen on deaf ears as he was pissed and they thought he wouldn't make the night. He finally got out of the changing rooms still wet through and he walked straight into Eddie.

'What the fucking hell have you been up to?' said Eddie in complete shock at the sight that met him.

'Swimming. And now I'm off to the room,' replied Greg.

'You're supposed to take your clothes off first you dippy twat'.

Then it dawned on Eddie, Greg was rooming with him so he took him back to the room and told him to take all his clothes off and not make a mess. Then he needed to get in bed as he needed to sleep it off.

'You're fucking joking we're all out at 5 and I'm not missing that,' yelled Greg.

'But you're pissed,' pleaded Eddie thinking what state would he be in on the night if he carried on drinking.

'Merry Eddie, merry, not pissed yet. If I can stand I'm not pissed. Now I need a shower, see you in the bar.'

Greg proceeded to take his clothes off and throw them all around the room, to Eddie's dismay. Eddie was a neat and tidy man who liked things just so. The room looked like a tornado had hit it and within five minutes the place was a mess, socks on the bedside light and his pants on the table next to the window, dripping wet.

'I'm going to the bar Greg, see you there and give the room a tidy, eh? I mean we don't want to live in a pig sty do we?'

'Alright, don't worry - I'm the tidiest in our house you should see our lass scruffy cow, stuff all over, I'll see you down there'.

Eddie had made the biggest mistake he had ever made as he walked in a daze to meet the others in the bar. They had all got changed and were ready to go out for the night.

'Something up Eddie?' asked Matt.

'It's Greg, I can't handle him, the room's a mess and he reckons he's the tidy one at home. The scruffy twat, there's stuff all over the place.'

'Sit down and have a drink, you know what they say it's always the quiet ones you have to watch. He'll be the one to bring back a prostitute and then you'll know about it Eddie,' said Daz winding Eddie up, which worked.

'He fucking won't, I'll locked the bastard out.'

'Only joking Eddie, only joking.'

With that the receptionist called Eddie over to inform him that one of his party at 4.30 had thrown the pool attendant into the pool and had ruined a £400 walkie-talkie radio. Eddie's face drained of colour and he looked like he'd aged 10 years. Just then Skip came up and asked what the problem was. 'What's the matter Eddie?'

'One of you silly twats has thrown the attendant into the pool ruining his £400 radio. Honestly that's it this is the last trip I do.'

'I was the last to leave and none of our lads were in there. These blokes from Oldham had just turned up on a trip. What time was it anyway?' asked Skip.

'4.30' Eddie informed him.

'Can't have been any of us, we all left after Greg the great did his party piece at just after 4.00. Go tell her it wasn't us.'

Skip went with Eddie to sort out the quandry.

'It was the rugby trip the attendant said' said the receptionist.

'Yes and we're not the only rugby trip here there is one from Oldham and one from Wigan and one from Halifax. So try asking them because I can tell you now we left the area after 4,' protested Skip.

Just then the attendant arrived, soaked to the skin.

'It wasn't these lot, it was some fat blokes they just nudged me in, these lot had already been asked to leave as John Wayne was synchronised swimming.'

'I'm sorry about that I'll try the other party' said the receptionist sheepishly.

'That's alright love we understand the situation,' said Eddie sympathetically. As the two men walked away Skip had a few choice words for Eddie.

'Look Eddie we aren't fucking stupid now relax and enjoy the trip. If anything needs sorting me and the lads can sort it. Stop being all apologetic, as thought we're a bunch of kids who can't behave. We've paid our money like the rest so we have every right to be here. Have you got me? I know you get stressed but try to enjoy it.'

'You're right Skip sorry for jumping to conclusions,' said Eddie sheepishly. They continued back to the bar.

'Right then is everyone here who's coming?' asked Eddie.

'I'll wait here I said I'd give Thommo ten minutes to get himself sorted. I'll catch you up,' said Gaz.

'Tell Greg where we are he said he'd be five minutes but I doubt it, the state he was in the scruffy get. I hope he doesn't make it,' said Eddie.

'We aren't coming back it's straight into Covent Gardens after the pub so try and bring everything you need so you don't have to come back and that way no one gets lost, and if you aren't coming tell us and we won't wait for you,' said Skip.

'Fucking hell Skip it's not a school trip,' shouted Jonesy.

'I know but you don't want to be left in the middle of London on your tod do you now?'

'I suppose not, so are we off then?' said Jonesy. 'I want something to eat, I could eat a scabby horse.'

Skip then went to the reception to leave a message for Damo to tell him where they had gone and to meet them there when he arrived. Just as they were going out of the door Thommo walked into the foyer to a massive cheer.

'Jesus, it's the living dead. Did anyone order a zombie-a-gram?' laughed Jonno.

'It's not funny Jonno my arse is like a blood orange I think I've got food poisoning. I'm going to have some food and then I'll see how I am,' said Thommo looking like he'd just been dug up.

'Right then take me to the birds and I'll show you how to pull' everyone turned around and Greg was stood there wearing the worse shirt you'd ever seen.

'What the fuck have you got on? Did you buy it from a funeral directors or just pinch it from a corpse?' Daz blurted out.

'Why what's wrong with it?'

'What's right with it, are you allergic to irons then Greg?' asked Matt.

'Cheeky twat.'

'Have you tidied the room up? Eddie said you were too scruffy for him and you'd left the room in a state. Isn't that right Eddie?' said Skip stirring it up.

Eddie looked as if to say you mouthy twat.

'I didn't say that .All I said was I like to keep my stuff in a nice pile and that Greg well, each to his own.'

'Which translated means Greg, Eddie thinks you're a scruffy twat' said Matt.

'I aren't now our lass is but I'm really tidy.'

'Can we carry this on in the pub some of us have lost the will to live' said Skip.

Off they all went through the park and sure enough in the distance all 200 yards away was 'The Clipper'.

Outside there was a notice, which read '8 bottles of Pils for £8'.

'Jesus look at that what an offer,' said Tosser.

'That'll do for us, a quid a bottle,' said all the older trippers.

'But what if you in a round of five? That won't work' said Grant.

'You thick twat and you go to Uni what do you do there clean the toilets? If there's five in a round then ask who wants a bottle for a quid when you get three takers you've cracked it. Hardly rocket science,' said Tosser amazed at the stupidity of the student.

When they got in to the pub most of them ordered food and got the drinks in.

'How long are you staying in here for Skip?' asked Eddie.

'We'll see eh, depending how we go but probably until 7 or 8,' came the answer.

'I've left a message for Damo as to where we are but if he doesn't come by 8.00 then we'll go on and tell him where we'll be.'

Skip then enquired about the chance of taxis and the landlord told him there would be no problem just tell him half an hour before they wanted them and he would order as many as they wanted. The landlord was loving it the pub was full and he looked like he'd sell more beer in a couple of hours than he'd sold all week.

'You boys can drink can't you?' the landlord said to Tosser.

'We haven't started yet and with that offer you've got on we'll be spending a lot of time in here, so keep the beers coming.'

'Right whose going to ring Pete?' asked Tosser.

'I will,' Matt volunteered.

'Get the number and I'll do the business, but be quiet.'

So the number was dialled and sure enough Pete answered.

'Hiya Pete it's Matt just ringing you to tell you what a fucking great time we're having the hotels got a pool and we're in a boozer where the Pils is a quid a bottle. And hang on a minute the topless barmaid wants me to suck her tits, here's Gaz he wants a word.'

'Look will you stop ringing me. All me spots are killing and Sally's had to go and get me some lotion to stop me itching.' Pete was talking to himself as Gaz hadn't even picked up the phone.

'Pete shame you couldn't come it's great here, anyway don't scratch them you'll get a scar' and then Gaz hung up.

Pete went into a rant 'You rotten bastards, don't ring again because I won't answer do you hear me, I say do you hear me? Shithouses have hung up' Then he lay back down and tried to take his mind off the itching he felt...

Tag had nothing to do all day apart from check his bag a thousand times to see if he had packed everything to impress Suki. He hadn't felt like this since he dated his first girlfriend and that was when he was 13. He had butterflies and had been on the toilet most of the day. In fact he never felt this nervous before a game, which was saying something as Tag for all his bullshit and bravado was actually quite a nervous and weak person who put on a front to mask this fault, which worked most of the time. But scratch the surface and you could see the cracks and the emergence of this vulnerable person who just wanted to be accepted but thought the way to go about it was to act like a twat who everyone thought didn't care about anything.

Fay was the only one who he'd ever really stayed with for longer than a couple of months and she had seen this side to him. The fact that he wasn't as confident as people thought.

Suki had seen this side of him to as with her he didn't try to be the life and sole. He just used to chat and let himself go and express himself in a way he couldn't do with other people. Suki was a mystery to him and he would long to have her and imagined what it would be like to finally make love to her. Now normally he would imagine shagging a bird but not Suki he wouldn't shag her he would make love to her and in his mind the time for doing that was a couple of hours away. Suki had arranged to meet Tag at five and then set off and as soon as five came around Tag was ready - and had been for three hours - like a dog waiting for the door to be opened so that he could go for his walk. He sat near the door waiting for the master to come home, and then he could run through the fields and have some freedom. Five o'clock passed and Suki hadn't arrived. So he started to pace up and down and his nerves kicked in again and he had to go to the toilet again. He looked at his watch, ten past. So he rang work up knowing she would answer the phone but there was no answer. She wasn't coming, the bitch had chickened out and she was taking the piss and they would all laugh at him at work on Tuesday. Then he thought she was too nice to do that, but she had said five to avoid traffic so where was she? It was back to toilet as twenty past arrived and still no Suki. Just then he could hear a car pulling up outside so he shot off the toilet and looked out of the window, but he didn't recognise the car. Suki had a ford escort and this was a BMW so it wasn't her. He sat back down thinking he would give her 'til six and then would have to find some bullshit to give to his mother to explain why he hadn't gone to London. Then after that he would have to stay in hiding so that Fay didn't see him. Why didn't he just go with the lads to London, he bet they were having a great time.

Just then there was a knock on the door and when Tag eventually got off the toilet and he answered it, Suki was standing there.

'What are you doing here?' asked Tag rather pathetically.

'Picking you up silly, I got stuck in traffic as I went home to get ready.'

'Where's your car?' asked Tag looking puzzled.

'Over there, dad has let me lend his car for the weekend as long as I fill it up, so if I put my foot down then we'll be there in no time. I bet you thought I wasn't coming and that I had bottled it didn't you?'

'No, of course not, I was just pottering about. The thought never crossed my mind. I'll just get my stuff, come in.'

As he turned to go and get his bag and the chocolates and flowers he'd bought he forgot he'd put his bag near the door and fell arse over tit and ended up sprawled out on the floor in the hall. Suki didn't know whether to laugh or get an ambulance as Tag held his leg. Suki was a first aider at work and came to Tags aid she told him not to move as she bent down and asked him where it hurt. He had only banged his knee and as she felt the area Tag could smell her. He was in dreamland and he could also see down her top and up her skirt. She had a lacy thong on and from what he could see a nicely trimmed pubic bush - which was Tag's favourite bush, after a privet hedge that was trimmed in the shape of a chicken.

Tag grabbed Suki and started to kiss her and as the two of them snogged on the floor, Tag put his hand on her breast. He could feel no resistance, only her heart going ten to the dozen. Tag then pushed his luck even more and touched her erect nipples. Still no resistance so he couldn't stop himself and he slid his hand up her skirt. Still no resistance. He put his hand inside her knickers and started to play with her clitoris.

She was very moist and as he thought 'fucking hell, bingo!' and was preparing to enter her with his finger, he suddenly thought about where he was and that this wasn't how it was meant to be. After all the waiting and the preparation he was going to do it on his mother's old Axminster shag pile - pardon the pun - in the hallway where the dog used to shit if they didn't open the door in time. Plus his mother was due home any time and what about all the money he'd spent on the Blackpool trip? He could have saved that if she was going to let him do it on some old shit-stained carpet.

Time seemed to stand still as all these thoughts went through his head. Just then Suki solved his problem as she grabbed his hand and whispered, 'Let's wait until Blackpool, there'll be plenty of time later, we better set off.'

Tag was all mixed up now he was disappointed she had stopped him but thrilled that they seemed to be on the same wavelength and that she wanted it to be special as well. He was also that excited that he would have been no use anyway he would have ejaculated as soon as she touched him such was his excitement, which would have not been too impressive. From the little Suki had let him know about her in their snatched moments, Tag had come to the conclusion that she had been with two boyfriends before and was going to get engaged at one point. But didn't seem to be very experienced with the one night stand scene. In fact she made it clear that she had never had a one-night stand and she was proud of it. Tag had even bought condoms for the occasion in case she didn't have any protection. He must have been in love as he always used to boast 'I'm not wearing one of those, it's like going swimming with your wellies on' which wouldn't have washed with Suki as she would have just rejected him. She knew what she wanted and it wasn't aids or a sexually transmitted disease. So Tag had got the condoms.

As the both of them got to their feet Tag was so pleased that it would be special and that it was actually going to happen. She had even said it 'let's wait until Blackpool' so there it was confirmation, in Blackpool it was going to happen, after the long wait and weeks and months of wanting to actually enter her he had just been given the go ahead. He felt like asking her for it in writing, but thought her word was good enough.

So the two of them set off and Tag would be able to relax as soon as they got out of the city. The time was 5.30 and they would probably now beat the traffic.

Not too far away an hour earlier the mini bus for the girls had turned up at Tossers house. After dropping all the kids off at grandparents and alike for the night. It had all been sorted Clare had got the booze the food and she'd even had t-shirts printed with the words 'I like cock' on the front. She decided against the original message as the arrow would have made them too expensive. She had, 'It's never dull in Hull' printed on the back, these were bright orange and you couldn't miss them.

'I'm not wearing that,' said Cary, Trev's wife.

'Why, don't you like cock then,' Clare blurted out to which they all started laughing.

'Well yes but it's sending out the wrong message don't you think?'

'Bollocks half the blokes will shit themselves and run when they see us and the other half have got no chance anyway it's only for a bit of fun. Take it any way you don't have to wear it' said Clare.

'Get a drink down you and then we'll be on our way. I'll go and see the driver and tell him we'll be about ten minutes we're not all here yet,' said Clare who loved going away and had sorted the trip out in such a manner Eddie would have been proud of her.

'Who's left to come?' asked Fay looking puzzled.

'Slag and her mate didn't you know. Clare let it out of the bag and she latch on to it and so she didn't open her mouth to the blokes at rugby Clare let her come,' explained Mandy, Skip's wife.

'Have I missed something here, who are you talking about?' asked Fay again.

'Shaz and her mate are coming,' came the reply.

'No not her, I fucking hate her, she's always trying to get off with everyone. She's nothing but a slapper. Which mate is she bringing? Not that fucking Charlie bitch who hangs around after the matches?' said Fay thinking about going home.

'Look, they'll go their own way, besides they paid their money and I don't think they're that bad. I think they've just got a bad reputation. They both seemed alright when I went on that trip with them last month. So get a drink down you Fay and stop fretting,' said Mandy.

'I don't feel like a drink yet. I've been a bit sick at work this morning and I can't keep anything down, can I use your toilet?' asked Fay.

Fay went to the toilet and the tongues started to wag. Fay thought that Shaz and her mate were after Tag but it was the other way around, Tag was after a threesome with them and had told them so.

'What's up with her?' whispered Sue, Jonesy's wife.

'She thinks that they both want Tag but when I was talking to them it's the other way around. Tag's after them, the little shit. I feel so sorry for her but they say love's blind and she needs a fucking guide dog. She won't have anything said against him,' said Mandy.

'I know I hear all the rumours myself about him on a Saturday night and it's not like he tries to hide the fact that he's after other women,' chipped in Steph, Tom's girlfriend. The room went quiet as Fay re-entered the room.

'Are you alright love? You don't look too good, have you been sick again?' asked Steph.

'You're not pregnant are you?' Mandy blurted out, meaning only to think it but it slipped out.

'Tag hasn't got it in him has he Fay?' chipped in Clare.

Fay then burst into tears and told them all he was having trouble getting it up and that they'd only done it twice that week. This was more than most of them did it in a month and they were beginning to look at Tag as if he was a super stud.

'Twice in one week, Jesus wait while you get kids, twice is a marathon in our house, Jonesy hasn't even got it out of his pants and it's nearly all over,' said Sue trying to lighten the mood.

'Yeah but you're all older aren't you?'

'Cheeky bastard I'm only four years older than you,' said Steph.

'I didn't mean it like that, me and Tag haven't been together that long that's what I meant. You and Tom have been together years so the attraction might have worn of a bit,' said Fay trying to explain.

'Would you like some help digging that hole your in Fay or are you fine doing it yourself? We know what you mean,' said Mandy.

The doorbell went and it was Shaz and Charlie.

'Hiya everyone, hi Fay are you alright?' said Shaz who liked Fay but didn't know Fay couldn't stand her.

'I'm okay Sharron. How are you, brought your Durex?' Fay replied frostily.

'Well funny you should say that I have so if you need any come and see me,' replied Shaz who could be a bitch when required and she felt that the moment had arrived as she waved the pack of durex in the air.

'A twelve pack are you sure you'll have enough?' sneered Fay.

'Well Charlie's brought two packs as well, if we run out we'll have to go to the chemist's won't we?'

This reply from Shaz brought a laugh from everyone as she only had a box and she was on the pill. She was single and liked men, the condoms were for sexually transmitted diseases. Besides Shaz had a reputation but this was due to rumour and she wasn't really that bad. She worked behind the bar at the club and the lads often saw her as one of them, so she got invited along quite a bit. But she had never been with any of them.

'Right then, let's get this show on the road shall we? Get your gear and we'll be off,' shouted Clare and she locked the door behind them.

'Where's Sally?' asked Fay.

'She's dropped out Pete's got chickenpox,' answered Clare as they all set off towards the bus. The bus driver was loading the bags into the boot and as he bent forward hit his head on the boot as one of the girls nipped his arse.

'Nice buttocks driver do you work out?' asked Shaz.

The others had seen this and as the driver went bright red with embarrassment they all started to laugh, he was five foot six and very overweight and was in his mid fifties. Shaz then winked at him and said, 'I'll slip you my key, you can give my back a rub in the bath if you like.'

The driver just shut the boot and in a shocked voice said, 'Right then ladies have you got the details of your hotel please?'

'Here they are driver, what's your name by the way? We can't be calling you driver all the weekend can we now?' said Clare.

'Hmm, it's Humphrey,' replied the driver sheepishly.

'Is that Humphrey cushion or Humphrey Dumpty. Don't be falling off any walls,' shouted Shaz.

'It's Humpty Dumpty,' said Charlie.

'I know. I'm only having him on you daft cow.'

'Well Humphrey you'll have no trouble with us, unless you want some that is,' said Clare as she winked at all the other girls.

'If you need me to stop just come to the front and I'll do what I can ladies.'

'What while you're driving? You'll crash the bus you saucy old get,' shouted Charlie.

'Alright girls let's leave Humphrey to get on with his job, we don't want him getting all excited with all this talent on the bus, it'll send his blood pressure up,' said Clare.

'I've seen more talent at a tea dance,' piped up Humphrey.

'You cheeky bastard Humphrey, get driving or we'll have to de-bag yer, you old get,' said Mandy quite offended.

'You haven't got it in you and you'd get a shock if you did,' replied Humphrey giving as good as he got.

This sounded like a Challenge, so Shaz and Charlie ran to the front and started to try and undo his belt. Humphrey let out a scream that could have shattered a wineglass.

'Wh... wh... wh... what the bloody hell are you doing? Leave me alone,' cried Humphrey.

'You laid down the challenge Humphrey boy, we just accepted, you've got a right length on you there. We'll just zip the trousers up, we don't want that escaping do we now?' said Charlie.

Humphrey had decided at that moment after having his trousers nearly ripped off by two girls he was old enough to be the father of that he would just drive his bus and not get into anymore banter with these nutters. He was used to taking old folks on outings and not sex hungry vixens who would rip a man's pants off at the drop of a hat.

'Sorry Humphrey you can set off now, we'll leave you alone,' said Clare and the girls trip began.

The time was 5.10 and they pulled out of Tosser's street and headed for the motorway. They passed the street where Tag's mother lived and actually past Suki in her dad's car going to pick up Tag...

The barman at the clipper couldn't believe it he went to his manager and told him if they carried on at this rate they'd run out of Pils. Although the manager looked stressed at this he was thinking fucking hell this'll look fantastic when the brewery see it. The takings are going through the roof. A few regulars had left in disgust at the noisy rabble disrupting their Friday evening after work drink with a bite to eat. The manager didn't care as nearly all the rugby boys had bought food and were drinking like fish. He wasn't bothered that he'd lost a few sales of wine. All they ever drank was a few glasses anyway and they didn't spend as much as these boys were spending. Besides, his was the only real pub around that area, so they could lump it as they had nowhere else to go.

The boys were all there even the driver who had been given the weekend off by Eddie and the boys - he was supposed to take them to the game at Wembley - as a goodwill gesture for spraying his hair green and orange. And of course nearly killing him with a bow and arrow. So even the driver was enjoying the delights of £1.00 bottles of Pils. The only person who wasn't there apart from Pete was Damo, and he was on his way. Because some of the locals had ordered their food and then left in a rush before it came, the boys soon clicked on to the fact that food was coming out of the kitchen and no one was claiming it. So the wider boys of the group sat near the kitchen door and as the food came out and the order was called, when no one claimed it they would put their arm up and shout 'Is it paid for?'

If the answer was 'Yes', which it had to be as you had to pay in advance, then the response was, 'Over here just put it there'. So not only were they getting beer at virtually cost price they were getting free food. Most of them couldn't believe that someone would pay for their food and then just leave it and walk out. These southerners must be rich or mad.

The atmosphere was getting more and more boisterous and Eddie had to step in when Matt and Gaz had the fantastic idea of making a model of the Eiffel tower out of the empty bottles. They managed to get the base done and then there was a crash as a few bottles smashed, Eddie wasn't to pleased and actually tidied it up himself.

But the manager didn't mind a few broken bottles he just looked in the till and saw how much he'd taken that afternoon.

This happened all over London on this weekend, bar takings were up nearly everywhere as the invasion from the North came down to London for the Challenge Cup Final. They drank like fish and didn't cause any trouble, a landlords dream. They improved the atmosphere of most pubs and the deadest place was rocking after the rugby boys had entered it.

Skip stepped in and told everyone to calm down as they didn't want to get thrown out. Then came the shocking news the barman and the manager had been dreading. The Pils had ran out and it was only six o'clock, what were they to do? Skip was at the bar and the manager called him over to explain the situation.

'Mate we've ran out of Pils so the offers off as I won't be getting another delivery until Monday now and that's no good to you boys is it?'

'Don't worry what other beer have you got that we can do a deal on?' Skip said as quick as a flash spotting that the manager wanted to keep their custom.

'I suppose I could do the same deal 8 bottles for £8 with the Sol if that's any good?'

'Wait I'll ask the boys. Listen up boys the Pils has ran out' everyone began to boo .Skip waited until the noise subsided as the manager thought there was going to be a riot. 'Listen who fancies a little trip down Mexico way? Because we can have the same deal on Sol, is that alright?'

'Is that for the full weekend?' asked Daz who was thinking ahead to when the price would probably go up.

They all looked at the manager who knew he would probably get a bollocking for it but he said after a slight hesitation.

'Go on then' the place erupted. 'Ondala, ondala riba'

'Three cheers for the land lord' shouted Daz and everyone joined in.

'We're going to sing you a song' said Matt 'it's called the cow kicked Nelly' and with that the whole party sat on the floor of the pub to the puzzlement of the bar staff and the few remaining customers who quite enjoyed the liveliness of the pub for a change. Even the kitchen staff came out to see what was going on. Matt started it and it went like this...

'The cow kicked Nelly
In the belly, in the barn
The cow kicked Nelly
In the belly, in the barn
'The farmer said 'It'll do no harm.'

Second verse - same as the first – but a little bit louder - and a little bit worse...

Oh! The cow kicked Nelly... etc'

This went on for about ten to fourteen verses and each time they got to a new verse they would sing louder and would rise up a little bit higher from the floor. So by the 6th verse they were all standing. But by the 12th verse they were shouting and jumping up and down still singing the song. Most of them would give in after 10 verses as they would be laughing too much and be exhausted. The people in the pub couldn't believe it grown men ranging from the ages of 18 to 67 were joining in this strange song and dance routine, even the bus driver joined in. When it all ended the bar staff and kitchen staff and remaining customers whilst wiping tears of laughter away at what they had just seen gave them a round of applause.

'You can join in next time if you like?' said Skip.

'I've seen some sights in my time but I've never seen anything like you lot' said the manager still chuckling to himself.

The boys were ready to go and after the song they thought it best to go out on a high and they asked the manager to order them some taxis. The old guard including Eddie were maybe going to Covent Garden later but it was a bit early for them. Besides they couldn't understand that they'd just got a deal on cheap beer and they were all going to somewhere it would be double.

'What are they going for? The beers cheaper here' said Bert

'Birds and disco's and that,' came the reply from Eddie.

'Them lot get a bird, I think not all the pet shops 'ill be shut. That's the only bird they'll get is a bloody budgie. They must be crackers.'

All the old brigade nodded in agreement as they drank their Mexican lager because it was cheap.

'Not a bad drop this I've never had it before where's it from?' enquired Bert.

'Mexico amigo' said Skip.

'Mexico, that means I'll get the shits does it then?'

'Maybe if you were drinking it in Mexico you would but I doubt it here. Try it see how many it takes you before you shit yourself. Too late you smell like you already have Bert' said Jonno.

'You cheeky little sod, I'll flatten you' said Bert rising to his feet.

'Sit down Bert he's only joking' Eddie intervened.

'Look Bert you enjoy your night here amigo, Sol long, see you later' said Jonno as he tried to calm Bert down while still taking the piss.

With that a car horn could be heard and the taxi's had arrived, everyone who was going split up to make it fair so that everyone paid the same and they sorted out with the drivers so that they all got dropped off at the same point. Skip asked his driver the nearest pub to the dropping off point and then went back in to tell Eddie the name of the pub so that Damo could get there as well. The idea was that they would leave a message in every pub telling Damo the name of the next pub they'd gone in. This sounded good but realistically none of them expected to see him that night. So off they went into the town of London on a hot summer night. Ahead of them was a night of excitement and hopefully loads of women and a lot of laughter and frolics.

The pub was distinctly quieter when they had all left and the there was an air of gloom about the place. Although they were loud, boisterous, cheeky and clumsy they brought so much atmosphere to the place. This was a pub that was used to yuppies who spent little and demanded a lot in return, not like these boys they spent a lot and didn't expect anything in return except the fact that they could just let their hair down - those who still had some - and enjoy themselves.

'Are they always like that?' asked the manager.

'Yes I'm afraid so' replied Eddie 'never a dull moment. It's never dull in Hull'

'They aren't too bad though made this place rock a bit.'

'Put it this way son you be alright by them and they'll drink in here most of the weekend, you mark my words make them welcome and they will spend their money here as will we, won't we fellas?' Eddie directed his question at the few remaining party members who were know as the coffin dodgers because of their ages.

'Yep! As long as it's a quid a bottle that'll do us mate' said Doug who was an ex-player from the 50s and now loved it being with the young-un's on a trip.

'Don't worry I'll look after you lot' the manager said hoping that if they were going to kick the bucket they did it after closing time as although they were getting on by hell could they drink.

'What time did you have your first drink?' asked the manager.

'Must have been about nine this morning,' came the reply

'Jesus and your still standing. Have you got hollow legs?'

'No steady Eddie is the way just take it slow and you get to enjoy the full day then.'

'How do you all afford it?'

'We save all year round, a couple of quid here a couple of quid there, I collect it and they don't miss it that way. As soon as we get back I'll start collecting again for next year,' answered Eddie.

'Bit of a nosey bastard aren't yer?' shouted Bert

'No just wondering because you lot spend money like there's no tomorrow.'

'Where we're from there probably is no tomorrow. Live for the day, seize it, what's the point in pissing about, enjoy life, that's what I say' said Bert profoundly.

'So why are you such a miserably twat then Bert?' said Eddie.

'Yeah and a tight arse. Seize it only if it's free or on offer. That's why you're loaded you don't spend 'owt' agreed Doug.

'I'm not that bad, I go on holidays and that, I always treat our lass' protested an under fire Bert.

'Yeah sometimes you let her toast both sides of her bread.'

'Get lost anyway it's your round Doug so get that up yer.'

'Never miss a trick do you? All the years I've known you and you always know whose round it is.'

'Sure do so get 'em in. I quite like this Mexican beer, think I'll get a pizza later seeing as we've gone all exotic,' laughed Bert.

'Why have you ran out of dripping sandwiches then you tight get?'

'No I still have some of those in the room. However seeing as the beer's cheap I'm going to splash out on a pizza. Here barman what's your name?' Bert asked the manager

'John' came the reply.

'Well John I want a pizza, where can I get one from?'

'We don't sell them here you'll have to ring for one. Look in the phone book and they'll deliver it to the hotel for you later.'

Bert looked puzzled. He wanted one now in the pub. But as Eddie pointed out he couldn't bring his own food in, the man was already giving them knock down priced drink. Don't take the piss and bring your own grub in.

Bert looked in the yellow pages and there was one with a menu. As he scanned the menu the choice was all too much for him and then there was the price. And finally he got to the bottom of the advert, which said '£2 delivery'. That was it, no way was he paying £2 for it to be delivered.

'How far is it to this pizza place John?'

'Nearest is about two miles away.'

'Bollocks, give us some crisps, pizza's off, too expensive anyway for a bit of bread with melted cheese and tomato,' said Bert mumbling away.

So as the pub settled in for the night a few more rugby people joined the throng and they were all set to have a good night chatting about old times. Eddie decided to have a wonder back to the hotel to see if Damo had got there yet.

CHAPTER 5
THE FIRST ONE TO SEE THE TOWER GETS A PRIZE

The girls were well on their way by now and the drink was flowing, although Fay still hadn't had a drink yet and had no intention of doing so, she felt sick and was beginning to think that she should have stayed at home. This hadn't bothered the others although Cary was keeping an eye on her.

'Are you okay Fay love? How long have you been throwing up?' Cary asked in a quiet voice so no one could hear.

'It started this morning, but I feel a bit better now, I think I'll stay on the coke for now until we get there.'

'Look don't worry none of these will realise that you haven't had a drink, just try and enjoy yourself.'

'I will but it would help if certain people weren't on this trip' she gestured towards Shaz and Charlie. 'They really piss me off.'

'Look at it this way they've made the bus cheaper, don't let those two spoil it for you. Forget about them.'

'Then there's Tag I wish I could have told him about this. I don't know why it had to be a big secret?'

'Neither do I' replied Cary knowing full well that Trev already knew.

'Is everybody happy?' shouted Clare.

'Yeah!' came the answer.

'How long Humph?' asked Clare. But before he could answer Shaz shouted, 'About two inches by the look of him. But it's longer when you feel it, eh Humph?'

'I'll ignore that. It'll be about another hour, maybe more.'

'Well then get the drinks out. Where's that cheeky little red that was in the box, open it and let it breathe' said Mandy who liked a bit of wine and wasn't a real fan of lager.

'Oooh! let it breathe, are you going to sniff it and taste it, get a bucket someone she'll want to spit it out,' Charlie blurted out.

'There's nothing wrong with doing things properly, you let it breathe and it tastes better, you just carry on with your cider' Mandy bit back and added 'you little slag' under her breath of course.

'Wonder what those dozy bastards are doing now?' said Sue

'Pissed probably, not a care in the world and thinking that the wife and kids are at home making curtains and shopping for next weeks food and tidying up so the house will be ready when they get back from their big trip' answered Clare with more than a hint of sarcasm.

'They'd go ape shit if they knew we were on the way to Blackpool' Chris (Jonno's wife) chipped in.

'Did anyone get a phone call off any of them? No not a fucking chance, they got on that bus this morning and it was like going back to school with your mates. They're like a bunch of kids, all I've heard for weeks is the trip this, the trip that. I need a cowboy outfit, and I need a song,' ranted Sue.

'Calm down Sue you'll burst a blood vessel. Not too happy about Jonesy then are you Sue?' asked Steph.

'It's not that, it's if I ask him to do anything he hasn't got time but when he has to go and get a cowboy outfit it's come on down to Toys 'R' Us and it's the most important thing in the world. Not the fact that the kitchen tap is dripping or the bedroom needs re-decorating, no but when he has to dress up as the milky bar kid, then the milky bars are on him or should I say me.'

'Jesus Sue calm down.'

'Alright I will get me some of that wine that should do the trick.'

'Did anyone get shagged by a cowboy last night then?' asked Shaz, which was typical of her, but she had latched onto something as the bus went quiet, so she didn't let it go. 'Come on who got pumped by a Clint Eastwood look-a-like?'

'More like a Cunt Eastwood look-a-like' said Clare as one by one the hands went up all except Fay who didn't know what they were all talking about, Tag hadn't got dressed up.

'Didn't Tag get all dressed up Fay?' Shaz asked.

'No he said that it was sad.' Tag didn't say this but Fay didn't want to make herself look stupid.

'Well he'll be doing plenty of forfeits then, they'll have him stripped naked and strapped to the gates at Buckingham Palace' laughed Clare.

'That's his problem not mine isn't it' answered Fay wondering why he hadn't mentioned getting dressed up. he hadn't mentioned a song either, which was strange because he usually was the first to join in. Clare started the girls in a sing song as she said if they can have a load of songs to sing so can we and Fay soon forgot about Tag not getting dressed up as they all started singing and the atmosphere on the bus was rocking. The only problem was no one knew a song all the way through, so it was one or two liners all the way but no one cared they were having a laugh.

Talking of Tag he was well on his way and Tag now felt like he could relax as they got onto the motorway. He had done it, convinced everyone he was going to London and the plan had worked, no one was any the wiser. Fay thought he'd gone to London, Suki didn't know about Fay so she thought everything was normal. It all seemed perfect, the hotel was booked they were travelling in style and he was in for a night of passion.

'Alright Suki? Drives like a dream doesn't it?'

'Yeah it's a great car my dad's pride and joy, but he said I could use it as I would be safer in this than in mine. And seeing as you don't have a car then it was the only real option.'

Tag did have a car but it was Fay's really and he used to bike to work.

'Mum said you could come for tea next Friday and meet everyone.'

'That'd be great,' replied Tag, thinking fucking hell what am I doing. Then he looked at her legs and thought as Tag always did, fuck it, it'll be alright, I'll make an excuse.

'Seeing as we're going steady now I might start coming with dad to watch you play.'

'That would be fantastic.'

No it fucking wouldn't, then the shit would hit the fan. Luckily there was only a couple of games left and they were away.

'I'll come to your presentation and meet all your friends.'

There was silence, think Tag, think.

'Don't you want me to come? You've gone all quiet,' pushed Suki, noticing Tag's sudden mood change.

'No it's not that, it's just, I don't know when it is, I'll get the tickets and we can go.'

'Good, dad says he might come down and put some money in your club, he knows your chairman. His work might sponsor the shirts for next season.'

'Good we need the money, the committee's always moaning about being skint,' Tag replied, trying to act normal but inside he was shitting himself. But then in true Tag style he soon forgot all about it.

'So what do you want to do tonight?'

'Get a nice relaxing bath, and then go for a nice meal and then back to the hotel if you like.'

'Sounds good to me, sounds good to me.'

They were gaining time quite quickly as the car was top of the range. They were going that well that they passed the bus with all the girls on it.

'Looks like a hen party,' Tag observed not realising that his partner the woman he lived with was on the bus heading to the same place as he was.

'They'll be off to Blackpool for a girls night out and some men by the looks of them,' Suki observed.

The girls on the bus never even saw the car as it was going considerably quicker than the bus.

'We'll be there pretty soon, what's the name of the hotel?' asked Suki.

'The Adelphi, it's in South Street, just off the Promenade. You booked it.'

'I know but that was ages ago.'

'According to this it's got a car park at the back. Go along the front and when you get near the tower it's the second turning on your left when you're travelling towards the funfair.'

'You know your stuff, done this before?'

'No, it's just I have an eye for detail and besides I looked at the confirmation letter,' said Tag defensively. Really he'd been studying the confirmation letter so that he could impress Suki and it had worked.

'I like it, you really are organised aren't you. I find that sexy when a man knows what he's doing,' she smiled at him. Tag could feel himself getting aroused. At this rate he'd have to go and have a wank as soon as they got there, otherwise although he hadn't dressed as a cowboy that day, his gun would be going off before he got it out of the holster.

'Well I like to know where I am and what I'm doing. That's the kind of guy I am.' He was lying through his teeth. The truth was that Fay had packed his bag for him thinking he was going to London and had even made him a packed lunch which he ate at his mother's whilst in hiding. In reality Tag had trouble finding the front door of his house, he was like a big child who needed looking after.

'When we've got a place Tag, it'll be great that you're so organised as I can't stand clutter and mess.'

When we've got a place thought Tag, fucking hell, he was getting deeper and deeper, but in true Tag style he thought it'll be alright, he'll just shag her and dump her. This time it was a little different as Tag worked with her and he was falling for her, in fact he had fallen for her in a big way.

Meanwhile, back on the girl's bus the tongues were wagging as they had stopped so that Fay could go to the toilet. In fact they all wanted to go but Fay still hadn't re-emerged and Steph had gone to find her.

'She'll be throwing up. She's pregnant, as soon as we get there I'm getting her a pregnancy test. It's as plain as the nose on your face,' said Clare.

'She definitely is, can you imagine Tag as a dad?' added Mandy.

'No! That'll be two babies to look after,' came the unanimous reply.

'I can imagine him doing one of two things either loving it or doing a runner,' said Charlie who didn't like Tag much.

'What makes you say that then?' asked Cary.

'Oh you lot maybe think me and her' she pointed at Shaz 'are a couple of stupid slappers, which we're not by the way, but let me tell you I am very observant and I can tell you I've seen it all before Tag will shit himself or grow up. It happened to my sister, her bloke was pissing around behind her back just like Tag does. She got pregnant and he just stopped going out and they even got married. Where as my cousin, same situation, her bloke pissed off and no one has seen him since. Shit himself and ran away the bastard and she has had to bring that child up with no help.'

The bus was stunned as Charlie had said all that without pausing for breath.

'My opinion, Tag will stay put, but be unhappy. But do you know that the best thing that could happen would be for him to fuck off as he's nothing but a rake, a little shit who will try it on with anyone.'

The girls probably thought the same but no one said a word as Steph had found Fay being sick in the toilets and had brought her back to the bus.

'Are you alright love?' enquired Cary as Fay got back on the bus.

'Yeah, just a bit sick that's all. I think it's the journey and that. I only hope Tag is alright as he had the same ham as I had in his pack up.'

'Maybe it's not the ham love. Are you sure you're not pregnant? I mean all the signs are there,' Cary blurted out.

'Is your period late?' Sue joined in.

'I don't think so, I'm quite irregular anyway,' she then burst into tears. Cary put her arms around her and consoled her.

'We'll look after you, we're nearly there.'

'What was the name of your hotel?' the driver asked.

'Hang on a minute driver, I'll just get the letter, here we are, it's called 'The Adelphi' and it's on South Street,' Clare answered.

'Oh I know it well, really rough, you'll all fit in quite well,' said Humphrey laughing as he said it.

'What do you mean rough and we'll fit in? - cheeky get.' Shaz was offended.

'Well I'm only joking, you'll be giving it away but some of the girls there, they charge if you get my drift.'

Shaz looked puzzled.

'He means prostitutes hang out there,' Charlie came to the rescue.

'Is that why you know it well then driver. Do you use prostitutes then Humphrey? And we won't be giving it away we are respectable girls. However if the right man comes along he can have a free sample,' laughed Shaz.

'I was joking,' said Humph.

'Well keep your jokes to yourself. Especially if they paint us as being a bunch of whores,' Steph piped up.

'Here, here,' said a few of the others.

'But he's got a point, I mean with those t-shirts and that we could look like we fit in,' laughed Steph.

'What's it like then driver?'

'Quite nice actually, still full of stag and hen parties but nice for a small hotel. It's central so you don't have to get taxis everywhere, you can walk.'

'That's more like it Humph, you never know you might get a tip on the way home,' said Steph.

'I'll give you a tip now,' shouted Charlie. 'Never knock your granny when she's shaving,' the rest of them burst out laughing.

'How far is it now driver?' Fay asked in a quiet voice.

'About half an hour? If you want I know where there's a chemist open late, I'll take you.'

'What for?' asked Fay.

'Something for your sickness.'

'And a pregnancy test,' added Mandy.

'I'm not pregnant. I'm on the pill, how could I be?' protested Fay.

'I was on the pill with my second but I still got caught. You've got all the symptoms, and the test will clarify whether you are or not. You wouldn't want to lose it if you were pregnant, now would you?' said Mandy. 'Tag would go mad.'

'Fuck Tag,' Cary shouted out, and they all looked at her as Cary hardly ever gave an opinion let alone used the 'F' word.

'This is about you love and your health.'

'Yeah, don't worry, we'll get you sorted and if you're not pregnant then we'll get something for your sickness, alright,' Clare tried to reassure her, knowing full well that she was 99% certainly up the duff.

Meanwhile Tag and Suki arrived at the hotel and booked in. They went up to the room and Tag grabbed hold of Suki and wrestled her to the bed and they began to kiss. Then suddenly Suki pushed him off and said she was going for a bath and that there would be plenty of time for 'that' later. She got up and proceeded to the bathroom.

Tag was sprawled out on the bed devastated that she still hadn't let him have his way with her. This was going to be a tough one to crack. But instead of making him frustrated it made him want her even more. How good was it going to be when they did do it. He got off the bed and started to unpack his bag. He found the chocolates and champagne he had bought - he'd already given her the flowers - and put them on the bed. Tag thought he would try to get into the bath and he used the old line of 'Need anyone to scrub your back'. But the answer was 'No' and as he tried the door to go to the toilet, he found that it was locked.

'What do you want?' asked Suki.

'To use the toilet,' said a shocked Tag.

'Well you'll have to wait, I'll be at least another fifteen minutes.'

'I'll go to the bar and use the one there then.'

'Don't forget your key.'

'I won't.'

Tag was already getting pissed off with the situation and wondered how long he could keep it up. He had only ever been on a date with Suki that lasted about on average 3 ? hours and then he could go home and get back to normal. This was hard work, pretending to be someone he wasn't. He went to the bar toilet, then ordered himself a pint of lager and sat and talked to the barman.

'Where you from?' asked the barman.

'Hull, we're here for two nights.'

'We get a lot of people from Hull. I think the bloke who originally owned this place was from Hull. You married?'

'No, haven't even...' Tag then went silent.

'Like that is it, most of the people in here are like that. They come for one reason really - a bit of privacy. Usually when they live with their parents.'

'No, I've got a house and she lives with her parents. We work together and have been dating quite a bit, but still no sex, bit frustrating, you know what I mean?'

'Yeah, but I suppose it's a good thing she isn't easy'

'I know but Jesus, I wish she was.'

'Can I get you another?' the barman asked.

'No I better not, she might be laid on the bed waiting for me, you never know.'

'Good luck,' said the barman smiling.

Tag got up and walked past the reception to get to the stairs as they were on the second floor. Just as he took his first few steps, unbeknown to him a bus had just pulled in to the car park full of some girls from Hull. Yes, Fay and the rugby girls had arrived.

They all piled into the hotel and Clare told them to go for a drink while she got the rooms sorted out. They all went to the bar and had a drink.

'Where are you ladies from?' asked the barman.

'Hull,' answered Shaz.

'Well you've just missed one of your fellow Hullites, he was drinking here two minutes ago, come here with his girlfriend.'

'What was his name? We might know him,' asked Charlie.

'He didn't give his name, he only had one drink and then went. I think he was on a promise.'

'You might be later,' Charlie winked at the barman.

'Well, I'm here for the night but I think I'd be too much for you darlin'' replied the barman who was used to being chatted up and teased.

'Ooooh! get you. Here Shaz, he says he'll be too much man for me.'

'Well I don't mind joining in, it'll be like tag team shagging. When one of us has had enough we'll tag the other one and you can carry on with her.'

Even the barman went red in the face at Shaz' suggestion.

'Leave the poor sod alone you two,' said Sue trying not to laugh.

'Don't worry love, they don't bite, do you girls?'

'What do you mean that we're dogs?' said Shaz who was at the back of the queue when they gave brains out.

'No, I mean there's nothing to be scared of, you're harmless,' explained Sue.

'I don't mind, what can I get you ladies?'

'Who wants a drink?' asked Sue.

'All of us,' came the reply.

'Well, all put a fiver in and we'll have a kitty. So then barman, can we have nine halves of lager and a coke please,' asked Sue as she went around everyone getting their money.

While all this was going on Fay was in the toilets with Cary trying to have a wee to check whether or not she was pregnant. They had dropped off at the chemists before they got to the hotel for a pregnancy kit.

'What do I do again?' asked a nervous Fay.

'Just wee on the part it says that you wee on.'

'Alright, here goes.'

Fay then started to urinate onto the tester. As she finished she didn't dare look at the results.

'Well, has anything happened?' asked Cary from behind the door.

'I don't know, I can't look, will you look for me,' Fay said very nervously.

'Come out then, I can't see through doors and I'm not psychic. Let's have a look here,' said Cary.

Fay slowly opened the door and held out the pregnancy test. Cary actually thought she was being a bit wet as she was old enough to own her own house and have relationships yet she looked like a primary school kid handing her homework in late.

'Let's see, one blue line means pregnant - and congratulations Fay - you're pregnant.'

Fay burst into tears and fell into Cary's arms wondering how could she be pregnant and what would Tag think? They couldn't afford a baby and what would her family say? They went crazy when she said she was moving in with Tag. Now she would have to get married. Cary finally managed to calm her down and eventually got to wash her hands that were still covered in Fay's urine. And then they joined the others in the bar.

Everyone guessed the outcome by the look on her tear-stained face and they didn't know whether to congratulate or console her. Charlie eventually broke the silence.

'Fay you don't have to have it you know. You're not that far gone. If you go to your doctor he'll tell you your options and that's just one of them and no one needs to know.'

Everyone just stared, they couldn't believe the fact that Charlie of all people had actually said what quite a few of them thought.

'I don't know what I want. I don't think I'll come out tonight.'

'Well, I tell you what, get that coke down you and we'll all go to our rooms and get ready to go out. And if you want to come out then just don't drink, it's up to you. I think the best thing would be to come out and try and forget about it until you get home,' said Clare who had sorted the rooms out and didn't really want it all to go tits-up as soon as they'd got there.

'Okay, I'll get ready and see how I feel.'

'Good girl, right here are the keys to your rooms. We'll finish here and go get ready and meet back down here in three-quarters of an hour. We're all on the first floor so Mandy you're with me, Cary and Fay, Shaz and Charlie, Sue and Steph and finally Chris and Tracey. Any questions?'

Nobody had any questions so they finished their drinks and went to their rooms.

When Tag got back to the room he found Suki fully clothed and putting her make up on.

'The bathroom's free now, you get sorted and then we can go for something to eat,' Suki told Tag.

'Alright I thought we could, er, you know…?'

'What?' Suki gave Tag a puzzled look.

'Doesn't matter,' Tag said as he did as he was told and got into the bath to have a shower, which was just an attachment really.

He'd only been in for about five minutes when Suki asked him to hurry up as she was hungry. Tag was beginning to think that going to London would have been a better option. He had been in hiding all day and now he was being told to get a wash and get his clothes on just like when he was at school. The thing that was annoying him even more though was that he still hadn't got to make love to Suki. He had never before been this patient with a girl in his life. But this time he had no option but to go with the flow as she was his lift home and he felt sure that he would have her, it was only a matter of time.

'I've got your clothes out for you Tag, they're on the bed,' shouted Suki.

'Oh, thanks,' Tag replied, thinking what am I, mummies little soldier? And what had she been doing going through his stuff? Cheeky cow. But he didn't want to rock the boat so he let it pass. He came out of the shower and grabbed a towel. As he was getting dried he frantically flicked his knob to try to 'get a bit of blood in it' to make it look bigger, then he wrapped his towel around his waist and entered the bedroom. Suki didn't even look at him and said she would be in the bathroom, so he could get dressed in peace with no embarrassment. Tag thought this was a bit odd they would be having sex later on so why the fuss about seeing him naked.

When they were both finally ready, Tag looked at Suki and thought wow! she looks hot. She was a very classy lady and she knew it.

'Ready to go?' asked Suki.

'Yeah, if you are, but couldn't we just have a bit of a cuddle before we go,' said Tag.

He couldn't believe he'd said cuddle. What, was he in a 70's sitcom? He meant to say shag but Suki looked so nice he couldn't bring himself to say such a coarse word, but cuddle was even bloody worse.

'We've got all weekend for that, haven't we? There's no rush.'

'I suppose so,' Tag agreed and she gave him a kiss on the cheek.

Just as they locked the door and started to walk down the stairs the last of the girls disappeared into their rooms and so avoided meeting Tag on the stairs by a matter of seconds.

They decided, rather Suki decided that they could have a drink at the bar.

'You've just missed a load of girls from Hull, just left to go to their rooms, they'll be down again in half an hour,' said the barman.

'Where are they staying, what floor?' asked Tag thinking he hoped he didn't know any of them as then his little plan would be knackered.

'The first floor. What can I get you?'

'Pint of lager and a white wine please,' Suki said as she got her purse out.

'I'll get them,' protested Tag.

'No you paid for the room and you can get the next ones in. I work as well so I'll pay my way.'

Great thought Tag, a classy bird, bit of money and gets a round in, he'd won the pools. The next thought was to get out of there as quickly as possible so that he didn't see anyone who might know him. He drank his drink as if he'd been in the desert for a week without a drink.

'You must have been thirsty?'

'I was and I'm hungry too, barman where's the best place to eat around here?'

'Depends, there's a good Italian nearby or there's a Chinese but that's about a mile away.'

'I fancy Chinese, don't you Suki?' asked Tag hoping she'd say yes and they could get away from the hotel and have less chance of bumping into anyone they knew.

'Sounds great, can you get us a taxi?' Suki asked the barman.

'It'll be about 30 minutes you could walk it in that time, it's straight up the road. Tell them Tony from the Adelphi sent you.'

'We'll walk it then, it'll be romantic. Come on, drink up I could eat a scabby horse,' Tag blurted out dropping his well to do guard and taking control.

'Masterful eh? I like that,' Suki said as she drank her drink and they left to get something to eat holding hands, which was another thing Tag never did. Really Tag was a caveman but Suki seemed to have tamed him.

A few minutes later all the girls re-appeared in the bar. Fay had decided to go out and enjoy herself after all. The baby might bring her and Tag closer together, she thought. So she decided to have a good time, she was sure Tag was having a good time. They ordered their drinks and asked the barman whether there was anywhere for them to get something nice to eat. He suggested the Italian or the Chinese as he had with Tag and Suki. In fact he got free takeaways from both as he had an arrangement that he would send anyone who asked about 'somewhere nice to eat' to either the Italian or the Chinese.

'What's it to be girls, Italian which is around the corner or Chinese a mile away?' Clare put it to the girls.

'Italian, it's closer and if Fay isn't too good then she can come straight back,' suggested Charlie, who all the girls were beginning to warm to, as she seemed a very nice girl.

'Italian it is then, drink these and we'll go,' said Clare.

So the girls set off after their drinks for a night of fun, all equipped with the t-shirts on but which none of them felt comfortable wearing. From a distance they looked like a huge pumpkin walking down the street...

The lads all caught their taxis making sure that there was the same number in each so that no one ended up out of pocket.

They were all told that the first pub would be the 'Lamb and Flag' in Leicester Square. They were going to go to Covent garden but the manager from the Clipper had suggested Leicester Square. As this was the pub that Damo had been told to meet them in and would be the easiest for him to find. They all made their way there and it was a fair old ride as the meter clicked up and up and up. The lads were nudging each other, this was going to be expensive. The car that had Jonesy, Skip, Tosser, Trev and Matt in it seemed to be going around in circles.

'That's three fucking times we've passed big Ben, this fucker's taking the piss,' Jonesy whispered to Skip.

'I noticed that we've seen nearly every face of the clock,' Trev chipped in. Then out of the blue Matt came out with a question.

'You know when you're having a wank? Do you ever put your finger up your arse?'

'No, why do you?' asked the others in astonishment.

'No, no I don't,' protested Matt.

'You lying bastard, why would you ask if we did if you didn't?' Skip had cornered him.

'What's it for anyway, to get shitty fingers?' Trev said

'No it's supposed to make you come like a waterfall, there's a gland up there and it's very sensitive,' explained Matt.

'So you haven't found it yet then?' asked Skip.

'No not yet,' said an unsuspecting Matt.

'Fucking got yer, so you have tried it then, you pervy, dirty bastard Matt. Wait while I tell all the others.'

'Yeah! We'll have to start calling you shitty fingers,' laughed Trev.

'No, someone at work had this magazine and he said he'd tried it,' said Matt trying to get out of it.

'So have you tried it then, come on admit it,' coaxed Skip.

'Yes just the once, but it didn't half hurt. I mean it hurts when you're wiping your arse and your finger accidentally goes through the paper.'

'You didn't put it up dry did you? You should have used some baby oil or sommat,' said Trev

'Woo! Baby oil, Trev's tried it, or maybe it's what he uses when he's up Cary's arse, hey Trev?'

At this point Trev went very quiet and immediately Skip picked up on this.

'So, Cary takes it up the shit box does she then Trev?'

'What me and Cary do is our business and not any of yours thank you very much.'

'We're only joking Trev, I mean I've tried it with Mandy but she doesn't like it. You all must have at some point?' Skip said looking at the lads in the taxi. But no one replied so he thought he'd ask the taxi driver, seeing as he was chuckling to himself in the front.

'Driver do you give your lass it up the arse?' asked Skip.

'No, she left me, I'm divorced.'

'There you go, all taxi drivers get divorced, it's a well known fact,' said Tosser.

'I might go for a job as one,' said Skip laughing.

'Can I tape you boys talking? I'll play it to all my customers, you're really funny you fellas,' the driver chipped in.

'You can if you knock a fiver off the fare?' said Trev.

'Can't do that Guvnor, gotta make a living.'

The conversation stopped as they'd arrived at Leicester Square.

'That's the pub you want there,' the driver said pointing to the Lamb and Flag. All the others were there already and they started to applaud when Trev and the others got out of the cab.

'Where the fuck have you been?' asked Grant.

'Around Big Ben three times,' came the reply.

'How much did you get charged?' asked Skip whose taxi had cost £22. The prices ranged from £18 to £24.

'We'll try and get mini-cabs on the way back, them black ones are too expensive,' said Thommo.

'Right are we all here?' Skip took charge.

'Listen up we all stick together. Unless you want to piss off which is fine but tell someone if you're going, alright?'

'We aren't at school Skip,' Thommo quipped.

'Hello Thommo, off the toilet are we? Shit coming out of your mouth is it now? The reason I'm saying this is because you don't want to get lost in London miles from anywhere. So no one gets left, if you want to go your own way feel free but tell us, then we know you've gone okay? And we won't be dicking around waiting for you.'

'Yes sir, what are we doing now sir?' Thommo asked sarcastically.

'We're going for a drink in that pub there because that's where we told Damo we'd be. But first I'm going to ring Pete up to tell him what a great time we're having, unless someone else wants to rub it in.'

'I will, it would be a pleasure,' so as all the others went into the pub Gaz rang Pete up to gloat. However Pete was ready for the next call and had a bit of gloating he wanted to do himself.

'Hello is Pete there Sally?'

'Who is it?'

'Gaz from rugby.'

'I'll just get him. Pete it's for you, Gaz from rugby.'

Sally handed the phone to Pete with a smile as she thought it was very funny, because Pete would have done the same thing but was now getting a bit of his own medicine, and it wasn't going down too well.

'What the fuck do you want? I suppose you're having a great

time, women giving blow-jobs out in every pub and free beer and food. But don't talk out of your arse Gaz. You'll be in some dodgy pub with some old twats trying to make each other laugh by ringing me all the time. Am I right?'

'No, we're in Leicester Square and guess who I've just got to sign my wallet?' interrupted Gaz.

'Who, the fucking Queen?'

'No, Rod 'the god' Stewart, he was going into a restaurant and I just shouted him over and he signed something for all the lads.'

Gaz knew that Pete was a big Rod Stewart fan and that this would piss him off even more.

'Well then get this, tell all them bastards that their wives and girlfriends have gone to Blackpool for the night looking for cock.'

'Who's gone to Blackpool?'

'All the women Clare, Cary, Fay, Mandy, Shaz, Charlie, Sue, Steph, Chris and Tracey, they've had it organised for months, got t-shirts printed, the lot. So what do you think about that? Tell Skip to give me a ring and I'll fill him in on the juicy details.'

Then Pete hung up and punched the air in triumph he had wanted to tell Skip or Tosser but he couldn't hold it in any longer. Gaz was stunned but started laughing to himself, this was going to be good. He entered the pub and the first person he saw was Skip.

'Did you rub it in?'

'Yeah good and proper, I even told him I'd got Rod Stewart's autograph.'

'Great. I bet that pissed him off didn't it?'

'Yeah but he had the last laugh.'

'What do you mean the last laugh?'

'Well according to Pete all the wives and girlfriends are in Blackpool for the night on a secret trip they've organised behind your backs.'

'You are fucking joking right? I'm going to ring home,' and off Skip went to ring home. He rang his own house and then his mother-in-law's and the kids were there. It was true - the sneaky twats. He then went back to the pub and told all the others what had happened. Trev of course already knew but didn't let on.

'Listen boys you won't believe this but the women have gone and sneaked a trip behind our backs. I don't know who has gone and who hasn't, but they've gone to Blackpool,' Skip announced. Then Gaz went through the names of who was on the trip.

'What's the problem you're having your trip why can't they have theirs?' said Thommo who had managed three cokes without having to go to the toilet.

'I don't see what's wrong with them having a trip,' chipped in Grant.

'That isn't the point, it's the way it's been done, all sneaky and that.'

Skip was fuming.

'They must have been having their meetings at my house and I thought they were having Ann Summers' and clothes parties. Thinking about it I never saw any dildos, or clothes for that matter,' said Tosser putting two and two together.

This revelation had put a bit of a dampener on the proceedings as everyone rang home to confirm that it was true. Even Trev went through the pretence of ringing home although he knew that Cary was in Blackpool. Skip then remembered about Tag's little adventure with Suki.

'Fay has gone and guess who is in Blackpool for the weekend with his bird? Tag is well and truly fucked if they bump into each other.'

'Serves the little bastard right. I hope she does catch him, what he's doing is out of order,' said an angry Tosser.

This cheered everyone up as the thought of Tag getting busted far outweighed the girls' secret trip and the atmosphere got better especially when Thommo had to run to the toilet again as normality resumed.

'Where's he gone?' asked Jonesy.

'Where do you think? Surely he can't have just had the shits for this long. He must have had something dodgy to eat, he's got to have food poisoning,' said Skip.

This was all said whilst Trev and the two students were in earshot and they kept their silence, just giving each other the odd look and smile as though to say, we know why his arse is like the flag of Japan.

The pub they were in was actually a bit dead and so Skip decided that seeing as they were all there then they would move onto the next one.

'Go and see if shitty arse is finished while I go see what they call the next pub. Tell him we're going for an Indian'.

Trev volunteered to go just to rub it in a bit.

'We're ready to go Thommo, are you alright?'

'Not just yet. Oooh! My God no, surely no more, oooh!'

Trev had to bite his lip as he was outside holding his stomach, it ached that much. When he calmed himself down he delivered the ultimate line.

'Skip says we're going for an Indian if you want to come Thommo, or what about a nice greasy kebab?'

'Fuck off Trev, this isn't funny. I've got no skin on my arse and the shit won't stop coming.'

'See you outside then Thommo, we'll wait for you.'

Trev then went outside and burst into laughter.

'What's so funny?' asked Grant.

'That twat in there, he's in agony and sounds as though he's giving birth, go in and have a listen.'

So Grant and Mike both went to have a listen and all they could hear was moaning and a couple of shrieks.

'Are you alright Thommo? Sounds like you're giving birth.'

'I'm trying to wipe my arse, but it's too painful, so I'm dabbing it instead. Tell them I'll be there in a minute.'

They'd got the name of the next pub and told the doorman if an Aussie came and asked where they where then they had gone to the next pub. Just then Thommo came out of the toilet walking like he'd just ridden the 'Tour de France' using a razor blade for a seat.

'Fucking hell it's John Wayne, you don't have to stay in character all night cowboy.'

'Get stuffed the lot of yer, I'm trying one more pub and then I'm off, I can't stand this.' Thommo was nearly in tears as he tried to walk normally.

'Onwards and upwards to the next pub, out of here and straight ahead,' instructed Skip.

They got to the next pub 'The Crown' and Thommo went to the bar and the barmaid asked him what he wanted and he just bent over dropped his trousers parted his cheeks and said, 'Can you do anything for this?' Pointing at his bleeding ring piece. To everyone's surprise the barmaid didn't even flinch and went straight for the biggest soda syphon anyone had ever seen and proceeded to squirt it at Thommo's arse, emptying the full lot and soaking his trousers and everything else. She then asked if he wanted anything else and then served the next customer. Thommo pulled up his trousers and headed for the door saying he was going back to the hotel. Then he went outside, got in a cab and went back to get sorted out.

After the initial shock they all gave the barmaid a round of applause and carried on drinking.

'Well that was good wasn't it,' said Skip who had seen some sights but none as bizarre as that.

'Has he really gone or is he just pissing about?' asked Tosser.

'Yep he's gone, just looked out of the window and shitty arse got in a taxi,' confirmed Gaz.

Ah! shitty arse, that reminded Skip of something. He had almost forgotten about 'shitty fingers'.

'Now, gather round everyone for a quiz,' said Skip. 'Who sticks his finger up his arse while having a wank?' they all looked puzzled.

'Matt does, he admitted it in the taxi,' declared Skip.

'I didn't say that I'd tried it, I was just saying that it helps you come quicker that's all.'

'Fucking hell, I don't need any help in coming quicker, it's the other way round. Sometimes I think of you Skip so I don't shoot my load too quickly,' shouted Jonesy.

'I've had a bird do it whilst we were shagging, but it hurt as she had big false nails on and she cut my arse,' confessed Gaz who it appeared had done everything.

'Alright, can we change the subject please? One arsehole's gone home, we don't want to be talking about his relatives all night,' said Trev.

The boys carried on drinking and chatted about what the night was going to entail.

'Where are we ending up then Skip?' asked Grant.

'Don't know really, Daz wanted to go to the Hippodrome, didn't you Daz?'

'Too right, it's been my life's ambition to get in there and that's where I'll be tonight. If you want to come you're welcome but I'm going and so is Gaz and Thommo, shit he's gone, so it looks like me and Gaz.'

'How much is it to get in then?' enquired Mike.

'A tenner,' replied Daz. He knew this because he'd researched it. He was determined to get in mainly just to brag about the fact he'd been to London and been to a top London nightspot where all the famous people go.

'A tenner, have you robbed a bank? Then there's drinks,' interrupted Jonesy.

'Well don't come then, I'm not bothered,' replied Gaz who also wanted to go and was hoping to score.

'I'll see how the night pans out before I'll make a decision,' Jonesy carried on.

'Don't come then, there's more fanny for me Jonesy, I don't give a shit.'

'What time is it?' Skip asked.

'Just gone 8.'

'Damo should be here by now, at least at the hotel, drink up and we'll go to the next pub and I'll leave the usual message.' This went on for about another three pubs as the locals didn't seem too friendly, so the boys drank up quickly.

Eddie had gone back to the hotel earlier to await the arrival of Damo. And as Damo got there and was checking in a taxi pulled up and out got Thommo. He was still soaking wet and trying to explain to the driver he hadn't pissed himself in the cab and that it was just water. Thommo eventually sorted it out although he had to pay extra to the driver to let his cab dry out. Eddie asked what had happened. Thommo explained the full story and then went to his room as he said he'd had enough and his arse was killing him.

'Sounds like someone's slipped him a laxo,' said Damo.

'Get away, a laxative?' laughed Eddie.

'Yeah happened to a mate of mine back home, he was on the 'dunny' for a day then was alright after that. Whose room am I in?'

'You're with Butty, I'll order you a cab.'

'Make sure it's a mini cab and not one of those black bastards, they're way too expensive.'

So Eddie ordered the cab and Damo went and got a shower and changed.

CHAPTER 6
A LUCKY ESCAPE

Tag had finished his meal and was ready for the bill. He figured that the sooner everything was out of the way i.e. drink, food, another drink, it would be taxi and then shagging. However Suki had all the time in the world and wanted to have a coffee after the meal and let her food settle and then maybe take a walk and go to a club. Tag was getting more and more pissed off but didn't show it of course. Secretly he was thinking of being in London, pissed and taking his chance with some slapper. Every time he looked at Suki he thought of getting in her knickers as she was gorgeous, but she wasn't easy like his usual type. But it would be worth it in the end, he hoped.

The girls had also finished their meals and were heading into the town centre where Tag was. They had their t-shirts on, which was getting them lots of attention, which is why they wore them. Fay had managed to stop being sick and was quite enjoying herself, she was in a bit of a daze as it had only been a couple of hours since she'd found out she was going to be a mother and she was warming to the idea. As one of the women pointed out she'd had good practice living with Tag as he was like a baby. The conversation then turned to the men that were in London.

'Do you think they will find out about this then?' asked Sue worrying slightly.

'Will they balls unless anyone of us says out about it and then what are they going to do. I can't see any of them ringing up to see how we all are can you? Besides I've told me mother to tell him I've gone out if he rings, which he won't. They think were going on a night out anyway, the cheeky gets tried to organise one for us. But as I pointed out that I am not stupid and I can organise my own night out.' answered Clare.

'I know they never ring when they go away do they?' Tracey piped in.

'No and don't think it changes with marriage when you're hitched then they definitely don't ring, isn't that right Cary?'

'Actually Trevor always rings me a couple of times to see how I am and that and tell me he's got there safe.'

'So what's he going to do when he finds out you're not in, what excuse have you left with your mother to tell him?' probed Mandy.

'He won't ring this time I don't think.'

There was silence as Mandy mulled over Cary's last statement. Cary's silence gave it away.

'You've told him about this haven't you? You stupid twat, now we'll all be in the shit, he'll tell everybody and we'll go home to hell.'

'Trevor will not say a word, I can assure you he's known for three months from the very first meeting and he hasn't told anyone so why should he now?' Cary defended her husband, she was exaggerating as Trev had only found out a day or two before.

'Well what did he say?'

'He just said he didn't mind and wondered what the big secret was.'

'I think you must have a really strong relationship Cary if you can tell him that and he's alright with it,' said Charlie.

'It isn't that, if he's allowed a weekend away, then why aren't I? He just sees us as equals not like you lot, pathetically sneaking around behind their backs in case they disapprove, you lot want to get back into the 50s. Trev and me share everything and that goes for cooking, cleaning and working. I work full time so why shouldn't I get a weekend away just like he gets one?'

Cary then went to the toilet and left the others shocked and stunned.

'Well that's us knackered then' said Clare.

'Not necessarily, she told him months ago so he hasn't mentioned it or else they would have known and we're here and they're in London, so he can't have said anything.' Mandy was thinking out loud.

'Bollocks anyway, like she said if they can have a weekend away, why can't we? Fuck 'em, let's enjoy ourselves and keep quiet until they mention it,' said Clare.

'I don't like lying to Tag though and especially now I'm pregnant,' Fay chipped in pathetically.

'Sorry Fay but Tag is a little shit and believe me he would sneak a trip behind your back without a doubt,' suggested Shaz.

'So you're saying he'd go behind my back with you? In your dreams,' Fay said, claws at the ready.

'She never said that, all she was saying was if the boot was on the other foot Tag would do the same' Charlie said trying to intervene.

'You can shut up I've seen the both of you talking to him.'

'Yeah trying to tell him to fuck off' Shaz said under her breath.

'What was that? He would see through you two in a flash, always hanging around club eyeing up the men, a couple of slappers that's all you two are.'

'Hold on a minute I work at club and she meets me there, and as for hanging around Tag well we don't want to go there, not with you being pregnant and that.'

'What do you mean? Come on tell me are you two shagging my boyfriend?'

'No we wouldn't touch your grubby little twat of a man if he was the last one on earth. We can't fucking stand him, he's tried it on dozens of times with me and her and we've blown him out more times than a church candle. He thinks he's God's gift to woman. Why don't you wake up and smell the coffee and take notice of your brothers who think the same way I do, that he's a snivelling little shit who will bring you nothing but heartache.'

'Alright Shaz that's enough,' interrupted Cary who had returned from the toilet.

No one knew what to say as Fay burst into tears and headed for the toilet herself. Clare followed her as the others looked at Shaz with a look that said, you bitch.

'I'm sorry but why should I have to take that shit from her, calling me a slag, I know she's pregnant but to come out with all that crap about me is out of order, I'm fed up with it. I can now declare that I have no interest in any of your husbands or boyfriends. Now I will apologise to her and if she accepts it good, if not then what can I do?' Shaz then headed for the toilet where Clare was consoling Fay.

'What do you want Shaz? Not now.'

'I just want to talk to Fay and apologise for what I said I didn't mean to upset her.'

'Well you did, take a look.'

'Right I'll say what I've just said out there. I don't like being called a slag and the other thing is I am not interested in anyone's husband or boyfriend. As for Tag Fay he's bad news, I'll tell you to your face, maybe the baby will change him but he acts like he's still single with all the chat.'

'But that's all it is he's friendly and talks to anyone but that's all it is he wouldn't cheat on me.'

Clare just looked at Shaz and rolled her eyes, she knew that Tag was everything that Shaz had said and more but Fay couldn't see it.

'Right come on let's stop this. I didn't organise this trip so that we would be arguing all night with glum faces. Come on Fay let's sort your face out and we'll go onto the next pub and into town for a good night.'

So Fay got her face sorted out and the girls headed for the town centre and the packed bars and clubs...

Just ahead of them was Tag and Suki. They were in the tower bar under the famous Blackpool tower. This had a dance floor and various bars and was a huge venue and it was packed to the rafters with a twenty-minute queue to get in. It was relatively early in the night but the place was rocking as Tag and Suki danced. Suki was a great dancer and as Tag tried to keep up she was knackering him out.

'I'm off to the toilet, I'll meet you back at the bar over there,' shouted Tag as it was the only way to be heard.

Suki sat down and almost immediately she was getting chatted up by a gang of lads who were out on a lads' weekend. Suki just chatted back to them as they told jokes and made her laugh. Then her favourite record came on and one of them asked her if she wanted to dance and she said 'Yes' so off they went to dance.

Two minutes later Tag came back to the bar area looking for Suki. When she wasn't there he ordered two drinks and waited thinking she might have gone to the toilet.

Five minutes passed and there was still no sign of Suki. Now Tag was wondering where she was and he was quite worried. But his worry turned to anger as she came walking back with a guy and calmly said, 'This is Gary, we've just been dancing.'

Gary extended his hand and said, 'Alright mate she wanted to dance to her favourite song so I asked her, no offence like.'

'None taken, now you've had your dance you can fuck off,' shouted Tag not realising he was surrounded by Gary's mates.

'What did you say to my mate, you little shit?' the booming voice of a six foot plus giant asked. Tag just looked and then the penny dropped that he was surrounded by Gary's friends. Gary got him out of the shit by saying 'Look mate it was a dance nothing else, let's leave it. I know you're annoyed but it's not the fifties, she has a mind of her own. I'll give you some advice, if I had a girlfriend like that I wouldn't let her out of my sight. I'd take her to toilet with me.' Gary winked at Suki who blushed and then he went on his way with his mates.

There was a silence that seemed to last for an eternity until Suki asked if he wanted a drink. Tag just handed her the drink he'd bought her and didn't say a word, he was sulking.

'Grow up Tag, it was a dance and you don't own me, I do what I like, and I wanted to dance to that song preferably with you but you weren't here, so...'

'So you grabbed the nearest man available. I thought you were different?'

'Obviously I'm very different to the girls you're used to. I want to have a good dance and in my world if I feel like dancing I'll go and dance. I'm not your property and even if we were married you still wouldn't own me. Now I'm going to powder my nose and you better think while I'm away about what you want because I'm not changing. If you want someone you can tell what to do and order around then forget me because I do what I like. While I'm gone Tag feel free to have a dance.' Suki then left her chair and went to the toilet. Tag just sat there for a minute in shock it wasn't what he'd expected and he was wondering what to do. He really had fallen in love with Suki but she was different from all the other girls he'd known, she was feisty, opinionated and had balls which is probably why he loved her . Plus she had great tits and an arse and legs to die for. If he went off in a strop all that planning would go to waste and he would have blown it and never get to shag her. The plan now was to go with the flow and let her do what she wanted and tell him what to do. This could be quite exciting as he'd always been the more dominant in all of his relationships so being dominated might be fun. However Suki didn't want to dominate him, she just wanted to do what she wanted to do and be trusted by him. Like an equal.

As she made her return Tag smiled and said to her, 'Drink up and we'll go for a dance - that's if you want to? And by the way I'm sorry.'

The two of them then hit the dance floor, just as the girls were entering the first bar that Tag had been in earlier...

After being in about five pubs and leaving messages in each of them for Damo. They finally hit the pubs that had a friendlier feel to them and they were full and a lot livelier.

'This is more like it Gaz look at the fanny in here' said Matt like an overexcited kid 'even I might get a blow job you never know'

'Fuck off Matt these birds wouldn't even look at you twice. Firstly you don't speak with the right accent and your clothes aren't the latest fashion and what the fuck are you doing Matt?'

Matt had got right in the middle of a group of very fit and good looking girls and started to strip. He was down to his pants and the girls formed a great big circle and began to clap and started chanting, 'Off, off, off!'

Matt thought for a moment and then in front of the full pub took off his pants and swung them around his head and threw them into the crowd and they landed on the head of the bouncer who was coming to see what all the fuss was about. The whole pub erupted with laughter. The only person who didn't see the funny side was, you've guessed it the bouncer.

'Get out you twat, now!' he shouted as he took the pants off his head, to which the whole pub started to boo. Even the bar staff and the other bouncers joined in with the booing. Then a chant started up from the whole pub.

'Let him stay, let him stay' they all chanted, and the bouncer had no option but to let Matt stay but told him he was on a final warning.

They all ordered more drinks and the girls began to chat with the lads and asked where they were from and what they intended to do for the rest of the night.

'Who said they wouldn't talk to us?' Matt said to Gaz with a big grin on his face.

'You mad bastard, I thought we were going to get chucked out for sure.'

'I'll go and see the bouncer and say sorry like. I'd had them on all day nearly and they must have stunk, come with us Gaz.' They both approached the bouncer.

'Here mate, sorry about that I didn't mean for them to land on you, it was just a bit of fun, no hard feelings eh?'

'No, I suppose not.'

The bouncers reply wasn't too forthcoming as he scowled at the two of them.

'He's alright mate you go back to your friends, he's just sulking,' said the second bouncer trying not to laugh.

'I am not sulking.'

'Yes you are skid mark.'

'Piss off we'll have less of it. I'm going for a break, and I hope you twats aren't here when I get back.'

He then went into the staff area behind the bar.

'Don't worry, he's a bit serious.'

'Well tell him there were no skids in them, anyhow where are they?' asked Matt.

'Under that pile of people,' answered Gaz pointing at the floor.

'Where are you boys heading?' asked the friendlier bouncer.

'Hippodrome, why can you get us in?' asked Matt.

'No, but I've got some 'money-off' tickets you can have, here.'

The bouncer then produced thirty tickets and each had £3 off the admission price.

'Cheers mate, now we might get to meet some page three girls.'

'You are joking, they go into the V.I.P. area which has a different entrance altogether. It's a con all you punters come thinking the place will be full of famous women and they're in a different part of the club. But saying that there will be plenty of birds to go around.'

'Great, I'll tell all the lads. Cheers mate.'

They went back to everyone who was getting on great with all the women in the pub and they decided to share the tickets out with them. They had decided to have one more drink and then head towards the next pub, which was across the road from the Hippodrome.

In the mean time Damo had arrived in town and was heading for the first pub.

'Mate have a load of guys been in here? And did they leave a message for me?' Damo asked the bouncer.

The man on the door looked puzzled and then remembered the message.

'Go about 50 yards that way and that's the pub they went to but it was quite a bit ago, they might have moved on,' said the bouncer.

'Cheers buddy, I'll catch you later,' and Damo went on his way to the next pub where the same thing happened. In the next pub he decided to have a drink thinking that he was never going to find them. Damo did this for several pubs.

The main party had just moved on with their new found lady friends in tow and had just left a message with the bouncer of the last pub, thinking that it was a pointless exercise. Just as they left and got around the corner, Damo entered the pub they had just left and asked the bouncer if he'd seen the rest of his party and the bouncer helped him on his way.

The next pub was a little bit more subdued. They had to talk their way in saying that they were in couples as the bouncer who was a good 6ft 6 inches tall but seemed very edgy and thought that he was going to get beaten up. Everyone had just ordered their drinks when there was a loud booming voice.

'G'day, get to the bar and get me a drink you tight pommie bastards,' it was Damo.

The whole place erupted, they grabbed Damo and were hugging each other and shouting and singing his name. Everyone was wondering what was going on, not least the poor doorman who had decided for his own safety not to intervene. He had to when they got Damo on their shoulders and started to jump up and down and he nearly got his head cut off by the ceiling fan. They explained to everyone the fact that they'd left him messages at every pub and by a miracle he had tracked them down. They then decided it would be a laugh to ring up Pete so that he could join in the celebration of Damo finding them. So that's what they did and they got Greg to do the honours. Now Greg was pissed and had gone onto his favourite drink of brandy and coke and was very much the worse for wear. They got the whole pub to be quiet and they rang Pete. So that he wouldn't hang up straight away Damo spoke first as he was the most sober. The phone rang about ten times and just as Damo was about to hang up Pete answered the phone.

'Hello,' Pete answered in a croaky voice.

'G'day Pete, how's it going?'

'Not great Damo I thought you were in London,' Damo handed the phone to Greg who had heard what Pete had said.

'He is in London you silly bastard and he's covered in love bites from all the women we've pulled, you spotty bastard.'

Then Greg handed the phone onto Skip. Pete was on the other end shouting obscenities.

'You lousy bastards, I was asleep who is that calling me spotty?'

'It was Greg, you should be here mate it's unbelievable.'

'Yeah and you lot should be in Blackpool where all your women are getting shafted. Now fuck off.'

Pete slammed the phone down as in the background the whole pub was cheering.

'What did he say?' asked Damo.

'Couldn't hear him, but we'll give him ten minutes to get back in bed and then ring him again and tell him about the Hippodrome.'

'So Damo, where have you been?'

'I dropped my bag off and came straight out passing Thommo on the way. What has happened to him?'

'Dodgy takeaway.'

'Come on you lot, I said to Eddie someone's given him some shit juice.'

'Some what?' Skip looked puzzled.

'Laxo - you know, laxatives - slip it in his drink when he's not looking and he'll be crapping all day.'

'Have you heard this Damo thinks one of us has slipped Thommo some laxatives that's bullshit isn't it?'

'No' Mike shouted out forgetting about keeping it watertight and telling no one.

'You mean you gave him them?' asked Skip. Trev was fuming but thought Mike would just say it was a joke and that he hadn't really done it. How wrong he was.

'No I brought them for a laugh and it was Trev who slipped it into his drink' everyone looked at Trev who had the reputation of being rather square.

'Trevor you fucking rotten twat' said Gaz laughing.

'Well he had it coming, and after he put that bottle up his arse I wanted to kill him, but Mike here had a better solution. I didn't think he would be this bad though.'

'How much did you give him?' enquired Gaz.

'About a third of the bottle.'

'Fucking hell I'll be on 'ambulance watch' tonight there'll be fuck all of him left he'll have shit himself away. You might have got your wish Trev he could be dead.'

'Don't go telling him will you now.'

'Why are you scared of him?'

'No we can do without it can't we. We don't need anyone arguing now do we. It would have been a secret if Mike over there had have kept his gob shut.'

'Look no one mention this again, Trev's right we don't need anyone fighting, and let's face it Thommo did have it coming to him and what a fucking laugh we've had watching him squirm. Three cheers for Trev hip hip hooray' and they all joined in with Tosser as he lead the chant.

When it had died down a bit Trev went straight over to Mike and Grant and made it perfectly clear that they weren't to mention another word about him slipping something into Thommo's drink. Then he went to have a quiet word with Gaz to ask him not to say anything at least while the trip was on. Anyhow Gaz agreed that Thommo could be a bit much and that he wouldn't utter a word...

Tag and Suki were having a great time. They had been dancing for at least half an hour and Tag had actually never done that before. Tag usually only went on the dance floor to cop a feel or to ask a woman if they wanted a dance. He would dance for a maximum of two songs and if he hadn't got anywhere with his stinging chat up lines by then he would go back to the bar. He would try this until it worked. This was a theory he had that if you asked fifty women to dance some will say, 'I'm already dancing', some would say 'Piss off' and others would say 'Alright then'. Then Tag would bombard them with crappy chat up lines thinking he was 'all that' and at least one of them out of the original fifty would probably cop off with him. This usually worked but if it didn't he would go home to Fay. But tonight he was actually enjoying dancing and he had got right into it.

Suki was the one who suggested they go for a drink at the bar. So they did and then sat in one of the many booths that surrounded the area away from the dance floor. The booths were quite secluded and private so you could have a chat and enjoy your drink. Well that was the general idea but in reality they were shag pots where couples went to try and have a quicky, hoping that no one would notice. That was the reason there were three security staff constantly patrolling the area to sort out anyone who was trying to get a quick hand job or some finger pie.

The Tower was a big place and you could get lost in there. You could lose your friends quite easily. This was lucky for Tag as he'd only just sat down when at the far side of the club Fay and all the girls entered and went straight to the same bar that Tag had been at not ten minutes before.

A few of them went to the toilet and the others walked over to the bar. Shaz and Charlie went to the toilet to apply some more 'slap' to their already heavily made-up faces, to try and attract some unsuspecting victim. They all got back to the bar and decided the best thing to do was have a drink and then go for a dance. They also decided they should stick together as the Tower bar was huge and they didn't want anyone getting 'lost'.

No sooner had they all got back to the bar than Gary, a good-looking bloke from Stockport and his four friends swooped.

'Hello ladies and where are you lovely lot from then?' asked Gary.

'Hull. Why? What do you want to know for?' came the rather frosty and abrupt reply from Cary.

'Yes, we're from Hull and where are you lot from then?' Charlie quickly got in before the lads had been put off by the crappy way Cary had answered them.

'Us lot, we're from Stockport, we've just come here for the weekend to have a good time, how about you?'

'Just a girls' night out.'

'Long way to come for a night out isn't it?' interrupted Steve, one of the lads.

'No we're staying in a hotel and going home tomorrow,' said Clare.

'Good, it gives us time to get to know you then, where are you staying?'

'Bit nosey aren't you? Where are you staying?' said Shaz in a flirty way.

'Maxine's B&B just off South Street.'

'That's just near us, we're in the Adelphi on South Street,' Charlie shouted a bit too enthusiastically, which didn't go unnoticed by the lads.

'Right then I'm Gary, this is Dave, Steve, Alex and the dopey looking one there is Carl.'

'Piss off Gary, I'm not dopey,' said Carl trying to defend himself.

'Want to put money on it? I'd have a fiver with you,' Mandy said under her breath to Clare and Fay who both burst out laughing.

'What's so funny ladies?' asked Gary.

'Nothing, she's got a cat called Carl and we just found it funny that's all. So what are you lot up to tonight?' Fay said, rather embarrassed at laughing at them.

'Few drinks in here and then we're going to 'Pixies'. It's open until 3 so we'll try our luck there. That is if nothing happens here with you lot. I didn't catch your name what is it?' asked Gary looking into Fay's eyes.

'Fay,' she replied, turning red with the attention and the fact that she thought he was hot.

'Fay, I like it, would you like to dance Fay?'

'Erm, I don't really know,' Fay answered rather pathetically.

'Jesus Fay, you sound like Mavis Riley, go on Fay it's only a dance,' Mandy said as she shoved her gently towards Gary.

'Alright then,' Fay replied and went even redder as she walked with Gary onto the dance floor.

Charlie and Shaz didn't wait for the men to ask they did the asking and Shaz grabbed Carl's hand and Charlie grabbed Steve's.

'Come on you two you're with us.'

The two left didn't get chance to ask as the five remaining women grabbed them and they all ended up on the dance floor.

While all this was going on Tag had gone back to the bar to get some more drinks and had picked up a flyer with money off the admission to 'Pixies'. He got the drinks and showed the flyer to Suki and asked if she fancied it. They both agreed that they would have one more and then go to the pub opposite as they had a band on. Catch the last set from the band and then go and dance the night away at the nightclub.

Gary and Fay were getting on well as they danced and Gary chatted and Fay gave one-word answers and smiled.

'Is there something wrong? I don't bite you know?'

'No there isn't, what makes you say that?'

'Just the way you seem all up tight, just relax and enjoy yourself.'

'It isn't that easy I haven't had a drink like you lot have.'

'Well have one then, I'll get you one.'

'No! I don't want one' Fay shouted a little too loudly.

'Alright then there's no need to shout.'

'I'm sorry I didn't mean to shout it's just that I haven't been drinking so I aren't in the same party mood as you lot and…' there was a pause.

'Do you want to sit down and talk about it?' Gary was thinking fucking hell, got a nutter here, there was ten to choose from and I get the one with problems.

'It's just that I found out I was pregnant today and it's come as a bit of a shock, that's all.'

'Oh!' Gary said, thinking the two birds I've got on with tonight, one's with her boyfriend and the other's up the duff.

'So sorry you won't be copping off with me tonight. Not because I don't find you attractive, I do, but you see I'm with someone but if I wasn't I would be interested.'

'Look, no need to explain, just keep dancing I'm not bothered anyway, you've obviously just had a crazy day.'

'I'm a bit mixed up really, I hadn't planned to get pregnant so it's come as a bit of a shock really.'

'I bet it has, look do you want a drink?'

'No thanks I'm in a round anyway.'

'Well I'm going for one are you coming?'

'Alright then' and the two of them went to the bar soon to be joined by the rest of the group. The lads all took it in turns to be grab by the women for a dance and nothing else. The girls were having a great time.

Time was getting on and it was coming up to 10 o'clock and Tag and Suki were ready to go. Suki said she wanted to go to the toilet and then they'd go. So Tag went himself so they wouldn't lose each other and then they would meet outside the toilets. They were then going to see the band in the pub across the road and afterwards onto the nightclub. Fay and a couple of the girls also went to the toilet at the same time as Tag had gone. Just as Tag went into the gents, then Fay and the girls came around the corner and went into the ladies. There was a queue and as Suki finished in her cubicle Fay jumped in and Suki washed her hands and was on her way out, they had walked right past each other, and even used the same toilet. Tag had already finished and stood outside the toilets totally oblivious to the fact the two women in his complicated life were currently in the same toilets together. Suki came out they went out of the bar and on their way, walking about 10 feet from where the girls party were stood with the lads they had met. Two minutes later the girls came out of the toilet and walked past the very spot that Tag had been standing on not 5 minutes beforehand. They went back to the rest of the party completely oblivious to who had just walked past.

'Bloody hell that was a job and a half getting out of there, how packed was it?' Tag couldn't believe the amount of people who were in the bar and the queue outside to get in.

'The bar opens 'til 12 that's why they're all queuing it saves going to a nightclub. But wait while they all come out and try and get a taxi it'll be chaos. We're much better going to see that band and then going onto a nightclub, believe me,' Suki said with an air of someone who knew what she was talking about. And Tag just went with the flow marvelling at the fact he'd bagged such a clever woman. In actual fact she was just sensible but Tag didn't do sensible, partly because he was thick but mainly because Tag never planned ahead, he just went with what he felt and got wherever it took him. He quite liked being told what to do and where to go. He liked it until he got to the door of the pub.

'£2 each please,' the doorman announced holding his hand out.

'What to get into a pub, are you joking or what?' asked Tag.

'No, I never joke. It's £2, there's a band on and if you want to see them get your money out.'

With that Suki produced two complimentary tickets she'd picked up from the restaurant.

'Will these get us in?' Suki handed the doorman the two tickets.

'Yes they will, enjoy the band and have a good night.'

The doorman moved aside and Tag and Suki walked into the bar which was full and very noisy.

'Do you want a drink?' shouted Tag. Suki just nodded.

'I would have paid the money to get in you know, I'm not a skinflint,' Tag was explaining at the bar.

'I am, I wouldn't let you pay £2 for what, an hour? The bands already done their first set and they'll only do another half an hour max.'

Wow! Tag was in dreamland she was great, she was clever, she knew what was what and of course she was as sexy as they came. What Tag failed to realise was that it wouldn't be too long before someone as clever as Suki would find him out. They got their drinks and settled down to watch the band.

Back at the tower bar they had been dancing and talking to the group of lads they had met. Shaz and Charlie had already decided what they were going to be doing that night as they were hooked up with Steve and Carl. The other seven were ready to sit down for a bit and were chatting. This left Fay in a bit of a quandry she had been with Gary for the whole duration since they'd met and they had got on really well, but Fay felt that if she didn't join the others she'd get stuck with Shaz and Charlie and she didn't want that. Fay also didn't want Gary to get the wrong idea as although she was attracted to him nothing was going to happen as she was with Tag and now with child, but if she hadn't have been who knows. She kissed Gary on the cheek and thanked him for the dance and then joined the others.

'Alright Fay?' enquired Clare.

'Yeah, why shouldn't I be?'

'No reason just the way you looked at that lad, you like him don't you?'

'He was alright.'

'He was more than alright Fay and he liked you.'

'But I'm with Tag and I just couldn't, not after meeting someone only hours before, I'm not a slapper, not like those two.'

'There's nothing wrong with having a good time as long as no one gets hurt. That's all that those two are doing, what single women do. And be honest, if you were single you're not telling me you wouldn't be tempted by gorgeous Gary,' said Mandy.

'Well maybe I would, he is nice but...'

'We know Tag and the baby, get your drink down you and forget about it, have a good time with us lot.'

They were actually sat in the same booths that Tag and Suki had been sat in earlier.

CHAPTER 7
DO YOU DO DISCOUNTS FOR COACH PARTIES?

The boys were on the last leg of their quest and as they left the last pub they turned the corner and saw it, the bright lights, the mystic, the glamour, but most of all the birds inside it. Yes they could see the Holy Grail, well Daz's Holy Grail, 'the Hippodrome'. But first there were two more pubs to fit in and although Daz was determined to get in some of the others wanted to know the price. So Daz ran across to see how much it was to get in with the tickets the bouncer gave them and he got back all excited.

'How much is it then?' asked Trev.

'£5 to get in after 11 o'clock or £3.50 before 11 only with these tickets though. We've got loads of them as well.'

'We're better off getting in some beers out here as they'll be expensive in there and going in after 11, we'll save £1.50 on the price of the beer' Skip said. So they all went into the next pub, and the bouncer was about six-foot six and built like a brick outhouse, but seemed very nervous.

'You can come in but don't cause any trouble will you? Are you football fans?' asked the bouncer.

'No, we're rugby league fans, we're down here for the Challenge Cup Final tomorrow and I promise you, you will not get any trouble from us but if someone else starts anything then there are no guarantees,' Skip assured him.

'Okay then, you can come in, we've had a few 'egg-catchers' in tonight already.'

Skip then led the way and the flock followed and immediately started to dance and jig about as the music was blasting out. After about ten minutes Matt saw the bouncer was bricking himself so now was the time for 'The cow kicked Nelly'. So they all sat on the floor and started, which got them a bit of an audience, some of them even joined in. The bouncer came over to see what was going on and was told by Tosser it was nothing to worry about and so he went back on the door. He figured that he was by himself and if it did kick off he was in the best position to escape. They all did the song and the pub went crazy with laughter and they all joined in and only a few drinks were spilt mainly over each other. When it all died down a bit Skip went over to the bouncer to ask why he was so nervous.

'How's it going mate?' asked Skip.

'Fine why do you ask?'

'You seem a bit edgy that's all'

'I'll be better when all you lot go I don't like large crowd of blokes from out of town, and I'm on my own the other doorman hasn't turned in.'

'Look the only hassle you'll get from us is to your ears we won't cause any trouble, we're here for a good time that's all. Can you get us cheap tickets for the Hippodrome? We've got these discount things but maybe you know a better way? If you get my drift?'

'Now you are joking, this is how it works, they only give cheap tickets out to the people who get in before ten and then that's only so they can get someone in, the place is dead until at least twelve. They give them ? price tickets but get their money back on the first drink alone, the drinks are really expensive.'

'So drink out here and then go in. What's it like inside?'

'The whole place is over-priced and over-hyped you won't see anyone famous they have a different bar and different part of the club. The whole place is shit in my opinion but they never have any trouble filling it because they hype it that much and mugs like you lot pay to get in to see what it's like and that's how they do it. Full of out of towners who've watched 'Hitman and Her' or foreigners. I wouldn't bother if I were you.'

'Where do you go then?'

'I go to local clubs which are for members only and they are mainly full of locals who know each other. You lot would hit trouble as they wouldn't like you on their turf, you get me?' warned the doorman.

'Yeah I see what you mean, well thanks for the advice and we'll see how we go.'

Skip went back to the lads and immediately was bombarded with questions.

'What did he want?' asked Tosser.

'Nothing I went to see why he looked so nervous.'

'Well what did he say?'

'Oh! just that he's shit scared of us because we're from out of town and he doesn't want any trouble.'

'Fuck off Skip, you're full of shit, look at the size of him,' said Daz.

'Honest, anyway he says that the Hippodrome is shit and it's really expensive for drinks and that they have a different part for famous people. He said it was a rip off and we shouldn't bother.'

'Now I know you're talking shit. My mate's been and he told me that the fanny is unbelievable in there,' Daz protested.

'I'm not sure I'm going are you Tosser?' said Skip.

'No what about you Jonesy?'

'No sounds shit.'

'Well you rotten bastards I'm still going and so are the rest of us aren't you?' Daz posed the question to Grant and Mike and Matt who all looked and finally Mike said 'Sounds too expensive to me, I'm only a student.'

'Right I'll go by myself then, I'll drink up and go on me tod, you bunch of fucking pensioners, full of shit. Where are you going tomorrow a tea dance?'

Everyone started to laugh at Daz who had gone on and on about the Hippodrome for months. They were only winding him up.

'Course we're going with you, you daft twat' Skip assured him.

'Well that's alright then, I knew you wouldn't let us down.'

'Well pick your lip up off the floor then sulky.'

'Do they have a pensioners discount for us lot like seeing as we're boring and all that. Where is that tea dance tomorrow Skip?' said Tosser.

'I didn't mean it like that Toss but you know how much I want to get in and I'd like everyone to be there,' said a relieved Daz.

'Well we're going, we get student rates which is £2,' gloated Grant.

'Get us in with you,' Matt shouted.

'Can't you have to show your card with a photo on it. here it is the beloved NUS card the students friend,' replied Mike.

'I fucking hate you students, I'm at work all day slaving away and you do fuck all then when it comes to doing stuff that's good you bastards get in less than ? price, the world's gone mad,' said Matt.

'And we get discounts for pictures and even at shops and with some takeaways,' Grant boasted, knowing full well that he was rubbing it in.

'Does she give you discount, that old prossy from the flats whose chips you nicked?'

'Fuck off Matt, not funny,' snapped Grant.

'Ooooh! Touched a nerve have we?'

'I'll be touching a nerve when I get in the club for £2,' Grant replied quickly, which really annoyed the others. He was a bright young man with the world at his feet and a future and most of these blokes were stuck in a rut, which is why they gave him such a hard time.

'Right, drink up and on to the next pub and then the nightclub,' Skip shouted rallying the troops. So they all drank up and made their way into the street and thanked the bouncer as they went each shaking his hand.

'See you tomorrow night we'll bring the livelier ones from the trip in,' joked Skip as the bouncer's face sunk.

'Don't worry mate these are as bad as we get, we'll catch you later. Cheers.'

As they all departed Greg who had been on brandy and coke all night led the way. And although the next pub was only 50 yards from the last one, he turned and started pointing at the pub and shouting for them to hurry up, as this was the pub they were going next. As Greg turned around he didn't notice the coffee sign on the pavement and he fell arse over tit over it and landed in the gutter. Everyone fell about laughing apart from a few tourists who asked if he was alright and showed some concern. All the lads told him to stop pissing around and to get in the pub. Greg slurred something about being alright so they all left him there to get up himself. In the pub Tosser was at the bar and as the barmaid was not very good at English, especially regional accents, he thought he would have a laugh.

'Here Skip, watch this. Love, can I have one Guinness, two lagers and two pints of draught shite?'

'Two lager beers, one Guinness beer and two shite beers,' the barmaid repeated.

'Yes that's right, thank you,' Tosser replied with a straight face, while Skip was pissing himself in the background. Word soon got around as the barmaid pulled the Guinness and then the two lagers. She was looking for the draught shite but couldn't find it and seeing as it was only her second night she didn't want to ask the manager as he would think she couldn't do the job. So she just kept looking. In the end when she couldn't find it, she asked the other barman who told her it didn't exist and what to say. She went up to Tosser who by now had a crowd all waiting to see what she had to say.

'Sorry sir, but we are all out of draught shite we do however have a new beer called 'Spunky Bollocks', would you like two of those?' Tosser was speechless. He hadn't expected the answer he received and as he got over the shock he asked for two bitters instead. Skip told her to get one for herself and Tosser walked away shell-shocked.

'She was quick there eh Toss? Made you look like a proper dick,' laughed Matt.

After the barmaid had made Tosser look like his nickname described, he couldn't wait to get out of the place as people were pointing and laughing at him.

'Right are we all ready to go?' Tosser shouted as he had finished his drink.

'I am, come on get 'em down yer, it's Hippo time,' said Daz who was like a kid on Christmas morning waiting to open his presents.

'Greg hasn't had his drink yet where is he?' said Trev holding Greg's drink.

'Go check the toilets,' said Tosser, which Matt did and there was no Greg.

'He's not in there and I got a woman to check the ladies and he's not in there either.'

'What shall I do with his drink?' asked Trev rather pathetically.

'Drink the bloody thing and then we'll go and find him,' snapped Matt.

'But I don't like brandy.'

'Give me it then,' and Matt took the drink and downed it in one.

'Let's go find Greg,' said Skip sounding slightly worried.

'Well he better be around because I'm not looking all over for him the Hippodrome is about 70 yards south and I'm homing in on it, bollocks to Greg,' protested Daz.

'You rotten bastard Daz, he might be in trouble,' said Gaz

'He fucking will be if I don't get to that club,' Daz whispered under his breath.

As they got out of the pub Greg was there still lying on the floor, he'd managed to get out of the gutter just before a taxi had nearly hit him. He was just lying there like a turtle with his arms and legs in the air. He had a big crowd around him and they were quite concerned. All the lads just walked up and just looked.

'Pick him up,' Tosser said.

'What you doing down there?' asked Skip.

'Well he's either breaking a bar of chocolate in his back pocket or he's break dancing,' quipped Matt.

'Hiya lads, I was just having 40 winks, where are we going next?' Greg got up, his back was covered in dirt and he looked a sight.

'We're going to a nightclub but you're going back in a cab, you're pissed,' said Daz, thinking they wouldn't get him in.

'Nightclub, well that's the one for me, I love nightclubs, the Hippodrome we're going to isn't it?' Greg slurred.

'How did you remember that Greg?' asked Trev.

'Fucking hell Daz has been going on about it for months, it's seeped into his brain,' laughed Tosser.

'Right then let's go and keep him at the back until we get in,' Daz demanded leading the way. But already well up the queue were the two students. As soon as they saw Greg was alright they went to join the queue and they were nearly in.

'Look at those two poofs,' said Skip.

'You two, you're at the wrong club, they have women in this one,' Matt shouted as everyone looked around except Grant and Mike who pretended they didn't know them or who they were talking about. The queue went down and Grant and Mike got in and waved at the rest of them.

'The jammy little bastards, five more minutes and we're in,' said

Daz excitedly as he grabbed Trev by the arm, nearly pulling it off.

'Get off you idiot, it's only a club,' shrugged Trev.

'Wrong Trev, it's the club to be at, the club of clubs.'

The bouncer at the front was a poser all in leather with sunglasses on and he thought he was the bollocks. The lads got to the front and with about ten people in front of them Skip started up a conversation with the bouncer or tried to.

'Alright mate, are there plenty in?'

He got no answer.

'Are you busy mate?' Skip persisted.

'I heard you the first time,' sneered the doorman from under his shades.

'Fucking spark him Skip the cocky twat' whispered Tosser in Skip's ear.

'No just let's get in, play it cool, nearly there, three more people to go.'

With that Greg stormed forward and shouted about two inches from the face of the bouncer, 'Do you do discounts for coach parties?' and sprayed spittle all over the doorman's leather jacket.

'Right you lot fuck off you're not coming in, we're full,' announced the bouncer as he was joined by three other burly specimens.

'What you've got to be joking?' Daz shouted nearly in tears, 'I'm not with these just let me in.'

'No none of you are getting in,' the bouncer re-confirmed.

'You fucking twat think your hard dressed up like a village people wannabe, well fuck you I've heard your clubs shit anyway,' Skip blurted out.

The doorman sniggered to his friends as Skip rushed forward. Tosser and Jonesy stopped him and pulled him back, as the doorman sought cover behind the door.

'Don't waste your time Skip, we'll go find somewhere else,' Tosser said calmly trying to cool the situation. Skip was a nice fella but if he was pushed he was a real handful and would have probably knocked the doorman off his feet.

'You hide behind your door you big bag of wind,' Skip shouted but the doorman wasn't hanging around. He locked the door and that was the last they saw of him.

Back on the street there was a big lull and silence as they all realised that last orders had gone and they hadn't got into a club, the night was ruined. Greg broke the silence.

'Well never mind, let's go back to the hotel,' Greg said this through his gums as he had lost his front teeth when falling over but hadn't realised it yet.

'Go back to the fucking hotel. You fucking muppet. We were in 'that place you stupid twat until you came out of your coma and pissed him off,' Daz had to be restrained as he was going to kill Greg.

'Keep your hair on Daz it's only a club,' replied Greg innocently.

'No it's not, you fucking moron, it's the club to be at. Just keep out of my way you prick or I'll flatten you.'

'You and whose army?' Greg answered, giving as good as he got.

'I'll fucking kill him!'

Daz again had to be held back.

'Now then this is getting us nowhere, let's try the last pub we were in they might give us a lock in,' Skip said trying to calm the situation down.

They all went across the road to see if they could get in and all they got was a sorry boys no can do, try the clubs around the corner. They all went around the corner and after being turned away from three clubs they decided to go back to the hotel and began the task of getting cabs in London at 11.30pm and so it was every group for themselves. They all got something to eat before the dreaded task of getting a cab.

'I've just realised them two jammy bastards got in didn't they. I was just going to say to Grant get your discount card out,' laughed Jonesy. 'Well at least someone got in Daz, the two students can tell you all about it.'

'Piss off Jonesy, you're not funny.'

'I bet they're in there now with half a lager and two straws, sat shitting themselves wondering where we are,' Skip carried on.

'Just don't mention that club again, please, we were two yards from getting in. Two yards from the perfect night and then that stupid toothless retarded prick comes out with the immortal line, 'Do you do discounts for coach parties?'

'What club would that be then Daz the Hippodrome?' Trev said with a smile. 'Cheer up there'll be other times Daz.'

'Yeah you're right, I'll stop moaning and try and have a good time.'

It helped that they only had to wait ten minutes and they all got a cab and were on their way back to the hotel.

Meanwhile in the Hippodrome, Grant and Mike soon realised that the others hadn't got in and headed straight for the dance floor and immediately pulled two girls from Sweden. They couldn't believe their luck. The girls were staying in London for the week and were going onto France on the Tuesday. They were students and were all over Grant and Mike. They spoke perfect English and were staying in a hotel about two hundred yards away. Grant and Mike had hit the jackpot and couldn't wait to tell the rest of the boys, but first they had to play it cool and not seem like two kids in a sweet shop, which of course is what they were. They sat down and while the girls powdered their noses the two lads began to plot who would go for who. In fact it was the girls who would decide as they had been having the same conversation in the toilets and Ulrika sat next to Grant and Anna sat with Mike. The boys then got in some drinks and they sat and chatted and danced and generally had a great time. Then the girls got up and bought some drinks – the boys were in heaven. Two Swedish birds who spoke perfect English, had a hotel within spitting distance and they got the round in, jackpot! The only thing that would spoil it was if they turned out to be a couple of blokes in drag. This was one possibility the lads had discussed while the girls were at the bar, but it was soon dispelled as they couldn't see any stubble or an Adam's apple, always a dead give away when spotting a tranny...

Back at the hotel a fleet of taxi's arrived and they all trooped out of them one by one and headed straight to the bar where Eddie and all the others had been since 11 o'clock. Even Thommo had surfaced and was nursing a coke in the corner looking like an extra from a zombie film.

'Fucking hell, didn't expect to see you lot until the early hours,' Thommo piped up.

'Don't go there, please,' Daz snapped as he went to the toilet.

'Why what happened then?' Eddie enquired.

'We were about two yards from the front of the queue and just about to get in when Greg comes forward and shouts to the bouncer six inches from his face, 'Do you do discounts for coach parties?' Well, that was it, we got the big 'fuck off' you're not welcome,' explained Jonno.

'But for crying out loud don't mention it to Daz, he went crazy at Greg and nearly flattened him,' added Trev.

'He looks like he's hit him already, where's your front teeth Greg? And look at your shirt, it's covered in shit,' Eddie pointed out.

'Haven't got a clue Ed and I don't give a fuck at the moment I'm just here for a good time, I bet you're glad I'm rooming with you, eh Eddie?'

'So when was the last time you had 'em?' asked Doug.

'He had them before he fell over a coffee board outside a pub and collapsed in the gutter,' Skip answered for Greg who was becoming less and less coherent.

'I see Damo found you all, so the messages worked then?'

'Like a charm Eddie, like a charm,' Damo replied.

'Where are the babies? Grant and Mike, you've never left them by themselves. Grant's mother will kill me, I said I'd keep an eye on him,' said Eddie, genuinely in a panic.

'Don't worry Eddie those two jammy twats are in the Hippodrome as we speak and they got in on their student cards for £2 each. Grant doesn't need a wet nurse, it's your fucking room mate who needs one and if these lot hadn't have got in the way he would have needed a real nurse,' Daz said returning from the toilet.

'How come you never got in then Daz?' Doug was trying to stir the shit.

'Too good-looking Doug that's why, you old shit stirring bastard. I'm over it now, the moment has passed.'

'Have you rang your lass Eddie?' asked Skip.

'Yeah I have why?' Eddie replied looking puzzled.

'Was she in?'

'Yes, why?'

'Because we rang Pete to take the piss and he reckons that all the women have gone on a secret trip to Blackpool. We've rang home and there's no reply,' Tosser informed Eddie.

'Well let's hope Tag doesn't run into them then. Fay'll have his bollocks on toast.'

Eddie knew what Tag was up to but it came as a shock to him that the women had secretly got a trip together, good on them he thought.

'So this is everyone back apart from students Grant and Mike. Well they've shown you lot the way haven't they?' laughed Eddie.

'What do you mean?' asked a puzzled Matt.

'Well think about it, you lot are full of we'll go here and we've been here before and don't go here and don't go there and don't do that and they're in the Hippodrome with Pete Waterman and Michaela Strachan and you lot are with us, the domino gang. The pensioners drinking overpriced beer from the hotel bar. At least we've got the excuse of being too old but you lot, you were going to do this and that and it's all gone to shit,' Eddie winked at Skip and laughed.

'Would you like a drink Eddie?' asked Skip.

'Go on then Skip, a bitter please.'

The time was just gone twelve and the night seemed all over as they sat with other residents who were also rugby people and talked about the game and the up and coming Final...

Last orders was being called at the Tower bar it was ten minutes to twelve and they were pretty strict that no drinks were to be served after twelve and the whole place had to be empty by half past. The girls got one last drink and as they sat down Shaz and Charlie came over with Steve and Carl and asked if any of them were coming to the club. They told the girls not to wait for them as they would be alright as the club opened until 3, so not to worry. Gary asked Fay if she fancied it but she sheepishly declined, although deep down she would have loved to. Gary looked quite disappointed, but Fay knew what the other two girls would be getting up to and she didn't want to be left alone as she wasn't like them. Shaz and Charlie bid farewell to the girls and Gary said goodbye to Fay and they left the bar and headed for the club Pixies. Tag was already in Pixies and was dancing with Suki and having a great time without a care in the world. The rest of the girls decided to get something to eat as they walked back to the hotel as getting a taxi was virtually impossible as the tower revellers all hit the streets at the same time. They walked through the streets with their chips back to the hotel and to their surprise the hotel bar was still open and so they decided to have a bit of a party. The bar could fit in about 50 people and was full with residents and the atmosphere was good with a bit of music on. The owner was playing D.J. and as he worked Fridays he thought the best thing to do was if he couldn't go out and party, then bring the party to the hotel and the girls were having a great time.

Back at Pixies the nightclub Tag had been lucky as Suki knew the score as she had been before and knew that getting into the club before everyone came out of the Tower bar was essential if you didn't want to be queuing for an hour outside. Shaz and Charlie were queuing outside and everyone was becoming agitated at the fact the queue was moving so slowly. Gary was quizzing them about Fay.

'What's the story with Fay then?'

'She's with this lad from the rugby club I work at. He's a real knobhead always fucking about behind her back. In fact I bet he's with some slag now in London. But today she found out she's pregnant, so that's fucked with her head a bit as well and that's it really,' Shaz answered.

'And she can't stand us two, she thinks we're after her man, who is a twat we wouldn't be seen dead with. But we put her straight on that one earlier today,' added Charlie.

'Why what did you tell her?'

'Just that we wouldn't touch him with a ten foot barge pole and that it was him who was always trying to get off with us and that he made our skin crawl,' Shaz ranted.

'Yeah and that he's always trying it on with other women behind her back and that she should wake up and dump the loser as he's bad news,' Charlie said this without drawing breath.

'So, no chance for me then?' Gary wouldn't let it go.

'No way try your luck in here, you've got no chance. Look at the facts she's pregnant and lives with him and loves him by the look of it. Like I said no chance,' Shaz confirmed.

There was silence as Gary was hoping slightly that they could put in a good word for him, but he soon realised that a good word from these two wouldn't make any difference to what Fay wanted.

Actually Fay did fancy him but circumstances dictated she had to think with her head and not her heart.

Tag and Suki had been drinking cocktails inside the club and had been dancing nearly all the time. They eventually decided to sit down and ordered two more cocktails. They sat and kissed in one of the more private booths in the club and Tag let his hands wander and Suki kept slapping them, saying that here was not the place.

Finally, after a three-quarters of an hour wait Shaz and Charlie and the boys got into the club. They headed straight to the bar and got a quick drink and then they hit the dance floor. Gary and his two other mates were at the bar when Tag walked up to get some more drinks. Gary was looking at Tag as if he knew him.

'Can I help you mate?' Tag asked looking puzzled.

'No, but I recognise you from somewhere.' Now Gary was confused. Just then Suki walked up and asked Tag if he'd got the drinks and that's when Gary remembered where he knew him from.

'You're the bloke from the Tower who thought I was stealing your woman. Well looks like you've done better than me tonight. I'd look after her if I were you mate, good women are like rocking-horse shit.'

Tag just nodded and walked off with Suki wondering what the hell he was on about. Gary ordered another drink and then fell off his stool, he was pissed and his two mates had to carry him and plonk him on a seat, in which he curled up and fell asleep. Time had passed and Suki was ready to leave.

'Let's have one more dance and then back to the hotel,' Suki said as she got up and pulled Tag by the hand and led him to the dance floor. They had their dance and were on their way with Suki just popping into the toilet to powder her nose. And as Tag stood in the foyer all excited about the night of passion he was about to have, little did he know that his pregnant girlfriend was staying in the same hotel and was sat in the bar.

They both got outside the club and got in a taxi straight away. Back in the club the girls Shaz and Charlie, knew where they were spending the night and it wasn't back at the hotel.

Back at the girls hotel the drink had been flowing and everyone was having a good time. Even Fay had let her hair down and was in good spirits. The owner had stopped with the music and the bar had about 25 people still in there, with the remaining eight girls still chatting and laughing. Tag's taxi pulled up outside and the two of them kissed as they got out of the cab.

'Let's have a night cap Tag and then go to the room. We've got all night,' suggested Suki.

'No, we shall have champagne in the room,' Tag was adamant. As the two of them walked into the reception area, the door to the left was to the bar and the door to the right was to the stairway to the rooms. The two of them were giggling in that lovey way that lovers giggle and then they entered the bar area in full view of all the girls and Fay. But no one noticed them as the girls were talking and Tag and Suki didn't notice anyone else as Tag had his back to the girls. He was only about five yards from them but they didn't recognise who it was. It couldn't be anyone they knew the lads and Tag were in London. They didn't recognise him until he spoke.

'Barman can we have a bottle of champagne for our room, this is a special occasion?' Tag said loudly.

Immediately Fay's ears pricked up as she shouted, 'Tag?'

Tag's face drained of all colour as he turned around to see Fay, and he had his arm around Suki.

'What the fucking hell are you doing here? Who's this slapper? And what's the special occasion?' Fay shouted hysterically. Tag just stood for what seemed like an eternity, staring at Fay and the girls.

'Do you know this girl?' asked Suki, who thought Tag was single.

'Know me you bitch, know me?' Fay started to advance towards them but luckily Mandy saw it and got in between. 'He's my boyfriend and he lives with me.'

'He can't be, he's been seeing me for months now and he's never mentioned you,' shouted Suki.

But she was already beginning to put two and two together. That's why they always went out into the country on their dates and why they never really had regular dates. Plus she'd never been invited 'round to his house.

'Well he wouldn't would he, you silly cow, maybe you don't care you're obviously a slag or else why would you be here with my boyfriend?'

Fay was in full flow but Suki was not going to take this kind of abuse and returned fire.

'Listen, just calm down, I am not a slag, slapper or whatever else you want to call me. We have been seeing each other for quite a while now and this weekend was meant to be for us to get away and spend some quality time together. I had no idea he lived with someone or already had someone and if I had known then I wouldn't be here.'

'So where did you meet?' Fay continued her tirade.

'I work as the receptionist at his work and he asked me out,' Suki never looked at Tag or referred to him by his name. Tag still hadn't spoken and was rooted to the spot.

'So then Tag, who is it going to be, me or her?' Fay fired the question at Tag and before he could answer she added, 'And by the way, I'm pregnant. Yes one of the only times you managed to get it up and you did it. Got one past the goalie. I'm amazed you had enough in you after seeing her as well.'

This shocked Tag.

Fay pregnant? How could she be? She was on the pill.

Suki had heard enough.

'Let's get one thing straight, we haven't had sex yet so if he hasn't been getting it up as you put it then it's got nothing to do with me. And choose between me and you? There is no choice dear. I feel sorry for you. He's yours. I don't want that piece of shit anywhere near me.'

Suki then turned around, slapped Tag across the face and went to the room.

All the other people in the bar felt like applauding Suki but no one dared to start it off. Tag had tears rolling down his face as he realised that he was to become a dad and he just looked at Fay. Not knowing what to say or do. The barman asked Steph did she think they would be wanting the champagne with the baby being announced, Steph just shook her head and the barman rather embarrassed put the bottle away.

'Fay how long have you known?' Tag finally got some words out.

'She found out tonight, you fucking prick,' Mandy butted in thinking that he wasn't going to squirm his way out of this one. Fay was in floods of tears and Cary was comforting her.

'We made her have a test, as she's been sick all day. Not that you'd notice knobhead, and the test was positive,' added Clare.

'It's time to grow up Tag, you think you're a man, now it's time to grow up and prove it. You can't go on thinking you can shag anything that moves and get away with it. Look at her and make sure that image is burnt into your mind because she worships you and you just take the piss out of her, you rotten bastard.' Chris chipped in.

With that Suki re-appeared with Tag's bag and threw it at him. She then went over to Fay.

'Look it's not mine or your fault, but I'm sorry about all this. I hope you make the right decision and for what it's worth we didn't have sex I think that he thought that was what this weekend was for. But I made him wait and he did. A bit of advice make sure he treats you properly if that's what you want and make sure you're in charge. I tell you what everything I've asked him to do he's done make sure you wear the trousers from now on, good luck.'

Suki then walked straight past Tag and didn't even look at him.

Tag didn't know what to do, every time he tried to get close to Fay the girls pushed him away.

'Fay can we talk? Please,' Tag pleaded.

'Look Tag, go away, can't you see she's upset,' Mandy said pushing him away again.

'Don't push me,' Tag said, getting a bit annoyed.

'Why, what you going to do, you big man, hit me? Go on then and

I'll tell you what we'll all fill you in, you pathetic excuse for a man.'
Mandy could handle herself and was angry at Tag.

'Anyway did everyone in London know about this?' asked Clare.

'I think so but they didn't know you were coming here,' Tag answered.

'Look Tag just go away, I don't want to see you at the moment. I'm going to bed and I'll see how I feel in the morning about you and whether I want this child.'

Fay had stopped crying enough to talk.

'Surely you don't mean an abortion? I won't let you,' Tag pleaded.

'As I said I don't know what I want. But I do know I want some sleep and I'll decide in the morning, I'm going to bed now.'

Fay and Cary went up to their room, with the others stopping Tag following and giving the receptionist specific instruction not to give her room number out. Tag was shell-shocked, he didn't know what to do. It was obvious Fay was not interested in him so he better leave that alone until the morning. What about the lovely Suki, well she hadn't spoken to him at all and it looked like she'd totally finished with him, after calling him a piece of shit he thought that was a fair indication that she was a no-go area. He was well and truly in the doghouse. It wasn't like he hadn't been there before but this time he knew he'd messed up big time. What was going to happen with his house and work and would they have to sell the house and what if Suki suddenly started saying things at work. His only solace would be rugby and by the reaction he'd got from the wives of his friends, that place he could get away from everything had gone. Everyone and everything he did and liked doing had been put in jeopardy. He was just sat staring into thin air when Tracey who was Daz's wife and Chris Jonno's wife sat down next to him. They were the only two women who hadn't gone to their rooms. They sat next to him and asked him if he wanted a drink, but Tag just sat there staring.

'Well Tag you've blown it this time lad haven't you?' Chris said. Tag still didn't respond.

'Look, give it until the morning and see how things are. You'll have to change though Tag. You can't have your cake and eat it,' Tracey said feeling a little sorry for him. She knew Tag from school and he'd always been the same, but he would do anything for anybody and was always generous with his time and money when he had any. Tag loved kids but had never thought about having any, not yet anyway.

'If she takes you back Tag and you have that kiddy then you'll have to grow up pretty fast, no more women and going out 'til all hours.'

Chris tried to keep up the conversation and it worked as Tag spoke for the first time in about ten minutes.

'I'm going to be a dad. I can't believe it. I do love Fay it's just that I take her for granted and she lets me. Whereas Suki, she was the boss and I was told what to do. I feel really bad that I've fucked them both about.'

'Yeah but would you have felt bad if you hadn't have been caught?' Tracey added.

'Probably not I would have got this weekend out of the way and then looked at my options. I love both of them, Fay is great and always there for me and Suki is just unbelievably gorgeous. When I asked her to see if she wanted a drink when I first met her in a club, I thought she's way out of my league but when she said 'Yes' I couldn't believe it. She's way too clever for me and she said she'd go out with me and it just progressed from there really. We talked about all sorts of things and even tonight I've been dancing, I never dance but with her anything is possible and I've balls it all up.'

'But what about Fay? She needs you to be grown up and for you to do the right thing by her even if it means leaving her. Don't mess her around Tag she's too nice for that kind of treatment. She thinks the sun shines out of your arse and if you are only going to go back to her because your receptionist doesn't want to know, then you should make a clean break altogether. Because it's not a good enough reason. Not even a baby is good enough reason. You should want Fay, that's why you should go back with her if she'll have you and no other reason. So think on Tag do the right thing for once and think of Fay. Goodnight love and don't think of doing anything stupid.'

Chris got off her soapbox and went to bed and Tracey followed leaving Tag with his thoughts and his bag. He just sat there until the barman pointed out that he couldn't stay there all night and that the owner had told him to tell him he would have to go to his room. Tag explained that he wasn't allowed in his room as he'd had an argument with Suki. The barman took pity on him and gave him a spare for the room next door and told him to be out by seven or he would be in big trouble for letting him use the room. Tag thanked him and made his way to the room, passing the room where Suki was sleeping. He walked quietly into the room, which was being refurbished but it had a bed and he just lay there and began to cry. He cried until he cried himself to sleep, just as both Suki and Fay had done earlier.

What a mess...

Shaz and Charlie had left the club and were heading back to the lads B&B which if it was no good they were going to bin it and take them back to their B&B.

They managed to sneak into the lads B&B and got upstairs into their room. The other three lads hadn't left the club yet and Carl and Steve were sharing a room anyway. The room was quite big with a double bed and a single bed. Shaz jumped on the double and grabbed Carl and they immediately got down to having sex. Their clothes came off at rapid speed and Shaz was going down on Carl straight away, which was a bit embarrassing for Charlie as Steve was having a pee in the toilet and Charlie was left sat on the single bed trying not to watch Shaz and Carl at it. She was getting turned on by the two of them and was waiting for Steve to hurry up. Then she heard a crash and a bang and went to investigate. Shaz and Carl just carried on with Shaz now riding Carl like he was a bronco and Carl making loud noises like a pig hunting truffles. In the bathroom Steve had fell asleep on the toilet and fell off it and onto the floor. Charlie was trying to pick him up and after five minutes she got him up and into the bedroom where the other two were still at it. So Charlie thought fuck it, and started to undress Steve and then started to try and arouse him. She tried with her hand and then her mouth as she was getting caught up in the atmosphere coming from the other bed. Steve had come around slightly and was trying to get erect but not a sausage - pardon the pun.

Shaz was screaming wildly and Carl was still truffle hunting and they came to a crescendo and both fell asleep. So did Steve and he began to snore, leaving Charlie frustrated and horny, so she masturbated herself using Steve's fingers and then fell asleep, wondering what the hell she was doing. She needed a steady boyfriend this was no way to go on every weekend...

The hotel bar back in the Docklands was quite full and everyone was back except the two students, they were still in the Hippodrome with their Swedish conquests. The bar had died down a bit as most people had had enough to drink and were just steadily drinking what they had left. The barman sussed out the situation and put his coat on and headed for an early night, hoping no one would object. He made sure that they all knew the bar was closing and asked if any of them wanted a drink. The barman then served the punters with their last drinks, locked up the till and was on his way. Leaving a bar full of people who would dwindle as they went to bed gradually. His last act was to put the shutters down on the bar, which he did. However he only put them ? of the way down and then he cashed up and took the till tray and was on his way. No one noticed the shutters were only three-quarters of the way down as they were all pretty pissed. The boys from the Hull trip were there plus some parties from Oldham - the ones who threw the attendant in the pool - and another party from Halifax. Damo on the other hand did notice, as he was relatively sober compared to the rest of them. Damo went to the bar and lifted the shutter a bit and tried the tap on the beer. It poured so he put his glass underneath it. Damo sat back down to enjoy his free beer. As no one had noticed the bar was shut, one of the boys wanted a drink and was just about to go to the reception to ask, seeing as he was a resident he wanted a drink. Damo told him to go to the bar, which brought a look of bewilderment to his face. But he did as he was told and from behind the bar Damo appeared as he had lifted the shutters and climbed over the bar and started serving his mate. Damo was an Aussie and bar work was second nature to him as he'd worked in a bar back home for a couple of years when he was a student. Well everyone started coming up thinking the bar had re-opened and were handing money over, but Damo just said they were 'on the house'. No one was going to argue with that and the party had started again as everyone had got a second wind and after every round he poured he sat down and enjoyed a drink himself. He did this so that if any of the hotel staff turned up then they wouldn't see him behind the bar. Not knowing he wasn't the barman the Halifax and Oldham gangs thought it was great that they were on free beer thinking he worked for the hotel.

Eddie just shook his head, and the older guard couldn't believe their luck. They thought the joy had come to an end when Damo announced that the draught had run out. But he tried the fridges and told them all they had to have bottles, as the draught had ran out, which no one objected to. They drank the bottles of lager until they ran out and then went on to the ciders and the 20/20s.

Damo kept this up and he couldn't believe that no one from the hotel had come to check on the bar. Some people were falling over and struggling to drink what they had and this was funny to watch but then Trev and Jonesy committed the sin that was unforgivable on all trips. They did the unthinkable and went totally against the rules of all trips that are set in stone. They fell asleep. The only punishment for this was that they were now fare game and anything could happen to them. Skip and Tosser were rubbing their hands and had a quick meeting.

'What's it going to be?' asked Skip quietly, well he thought he was being quiet but in fact his wife could have probably heard him in Blackpool.

'Eyebrows?' enquired Tosser.

'No! not eyebrows' Eddie intervened. 'that could lead to a fight and not on this trip. I've seen it before it's funny for a day then they have to go to work when they get home.'

'You're right Eddie, Trev has been humiliated enough in front of his boss today, with Thommo and the bottle. He can't very well go into work on Tuesday with no eyebrows,' Skip agreed.

Then Tosser had an idea, he told Matt to go get his camera and asked one of the women from Oldham if she had any make up. The two requests were granted and so began the making up of both Trev and Jonesy.

Firstly Tosser touched their faces to gage any reaction. They were totally out of it asleep and Tosser was sniggering like a little kid. Slowly Skip and Tosser began to make Trev and Jonesy up, while everyone was falling about laughing, Matt was taking photos. The end product was they had full make up on, badly applied lipstick and they looked like two 'Aunt Sally' dolls from the telly programme Worzel Gummidge.

The finishing touch was every ashtray in the bar emptied on their heads and tab ends pushed up their nostrils, in their ears and one in their mouths. They had flowers from the hotel bar placed behind their ears and then loads of photos were taken. People were going to their rooms to get their cameras to get a picture. The Oldham and Halifax gangs were in stitches. Trev and Jonesy slept happily through all this and didn't move a muscle.

When it all died down and people had ran out of drink, they began to stagger their way to their rooms. The time was about 3 o'clock in the morning and everyone had had enough. The lads decided to wake up Trev and Jonesy who were oblivious to all that had gone on around them and knocked the fag ends out of their noses whilst stirring from their slumber. The bar looked like a bomb had gone off at a students' house party. There were bottles all over the place, the ashtrays had missed their intended target - Trev and Jonesy's head - and were on the floor. Eddie was going to clean it but Skip told him not to bother.

'I hope this is your lot?' Eddie pleaded with Skip.

'What do you mean Eddie?'

'Don't be wondering around the hotel causing trouble with fire-extinguishers.'

'Fucking hell Eddie, you want to spoil all our fun don't you?' protested Tosser.

'Yes I bloody do,' said a tired Eddie who still had to go to the room with Greg.

'Look Eddie, everyone's wasted, even if we wanted to no one would be able to. Go to bed and relax and read Greg a bedtime story,' laughed Skip.

Eddie's face was a picture, he'd forgotten about having Greg as his roommate.

'Yeah, you look after Greg, the toothless pisshead,' laughed Tosser. 'Come on Eddie we'll walk you to your room and see the useless twat's not killed himself.'

So the three of them left the bar tiptoed through the reception area and made their way to their rooms.

They got to Eddie's room and he opened the door. Well, the noise was like the giant snoring in 'Jack and the Beanstalk'. They all entered the room but Greg was nowhere to be seen but the snoring sound was deafening. Then they discovered where Greg was. He had fallen asleep in the bath, and the sound of his snoring was echoing around the room. Eddie wasn't at all pleased, unlike Skip and Tosser who thought it was hilarious that Eddie had to put up with Fred Flinstone's pet brontosaurus with breathing difficulties.

'Goodnight Eddie, we'll leave you and Dino in peace,' Skip sniggered.

'Come on lads help me get him in bed. We can't leave him here,' pleaded Eddie.

'Come on then Eddie get his bed ready,' said Skip.

The three of them then proceeded to get Greg into bed from the bathroom. Now Greg weighed in at a whopping 12 stones, but it felt more like 20 as he was a dead weight. Skip got his top half and Tosser got his legs and Eddie opened the door for them. They had just about managed to get him out of the bath and then they dropped him onto the floor of the bathroom with an almighty crash.

'What's happened there?' Eddie enquired rushing from the bedroom, as Greg just lay there.

'We've dropped him, the stupid bastard,' Skip said getting more annoyed.

'Toss, you get one leg and I'll get the other and we'll drag him.'

So the two of them began to drag the hapless Greg towards his bed. Then there was another crash as Greg hit his head on the chair by the side of the bed. Greg didn't even flinch.

'Jesus! How much has he had to drink?' Eddie enquired worriedly.

'The same as the rest of us Eddie. Right, give us a hand here and we'll get him on the bed,' Tosser said sweating.

The three of them managed to get Greg on the bed and put the cover on him. Then as quick as a flash he sat bolt upright and started singing 'Ring of Fire' at the top of his voice.

'We're off Eddie, not a big fan of Johnny Cash tribute acts, see you in the morning.'

Skip and Tosser then rushed out of the door and left poor Eddie with Greg who didn't know what day it was.

When they got into the corridor both of them fell about on the floor laughing and holding their sides as they imagined what kind of night Eddie was going to have. In fact Greg fell fast asleep but was snoring all night, much to Eddies discomfort and annoyance.

Skip and Tosser got back to their room and started to get ready for bed when Skip put his hand in his pocket to take his money out and he felt a sharp object that nearly cut his hand.

'What the bloody hell is this?' he yelped as he pulled his hand from his pocket to reveal Greg's front teeth.

'How the fuck did they get into my pocket?'

'It must have been when he fell over that coffee sign, they must have fell out and you must have picked them up.'

'I'll tell you what, that twat's not getting them back this weekend. He'll have to fucking liquidise his breakfast,' Skip quipped and they both laughed and then got into bed fully clothed and fell fast asleep.

Across town the two students Grant and Mike had hit the jackpot. They were at the Swedish girls' hotel and were getting a lesbian show. The two girls started to kiss and then to play with each other, until they had no clothes on and then started to lick each other. Grant and Mike didn't know whether they were dreaming or not. They sat watching with mouths wide open and knobs rock hard. The girls waved at the boys to come and join in and they ended up with them both doing the girls doggy style while they carried on kissing. They were looking at each other whilst shagging, which seemed really weird. Then they started to pull faces and make noises to put each other off. Firstly it was moaning and groaning then Grant started doing Tarzan noises, 'Arooaroooar' Mike nearly wet himself but the girls got even more excited. Mike couldn't last any longer and made a weak monkey noise and then withdrew from the Swede. By that time Grant had got his second wind and was pretending he was a rodeo rider trying to stay on, but after about five minutes he fell off. Both of them were amazed at how long they lasted. The two girls finally finished each other off, and Grant got into bed with Anna and Mike got into bed with Ulrika. They thought that was good manners seeing as they had just boned them. But to their surprise the two girls got out of bed and Anna got in with Mike and Ulrika with Grant.

They both immediately started giving oral sex to the lads and although it was pleasurable the two of them couldn't help but think that they had already played their best game and that repetitive strain injury could occur. The girls continued for another hour and the boys excelled themselves before finally falling asleep.

CHAPTER 8
BREAKFAST IN BLACKPOOL

Tag had only slept for two hours when he woke up with the feeling that he'd had a bad dream. However, he soon realised that it was no dream, he really had fucked up his entire life and was in the middle of one almighty mess. What made it worse was that it was all his own doing. He decided to get up and go for a walk, and he proceeded to the dining area where the staff were just preparing for the breakfast.

'You're a bit early love,' said the cook.

'What, don't mind me I'm just sitting here,' Tag said as he was miles away.

'I'll get you a drink. Do you want tea or coffee?' asked the cook who could see Tag was a bit distressed.

'Whatever's easiest thanks,' Tag was on another planet.

'It can't be that bad can it? It's never that bad love.'

'This is that bad though,' Tag replied but didn't elaborate. The cook made him some tea and left him to his thoughts. Funnily this was the first time in his life that Tag wasn't trying to wriggle out of some situation. He knew he was to blame and no one else. Tag knew that Suki was a 'no go' and that realistically Fay would have been to, except they shared a house and now she was pregnant. Tag thought long and hard and decided on his course of action - he was going to ask Fay to marry him. Firstly though he had to get her on her own as the others would tell her to tell him to get stuffed.

Time passed and the cook asked him what he wanted for breakfast. Tag didn't really hear her and just asked for whatever. So she took the cold tea she'd made for him that he hadn't drank, and replaced it with a fresh pot and a full English breakfast.

'Get this down you, it'll make you feel better. No good starving yourself. Whatever's gone on, there's no use wasting away now is there?' The cook smiled and Tag smiled back, said thanks, then started to eat the food. Just then Suki entered the room and Tag stopped eating.

'Look Suki I'm really sorry....'

'Save it, do you know what? I don't deserve this,' Suki cut Tag off mid sentence.

'I know and I wish I could…'

'Could what? Have fucked me and carried on with this pantomime, and played with my feelings. And what about the poor cow who you live with, what about her? If you can do this to her, it just shows how little you thought of me,' Suki again cut him off.

'Look if you really want to know it was a bit of a laugh at first. But then, and let me finish, I fell for you in a big way. I was going to get this weekend out of the way and leave Fay.'

'Pull the other one, you've been caught out and this would have gone on for as long as you got away with it, you need to grow up Timothy.'

Tag hung his head and agreed with her.

'Listen, believe me when I tell you that you're the first woman I have loved. I've never met anyone like you, beautiful, clever, sexy and great to be around and it's just a shame it hasn't worked out.'

'What about her, don't you love her?'

'Actually, thinking last night, I realised that I do love her but I suppose we got too familiar and I wasn't grown up enough. But things are going to change and I'm going to grow up.'

'Well you've blown it with me.'

'I know that, Fay's pregnant and I'm going to ask her to marry me.'

'Are you sure that's wise in the circumstances?'

'Look, I should have done it ages ago and not pissed around all the time.'

'Good luck, you'll need it because I'd tell you to sling yourself off the pier.'

'I meant what I said about us two. I really did love you. You made me feel like I'd never felt before.'

'For what it's worth, I loved you too Tag. I tested you to see if you were the one for me. I knew you wanted me and the feeling was mutual but I figured if you'd waited this long then you must be the one. How wrong could I have been. I'm going home now so you'd better have this.' Suki threw Tag the key to the room.

'You didn't think I'd stay did you? And I'm not taking you home. If you want my opinion Tag, stay here with Fay and get it sorted out and get a bus back on Sunday. Change the room though, I mean don't insult the girl's intelligence.'

Tag didn't know what to say, he knew Suki was decent but he thought even she would have tried to get revenge.

'Thanks, oh! I forgot classy when describing you. What about work?'

'Don't worry, I'm hardly going to say that you've been two timing me and made me look like a fucking idiot in front of a load of strangers am I now?'

'I suppose not, but can we be civil?'

'Well, it's only for two more weeks as I'm going back to Uni to study for the degree I've been running from.'

'You never said.'

'No, you helped me make my mind up last night, so thanks for that. But we could have had a future.'

'Look I….'

'No need Tag, do the right thing for once and tell Fay what you've told me and don't hold back and make the right decision. Don't play with people's feelings, it's not on.'

'Point taken. So this is goodbye then?'

'No, I'll see you at work. But I suppose it's goodbye for this situation, we will never be like this again. I'll be off then.'

'Goodbye Suki, I meant what I said.'

'I know you did Tag, goodbye and good luck.' Suki left the room and went straight back to Hull. She had seemed hard and unaffected but really she was deeply hurt and she balled her eyes out when she got out of view and was in the privacy of her dad's car. She really loved Tag and wanted to be with him for the rest of her life, he was the one she'd dreamed of but she realised that it had all been an act as far as he was concerned.

So Tag was left with his cold breakfast but he didn't care, he knew what he had to do. The first thing he did was change the room and then he sat and waited for Fay to come down for breakfast...

The night porter come doorman, barman and part time cook started to open the front door to let people come and go as they pleased. Within five minutes there was a commotion as Shaz and Charlie tried to creep in the front door and get to their rooms before anyone was any the wiser to them stopping out all night. Not that anyone was bothered that they had. They walked into the dining room and stood in horror at the sight of Tag sitting there.

'What's happened Tag? Is Fay alright? Has she had an accident? How did you get from London so quickly?'

The girls couldn't get the questions out quickly enough. When they finally ran out of breath, Tag answered them.

'Well I suppose you'll only find out sooner or later.'

'Find out what?'

'I didn't go to London and Fay is in bed. I came here with a girl from work who I've been seeing behind Fay's back and bingo! Walked in here last night and Fay was sat there and it all kicked off.'

'You fucking prick Tag. How could you do that to Fay?' Shaz said angrily.

'Yeah, we've slagged you off for being a twat and now you've just proved it,' Charlie chipped in.

'Cheers girls, thanks for the support. Look please don't tell anyone about this, I'm hopefully going to sort it out in the next couple of hours.'

'Why have you got a magic wand Sooty?' quipped Shaz.

'No, I'm going to sit down and sort it out with Fay if she'll agree to stay with me. I really want to be a good dad.'

'Fat chance of that dickhead, anyway where's this other slapper?'

'She's not a slapper, she was as shocked as Fay, she didn't know about Fay either.'

'What? How the fuck do you do it Tag? You've got more secrets than James Bond. So where is she?'

'On her way back home to Hull, she's fucked me off. Doesn't want to know.'

'So that's why you want Fay is it, last chance saloon with the only person who will take all your bullshit and come back for more.' Charlie was livid, she actually liked Fay and wasn't bothered that the feelings weren't reciprocated.

'No, I know it looks like that, but I've done a lot of thinking tonight, well last night and I want Fay and the baby. But most of all I want to grow up and treat Fay like she deserves to be treated.'

'Talk's cheap Tag and actions speak louder than words. So answer me this, if she has you back and has the baby and there's a lads' night out and this stunner comes onto you what are you going to do?' Charlie quizzed him.

Tag didn't take long to reply.

'I would say no thanks and that's the truth. The way I feel now I just want to get Fay back home and sort this mess out.'

'Well Tag I hope she can forgive you because I'm not sure I could. Do you know how much she loves and defends you even when everyone is slagging you off?' Shaz joined in.

'I know she loves me and now it's time to give her back what she's given me all these years. I just want the chance. Maybe you could put in a word for me.'

'Look, she's hardly going to take notice of us two is she? She doesn't like us for a start and it's you who has to sort this out, no one else,' said Charlie.

'I suppose so, I'll sit and wait for her here. Anyway where have you two been?'

'At the B&B around the corner, we copped off with two lads,' said Shaz.

'Well you copped off Shaz, mine was a corpse that snored and couldn't get a hard on,' Charlie butted in.

'Anyway never mind us, we're single and we can do what we like. Now we better get changed then come back down for some breakfast,' said Shaz.

'And you better get some knickers on as well. Seeing as you lost the last pair,' laughed Charlie.

'Fuck off, don't tell him that.'

'Your secret's safe with me,' Tag shouted as the two of them went to get changed.

Tag sat for what seemed like an eternity, just staring and thinking what a prick he'd been. Just then the door opened and in walked Fay with Cary. She saw Tag and burst into tears and began to walk out. Tag got up and followed her.

'Fay, Fay can we talk?' begged Tag.

'Fuck off Tag, I don't know why you're still here. Anyway where's your girlfriend? Left you has she?' Fay shouted.

'Can we have a bit of quiet please, there are people still in bed,' interrupted the owner, chef, porter.

'Sorry,' Tag said.

'It's a shame you weren't sorry when you were fucking that piece from work,' Fay just kept walking away from Tag, as he and Cary were trying to catch her up. The scene was a comical one. It looked like a race and Fay was the pacemaker and the other two were trying to keep up. The obscenities were flying around as finally Fay settled in a chair in the dining room and again told Tag to piss off and leave her alone.

'Look Fay I want to talk to you. Suki went this morning and before you ask I didn't spend the night with her. In fact we never had sex at all.'

'It doesn't matter whether you did it or you didn't, the intention was to carry on behind my back. No, but this weekend was the biggy wasn't it Tag? You were going to get your rocks off this weekend weren't you? You'd planned it hadn't you?' Fay seethed at him.

'Yes, that was the plan, I won't lie, I've stopped lying and pissing around from now on. I thought long and hard last night and I want us to make a go of it.'

'You mean she fucked you off so I'm your last chance. The first prize went so you don't mind having the second prize. Or am I the booby prize, is that it? Well I thought we were making a go of it already? You know, buying a house together and now having a baby, silly me and I thought we were just playing at living together.'

'No I mean I want to sort all this out and be a good partner and father and stop pissing around all the time. I'll stop going out and we'll do more things together.'

'Like what - taking me to Blackpool and staying in a hotel, like you did this weekend with her? Do you realise how hurt I am you bastard?'

'I know and I want to make it up to you. I've booked a room tonight here if you want to stay, and before you ask no it isn't the one

Suki and me had or were supposed to have.'

'My bus leaves at 5 o'clock, how am I going to get home?'

'If you stay I'm going to go and book us on the train or a bus tomorrow. So come on, what do you say? Let's give it a go. I know I've been a prick and I promise I'll change, just give me another chance.'

Fay looked at Cary for advice.

'Don't look at me Fay it's your life, Tag seems pretty genuine, but I don't live with him and you've got a lot to sort out. If you go home it could all kick off with your families, so I would stay here and get it sorted, if you want it sorting.'

'Look Fay, I'll be in the bar, if you decide that you want to stay come and see me. By the way it was always going to be you out of Suki and you. Last night really hit home how badly I've mistreated you and I want to make it up to you. And Fay, I do love you.' Tag then went to the bar to read the papers and wait for Fay to come to a decision...

The dining room filled up slowly as all the girls came down for breakfast, all except Shaz and Charlie. The atmosphere was quite odd as no one dared speak and then Fay broke the silence.

'Look everyone, I hope you're not quiet because of me. Carry on the weekend, don't let that prick spoil it.'

'Have you seen him this morning Fay?' asked Clare.

'Yeah and he's asked me to stay here tonight and get the train or bus back in the morning with him.'

'Well what did you tell him?' asked Mandy anxious to know.

'I didn't tell him anything, he's in the bar waiting for my answer. And he'll be waiting a long time because I've made my decision but he won't find out until I've had a day out with you lot as we planned. We're going to the funfair aren't we?'

There was silence.

'Too right we are love,' Clare shouted.

'You mean you're going to tell him that he'll have to wait for your decision all day?' asked Cary in horror.

'No you're going to tell him for me and leave him hanging. If we do get back together I will be wearing the trousers from now on and where better to start than now.'

'Good girl, finally you're taking the firm hand that he's always needed,' said a relieved Clare who knew Tag needed bringing down a peg or two.

'Do you want me to go now?' asked Cary.

'No, let the little bastard stew,' laughed Fay rather enjoying her new found strength.

'So come on then, tell us what you're going to do?' Steph said excitedly.

'Well what do you think? I live with him and have a mortgage with him and now I'm having a baby with him. My decision is I'm going to tell him…,' then she paused.

'What? What? Come on you silly cow tell us,' protested Clare.

'Well, I'm going to tell him to fucking sling his hook, the dirty, no good, cheating bastard.'

The room went silent as they fully expected the answer to be, 'I'll give him one more chance and he's not that bad'.

'Well if that's what you want love,' said a stunned Cary.

'Of course it isn't, but don't let him know that. He'll get his last chance, but before you think I'm going soft it will be his last chance, anymore fucking around and that's it.'

'Shall I go and tell him?' Cary asked.

'No, don't you get it? We all know he's not finding out until later. She's making him sweat a bit, and I for one think you've made the right decision,' said Mandy.

'Go and tell him I'll let him know at 4 o'clock today and not a minute earlier. Tell him I need to think. I'll give him my decision back here in the bar,' said Fay.

So Cary went into the bar and told Tag the latest. Tag's eyes lit up when he saw Cary. But she soon put a dampener on the proceedings.

'Fay said she hasn't made up her mind yet and she'll tell you what her decision is at 4 o'clock in the bar. We're all going to the funfair as planned and she said she's not changing her plans.' Cary sounded like a schoolgirl passing on a message for her lovesick friend who was packing her boyfriend in.

'Alright Cary thanks, I'll just hang around until then,' answered Tag looking all forlorn and lost.

Cary felt sorry for him but knew it would do him no harm in the long run. If Trev had done the same to her she would probably have stabbed him with the butter knife at breakfast. She left Tag and returned to the dining room to tell Fay the message had been passed on.

'What did he say then?' asked Steph who was quite enjoying the morning of betrayal and goings on, it was better than the soaps.

'He just looked very sorry for himself' and said, 'Thanks', replied Cary.

'So he should the shit head after what he's done to me,' Fay exclaimed.

Then the door opened and in came Shaz and Charlie.

'Look what the cat's dragged in,' Steph shouted. 'Where have you two been?'

'In the room having a shower,' Shaz replied.

'What time did you get in then?' asked Sue.

'This morning, why?'

'So did you pull then? Come on tell us what went on,' asked an excited Clare.

'Well she got pumped and I got sleepy. Mine tried to get a hard on but it was never going to happen and Shaz got shagged, and lost her knickers in the bargain. Thinks she's left them in the room.'

They all started laughing at this even Fay.

'We saw Tag Fay and he seemed really upset and was distraught at what had happened. I've never seen him that serious before. Is he still here?' asked Charlie.

'He's in the bar waiting for my decision as to whether I'll give him another chance or not. But he'll have to wait until this afternoon because after breakfast we're going to the fair for a good time.'

'Good on you, you let him know who's boss,' said Charlie.

'Right then girls let's have some fun,' Fay shouted. 'You never know we might score at the fair.' This was said loudly enough for Tag to hear and they all walked past the bar where he was sat and all giggled as they past him.

Tag cut a lonely figure and was genuinely hurt and nervous that the answer from Fay might be 'fuck off Tag'. Fay seemed very sure of herself and Tag had never seen her like that before. He decided it was too early for a drink so he went to his room and fell asleep...

Eddie was up bright and early on the Saturday morning to see what kind of a state the boys were in after their marathon session. He loved this part of the trip as long as no one had caused any trouble. He sat and ate his breakfast and read his paper and was quite glad to get away from Greg who had spent the night in the bath with his quilt. Despite being put back in bed by Skip and Tosser he got back up and went straight back into the bath and fell asleep. Eddie had tried numerous times to wake him up but to no avail, so he just left him fully clothed in the bath.

Room by room they began to stir, all the worse for wear and laughing at the same time wondering how grown men could get into such a state. Skip and Tosser had both fell asleep fully clothed and Tosser woke up with chocolate all over his head as he'd slept on the complimentary confectionery. The room looked like a bomb had just dropped. There was brown powder all over the sideboard, it was when Skip had tried to make a hot chocolate for himself and the packet exploded all over. Next to the brown powder was Skip's money and next to that were Greg's front teeth.

'What the fuck are they?' asked Skip.

'Greg's teeth don't you remember he lost 'em and we must have picked 'em up.'

'Well he's not getting 'em back 'til the weekend's over,' and they both laughed.

'Right shower and get the troops together. What time is it?' Skip enquired.

'Half eight, no wonder I still feel shit we didn't get to bed until about three.'

'What a good night though wasn't it. How the hell did Damo find us?'

'How the hell did he get behind the bar. I think the shit will hit the fan about that one, we better tell everyone that no one knows anything if asked.'

The two of them got a shower and started going to everyone's room to brief them. Skip did what he always did, he got a room listing of everyone so that he could terrorise anyone who was getting too cocky.

The first room they went to was Thommo and Gaz's. They knocked on the door and after a few minutes Gaz answered looking terrible.

'What?' croaked a blinking Gaz, looking like he'd just been born and sounding like he'd just spent a month in a cigarette factory with the beagles.

'Come on breakfast Gaz, don't you want a runny egg and some greasy bacon?' asked Tosser laughing.

'Fuck off, not funny.'

'What's that smell?' asked Skip reeling from the smell.

'Thommo, he pissed the bed so we've put the mattress on the radiator to dry. It doesn't smell that bad does it?'

'It doesn't smell that fucking good from where I'm standing. Look if anyone asks, you didn't get anything free in the bar last night, alright?'

'Oh yeah! Damo got yer. Well I shall see you two in about ten minutes,' and with that Gaz shut the door.

The next room they tried was the students' but they got no reply. So they went to Daz and Matt's room.

'Wakey, wakey come along you two, breakfast is waiting,' Skip shouted as the door opened and a fully clothed and showered Daz and Matt walked out to greet them.

'That bastard Greg better keep away from me today,' announced Daz who was still livid about the Hippodrome.

'Are you still going on about that Daz?' Tosser quipped.

'He's been going on about it in his sleep,' Matt joined in.

'I know but the bastard, I was nearly in there. Them fucking students got in as well.'

'We've just knocked on them and no answer. I bet they've pulled a couple of page three birds,' scoffed Tosser.

'Those two couldn't pull a budgie or a muscle. They'll have got up early to buy a comic,' said Daz and they all laughed.

They all entered the breakfast room after giving their details to the Gestapo officer who guarded the breakfast door with his life. Nothing got past him, not one hash brown or piece of toast, not even a butter packet. If you hadn't paid for a breakfast by crikey you wouldn't get one, not on his watch. They sat down at the table next to Eddie and immediately started the wind-ups.

'Where's Greg?' asked Skip.

'In the bath, with all his clothes on,' Eddie replied.

'What is he mental?' Daz butted in.

'No he fell asleep in there. Skip, Tosser and me got him back in bed but he must have got up again and got back in the bath and hasn't moved since.'

'What's your room number Eddie?' Daz was hatching a plan. The plan was go to the reception, say that he'd lost his key, get a spare, go into the room and turn the shower on above the unsuspecting Greg. But Eddie knew all the tricks and his in-built security system was flashing red.

'I'm not telling you so that you can go and soak him and make a mess of my room.'

'Eddie, the thought never crossed my mind,' said an angelic looking Daz.

'It had mine, give us your key Eddie and I promise all we'll do is run in turn the shower on and run out.'

Matt was pleading with Eddie and to his surprise it worked.

'Here then, just turn the shower on and away,' said Eddie handing over the key.

Greg thought he deserved it after being a pain for the full day.

'Good lad Eddie,' Skip said as he snatched the key then led all four of them to the room.

Slowly they entered Greg's room and could hear him snoring in the bath. They then tip-toed over to the bath, trying not to laugh, and worked out which button to press for the shower. They set the shower to cold and then on the count of three they hit the 'on' button before running out of the room. Then, creased over in pain through laughing, they heard screams coming from the bathroom as Greg desperately tried to stop the shower from working...

They all ran back to the breakfast room, but first Skip had to ring Pete to tell him about what had happened so far. Pete thought the joke had ended on the Friday and that they would have forgotten about him by now. But how wrong he was as the phone went. He answered it as Sally had gone to the shops.

'Hello.'

'Pete, how are you mate? All got a shag last night, in fact haven't been to bed yet and we got a free bar at the hotel. Just going for a massage in a minute from one of the Thai birds that work here. What are you doing today, itching?' gloated Skip.

'Staying in you dick, I'll get you back for this Skip.'

'Don't pick those spots too much, they'll leave a scar. Get the calamine lotion on them and you take care this afternoon while we go to the game and get loads more drink down us and shag loads more birds.'

Skip was wasting his breath as Pete had hung up. Skip and the others then returned to get their breakfast and to plan the day ahead. Eddie waited while everyone had come down from their rooms and then gave out the tickets for the game. The only people from the party that were missing were Greg, plus the students, Grant and Mike.

'Where are those two little buggers? I told Grant's mother I'd keep an eye on him,' Eddie fretted.

'The last time anyone saw them was going into the Hippodrome. Did you see them in there Daz? Oh! sorry you never got in did you?' laughed Tosser.

'Fucking funny Tosser, ho, ho, ho,' Daz was mellowing slightly.

'Sorry mate, couldn't resist it.'

'Well I hope they're alright.'

'Eddie, they'll be okay don't worry. Grant's used to sticky situations, look at that pensioner he was shagging.'

Just then Greg appeared, toothless and looking rather pissed off. Matt saw him and started to wind him up.

'We've got one of them power showers in our room, great they are, have you had a shower this morning Greg?'

'So it was you then?'

'What was me?'

'The funny bugger who turned the shower on with me in the bath.'

'Don't know what you're talking about Greg me old son. Anyhow where are your teeth?'

'Lost 'em last night didn't I?'

'Maybe that bouncer at the Hippodrome's got 'em after you spat your words into his face,' Daz cut in.

'Fuck off Daz.'

'Good job you haven't got 'em or else after last night I would have knocked the bastards out.'

'Why, what did I do?'

'Well you fell over a coffee sign outside a pub and laid in the gutter for twenty minutes. Then you shouted at the bouncer, who then wouldn't let any of us in the club. That's why I'm pissed off with you.'

'Sorry Daz, I just had too much to drink, I apologise. But does anyone know where my teeth are?'

There was silence as they all just shrugged their shoulders. Skip and Tosser kept a straight face.

'You haven't lost them in your room have you Greg? I mean they're not in the bath are they?' Skip broke the silence and was taking the piss.

'No, I looked and I couldn't find them,' Greg continued not realising.

'They haven't gone down the plug hole have they?' Skip carried on.

'They're too big to go down the plug hole.'

'Maybe they're in that curb you tried to take a bite out of last night when you went down like a sack of shit outside that pub, when that bloke Ken tripped you up,' Tosser joined in.

'Who's this Ken you're on about?' Greg looked puzzled.

'You know, that coffee bloke, Ken, second name Co.'

'Kenco who's that?'

Then came a pause as Greg mulled over the information in his mind before realising they were taking the piss.

'Look, very funny, but do you know where my teeth are or not?'

Everyone to a man began to search their pockets and wallets pretending to find the missing teeth and then all shouted as one, 'No one knows where your teeth are.'

'That's all you had to say.'

'We did about ten minutes ago, you twat,' said Daz looking pissed off.

Greg got on with his breakfast and tried to eat it the best he could. But with no front teeth he was finding it increasingly difficult. Everyone was looking forward to the excitement of another fun-filled day and were about to plan what it would entail. They congregated at the breakfast area and swapped stories of what had happened the night before. Well what they could remember, this was a good time to put the pieces of the giant together of what had happened as someone always remembered something someone had forgotten. After this Skip told everyone to meet in the hotel foyer at 11 o'clock and then they would be on their way for the day. Eddie was becoming increasingly worried about the two students and as to their whereabouts.

'Before you go to your rooms, think hard have any of you seen Grant and Mike this morning? Because they never came back last night.'

'Get Nick Ross and the Crimewatch team on the phone,' Thommo shouted.

'Not funny Thommo, they're only young lads, they might be in trouble,' said Eddie.

No one said a word, then Greg blurted out, 'There they are!' as he pointed to the reception area. Sure enough the two of them had just got back into the hotel and were asking where breakfast was being served. As they entered the breakfast room the place erupted with noise as the insults began to fly.

'Got a bit of bum action last night did you? You couple of homos,' Matt started.

'You've never walked it home from the Hippodrome have you?

'You tight, greedy, student bastards,' came another insult from Thommo.

'Don't tell me you picked up a granny and the home she lives in lock the doors, so you've had to wait to be let out?' Skip joined in. Eddie was really pleased to see them and told everyone to leave them alone.

'Come on then you bastards, tell us what happened in the Hippodrome?' Matt was dying to know.

'They will have had a drink and run out of money - and then they'll come out with some bullshit to piss us all off,' said a rather jealous Daz.

'Well,' Grant began, 'you won't believe this, we got in the bar and bought a drink and just stood there looking around, when these two stunners from Sweden, what were their names Mike?' Grant knew how to milk the situation.

'Ulrika and Anna,' Mike replied.

'Well, they came up to us and asked us to dance and that was it really.'

'What, that's all you did, dance?' interrupted Daz.

'No I haven't finished yet. Then we sat down with them and got some more drinks in and then danced some more.'

'Fucking big wow, drinking and dancing, is that all that happened?' Thommo interrupted.

'No, no, no, dear Thommo, we were then asked by the ladies if we would like to go back to their hotel room, which was just around the corner from the nightclub. Now I'll let Mike take up the story.'

They had rehearsed this in the taxi coming back to get the maximum affect and it was working. They had everyone on the edge of their seats even the old guard had stayed to listen. Eddie was loving it, watching all these so called men of the world, who had given out so much advice to the students on what to do and what not to do in London. None of them had ever got a sniff of a bird in all the time they'd been coming on these trips and here they were hanging onto every word these two young lads were saying.

'Thank you Grant, I shall continue. We got back to their hotel, had a drink at the bar and then proceeded to their room. Once in the room there were two beds and we sat on one while they got out a bottle of vodka and poured four glasses out and put in some orange from the fridge and we had a drink. Now I shall pass you back to Grant to continue, Grant.'

'For fuck sake you two little bastards, better hurry up, the game kicks off in five hours,' Daz was getting pissed off.

'Alright we will end the story there,' Grant announced.

'No you won't! Fucking sit down and continue, I'm getting a hard on here and that hasn't happened for a long time,' said Bert, 'You carry on lad'. Everyone burst out laughing at Bert, who was deadly serious.

'Where was I?' Grant continued.

'You were on the bed drinking vodka and orange,' Bert excitedly filled him in.

'Right, then they began to whisper and started to laugh and both went into the bathroom. We just looked at each other and thought they were going to tell us to fuck off but a couple of minutes later they came out and started to undress each other and play with each other. It was unbelievable, they were playing with vibrators and licking each other. We couldn't believe it.'

'So you just sat there?' asked Skip.

'No, they put on a show for the girls in return and wanked each other off, a bit like a sexy foreign exchange,' said Matt.

'Look, do you want us to tell you the rest or what? Well I'll pass you back to Mike and he'll continue.'

'Well, they carried on for a while and then stopped and got us over. I took Anna onto the single bed and he had Ulrika. Then we swapped and I had Ulrika and he had Anna.'

'You lying pair of twats,' Daz said having none of it.

'Don't believe us then, we were at it all night in every hole as well. I am absolutely knackered and my cock is red raw,' said Grant.

'You'll get a chance to meet them tonight, we're meeting them again and it's our home tie tonight, they're coming here to stay.'

'Anyway Daz, did you have a good time playing dominoes last night?' scoffed Grant.

'Fuck off. You two twats never pulled last night, you've made all that up,' Daz laughed at them.

'All true I'm afraid Daz, you've either got it or you haven't,' Grant was continuing to rub it in.

'Well, true or not boys, it's a great story and I for one am looking forward to meeting the two girls tonight,' said Skip plotting their downfall if it was true. Everyone went on their way and all knew where to meet at eleven.

The two students got their breakfasts and were still in shock at the night they had just had. Eddie had joined them and asked if they were lying.

'Honestly Eddie, they picked us up and shagged our brains out and they want to do the same tonight here.'

'You've got no chance of doing that here boys,' Eddie explained.

'Didn't you see Skip he'll get you as soon as you get into your room. He'll get the spare key and barge in on you while you're at it. Now we could have a bit of fun here boys but this is between just us. Come to the reception with me and I will tell them you want a different room as you're not happy with the one you've got. You move to a different room and get on with it tonight. Now Skip's got your old room number, so when you go to bed he'll give it half an hour then he'll bring the mob and try and fuck up your night. But he won't be able to as you will have moved to another room, so the laugh will be on him.'

'Eddie, you are a fucking genius.'

'I know. So finish your breakfast and then we'll do it. Now all you have to do is hold onto your birds because these lot will be like flies around shit, believe me.'

The two students finished their food and swapped rooms, and then went to get their stuff to put into the new room and tried to get half an hour's sleep.

Thommo and Gaz had hatched a plan and were trying to sell their tickets for the game to a couple of guys in the hotel bar. They were planning on going into central London and getting a massage with the money from the tickets. The guy who was at the reception had recommended a place that was supposed to be good. They eventually persuaded the couple who were from the USA that it was a traditional northern English ritual to go and see this game, and they bought it. The rest of the boys had got down from their rooms and were congregating in the bar, which was closed. Then a couple of the people from the other rugby party who had been in the bar the night before started chatting with the lads.

'Eh up, what a good barman he wor last nite, we didn't pay for owt after about ? twelve.'

'Jesus mate keep it down, that wasn't the barman it was one of our lot and if they find out we'll all be in the shit, so keep it quiet,' said Skip.

'Sorry lad, we didn't realise, we thought he just didn't give a shit. I'll tell the rest of our lot to keep it quiet.'

'Good night though wasn't it?'

'Cracking nite, who do you think'll win game today?'

'Wigan by a mile, Cas have got no chance,' said Skip.

'I know it's getting boring with those twats winning everything year in, year out. Where are you lads heading before the game?'

'We're going to that pub through the park. They've got an offer on £1 a bottle as long as you buy eight at a time. The barman loves us, we supped him out of beer yesterday. Then we're going to 'Hog in the pound' on Bond Street.'

'Eh up that's where we're going and meeting up with a load of lads from our club. Might see you in there because it looks like our taxis are here. If we don't see you there might see you in bar tonight. Catch you later, have a good day.' Then they got in their taxis and left.

'Catch you later mate,' said Skip who now was turning his attention to seeing if everyone was ready to go.

'Is everybody here and remember if you're with us make sure you've got your ticket and money because we aren't coming back.'

'We're all here. Grant and Mike know where to find us, they'll be down in ten minutes,' shouted Eddie and they all set off for the Clipper to get some cheap beer and then off into London. In the Clipper the offer was still on but after half an hour the manager called Skip over and announced that they had ran out of Sol and that the only bottled beer they had left was Heineken export but he couldn't do that for a pound. It would have to be £1.20 a bottle. Skip took the offer back to the lads and they agreed that it would be alright. The barman began to serve the export and the beer was flowing. The two Americans had tagged along and were getting into the swing of things but were getting quite tipsy as they hadn't drank as fast before. Skip went to the bar and ordered some taxis to take them into London and to Bond Street to the famous meeting place on these trips 'Hog in the pound'.

Straight after doing so he rang up everyone's favourite spotty bloke, yes you've guessed it, Pete, who refused to come to the phone and was still refusing to come to the phone the fifth time they rang him. In fact Sally told them to grow up in the end and unplugged the phone for an hour hoping that would stop them and it seemed to work. The lads tried a couple more times and then gave up after getting a dead tone.

'We'll leave it until we get to the ground and then we'll surprise him.'

Skip laughed as he thought this was great because Pete was one of the biggest wind-up merchants going and was finally getting a taste of his own medicine.

Finally the taxis arrived and they were off to Wembley via Bond street and the famous meeting place for all fans 'Hog in the pound', they met there every year and congregated for a couple of hours and chatted about the forth coming game. Some of the people down Bond Street were in fancy dress, others were just loud and it all added to the colour of the Wembley weekend. The pubs loved it as these northerners drank like it was going out of fashion. They could really knock it back and they didn't cause one bit of trouble. They had to put on extra staff for these weekends as this was the busiest weekend of the year. There was never any trouble as if anyone got too boisterous the other rugby people sorted it out amongst themselves. The Hull boys all arrived and immediately headed for the bar. They got their drinks and headed for the door to stand outside as it was a lovely sunny day and watch the passers by and to have a bit of banter with each other. Skip had brought a couple of song sheets with him and as soon as everyone was ready with drink in hand they started. Skip stood on a chair, which was out of the bar and held up the song sheet. The song was 'Rhinestone cowboy' and within a couple of minutes the whole of the pub was singing this in unison. All the shoppers were standing and looking in amazement at the spectacle of a couple of hundred northerners singing a cowboy song on the streets of London. They weren't in tune but no one cared. With that just on the last chorus two policemen on bikes arrived to see what the crowd had gathered for and they just sat and watched along with the others and even joined in the chorus as this small part of London became a country music haven. When the song had finished all the on lookers applauded. Skip looked at the policemen and they didn't seem bothered so he began to belt out the clubs anthem Tom Jones's 'Delilah' and again the whole crowd joined in, only this time the police had to tell them to stop after the song due to the fact that they were beginning to cause an obstruction. There were that many people there stopping and looking. Skip thanked the policemen for their patience and the singing stopped. The police had in fact got used to the crazy drinking northerners who put away huge amounts of ale and never caused any trouble. It made a change from the football hooligans they encountered on a regular basis, they actually enjoyed the singing. Then they went on their way leaving the boys to it, safe in the knowledge there would be no trouble.

Skip told everyone to be ready to go at half one as they still had to get to Wembley via tube. Just then it happened as it had happened for the past five years and no one knew who it was or how he did it. Outside the pub you can see the tube station which is about twenty yards away. Now the entrance to the station is through a shopping centre and one of the shops has a display in the windows which faces into Bond street and looks directly onto the pavement outside the pub. Well one of the rugby supporters always gets into the cabinet display every year and strips off. So this year all of a sudden there was a roar and they all turned around to see this bloke with no clothes on standing like a statue with the other manikins.

'What's he doing?' asked a puzzled Grant.

'He does it every year mate, wait while he starts performing,' said one of the crowd and with that he started to undress one of the other dummies and put her clothes on much to the amusement of the crowd. In the background you could see the staff frantically trying to get him out as soon as they realised what he was doing, but this man was a pro he had blocked himself in and locked the display cabinet from the inside. The manager of the store was now outside trying to plead with the man to stop it and that the joke was over, but the only thing he succeeded in doing was making him crave more attention, as more people gathered to see the spectacle. He picked up the dummy and began to dance with it and then he started to kiss it and roared on by the crowd he finished by bending it over and pretending to mount it. At this point the police had arrived and were trying to keep a straight face in front of the manager who was distraught at what had gone on in his display window. The police half-heartedly tried to get to the display area but as soon as the man had seen them he was off and had survived another year. The police then told the crowd to be on their way as they had to take a statement from the manager about the incident.

'Does he do that every year?' asked Mike.

'Well every year I've been coming here he does and it's always the same he does it for so long and then runs away. He's fucking priceless,' said Tosser still laughing at what he'd just seen.

'Right then boys drink up, and we'll be on our way. Wembley here we come,' announced Skip.

'Are we going?' asked Brad, one of the Americans who had tagged along.

'Yes we are my old American friend. How did you like the side show?' answered Tosser.

'Well it was different, in the States he would have been arrested. But here the police seemed to just let him go.'

'Well what harm has he done?'

'None I suppose, it sure was funny.'

'Drink up and we'll show you a real sporting event, none of your shitty Super bowl here.'

They all drank up and made their way to the underground and got their tube tickets. Thommo and Gaz stayed behind and got another drink in and then made plans to get to the massage parlour. They were bricking it and looking forward to it at the same time. It was like Christmas Eve.

Within twenty minutes the pub was almost deserted as nearly all of the customers had gone to the game. All that remained were Thommo, Gaz and a few regulars, it was as if the place had just been declared a no go zone. The silence was deafening apart from the odd siren. You wouldn't have believed that only twenty minutes earlier the place had been rocking to the sound of laughter and mischief and the ringing of the tills...

CHAPTER 9
DO YOU DO EXTRAS?

'You not going to the game then?' the old man sat in the corner asked Thommo and Gaz.

'No, we had a ticket but we've sold it. The game will be too one sided. Besides we're going for a massage,' Thommo announced as if it was something that no one had ever done before.

'Well you go careful those girls will get all your money if you don't watch out, they have special techniques, you know. Once they start rubbing you even the man with the strongest will can go weak at the knees. I know I've seen it time after time.' The old man knew a thing or to about getting ripped off in London as he'd seen it all before.

'Don't worry about us we've made a pact. Gaz here is looking after the money and we only want what we can afford. Isn't that right Gaz?'

'Yes we'll haggle if we have to but on no account will we spend what we haven't got.'

'Well as long as you're careful and stick to that principal you'll be alright. Enjoy it,' the old man smiled.

'Oh, we will don't you worry, we will,' said Thommo.

The two of them drank up and got on the tube to find the address they had been given in Soho by the hotel barman. They walked past the place about four times until they eventually found it after they asked a weird looking man who was hanging around. For all their bravado they were like two kids playing truant and felt like they were being naughty.

'Excuse me could you tell me where this is?' Gaz plucked up the courage to ask, pointing at the address on the piece of paper the receptionist had given him.

'Let's have a look, yes you turn around and walk two yards and it's on your left,' the man said trying not to laugh. They were stood right outside of it.

'Cheers mate' they both said feeling rather foolish.

The place was just a door with a number on it and a bell. Nervously they rang the bell and waited, there was no immediate answer so they rang it again. Straight away there was an answer.

'Bit impatient aren't we? What do you require?' asked the lady.

'Two massages please,' they answered sounding like Oliver asking for more.

'Push the door when I buzz and we're on the second floor.'

The door buzzed and they began to walk up the stairs to the second floor and had to press another buzzer to get in. They were greeted by a scantily clad girl in a sort of beautician's uniform, which was about three sizes too small.

'Just take a seat over there and we'll be with you in a minute,' the girl said pointing to the comfy looking chairs that were next to the table with all the reading material. The two of them looked at each other and then at the mags which were nothing like you could buy in the local newsagents, these were real hardcore. Sat opposite them was a big, huge black guy.

'Been waiting long mate?' asked Thommo nervously as if he was due to have all his teeth out.

'All my life man all my life. I work here. Maybe I'll be the one who gets to give you your massage,' The man said with a straight face. The look on Thommo and Gaz's face was a look of total horror. Then the man started to smile and put them out of their misery.

'I'm the one who you answer to if you can't pay or you cause any problems.'

'Don't worry you won't get any trouble from us mate. Maybe premature ejaculation eh Gaz?'

'You might but I won't, cheeky get.'

'Listen boys just relax. The girls here are good and as long as you don't cause any bother then you'll have a good time. You have to pay first before anything anyway. You two just enjoy it,' The guy assured them.

With that it went quiet as the two of them nudged each other in excitement and anticipation of what was going to happen. Then a small, old women came out and asked them if they'd seen a price list. They hardly dare speak as they shook their heads and quietly said 'no'. The women then glared at the big guy and told him to 'pull his fucking finger out or else'. The huge man seemed to quiver at the thought of what might happen to him and he quickly handed the two of them a menu which had all the prices of the services offered and the price of the drinks and such like. The two of them browsed the sheet of paper and looked at each other. There was no account of sexual encounters that the hotel guy had told them they could have. The price of a massage full body was £30 each. They thought this must include a wank at least. But before they could think the man asked them what they wanted. Knowing he was now being watched by the old women who looked like she ran things.

'So boys what will it be, can I interest you in a drink first? Or is it just a massage?'

Seeing the prices of the massage and the fact a pint of lager was a tenner the two of them were having second thoughts about whether they had made a mistake. They felt like putting their hands over their eyes like school kids do and when they removed them they hoped the man had gone away. Unfortunately this wasn't a playground this was a 'massage parlour' in central London and the prices were central London prices.

'Err, I'll just have the massage for now' said Gaz perusing the menu like he was in a fine dining restaurant trying to decide which wine went best with the dish he'd ordered.

'Yes and the same for me' said Thommo nodding in approval of Gaz's decision.

'That'll be £30 each then gentlemen. By the way any extras you have negotiate with the girls.'

They both handed their money over thinking shit, that £30 didn't include a hand job after all. But what the hell they might as well enjoy it now. The man checked the money and then lead them to another room which had a massage table on it.

'Just wait here boys and someone will be with you shortly, enjoy it.' The man then left the two of them in the room for what seemed like an eternity.

'Fucking hell, this has cost an arm and a fucking leg Thommo. Right whatever you do, don't ask for fuck all else, we'll have to work here to pay it off. And I'm not rubbing anybody. Get the massage and we go okay?'

'Look I'm not stupid here you take my money if you don't trust me.'

'We won't get out alive if we do anything stupid.'

'Tell you what I'd rather fight the fella rather than that women, she was scary, did you see him shit himself, she must be one nasty bitch.'

'I know probably a witch or more like she owns the place and has even bigger nastier people to deal with him.'

With that they both shut up as a side door opened and two girls with the tightest of outfits walked in and handed them a towel each and told them to undress and wrap the towel around themselves. Then they departed. The girls had very tight beautician/nurses outfits on that were too small and very short. The lads looked at each other and couldn't wait.

'Fucking hell Thommo I've nearly got a lob on.'

'Me too, for Christ sake don't come as soon as she touches you, that would be embarrassing.'

'I know but fucking hell did you see 'em? Virtually fuck all on. This is better than watching a stupid fucking rugby match and they haven't even done anything yet. Look Thommo don't get carried away keep your money in your pocket.'

The girls returned as the two of them stood there like kids waiting for a locker at the swimming baths.

'Put your stuff on the chair and then we can start' said one of the blondes. The lads did exactly what she said and then she took Thommo by the hand and led him to the other room. Leaving Gaz in the room alone with his girl. Thommo was getting really excited and then had a stroke of genius. Have a wank before the massage and then he would be able to resist temptation. So he asked to go to the toilet and cracked one off in no time as he was that excited.

Gaz was already hearing the soothing sounds of whales mating and smelling the warm oils that were about to be rubbed into his body. Good job he was on his front as he could then control the embarrassment of his erection. He was trying to think horrible thoughts of naked teammates doing bizarre things to take his mind off sex. And he gradually was getting the hang of it until she started to touch him and rub him. He couldn't believe it when she did what she did next. She got his hand and put it up her outfit and guess what she had fuck all on.

'No poking that's the rule you can touch but no poking' said the girl.

So Gaz just felt his way around while she rubbed him. He was in ecstasy when he discovered that she had a 'shaven haven' and he was happily playing with her clit and tickling her bum hole. The girl didn't even flinch and just carried on as if it was just another day at the office. He however was getting really excited and thought he was going to come.

Meanwhile in the other room Thommo who had relieved himself earlier was getting the same treatment and same instructions. It was a good job he had been for a wank as he would have shot his dust by now as the girl was straddled on his back rubbing his neck and shoulders. He could feel her warm fanny rubbing against his back and this excited him even more. The two girls knew exactly what they were doing and the two boys wished they would stop as they didn't have enough money to go any further. Then it was time have their legs and arses rubbed and this was pure ecstasy as the warm oil went down their arse cracks and the girls started to massage their buttocks and pulling their cheeks apart and rubbing their knackers and the bit between their knackers.

Then it was turn over time and both of them had hard ons which is what the girls wanted. They teased the boys by massaging their legs and upper thighs and occasionally as if by accident but on purpose they would stroke the base of the penis. The boys were doing quite well as they hadn't come yet and had been holding on through the thought of the embarrassment of coming whilst not being touched. They weren't very up on the etiquette of the massage and didn't know whether premature ejaculation was allowed. In fact the girls were used to men shooting all over the place as soon as they touched them, that was what the towel was for.

The girls then straddled the lads and rubbed their chests and upper bodies. They could feel the hot, sticky minge on their skin and they started to play with the girls again and this time they even got their tits out. But were told 'no sucking or biting'. Thommo was having a great time and found that the wank before hand had done the trick. As she rubbed his chest and nipples he fondled her breasts, which were perfectly formed and the nipples were just nicely erect. Chapel hat pegs Thommo thought for one brief moment and then he thought about what he'd like to do as the girl got off him and reached across him on purpose putting her tits near his face whilst she reached for the oil to rub on his chest and groin area. In the other room the exact same thing was happening to Gaz who hadn't had the foresight to relieve himself before hand and was now really struggling to stop himself from ejaculating all over. Gaz was quite relieved when she got off him as she had been touching him all over and he thought he was going to explode. Just as they thought they couldn't be teased anymore the girls lay on top of them and wriggled about in the oil and writhed all over them as the two lads just couldn't believe what was happening. This was better than watching some poxy rugby match. Gaz was the first to finish as the hour was nearly up and then came the immortal line 'Do you want extras?'.

'How much?' asked Gaz who had told Thommo 'what ever you do just get the massage' was now contemplating sex.

'£50 for a hand job there's nothing else on offer, we aren't prostitutes' said the girl.

Gaz thought for a minute well you aren't far off. But if the massage was that good what would the wank be like. You're only here once Gaz go for it and before he knew it he had said 'yes'.

'Money upfront' demanded the girl. So Gaz went over to his jeans and got out his and Thommo's money there was £60 left and he took the £50 and left two fivers in his pocket, then handed over the money.

'Lay back down on the table, and you can suck my tits and finger me if you like, but once you come that's it end of the session,' said the girl as a matter of fact. Gaz thought she was going to add and no video taping or flash photography is allowed.

'Alright that sounds fine' said Gaz as if he was ordering some food in a restaurant.

The girl then proceeded to stroke him all over getting him excited and Gaz was getting his moneys worth he had his hands all over her playing with her and fingering her whilst sucking her tits. She then got to his penis and started to stroke it up and down with oil and then proceeded to go up and down, try as he might Gaz just thought go with the flow and after about two minutes he came all over his chest whilst she kept pulling his dick he lasted as long as he could until it became painful. And the whole experience was over as he signalled that he'd had enough and she collected her oils and said 'thanks for the business see you again ' she left him there. Meanwhile in the other room Thommo was still at the stage where she was on top of him and then she asked the question 'do you want any extras?' and Thommo thought fuck it the same as Gaz had.

He went into the room where Gaz was, to get his money and saw Gaz laid on the table flaked out with a big smile on his face.

'Where's your jeans? I need some money I'm going for it' Gaz pointed over to the chair and Thommo searched frantically through the pockets for his money.

'Where's the money?' he said looking at Gaz.

'I've spent it' Gaz replied pointing to his spunk covered chest.

'You bastard Gaz after all you said. I'm taking the rest of the money.' So Thommo took the cash all £10 of it and went back into the room.

'Thought you'd pissed off' said the girl as she was packing her stuff away.

'I've got a tenner what can you do for a tenner?' asked a desperate Thommo as he watched her pack up and walk out, leaving him naked, except for the towel. He stormed into the room Gaz was in.

'You twat Gaz after all you said to me.'

'Keep your voice down or else that witch will be in and you know what that could mean us getting filled in, or even worse a curse being put on us,' Gaz said with a straight face.

'You bastard Gaz, you fucking bastard, I've got no money left hardly,' Thommo whispered.

'Don't worry I'll pay you back when we get back to Hull'

'What the...?' Thommo had steam coming out of his ears.

'Only joking, I've got the money back at the hotel. We've got time to have a beer and watch a bit of the game and then we'll have to get a cab and get ready for tonight. Tell you what fucking hell I've stored enough up in the memory bank to have another tug.'

'I know mine was unbelievable she let me touch her and all sorts. But she wouldn't let me touch her tits. '

'Jesus you're going to hate me for this but as soon as I paid for the wank she said I could suck her tits and finger her and I only hoped I could have lasted longer than two minutes, and even that was a struggle.'

'I had a wank before she massaged me so I was prepared, but even then I struggled to hold it in. The crafty cow was touching just near my dick and kept accidentally touching it a few times.'

'Yeah mine did that to they must do it on purpose. Anyway get your gear on and we'll go.'

Just then the bouncer came in.

'Having another go boys? Well if not hurry up you're well past the hour. Was it good?'

'Too right it was' said Gaz.

'And did you go for the extras?' enquired the man.

'I did he couldn't afford it,' Gaz nodded in Thommos direction.

'Well I didn't get much choice did I seeing as some bastard spent my money.' Thommo was still angry.

'You boys are funny, so you got the hand job then?'

'Well yes but why do you want to know?' asked Gaz.

'She has to share the money out at the end of the day, she doesn't get to keep it all.'

'Do you ever have a go then mate?' asked Thommo.

'No mate I wouldn't let them two slags touch me they are not that nice as far as this game goes. The last place I used to work was twice as pricey but you got the better type of slapper. Anyway time is money and if you've got no more money left I'll show you the door, but do feel free to call again.' The bouncer showed them out and the two of them went to the nearest bar to swap identical stories...

The girls had all gone to the fair for a couple of hours before going back to the hotel and departing for home. Fay would give her decision to Tag, which everyone but Tag knew what it was. They headed for the amusements and some fun. They were all sporting thick heads from the night before and it was a while before they got to the funfair. Fay was feeling alright and knew that she was making the right decision about Tag. She had never seen him look so serious about them as a couple before she had good feelings about it. They walked around an open market and all bought the good old 'kiss me quick' hats and they finally settled for a game of bingo after ringing home to see how the children were. They won a few games each as they were the only ones playing and they all put their winning tokens together so that Fay could get the baby its first cuddly toy. This nearly caused a row in the amusements as they had won twenty tokens and they went to get a prize and were shown what twenty tokens would get. It was far from impressive it was a little scrawny fluffy thing.

'You are joking mate twenty tokens for that, it's got fucking alopecia, come on mate she's having a baby how about that big one there?' protested Mandy, pointing to the biggest cuddly toy of the complete stand.

'Well that's supposed to be for fifty wins,' the man replied.

'Have a heart mate no one is going to win that and if you give us it we'll tell whoever we see to come and play and tell 'em we won this on your stall, come on what about that?' Clare chipped in.

'Go on then but don't tell 'em you bloody hoodwinked me' and he got the teddy down which was about three foot tall and handed it to Fay.

'Cheers mate you're a good un,' said Clare.

Fay couldn't believe the cheek of them but felt touched that they all gave her their winning tokens and got the baby something. So she had her first toy for the baby and it finally sunk in she was expecting and she began to feel quite apprehensive. Cary saw the look of horror that had overcome her at the realisation of the situation, and had a quiet word with her.

'Don't worry we all have doubts Fay it'll be alright believe me you'll be a great mother.'

'Thanks Cary it's just….'

'I know it's scary at first but just enjoy the rest of the afternoon and talk about that to Tag and make sure he knows how you feel.'

'I will and thanks again, you've really looked after me this last couple of days.'

'Not a problem Fay, you're okay and should be treated accordingly.'

The girls proceeded into the funfair and had bought some ice creams and were generally enjoying the day. In the distance there was a loud noise coming towards them and they couldn't make out what was being said. But it all became so clear when the crowd got nearer. It was Gary and his mates from Stockport and they were shouting of Shaz and Charlie. Carl the lad that had shagged Shaz had something on his head and it soon became clear what it was.

'Shaz we thought you'd be here, so we brought you something you left. I bet it's been draughty without them,' Carl said as he pointed to his head on which he was wearing Shaz's knickers from the night before.

All the girls started laughing as they knew what the girls had been up to but it was still funny that she'd left her knickers behind.

'I hope you've washed them?' retorted Shaz, which took the sting out of their tail. Shaz could laugh at herself and saw the humour in it.

'We tried but we couldn't get the stains out' said Steve laughing as he thought he was a bit of a comedian. But he was soon shot down in flames as Charlie chipped in.

'I hope you tried a bit harder than you did trying to get a hard on last night you floppy bastard. You were fucking useless and then you fell asleep.'

The rest of the lads just looked in amazement at Steve, then Gary spoke, 'You lying bastard you said you gave her a good seeing to and that she couldn't get enough of you.' And everyone averted their gaze towards Steve awaiting a reply.

'Well stud what happened really? Come on tell the boys and girls Stevie.' Charlie was secretly fuming and was determined to embarrass him for lying.

'Well I tried but I'd had too much to drink and...'

'And what you're a fucking light weight who can't get a hard on or was your hard on that big that all the blood rushed from your head and you passed out. Firstly you fell asleep on the toilet then fell off it and when you finally got into bed you fell asleep straight away and snored all night. In future don't fucking bullshit people, yeah, you could sleep with me I was willing but don't lie, I can't stand liars,' Charlie finished his sentence off for him as Steve just wished a hole would appear for him to fall into.

'Well she shafted you there Steve' Gary pointed out.

'Can I have my knickers back or do you want them as a memento?' Shaz asked Carl.

'You can have 'em back, I was only joking love no offence.'

'None taken, you can pay for me and Charlie to go on that big ride.'

'What?'

'As an apology you can pay for us two to go on the 'Big one' seeing as neither of us got a chance to go on a big one last night and you can both ride with us.'

'Alright Steve can pay for Charlie and I'll pay for you, alright with that Steve?' said Carl who knew Steve was scared of rides.

'I suppose I'll have to be won't I,' said a rather reluctant Steve who hated rides but had lost that much face he thought he'd better try and get some back. So they set off to get the tickets for the ride and Gary took his chance to have a word with Fay.

'How's it going Fay? You seem quiet, are you okay?'

'You would be if you'd had the 24 hours I've had.'

'Why what's gone on?'

'Well I found out I was pregnant and then goes back to the hotel and my boyfriend is only there with his knock off piece. I thought he was in London and he thought I was at home.'

'Fucking hell what did you do?'

'Nothing he's at the hotel awaiting my decision as to whether I want to know him or not.'

'Do you know what you're going to do?'

'Yeah, have him back but on my terms and if he fucks about again then it goodbye.'

'I'd have said goodbye anyway. But I suppose there's the baby to consider.'

'That's why he's getting a second chance and the fact that I do love him, even though he treats me like shit.'

'Listen I'm not just saying this but I would never do anything like that to you. I'm the one who always gets pissed around and hurt in relationships.'

'Don't worry you'll find somebody one day who will treat you right and will appreciate you for the nice bloke you are.' Then Fay kissed him on the cheek. This tender moment was interrupted by the screams from the ride, as Steve had lost all control and was whaling like a banshee,well a big girl. On the ride the two girls couldn't stop laughing at him. He was like a small girl who was locked in the ghost train. When his torture had finished they all got off the ride everyone was pointing and laughing at him.

'Shit scared of a ride and can't get a hard on not your weekend Steve is it?' giggled Charlie.

'Piss off I think I'm going to be sick'. was Steve's reply as he made his way to the toilets.

They all got back to the rest of the gang.

'Where's floppy?' asked Mandy.

'Oh, he got a nose bleed and he's gone to be sick and to see matron the big poof' answered Shaz.

Steve then emerged from the toilet looking like he'd had a tonne of flour poured on him.

'Jesus you look rough Stevo' said a shocked Gary.

'I feel fucking rough, I've just brought breakfast back up and last night's pizza.'

'Too much information son just the fact that you'd been sick would have been enough' said Cary.

'Balls to this I'm off for a lay down' and Steve walked off.

'Where's he going? He'll not get in the hotel they'll be cleaning the rooms.' Carl asked.

'Leave him he'll be back soon enough,' Gary informed them.

With that Steve just lay down on a bench and tried to get his focus and the feeling in the pit of his stomach to go away.

'You rotten cow Charlie, look at him the poor lads ill,' Mandy had a dig at Charlie.

'I couldn't give a shit he shouldn't lie about having his way with me when he didn't, serves him right.'

'I agree with you there Charlie, men who tell lies should always be made to pay,' agreed Fay to everyone's surprise.

'Well what time are you girls going home then?' asked Carl

'About four after some dinner,' Shaz answered.

'We're going in a minute as soon as Spewy gets himself together. Get back to the pub for an afternoon pint and then back around Blackpool for the Saturday night. 'Why don't you stay Shaz?'

suggested Carl.

'Where would I sleep?' asked Shaz innocently.

'You could stay with us in my room.'

'Can Charlie stay as well?' asked Shaz

'Fuck off I'm going home, I'm not staying. If you want to stay Shaz you'll be on your own. Besides how will we get home?'

'Well that's a no then Carl, sorry, I never thought about getting home tomorrow.'

'Never mind I thought…'

'We know what you thought Carl well tough,' teased Charlie

Steve then walked up and told them he felt better and they decided to go on there way.

'Right we'll be on our way then, nice to have meet you Fay,' said Gary as he kissed Fay on the cheek.

'Like wise Gary I might see you around, I'm staying tonight.'

'I hope not because I might have to say something to that dick of a boyfriend you've got.'

'Please don't if you do see us' pleaded Fay.

'I won't don't worry.'

They all kissed and shook hands and bid their farewells. Shaz got her knickers back and the boys left and the girls went for some dinner.

'He was nice Fay do I sense some regret?' asked Mandy.

'Do you know what Mandy if I wasn't pregnant and I found out what Tag was doing I would be shagging him right now he was not only gorgeous he was the most thoughtful bloke I've ever met and I would have dropped 'em for him any day knowing what I know now. And do you know what I'd have stayed the weekend with him to. But all of that is irrelevant because I am pregnant and I am with Tag.'
Everyone just stood with open mouths in amazement at what Fay had just said until Mandy broke the silence with a typically funny line.
'Well who's for chips?' And they all went for something to eat...

Tag was back at the hotel thinking about booking the tickets home for the next day and was planning to book a table at a restaurant but he could do neither as Fay hadn't given him her decision. He only hoped that she would see that he was genuine in his plea that he wanted not just the baby but her as well. He decided to go for a walk and buy a paper and try to relax, and wait and wait and wait...

The boys got to the stadium in plenty of time and the Aussies couldn't believe it, they were actually at Wembley. They got off the tube and then were greeted with the sight of the half a mile walk down Wembley way and the volume of people was something they hadn't seen before. Then they could see the twin towers in the distance. The only time they had seen this magnificent, iconic landmark was from 12,000 miles away on television at four in the morning watching the Challenge Cup Final and seeing which lucky countryman had the fortune to play at this venue of venues. They got their cameras out and were clicking away to capture the memories they would hold for a lifetime and the photos they could show their unborn kids in years to come.

Now Eddie had given them all their tickets and none of them had looked at the seat row or number, this included Eddie himself. So when they started the assent to their seats they went up the stairs as you always do at Wembley to get to your seat. But then there was another flight of stairs then another.

'Fucking hell what are we sat in the blimp? The oxygen is getting thinner Eddie I don't think I'm going to make it,' said Tosser.

'Well you lot said get the cheaper tickets they're all the same,' replied Eddie who was beginning to wonder how many more stairs they had to climb.

Then they came to the entrance number 218 upper.

'This is it' shouted Eddie with relief.

'Thank fuck for that' a few of them said in unison.

They all got through the entrance and they could now see the green grass and the magnificent stadium before them. There is no finer sight than that of a sporting event waiting to happen, the band on the pitch the colours of both supporters, the atmosphere it was just magic. Then came the shock as they asked the steward where they were sat and he pointed them in the right direction.

'This isn't that bad Eddie' said Skip.

'We haven't got to our seats yet, what row are we on?' asked Tosser.

'Let's look here, Jesus Christ it's row Z upper, we're on the fucking roof,' Trevor blurted out.

'Yes you're right it does appear we are on the roof,' agreed Eddie.

'The shittest seats we've ever had Eddie,' Jonesy chipped in.

'Well you boys did say get the cheapest and that's what you got.' Eddie was laughing to himself and they were right the seats were shit if an up and under was put up you lost the flight of the ball because of the stadium roof.

'It's not that bad lads come on let's start joining in with the singing,' said Skip trying to take the pressure off Eddie. Although Eddie was feeling no pressure. The band struck up and they played the traditional Wembley anthem 'Abide with me' and a few of the boys had a tear in their eye and a lump in the throat and these were tough blokes as tough as they come. The Aussie boys didn't understand the tradition of it all. The two Americans had got lost and hadn't yet made it, they were still down Wembley way. And then the two teams came out of the tunnel and as soon as the crowd caught a glimpse of their heroes the whole place erupted and nearly lifted the roof off (which would have been handy, they could see everything then), now the Aussies knew what all the fuss was about, the noise was deafening. The national anthem was played and the players were introduced to the dignitaries and then the teams sped off one by one as their names were announced to huge cheers and went to the end their supporters were, to begin the game. The two captains tossed the coin and they were away ready to go.

Whilst all this was going on back home Pete was putting his feet up and was having a drink to quell the pain of not being there and then the phone went. Pete thought he'd ignore it and as Sally was out it might be an emergency and surely the game was about to start no one would be ringing from London. How wrong could he be it was Tosser who had been assigned to find a phone and give Pete an update of the days events.

'Pete it's Tosser, great atmosphere Pete we've all had loads to drink and now we're going to watch the game shame you're missing it mate, it's just not the same on the telly…'

'Fuck off Tosser you twat' and Pete hung up but it was too late Tosser had already done the same and was on his way back to his seat to tell the others and he was laughing all the way. The game got under way and it was the usual Wigan final. Totally dominant and Castleford could only hope to keep the pace but as it had been for years the inevitable was going to happen and after Wigan had taken an early twelve point lead some of the boys went to get some beers. The Aussies were still mesmerised by the whole thing and couldn't wait to tell everyone back home how cool it was. They didn't care who won they were just bothered about being there. The crowd noise never waned and the atmosphere was at fever pitch all of the first half. The good thing was Castleford were giving as good as they got and just when you thought the crowd couldn't lift anymore they did and nearly lifted the roof off the stadium as Castleford scored. The whole place went crazy as all the neutral fans were rooting for Cas' as they all hated Wigan. Wigan were full time and had all the best players and all the money and were probably the most hated team in the land.

The hooter went for half time and everyone went for a walk either to get a drink or to go to the toilet.

Back in Hull Pete's phone had been ringing on and off for the past five minutes. It was Sally trying to get in touch with him, but Pete wasn't answering. Finally after the tenth call he answered it.

'Look fuck off, you're not fucking funny, you're a bunch of childish silly bastards and I'm going to flatten the next one of you that rings. What have you got to say about that then?'

'I only rang to say take the chicken out of the fridge and put it on timer for two hours for tonight's tea,' said Sally.

'Oh Sally sorry I thought it was those soft twats pissing around again. they even rang at kick off.'

'Look relax and forget about them, I'll be home in an hour, see you love.'

'Yeah see you.'

The phone went again and this time Pete answered it straight away thinking it was Sally, but no this time it was Jonesy and Trev.

'Pete, Pete, Pete you're missing it mate it's fantastic here great seats, just seen the Prime Minister in the toilets that's how good the seats are. Anyway got to go Michael Parkinson is calling us over, we're coming Parky you just wait there, impatient get, see you Pete.'

Pete had hung up straight away and sat and laughed to himself, what a bunch of shithouses but deep down it was all part of it and it wasn't meant to be malicious, it was just banter between mates. The two of them thought he was still there and were laughing to themselves. They went and sat with the rest of the lads and had a half time beer and told them what they'd said to Pete. Eddie was feeling sorry for Pete but at the same time loving the humour of it all, at how cruel they could be to one of their mates.

'Why don't you give him a bit of peace lads?'

'Yeah we will Eddie, until full time and then until we get back to the hotel. Piss off he would be the first to rub it in. he's worse than all of us put together,' said Tosser.

'We haven't forgot the time he got into that club and we never. He came out with a t-shirt the works and never stopped going on about it all the way home from Blackpool,' Skip joined in.

'Talking of Blackpool what about them crafty cows going behind our backs,' laughed Jonesy.

'I know why do it in secret, I'm not bothered if they want to go to Blackpool and I don't know anyone else who would be,' said Skip.

'I think they thought we'd all kick off if we knew' Trev chipped in trying to sound like he was as surprized as anyone.

'Well I hope they haven't bumped into Tag and his bird Suzuki or else the illuminations will be on early, the night sky will be alight if Fay sees him.' Tosser said this really hoping that they had bumped into each other and that Tag had finally dropped himself in the shit. The boys finished their beers and regained their seats on the roof at high altitude for the second half...

The girls had been to the funfair and had eaten and had a couple of drinks. They had bought presents for the kids and were ready to go home. The bus was due to pick them up at four and the time was now a quarter to as they got into the hotel foyer they could see Tag nursing a cold cup of coffee. It was his fifth and he was just sat staring into thin air. He didn't even notice the noise the girls were making he seemed in a world of his own. He had just spent the longest couple of hours of his life sat thinking yet again what a prick he'd been and how badly he'd treated Fay. It was Shaz who broke him from his daydream.

'Tag we're going now.'

'What? Where?' mumbled a startled Tag.

'We're going home are you coming to see Fay?'

'Er, yeah where is she?' he got up and then realised what was going on, it was decision time. His heart was pounding she was going home, Shaz has said it 'we're going now' we're, meaning all of them. Tag virtually ran out of the bar and nearly fell over the bags in the foyer.

'Fay wait don't go I've sorted the room everything, I've booked a table for tonight and got tickets for tomorrow. Please don't go' begged Tag looking quite the pathetic sight really seeing as 24 hours later he was Mr Cool with a lady on his arm about to have a night of passion behind Fay's back. Now he just looked desperate, which of course is what he was desperate for Fay to have him back.

'Well Tag I've come to a decision, and the decision is that I'm going to stay and sort things out…' Tag ran forward and hugged her, but she pushed him off and continued 'but believe me Tag things have got to change no more going out with the lads all the time and no more pissing around with other women. You have got to grow up, because we are going to have a baby and that is the only reason you've got away with this for now. Do you understand me?' Fay said with some assertion which surprised everyone including Fay.

'Yes I do and I've been doing a lot of thinking and I want us to get married, what do you think?'

'No chance Tag ask me again when the baby's born and we've been at it for a couple of months and I'll think about it.'

Which was not the answer he was looking for but he was up shit creek. He thought she would be all over him and accept but Fay had changed in the last couple of hours and was now finding a new strength and wasn't prepared to cut Tag any slack at all. She had been chatted up on several occasions by a cool good looking man and was feeling wanted again and she had found new confidence in that. The boot was on the other foot and instead of Fay doing all the chasing it was now Tag who was desperately clinging on to their relationship.

The sound of the horn from the bus could be heard and the girls all got their bags and put them on the bus. They had the same driver as they'd had coming and he was trying not to get them going.

'Now then Humphrey did all the kings horses and all the kings men manage to put you back together again?' Shaz shouted out.

'Get your hole filled last night did you?' Humphrey came back with as quick as a flash.

'Oh very quick Humphrey very quick' Shaz was shocked at his response, 'Yes I did get my hole filled, did you get to fill a hole though?'

'Well if it was as big as yours I'd have fell in' this left Shaz gobsmacked, much to Charlie's amusement.

'Bet you didn't lose your knickers Humphrey though did you?' Charlie added pointing at Shaz, who wasn't enjoying suddenly being the butt of the joke.

'Cheers Charlie tell the whole fucking world.'

'Well leave the poor bloke alone, he's beating you hands down anyway' Charlie added as she gave Humphrey a little wink, which brought a smile to his face.

The bus was loaded and they all went to say goodbye to Fay and wish her all the best and gave Tag some advice.

'Don't fuck this up you useless twat, we've all got our eyes on you and if you piss her about you'll have us lot to answer to got it?' Mandy was spokeswomen.

'Yes I get the message loud and clear' Tag replied.

'Take care Fay and we'll have a night at mine next week and have a chat,' Clare said cuddling Fay.

'I tell you what we could have a girls night once a fortnight at each others houses, are you all up for that?' announced Mandy.

'I think we should have an annual trip to somewhere just us girls and this time no secrets,' said Cary who'd already told Trev anyway.

'Great idea Cary, we'll sort it out,' Sue agreed.

They all started to get on the bus when Fay got hold of both Shaz and Charlie and apologised for being a bit of a cow. She now realised it was Tag hanging around them and not the other way around and that they were only single girls out for a good time. In fact all the women had warmed to the two girls and no longer saw them as a threat to them. As Charlie had pointed out 'why would I want a married man when I could have some young randy hunk without a beer belly.'

The girls got on the bus and waved at Tag and Fay who just stood on the pavement until the bus turned the corner and went out of sight. The two of them stood silent for what seemed like an eternity like two strangers who'd never even met. Neither of them knew what to say to each other, all the years they'd been together and neither of them knew what to do or say. Tag broke the silence.

'Shall we go inside and I'll show you the room?'

'If you like' Fay's reply was quite frosty.

'Look I know I've been a prick and a fucking idiot Fay but can you please talk to me in a civil manner.'

'Have you swallowed a dictionary Tag?'

'Look I'm trying my best here.'

'Sorry but I'm still pretty angry with you and it may take some time to go. 24 hours ago I got the news that I was pregnant and then I find you with a bit on the side, it's all a bit much to take in.'

'I know, I know and I'm really sorry for that but I can't change the past, I can only make the future better.'

Fay picked up the big teddy up the girls had got her, as she'd left it in the hotel doorway.

'Is that yours?' asked Tag.

'No it's the baby's, the girls won it for us.'

'That was good of them.'

'Yeah it was wasn't it, they really are a great bunch, we've had a great time, apart from the other things that had gone on.'

They eventually got to the room and Tag opened the door and put the bags in that he'd carried for Fay.

'By the way this wasn't the room that me and Suki had'

'I know Tag you're stupid but not that stupid.'

'Do you like it?' Tag was referring to the room he'd arranged flowers and there were a couple of presents he'd wrapped himself, and he'd really made an effort. In the flowers there was a note which read 'I'm so sorry for the hurt I've caused you it will not happen again, all my love Tag'. Fay then burst into tears and Tag held her and hugged her. Then Tag started to cry as Fay asked him what she had done to make him look elsewhere and was she really that bad a person that he had to try and find someone else.

'Look it has nothing to do with you Fay, it was me I was an immature prick who thought that he was a big man getting off with women. That I could be classed as someone people thought was a stud. But do you know what I've been blown out more times than a candle on a birthday cake.'

'So how long have you been seeing Suki?'

'Look it's in the past now I don't really want to talk about it,' Tag tried to shy away from the question unsuccessfully.

'No Tag I need to know, and why did you find the need to look elsewhere. We do everything in the bedroom don't we? So then why? I keep it interesting don't I?'

'Yeah you're great but I suppose it was a case of the grass is always greener on the other side. I started to talk to her about my overtime sheet and you must admit she is pretty nice. Then I said I bet your boyfriend gets jealous you working with all these men, and she said she didn't have a boyfriend and I asked her out never thinking that she'd say yes. Actually I saw her at LA LA's and we arranged to meet, after that I tried a line and she took it.'

'Oh Tag, very Mills and Boon, and didn't she ask if you had a girlfriend?'

'Well yes and I said, 'No' and we went out for a drink and it went from there and then I brought her here to have a weekend with her.'

'You mean a dirty weekend?'

'If I'm being honest yes, a dirty weekend. You see we never had sex and this was the time I suppose. You see I'd never met anyone like her, she wasn't easy she had a bit of class and was sort of a challenge, I thought she was out of my league so she was a bit of a trophy I suppose - look what I can pull, kind of thing.'

'So I'm easy then, is that it?' said an offended Fay.

'No you know what I mean, we did do it on our third date after a week. You know what I mean?'

'Well Tag I met someone last night who wanted me and was willing to take me out baby and all. And do you know what I did? I told him I was with someone and that we were going to have a baby. But I was tempted Tag, boy was I tempted. How would that have made you feel Tag?'

'I don't know, probably angry.'

'You got it Tag, angry and let down and hurt and just you keep that thought in your mind and multiply it by a hundred because that's how I felt yesterday.'

'I'm sorry Fay, look can we start afresh?'

'We can when I've finished with what I have to say to you and that might take a day, a week or a month I don't know, I'm that mixed up at the moment. It will take time Tag, and only then will we be able to try again.'

'Who was he then?' asked a jealous Tag.

'Why are you jealous? His name was Gary and we've just bumped into him at the fair this afternoon. Do you know what Tag I wanted to last night because he was gorgeous, but I had principles and thought about you. Do you see the difference between me and you?'

'Yes, you've made your point Fay and I am jealous.'

'Why? Because nothing happened, we only talked for a brief while. Do you see how I feel? You were at it for what was it, three months, behind my back. So why do you feel jealous?'

'Probably because I really care about you and I love you.'

'Good, because I love you, God knows why, you treat me like shit and take the piss out of me.'

'Like I said I've seen the error of my ways and I'm going to put it right.'

'Well Tag, time will tell because words are cheap.'

'I know actions speak louder than words and you'll see I'm going to change.'

The two of them then held each other and cried some more..

CHAPTER 10
ARE YOU HUNGRY?

Back at Wembley the game had finished, petering out in fact as Wigan had blasted Cas 'off the park'. It was another trophy for the Wigan machine to lift to a half-empty stadium as a lot of fans were getting fed up of seeing them win everything. Most of the Castleford fans stayed to cheer their team on their lap of honour. The rest of the fans, the neutrals, they had long gone most of them were on weekend trips and they had gone to catch the tubes that would take them back into London. The Dockers lot all saw the trophy being presented as the Aussie boys wanted to see it and then they rang Pete for one last time and they were on their way. They hit the queue and had a bit of banter with the police who were on horseback. The coppers, by their own admission loved policing the Challenge Cup Final as they never got any trouble as the fans all mingled with each other, and although they all had a drink they always behaved themselves.

The queue was soon sorted out as train after train came and soon got rid of the crowds. The lads were going to head for Baker Street and the Globe pub opposite Madame Tussauds. This pub was usually full of rugby league fans and the day would continue. The tube was packed and very noisy as the northerners chatted and burst into song whilst their southern counterparts didn't make eye contact with anyone. Suprizingly they got to Baker street by quarter past five and had a couple of drinks and then some of them made their way back to the hotel. It was mainly the two students who had arranged to meet their Swedish dates from the night before, and the rest, about eight of them went to the all you can eat pizza restaurant across the road from the Globe. Now Skip, Tosser, Jonesy and Trev were not small men and if you added Matt, Daz, Damo and Jonno you had the biggest nightmare a pizza cook could have if there was an all you can eat offer on. The offer ended at 6.30 and the time was now 5.40.the waitress came and asked what the order would be and all of them said the all you can eat, all except Matt he just had to be different.

'I'm starving can I have two of the all you can eat please?'

'You will only need one sir it's all you can eat,' the waitress stressed thinking she was being informative and totally misunderstanding the fact that he was messing her around.

'But I'm starving, I'll have two,' insisted Matt.

'But sir you can't have two, you can only have one.'

'Why you don't know how hungry I am and how much I can eat.' All the others were hiding their faces as they were laughing but biting their lips. The poor waitress kept trying.

'It's 'all you can eat' sir, you will only need one.'

'Will one be enough, I mean I'm really hungry?'

'Yes one will be enough it is 'all you can eat' sir.'

'Well I suppose so then, one will have to do but you don't know how hungry I am.'

'You just keep going up to get more if you're still hungry sir.'

'Alright then one it is please.'

So every time a pizza was brought out it vanished. There were five varieties and every time pizza was brought out they took it and seeing as there was no one else in the place the boys took full advantage.

In fact the poor waitress should have known something was afoot when as they walked in Matt turned the open sign around to closed and said 'you'll be busy with us'. Every time the pizza ran out they asked for more, which was getting on the manager's nerves. And the more they shouted for the pizzas, the less toppings were being put on them, so it ended up with just bread and a bit of tomato puree and a bit of cheese.

All in all fifteen pizzas were eaten which sounds a lot but some of them were pretty poor excuses for pizzas. When the lads had all had their fill of food, they gave the waitress a big tip and then it was back to the hotel to get ready for the big Saturday night out. They flagged down two taxis and made their way back to the hotel. They started to talk about the two students and what they would do to them if they brought back the two Swedish girls.

'We'll have to be all nice and then wait while they get into their room and then bingo, bombard them with fire extinguishers,' said Tosser.

'Yeah and have you seen those icemakers in the corridors, we can fill the ice buckets and chuck all that in as well,' added Jonno.

'We'll see, why don't we just leave 'em to it lads?' asked Skip.

'Fuck off Skip, if they get cocky which they will, then they've had it. That's if they bring them back to the hotel that is,' Tosser said with a real determination to get the students.

'That's if they actually met two birds last night, I mean they could have made the whole story up,' said Tom.

'I don't think they did, you know they looked pretty pleased with themselves, and if they were telling the truth they are one pair of jammy bastards,' said Skip.

'I know how many trips I've been on and not so much as a

'Barclays bank' from a bird,' added Tosser.

They arrived at the hotel and paid the driver. They all then decided to order mini cabs for the night out as it would be far cheaper. Once the cabs were booked, they all went into the bar where only Eddie and a few of the others were.

'I've told everyone 7.30 in the Clipper, alright Skip and we'll set off from there,' Eddie informed Skip.

'Great Eddie, then it's on to the old George in Bethnal Green isn't it?'

'Yep, that's where the action is tonight, it's usually packed with everyone from Hull and the bands they have on are top notch - and they open 'til 12.30 so we can get back here and have a nightcap.'

'Spot on Eddie, we'll see you in the Clipper at half seven then.'

Then Skip and the rest of them all went up to their rooms to dress to impress. The order of the day was suits and ties. They all got showered and splashed on the old Blue Stratos and they were ready to hit the night in the knowledge that some lucky cow was going to get lucky that night. This knowledge was totally unfounded as no one ever got a bird, the only bird anyone had ever pulled was coated in a secret combination of herbs and spices and deep fried. It was 10 out of 10 for effort but they always went home alone, which was great as they all had a laugh but most were married and it wasn't worth it. A quick shag wasn't worth swapping for a night of laughs. A woman would get in the way if they managed to get one. There was more fun to be had taking the piss out of each other.

The two students Grant and Mike had already gone out to meet Ulrika and Anna and had told Eddie that they would be back tonight but they might join the rest of them in the George depending on how things panned out. Eddie thought this was extremely funny as the two of them were showing that they weren't as naive as everyone thought they were. But to bring the girls to a pub to show them off would be suicidal as the lads would rip them to pieces, and Eddie was trying to warn them that this wouldn't be wise thus the reason he told them to swap rooms.

As they all began to arrive at the Clipper the anticipation of the night out was reaching fever pitch, even the old guard were excited and were willing to give up the cheap beer deal they were still enjoying. The manager was over the moon as he had a full pub for the second night and money was coming over the till in its droves. Eddie counted heads and ordered the correct number of cabs from the local mini cab place, as Skip hadn't ordered enough. The taxis were ordered for 8.15 so they still had twenty minutes of cheap beer to get in. Some of the locals had taken to the lads bringing a bit of atmosphere to the place which was dead from Friday to Monday, they even had a bit of a sing song which none of the usual customers would ever have done. The manager loved it having a vibrant pub with atmosphere but it was only going to be short lived as he knew that once they all went it would be back to the old boring lot who hardly spoke.

'What time are you open tomorrow mate?' asked Skip.

'Twelve, why?' replied the manager.

'We'll probably pop in for a drink before we get on our way if we get the time.'

'Great you boys do that, it's been great having you here, not only for business but for the crack.'

'Tell you what come over to our hotel for a beer with your staff if you like, we'll be back there at about one.'

'I might just do that, thanks.'

Then the horns sounded and the first of the cabs had arrived and they started to get into them group by group and then on to Bethnal Green. Now mini cabs are a totally different kettle of fish to your black cab, they usually have a set price and the more jobs they get in the more they earn. The boys soon found this out when they were up kerbs going through red lights and generally knowing what it felt like to be in wacky races with Dick Dastardly.

They all eventually reached the venue and topping the bill was a Terence Trent D'Arby look a like. Firstly though it was one last call to Pete to say what a great time they were having. Pete was sat on the settee with Sally and he'd taken the phone off the hook, so that had pissed on their chips and after about ten tries they gave up. They looked in the pub and it was fairly empty so they decided to have a couple in a pub down the road, so they all went in and ordered their drinks. At the other end of the bar there was this stunning long legged beauty sipping on a cocktail and all the older crew were besotted.

'Fucking hell, look at her,' drooled Doug.

'I know she could rub me down any day' said Bert.

'The legs on her she could wrap them round my face anytime Bertie boy.'

'Excuse me, can you tell me where the toilets are?' Skip asked the barman. He pointed Skip in the direction of the woman. So Skip walked past the woman and noticed she had an Adam's apple the size of a melon. So he couldn't wait to get back and tell the others. He finished his wee and rushed back to the others.

'You won't believe it, she's gorgeous Doug and I think she fancies you, mind you if she wrapped her legs around you where would you put her cock?'

Doug looked at Skip with a puzzled expression, as did Bert.

'What do you mean?'

'She's a fucking bloke in a dress you idiot - you want to see the Adam's apple on it,' Skip explained.

'Fuck off,' the two older men exclaimed.

'Go and look for yourselves, she's a tranny.'

So Doug and Bert braced themselves and pretended to go to the toilet. They went passed and stared at the woman/man and she/he stared back and they proceeded to the toilet. With that the door opened and in walked the woman/man, hitched her tight dress up and started to pee much to the astonishment of the two men who thought they'd lived a bit.

'Evening boys. You're not from 'round here are you?'

Bert and Doug just shook their heads with their mouths open looking like two scared schoolboys.

'Well you might get lucky if you hang around. I've got a couple of friends who are meeting me here in a bit,' and she/he patted them both on the head after she'd put her cock away and pulled her dress down. They tried to look cool about the situation as they fled the toilet and virtually ran back to the group.

'Well am I right?' said Skip.

'Too fucking right, drink up I think we've pulled, she/he's got a couple of mates coming and I'm not hanging around, she/he fucking fancies us and said we might be lucky if we stick around. Fuck that she/he's got a cock an half on her/him.' Doug couldn't get his words out quickly enough as he and Bert drank up and fled the pub in the direction of the George. All the others burst out laughing and couldn't believe it. This soon turned to panic as the 'lady' in question came over and asked if anyone fancied a dance. They all drank up and the pub emptied faster than you could say Jacqueline flash. The tranny in question had of course done it on purpose but crikey, did she put the willies up them so to speak. They all ran up to the George and weren't bothered if there was no one in.

The George was now fairly full and the number of familiar faces made it feel like they were back in Hull. They had a tale to tell much to the amusement of the landlord of the George.

'So you went into Davina's did you, well that tranny is Dave and he owns the place, they come from far and wide to drink in there. Great atmosphere in there, he loves to wind blokes up does old Dave and by the looks of you lot he's had a field day,' said Tony.

'Here Mike, they've just done what you did a few years ago, they went into Davinas, only difference is that Mike pulled.'

'Fuck off. I pulled a muscle getting out of there, I've never moved so fast, one of the bastards grabbed me arse,' said Mike, who was the landlord of their local back in Hull and he had his usual entourage with him. Mike Shoebottom was his name and he was a great and popular character who would do anything for anyone, plus he was a shrewd bugger when it came to running a pub. 'Shoey' knew his stuff about getting punters in and keeping them in. In fact he was better at socialising and mixing than pulling a pint. He usually left the pulling to his long-suffering wife. Mike would sometimes have a couple of Sunday lunches just to be sociable with his customers. This had a bit of a down side as he was quite a big fella and was prone to falling asleep, sometimes whilst driving his car, which would shit anybody up who he gave a lift to. But the other thing Shoey was good at was belting out a tune and he always did a turn at the George every year without fail. Well he did one song, usually 'New York, New York', which he still didn't know the words to, but every year he got up and with his beer mat in hand with the words on it he would sing his heart out. Mike was good friends with the owner of the George and it was through him the place was packed every year when the final was on. It was quite early and the band was setting up and the place was starting to fill up nicely and the atmosphere was good. People were talking about the game and what they'd been up to and what they were doing the next day...

Across town Grant and Mike were in Chinatown having a banquet with the two Swedish girls who were looking stunning. The two boys had been to the toilets and talked about how much sexier they were. The night before had been a bit of a blur as they'd been drinking all day and although they weren't drunk, the fact was that now they hadn't had much to drink, they realised how lucky they'd been to meet them.

The two lads didn't want to take them back to their hotel as the lads wouldn't leave them alone so they tried to persuade the girls to go back to the girls' hotel again. This didn't work as the girls had set their hearts on seeing Canary Wharf at night as the two students had told them how beautiful it was. They carried on with their Chinese and then went onto Leicester Square and Covent Garden for a couple of drinks. Grant said he had a bit of indigestion and went to the nearest chemist. He was of course lying he wanted some condoms for the night's forthcoming sexual conquests. Why he had to lie about this was anyone's guess as the girls knew what was going to happen later on, it was no secret.

Back in Blackpool Tag and Fay had got ready for their night out, which was going to consist of a quiet Italian and a walk on the sea front. The Italian restaurant was right next to Gary and the lads' hotel and as soon as they walked past the hotel they bumped into Gary and the lads.

'Hiya Fay,' said Dave, Steve, Alex and Carl.

'Hiya lads going on the pull? Where's Gary?' and as she uttered the words Gary appeared and stood staring at Fay and Tag. Tag stared back and there was a silence, which seemed to last forever until Fay finally broke it.

'Do you two know each other?'

'Not really Fay,' Tag said first.

'Well we did speak last night didn't we mate in the Tower bar?' Gary replied.

'I don't remember,' said a puzzled Tag.

'You do, you thought I was chatting your girlfriend up at the bar and I said if she were mine I wouldn't leave her for one minute.'

'I think I do remember now,' said Tag starting to recall the situation.

'Well mate, it seems I had a pop at both your ladies last night because the same applies here if she were mine I wouldn't do what you did in a million years, she's too good for you mate, you don't deserve her,' Gary was getting irate.

'Calm down Gary, there's no need,' said Carl.

'Leave him he's right I have been a prick but I'm trying to put things right,' Tag said sheepishly as he knew that Gary was right.

'Well make sure you do mate, make sure you do.'

'Oh he will Gary he will,' Fay interjected.

'Good have a good life Fay and don't let him piss you around,' and then Gary walked off with his mates trying to catch him up.

'Who was that?' asked Tag.

'Some really nice guy I met last night and chatted to for a long time about things.'

'About us?'

'Yes about us, if there had been no us and no baby, I would have probably shagged him Tag.'

'Oh!' said a shocked Tag.

'Yeah, oh! How does that make you feel Tag? Gut wrenching isn't it well think on, think on. Now let's get some food, I'm starving.'

They both went into the Italian and tried to have a good night as well as talking things through. Tag was taken aback by Fay's admission and didn't know how to handle it, she had become assertive and really confident over night. It appeared she was wearing the trousers now and it felt strange to him, the worm had definitely turned. Fay on the other hand had decided that she was going to be as hard as nails from now on with Tag as this seemed the only way he would take her seriously. Tag was still feeling like a shit for what he had done and Fay sensed this and was playing it for all it was worth. The night would be an interesting one.

In the George the night was now getting a lot more livelier. There was a queue to get in, and the place was jumping as the D.J. had started to play the music. It wasn't long before the lads realised that Thommo and Gaz had been quiet and they soon started to grill them about what they'd been up to that afternoon.

'So then where did you two go this afternoon?' enquired Skip.

'Don't fucking ask,' snapped Thommo.

'Oooh! touchy bastard, Thommo what's wrong with you then?'

'Ask that twat there,' Thommo pointed at Gaz, who was smiling at this point.

'Well Gaz where did you end up?'

'We sold our tickets to those two yanks.'

'Yeah and did they get excited by the game they loved it. We fucked them off in the end all that whooping and that, embarrassing,' interrupted Tosser .

'Yeah Tosser let him tell the story, carry on Gaz' Skip said dying to know what had gone on.

'Well we asked the guy at the hotel desk where the best place to get a massage would be. He asked where we were heading and he told us this place in Soho. It took ages to find it but after we'd asked someone, it was just a door that lead into this stairwell and at the top was this big reception and bar. So we went up and asked how much a massage would be.'

'Well how much was a massage?' asked Jonesy.

'£30, which we thought better than watching Wigan hammer Cas.'

'Fucking £30 for a rub, did that include extras' said Jonesy who was now getting quite excited.

'Look Jonesy let him tell the story and you can quiz him after. Carry on Gaz,' Skip said again.

'Anyway we decided to go ahead with it and this big guy took our money and told us to wait. He then said if we wanted extras then we should negotiate a price with the girls.'

'Yeah, then he tried to charge us £10 for a pint,' interrupted Thommo.

'I thought you didn't want to talk about it Thommo?'

'Well you'll see why in a minute.'

'Right, I'll carry on, so we waited a bit and then these two girls came in with really short tight uniforms on, both blonde and both stunners. They lead us to this room and told us to take our gear off and leave it on the chair.' Gaz had everyone hanging on to his every word.

'Yeah and I had this twat in my ear telling me whatever I did don't let them con me into any extras,' Thommo fumed.

'Anyway Thommo's bird came in and took him into a room and mine told me to put on a towel and lie on the table face down. Well I had a job trying not to get too excited, I mean that would have been embarrassing shooting my load as soon as she touched me.'

'Well I made like I wanted a piss and had a sneaky wank and even

I had to stop myself when she touched me,' Thommo exclaimed getting excited at reliving the day's events.

'So she starts rubbing me all over and then straddles me and I can feel she's got no knickers on and I can feel it rubbing up and down me. Next she turns me over and says I can play with her if I like but no poking. Well, this was tough, my knob was as hard as it had ever been and then she starts massaging my front and keeps touching my dick on purpose and then she gets on top of me and rubs my chest.'

'Jesus, I would have whitewashed the ceiling by now, how did you cope with that?' asked Skip.

'I thought of you Skip with no clothes on, complete turn off.'

'Cheeky bastard.'

'Anyway she was at this for about three-quarters of an hour and then she eventually uttered the words, 'Do you want any extras?' which included finger pie and full access to her tits and a wank.'
Gaz then went silent and had a sip of his drink to build up the impact and suspense.

'Well, tell us what happened?' they were all shouting.

'I'll tell you when I get back from the toilet, I'm busting for a piss.'

'Come on Thommo what happened - is he lying?'

'No straight up that was what happened to me as well but because I'd had a wank already I could enjoy it a bit more and then that twat did...'

'I'm back, now where was I?' Gaz ran back not letting Thommo steal his moment.

'She's just asked you if you wanted extras,' Skip helped him out with the point he'd got to before he went to the toilet.

'Oh yeah, well I know I'd been lecturing Thommo about temptation and that. Well Thommo left his jeans in the room I was in as a precaution so that he wasn't tempted and well....'

'I'll take over from here he took my money and got himself some extras, didn't you Gaz, the lousy bastard got himself tossed off on my money.'

Everyone burst out laughing as did Gaz but Thommo wasn't seeing the funny side of it.

'Look, look let me explain I couldn't help myself and the best bit was when Thommo. Can I tell them Thommo?' Gaz looked for Thommo's approval to carry on with the story.

'You might as well you shithouse, I suppose it's quite funny and I'll see the funny side of it maybe by Christmas.'

'Come on what happen next?' They were all shouting.

'Well I lasted about two minutes, tops. I was fingering her and licking her tits and she just started pulling my dick really slowly with her oiled up hands. And I couldn't hold on much longer and I came all over my towel and my chest and then I just lay there as she packed up her stuff and left. Well two minutes later Thommo comes bursting in and asks where his money is and he's going through his jeans when I say 'I've spent it' and pointed at my spunky chest.'

'What did you do then Thommo?' asked Jonesy.

'Well I had a tenner left so I rushed into the room and asked what I could get for a tenner? And she just looked and packed up her oils and fucked off.'

'I have said I was sorry and I've given you your money back Thommo. What else do you want from me.'

'I know but the fucking earache you were giving me about the temptation and that and then you fold and give in straight away.'

All the lads were in fits of laughter, this was priceless.

'You two are fucking unbelievable, you paid £80 for a rub and a wank, unreal you must have money to burn. I'd have put her in the wank bank and tugged myself silly back at the hotel all afternoon,' proclaimed Tosser.

'I tell you what everyone of you would have done the same, and don't worry it's up there mate and I can recall it at any time. In fact I'm getting all hard thinking about it now.'

'I must say it was a great hour apart from the last five minutes, the girls were top notch and knew what they were doing the crafty cows,' Thommo added. 'Even though I didn't get the extras, anyway you're getting the beer all night so get to the bar.' Thommo pointed to the bar.

Gaz did as he was told and within five minutes the whole bar knew the story and Thommo had people coming up to him and laughing. Thommo actually took it in good faith.

'I tell you what Thommo you've had a shit weekend so far. Had the shits all day yesterday and then someone spent your money on a wank, have you broken some mirrors?' Skip pointed out with delight.

'Look Skip I'm going to enjoy the rest of the weekend. I reckon somebody spiked my drink yesterday. You don't shit that much from a dodgy curry that I do know.'

'You can if you get food poisoning, what curry was it?' Trev was trying to get Thommo off the subject seeing as it was him who spiked his drink.

'Chicken madras Trev, why?'

'There you go then if the chicken wasn't cooked properly you would have got food poisoning.'

'But I'm alright now, I can't work it out.'

'Well stop trying to and just enjoy yourself if you feel alright then what's the problem.' Tosser had got him off the subject much to Trev's relief.

'I suppose so right let's get stuck in to the beer,' agreed Thommo as he drank a couple of lagers and forgot about the traumas of the weekend so far.

The locals were loving the fact the place was packed to the rafters and they didn't seem to mind that it was taking ages to get served at the bar, and that was with Tony putting on extra staff. The pub was bouncing bringing back memories of yesteryear when from Thursday to Sunday it was chocka block. Now it was barely half full unless they had a good band on with a bit of a following. The old guard were deep in discussion about the usual subject that the current team wouldn't have beaten their team and that things weren't as good as they used to be. Even the music was shit yet it never stopped them enjoying it although you wouldn't have thought so. Skip came over for his usual chat and to take the piss out of the oldies although they didn't know he was winding them up.

'Tell you what Bert the games not what it was is it?' Skip started.

'You're right there Skip it was better in my day' agreed Bert.

'No I meant it's better now Bert, faster more exciting even the kits are better and the boots and the tracksuits.'

'You're talking out of your arse there Skip. Here Doug have you heard this twat saying the games better now than it used to be.'

'Who said it's better now?'

'Skip did.'

'Well it is, it's faster, tougher you have to be fitter the lot. There's more skill involved the lot.'

'Bollocks, Skip bollocks you're talking rubbish.'

Doug was getting irate which is what Skip wanted.

'Tell you what I bet in your day you wouldn't have lived with us in a match, we would have been too fast for you' Skip continued.

'You young 'uns think you know it all'

'Tell you what Eddie can settle this, he's seen both eras. Eddie who would have won in a match us or the old guard?'

'Well you because the oldies would be too busy trying to kill you and you lot don't give penalties away.'

'Cheers Eddie this is the last trip of yours we'll be coming on' said Doug.

'Good I've been trying to piss you off for years Doug' and with that Eddie walked off leaving the two old blokes dumbfounded.

'He's only kidding Doug and so are you, what other trip could you go on where you get beer for a quid a bottle and then get the chance to get off with a tranny. I bet you and Bert will be back in there before the nights out,' said Skip as he trotted off laughing to himself as he joined the others he told them he'd wound up the old coffin dodgers and as per usual they had fell for it. Doug was fuming, but then Bert pointed out that he was only having a joke with them. Then Skip came back over and shook Doug's hand and said, 'Got you again you old bastard, it's a good job you're not a fish Doug you take the bait every time. Mind you I still think we would have beaten you lot and I think you and Bert would have tapped off in that pub.' Skip then smiled and went.

'Piss off you cheeky get,' laughed Doug.

Skip returned to the rest of the lads who were by now quite merry and it was only 9.30. There were a few locals who used the pub all the time and they were getting on in years and it was one of their birthdays. Enid was 64 and the D.J. announced it on the mic and the full pub sang happy birthday to her. She got up on the stage and the landlord gave her a cake and some flowers and the whole place cheered. Enid then went and sat back down with her best friend Dora who she'd known for years. The boys all chipped in and bought the two of them a couple of port and lemons and took them over and congratulated her.

'I thought the stripper had come on when you got up,' joked Daz.

'No I used to do that but not anymore my hip gives me jip' was Enid's quick as a flash reply, well Daz didn't know what to say.

'She's joking son. We tried to get a stripper-gram for her but it was too expensive,' explained Dora.

With that Matt came from the bar and joined Daz.

'What's too expensive?' he enquired.

'Oh! A stripper-gram for Enid'

'Why how much do they charge?'

'£30 son and that was too much, I'd have paid a tenner but not thirty, that's way too much.'

'I'd have done it for a tenner, I can dance and underneath this clothing beats the heart of a beast of a man,' claimed Matt.

'Well I've spent the tenner now I got her some slippers and a hat,' said Dora.

'Here Daz I've got an idea, I'll go and see the D.J. and put when I'm 64 on and I'll strip,' whispered Matt.

'Fuck off, no way will you do that,' answered Daz.

'You watch me it'll be a laugh. I'll give you the signal you get all the boys around the table and then I'll do it. But I need to fiddle with me knob so it looks bigger and try and get a bit of blood in it.'

'Are you serious?' asked Daz.

'You only live once and no one knows me around here anyway.'

So the two of them said goodbye to the old ladies and went to get sorted. Daz went to tell the lads to gather 'round the table and Matt went to see the D.J.

All the boys started to congregate around the ladies table and waited for the announcement, which wasn't long coming.

'Ladies and gentlemen we all know it's Enid's 64th birthday today and now making a special appearance for one night only it's

'Massive Matt and his Massive Member' take it away Massive Matt.'

All the boys parted as the Beatles came on and Matt danced his way through to Enid and Dora's table. Everyone had gathered around and people were hanging onto the bar, stood on tables to get a better look. Matt was going for it and was looking good. Firstly he took off his shoes and then invited Enid to take off his socks, which she did with a bit too much vigour she nearly pulled his leg off. Then he did a bit of a dance and then took his jacket off and his tie which he wrapped around Enid's neck and pulled her close as if to kiss her which Enid was up for but Matt very professionally pulled away leaving only the tie. Then came the shirt, he undid each button and showed bits of chest before working the crowd up into a frenzy and they were all shouting 'off, off, off' he took it off and threw it into the crowd. This got a massive cheer, and then he started rubbing his nipples and invited Enid and Dora to join in but Dora got far too excited and bit him on his left one.

This didn't stop Matt though he was enjoying this and now for the finale, his trousers and then the undercrackers. He could dance could Matt and he started to gyrate like Tom Jones as the Beatles record had ran out and Tom had been put on and it was 'It's not unusual' so Matt was well away the crowd were clapping as he undid his belt and put it in his mouth and then he undid his trousers and again got the crowd to shout 'off, off, off', he took them off slowly and swung them around his head. Well a few people were laughing that much they fell off the table they were balancing on. He then took his belt from his mouth and put it between his legs and started pulling it backwards and forwards as if he was polishing his balls, in fact he hit himself and caught one of his testicles which normally would have winded him but his adrenaline got him through the pain. He had to knock away Dora's hand as she tried to touch him. Matt got a bit carried away at this point and did something he would regret later. He gave Enid his belt and bent over and invited her to spank him with it for a bit of fun. Well he got more than he bargained for as Enid gave him a little slap on the cheeks with the belt, but then the crowd led by Tosser started to shout 'harder, harder' to which Enid obliged and gave Matt a really hard slap across the buttocks. Matt shot about three feet in the air and quickly beckoned to Enid, no more.

Matt had had enough but the crowd wanted to see how massive he was and started chanting 'off, off, off' again so Matt limped his way to the end of the song and pulled his underpants off swung them around his head and threw them. They hit the ceiling fan spun around a couple of times and landed on the landlord's head. He then sat on Enid's knee crossed his legs and gave her a kiss and the whole pub went ballistic. What a show, what a show, Matt took a bow and everyone that could still stand and weren't doubled up laughing applauded. Matt was exhausted and the weight of the slap finally hit him. His backside was sore and he had a huge mark on his buttocks.

The pub went back to normal pretty soon and the landlord got Matt a drink and gave him his kegs back and said he'd seen some sights but that was brilliant and could he book him every week. Now Matt had a problem he had his underwear but no one seemed to know where his clothes where. He did a couple of laps of the pub trying to find them but they'd vanished. He then went to the D.J. to make an announcement that could he have his clothes back. Skip had already collected them every time he took them off and put them behind the bar but he thought it would be funny for Matt to walk about with just his belt and kegs on for a bit. Now the pain from his backside was becoming unbearable, God knows what it would be like in the morning. He asked Daz to have a look in the toilets.

'It's fucking killing me Daz, what's it look like?'

'Jesus you better tell Anna as soon as you get home the full story, it's a big purple strip right across your arse.'

'Fucking Tosser getting her to do it harder.'

'Tell you what though you were fucking brilliant mate, top notch you could do that for a living.'

'I'm off to ask for my tenner, she said she'd pay a tenner.'

'You can't ask for any money she's a pensioner'

'A fucking strong pensioner by the way my arse is feeling.'

'Come on we'll try and find your clothes, I'll help you,' said Daz who already knew where his clothes were.

They came out of the toilet and everyone who saw Matt shook his hand and laughed and congratulated him on his performance. Some asked what had happened to his massive member did he not show up, but for overall entertainment, 10 out of 10.

'Your bird wants you over there,' said Eddie

'Yeah right Eddie, just help me find my clothes.'

'No really she wants you,' insisted Eddie.

Enid was waving him over, so Matt took Daz with him.

'Did you want me Enid?'

'Yes this is my daughter Karen,' Enid then introduced Karen who was beautiful.

'Pleased to meet you Karen, did you enjoy the show?' asked Matt trying not to look at her enormous breasts.

'I missed it, the bus was late, mum really enjoyed it and she's bought you a drink.'

Karen handed him the drink, it was a double whiskey.

'Thanks son that was the best birthday present I've ever had, are you a professional?'

'Not with that winkle,' Dora laughed.

'Ooh! Dora I've seen smaller, mind you I've seen bigger to,' Enid confessed.

'Mum you are embarrassing,' Karen said looking at Matt as if he had two heads. She couldn't work out why he was in his pants and a belt. Matt sussed this and told her. 'Oh I did have clothes on but it appears someone is hiding them or they've been nicked.'

'Well I was wondering what you were doing?'

'I'm going to find my clothes so I'll see you later Enid, Dora and Karen, are you coming Daz?'

'In a minute Matt' said Daz who was taking a fancy to Karen and he started to chat to her.

'Is this your local then?'

'No, not really I only came because my mum was having a drink here for her birthday. It's a bit dead usually but it's lively tonight, where are you lot from?'

'Hull, you know that little fishing village on the East Coast with a population of about 300,000.'

'I've never been north of Watford so I don't really know where you are.'

'Well it doesn't matter really does it then, so do you live around here then?'

'Yeah all my life, went to school around here, and now I work around here.'

'What do you do for a job then?'

'I teach at the local primary school, why what do you do? Sorry I don't even know your name.'

'It's Daz and I'm a joiner, hardly James Bond but it pays the bills.'

'Where's your boyfriend then Karen has he let you out by yourself?' asked Daz trying to assess the situation.

'I don't have one I'm a lesbian' Daz's face dropped as he thought he was getting on well with her and was planning to make a move before Matt got back.

'A lesbian, well you don't look like one.'

'Why what does one look like? I'm joking by the way I'm not a lesbian. Why are you married?' Daz had took his ring off and left it in his bag back at the hotel.

'No I'm a lesbian to, can't get enough of the lady garden me, yes 100% lesbian.' This made Karen laugh, and Daz thought I'm in here if I play my cards right. He could see the lads taking the piss out of the corner of his eye and he knew he had a battle on his hands if he was to get her back to the hotel he had to make his move quite quickly and be very cunning.

'Do you want a drink Karen?'

'Go on then a quick one I'm meeting a friend at a club in ? an hour, I'll have a bottle of Becks.'

'One bottle of Becks coming up' said Daz as he walked to the bar cursing his fucking luck, meeting her mate and doesn't just want half a lager, oh no bottle of fucking Becks. What Daz didn't realise was that Karen fancied him and was going to go to the club and ask if he wanted to come. Enid called her over and asked if everything was alright.

'You won't get much better than that Karen my girl, if I was 20 years younger I'd have him,' said Enid.

'Mum you are embarrassing please don't say anything, because I'm meeting Ali and he's with his mates."

'Are you that slow, get his bloody hotel number and if the club and the night out is crap you and Ali turn up at the hotel and Bob's your uncle,' chipped in Dora who in her day had been a right handful. Daz came back from the bar after taking some stick from the lads about buying her a drink.

'One Becks, sorry Enid I never asked…'

'Don't worry son we'll get our own' said Dora.

'So where were we then? So you're going to a club? Where is it? I mean we might come if it's any good.'

'It's only open 'til one and it's not really my kind of thing, but my friend Ali asked me to go so I'm stuck really. What hotel are you staying in?'

'The Scandic Crown on Canary Wharf. I'll tell you what, why don't you come with your mate Ali back to our hotel and we can carry on there with the night and have a few drinks.'

'Are you lot rich? Those hotels are really classy.'

'I know I think we got a deal, because there's no one in them. I'll show you my room it's great looks over the river it's fantastic. Oh I didn't mean it like that I meant…'

'I know what you meant it's okay, I'd love to come to your room to see the view and who knows what else.'

Daz went red at this point his heart was pumping he'd never felt like this, it was like a movie when the leading man gives a throw away line and the girl takes it and rides with it. Daz never chased women but now his heart was beating like a drum. Although he lacked experience of being cool with women, he was beginning to like the fact that she'd noticed him, now all he had to do was not fuck it up or not let the others fuck it up for him. While he was dreaming of his rendezvous later he failed to notice that Karen had finished her drink and was kissing her mum and Dora goodbye.

'I'll see you later then Daz, have you got that address of your hotel? I'll bring Ali along for your stripping mate, she'll like him and we can have a drink together.' Daz scrambled for a pen until Dora saved the day with her bingo marker and beer mat. Daz scribbled the name of the hotel down and his room number and handed it to Karen.

Then Karen kissed him on the cheek and left. Daz couldn't believe it and was going to tell Matt who still hadn't found his clothes. Then there was an announcement from the D.J. and compare for the night. 'We have a special presentation to a very unusual act, in fact he could be done under the trades description act I mean 'Massive' is hardly the word I would have used to describe it but what a good sport and a great laugh. So can we have Matt 'Massive Matt and his mini member' on stage.' everyone cheered as Matt got up thinking he'd won something and was waving at the crowd, who were chanting 'Massive, Massive' whilst wiggling their little fingers indicating he had a small knob. Then the D.J. got the landlord Tony up to present Matt with a prize. Matt looked in excitement as Tony got up with a huge bag, which was full of something that Matt had won.

'Over to you Tony,' said the D.J.

'Thanks, well Matt you have been one hell of an act so we at the George thought you deserved a present.'

'Well I only did it for a laugh I hope you enjoyed it,' said Matt as he thought they'd got him a present.

'Here Matt you can have you clothes back' and Tony handed him the bag, which was full of his clothes. Matt couldn't hide his disappointment as he'd forgotten he had no gear on and thought he'd won a prize. All he could manage was a downhearted 'cheers for that'. All the lads were doubled up again. Matt left the stage and headed for the toilets to put his gear on. Daz saw him and as quick as a shot went to tell him the promise the two of them were on later.

'Matt, guess what?' whispered Daz as he checked the toilet to make sure they were alone.

'What?' Matt replied still pissed off about not getting a present.

'Do you know that Karen? Enid's daughter?'

'What about her?' Matt was trying to put his trousers on without getting them on the piss stained floor.

'Well she's meeting me back at our hotel and she's bringing a mate for you, how fucking good is that?'

'How good is what?' came the reply from the freshly opened door as Tosser stood there.

'Err, the fact that the barman said he could have any drink he wants on the house, Enid's buying him one.' Daz was quite quick and Matt said he'd see when he got out.

'See that bird blew you out Daz, you bought her a drink as well, you never learn do you?' Tosser scoffed.

'Fucking hell Toss I can't see you beating them off with a shitty stick, at least I managed to talk to her for a bit you usually grunt and they fuck off.'

Daz was pissed off with the fact Tosser thought he knew everything about women and he knew nothing. Rumour had it he didn't even ask his wife out and she proposed to him in a leap year.

'Cheeky get you want to see some of the birds I've turned down. There's plenty of foxy chicks had their hearts broken by old Tosser here I'll have you know.'

'More like turned you down.'

'Yeah your probably right Daz I am shit with the women,' Tosser admitted.

Daz left the toilet and went to the bar and waited for Matt to emerge from the toilet. Matt came straight over to ask what he was talking about.

'What was that you were saying?'

'Look me and you are on tonight my friend if you want, Karen is coming to our hotel with her mate for you. I can't believe it I started going on about how nice the hotel is and that and she said she'd like to see the view from the room and then maybe something else. Fucking hell Matt we've cracked it.'

'Are you mad Daz you and I both know that we are happily married and the thought of guilt free sex on a weekend away should never enter our heads.'

'So you're not up for it then?'

'Are you fucking joking, if they turn up I'd be mad not to be. When are they coming?'

'About one-ish, but don't tell these bastards or they'll fuck it up for us. As soon as we see them get them to the room and well you know,' said an excited Daz who had forgotten he was married.

They both looked at each other and smiled and rubbed their hands. Tony then got hold of the mic and announced the act that would be entertaining them for the night. This was a bit of a throwback to the old club turns and no one really took much notice even when this six foot plus black guy came to the stage they all thought he'll be shit otherwise why would he be in a pub singing. then he started to sing and he started with 'Wishing Well' by Terence Trent D'Arby, and the whole place was transfixed on the stage as this guy was fantastic. He actually looked and sounded like Terence Trent D'Arby. He finished his first song and the whole place was applauding like crazy. He sang two more songs and then went off stage as he'd completed his set. He went to the bar and got a drink and was due on in about an hour. Skip got talking to him and asked him if he only performed in London and would he like to come to the Dockers presentation and how much would he charge. Then Terence explained he'd only been doing it for a bit of pocket money and that he only really knew three songs the ones he'd sung. He really needed to learn some more before he could take it more seriously.

Tony was on the mic again announcing the act they'd all been waiting for.

'Can I have your attention please ladies and gentlemen, we now have an act on that will thrill you and entertain you no end. He does one gig a year in London and usually sings the same song but what a song and what a singer. I give you because nobody else wants him, the world famous just come from a tour in Vegas where he's been performing to sell out audiences, here he is the one and only Mike 'Shoey' Shoebottom from Hull' the whole place went crazy, but Mike never came to the stage. Tony went to see what was wrong and came back on the mic to explain. 'Sorry ladies and gentlemen a slight technical hitch there 'Shoey' was still getting the words written on the beer mat for him, this is how much of a pro this guy is. But now he's ready so give it up for the one and only Shoey.'

Shoey got his very large frame on the stage and immediately started to sweat profusely under the lights. He was just about to start went the chorus went up from a small section of the crowd and was soon to be all of the crowd of 'you fat bastard, you fat bastard' at this point Shoey started to conduct the crowd in the chorus and do a bit of a dance. Then when they had died down a bit, typically Mike started them again with the line, 'You forgot 'who ate all the pies'' so they all started with that one and again Mike conducted them.

'Who ate all the pies, who ate all the pies, you fat bastard you fat bastard you ate all the pies.'

'Now have you finished? Then I shall begin' and Shoey belted out the Sinatra classic 'New York, New York'.

Some in the audience thought that he may need oxygen half way through it, as his head was getting redder and redder but no Mike completed the song and got a standing ovation from the crowd. Then promptly sat back down and had a drink. He had knocked himself out and refused an encore, as he was knackered. Looking like Pavarotti he was wiping his face with a beer towel, as all the punters were shaking his hand and congratulating him on another superb performance. The D.J. started with the music and told them the acts would be on again in about half an hour. The pub settled into some kind of calm after the recent events.

CHAPTER 11
NICE HOTEL
ISN'T IT?

Tag and Fay had finished their meal and it had gone well they talked and opened up a bit to each other about how they both felt. Tag again apologised and Fay told him that it was going to be hard for them as she couldn't forget what he'd done overnight. But she said she'd try and not bring it up every five minutes. All she wanted and had ever wanted was him and he was on his last chance baby or no baby. Tag told her he'd done nothing but think about how much he'd took her for granted and he was going to change. He said he meant it when he said he wanted to marry her and settle down to normal family life.

They asked for the bill and decided to have a walk on the front and go into the amusements just like they had when they first met and used to go to the coast to get some privacy when they first started to see each other. They used to go to Withernsea in Tag's clapped-out old car and shop a bit at the market, then go into the amusements for an hour before getting fish and chips and eating it in the sea air. They would stroll hand in hand to the car and back home and to Fay's house where Tag would be closely watched by Fay's brothers who didn't like him, as no one was good enough for their sister. This was only a few years ago but seemed like a lifetime away, they were in love then and it was only when they moved in together did the relationship dwindle a bit. Tag started to feel trapped and Fay started to nag, and it just seemed to go sour. This walk and doing something simple reminded them of how they actually did get along and most of all did love each other, it was just when they were at home it all seemed so drab. But now they had a new focus in life. They were going to be responsible for another human being that they had created. This seemed to have brought them together again and not just because it seemed the right thing to do but because they actually discovered that they were in love again. It was as though their love for each other had been in hibernation and now it was spring and their love was to blossom again.

They finished in the arcade and bought an ice cream and walked and talked arm in arm. This was amazing as less than twenty-four hours earlier it had looked as if they would have to sell the house and go their separate ways. Now though they seemed to be on the right road to happiness even though it was early days. They had been enjoying each other and were that wrapped up in each other that they actually walked about a mile out of their way and had to go back on themselves. This didn't matter as they were in love. They got back to the hotel and had a drink in the bar and then went straight to the room and laid and kissed and cuddled and then fell asleep in each other's arms.

The journey back to Hull was a quiet one for the girls as most of them speculated as to what would happen with Fay and Tag. Most of them saw a change in Tag and hoped that he could change for both of their sakes. The rest of the journey was mainly them dozing off as they had all had a late night. They were looking forward to seeing their kids again, the ones that had them anyway. Shaz and Charlie were going to drop their bags off at the club and go straight out to town. Humphrey was pleased they were all knackered as he could do without his arse being felt again and being subjected to questioning by girls who were young enough to be his daughter. The girls had a whip-round for him and then asked if he could drop them off at their houses. They stuck a quid in each and it was cheaper than a taxi. They were all soon to find out that their husbands and partners had all phoned to see where they were and had found out about the weekend, all except Cary who had already told Trev.

They soon started to ring each other up to see what to say and the general feeling was summed up by Tosser's wife Clare, when she said, 'What are they going to do divorce us? We've had the weekend and that's all there is to it. They've had their weekend and we've had ours. Only next year it won't be a secret, because we're all going to go on a regular trip.'

They had all enjoyed it and were going to make it an annual thing. They all settled in for the night and gave the gifts they'd brought their kids and then most of them went to bed early as the twenty-four hours they had enjoyed had taken its toll on them. None of them expected a phone call from their husbands or boyfriends and they were right to, as none of them received a phone call.

The only two that made it past eleven were Shaz and Charlie and even they were flagging at midnight and decided that a nightclub wasn't on the cards but instead they got a takeaway and went to Charlie's and ended up falling asleep on the settee watching 'The Hitman and Her'.

Back at the George the party was in full swing, Matt and Daz were like two schoolboys waiting on Christmas Eve for Santa to come. Daz had even bought Greg a drink and had buried the hatchet about the Hippodrome. Daz hadn't thought about the fact that he was married at all and neither had Matt, but nothing was in concrete yet and those guilty feelings wouldn't materialise until the girls turned up. Which truth be known neither of them thought they would turn up. Skip was over at old fellas table and this time most of the lads were with him.

'Doug do you want a drink?' asked Skip.

'Ey! go on then but don't expect me to get in a round with you lot, I'm not that loaded. I'll have a whiskey please.'

'Bert do you want one as well?'

'Well I'll not be buying you one back,' said a suspicious Bert.

'Fucking hell you two are something else, don't worry I was going to buy you a drink from our kitty. Do you still want one?'

'I'll have a rum, then Skip,' Bert finally accepted.

'Is it true Bert that you were that tight that when your kids were little you told them you were going to take them to see the animals and they thought they were going to the zoo? But you took them to the abattoir to see the animals just before they got slaughtered,' Tosser asked Bert, knowing that it was true, as Tosser's dad knew Bert well and this was a well know fact about him.

'Cheeky bastard,' retorted Bert.

'Well come on Bert is it true?' asked Trev.

'Yes and he knows full well it's true, but in them days we couldn't afford zoo's and stuff like that and my two liked cows and that.'

'Why didn't you take 'em to the country to see them, instead of just before they were made into burgers,' Trev was persistent.

'Cost too much to go to the country, I mean it's only three miles out of Hull. Come on kids let's go see the cows on death row,' Tosser said making actions of counting money with his hands and doing his best Scrooge voice.

'You lads are a bunch of piss-takers and you think your funny don't you?'

'We don't think Bert we know,' said Skip who was back from the bar with the drinks. 'There you are you old bastards, get them into yer.'

'Cheers lads, much appreciated,' Doug said raising his glass. Then they all looked at Bert who had downed his in one and wiped his mouth.

'What are you lot looking at?'

'You, yer miserable get,' Jonno shouted. 'Thank you Bert.'

'Why I've done nowt,' Bert looked confused.

'No stupid, say thank you we've just bought you a drink.'

'I thought that was because he'd been cheeky,' Bert still wasn't getting it.

'For crying out loud Bert thank the lads, even if he was cheeky they have bought you a drink, it's good manners,' Doug glared at Bert as he said this.

'Thanks lads,' Bert said finally getting what everyone was talking about.

'You're fucking priceless Bert, I hope it gives you heartburn, you clueless twat,' was Skip's final remark and they all walked off. Doug looked at him and said. 'I've known you for years Bert and I tell you what you're getting worse, now get to the bar it's your round.'

'Are you sure?' Bert quizzed Doug.

'Yes I'm sure I got the last one in and there's only two of us in the round. I'm surprised you don't argue with yourself when there's only you out.'

'Do you want half seeing as you've got a whiskey there?'

'No I want a pint, and I don't know what your moaning at it's only the second full priced round you've bought.'

Bert went to the bar as he was told and Doug just shook his head. He knew he was a tight arse but he was getting to be a nightmare. Tony got back on the mic to announce Terence Trent D'Arby was coming back on stage.

'Give it up for a superb talent that we all believe is going places- it's Terence Trent for his final set of the night.'

Terence took to the stage and the crowd went wild. That was until they realised that he was singing the same songs he'd sung in the first half. He was good but like he'd admitted, he only knew three songs all the way through. He was halfway through 'Wishing Well' and the old women Enid and Dora threw Enid's spare pair of knickers on stage, the ones she took out with her in case she had an accident. Well if you could call them knickers they were more like a marquee. Terence didn't know where to look but he carried on anyway as the crowd was laughing at the old girls. Terence finished his set and the lads started shouting 'More, more'. This caught on and he decided to sing 'Wishing Well' once more. He got the first couple of lines out and Matt jumped on stage and got him in a head lock and started to play wrestle with him whilst he was still singing and then let him go. Terence carried on singing and Matt joined in. Terence then did 'Twist and Shout' with Matt prompting him with the lyrics and the whole place was up dancing. Matt was enjoying his newfound fame and got a little carried away, he took the mic from Terence - whose real name was Duane - and started to get the crowd going.

'Give it up for Terence Trent D'Arby.'

'It's Duane,' Duane whispered in his ear.

'Sorry, give it up for the magnificent Duane Pipe.'

Everyone got the joke except Duane himself, who seemed quite miffed as it wasn't the first time he'd heard the joke, but he took his bow and left the stage. Matt was still going on and to his amazement no one had turned the mic off, so he carried on.

'Right then I would like to round the evening off with a song, you can join in if you like it's quite easy to pick the words up. I shall sing it first and then we'll do it again and you can all join in.'

Everyone wondered what he would sing. Would it be the Beatles - or the Stones? No one had ever heard Matt sing before.

'Here we go, I shall be doing this without any music. I believe it's called Acapulco.'

At this point the pub was waiting for something special and memorable, well it turned out to be memorable. Matt started…

'She's a big fat bastard, Twice the size of me,
With the hair on her fanny, Like the branches of a tree,
She can hop, skip and jump, Catch a barrel up her cunt,
She's the girl for me.'

Well the whole place was silent, there was tumbleweed blowing through the bar. Matt had scored a massive own goal but hadn't realised this and he tried to carry on.

'So you can all join in.'

Skip and Tosser got on the stage and quickly got Matt off before he could humiliate them anymore. Tosser was left with the mic, and Jonno shouted out, 'Give us a song Tosser.'

'Alright you can all join in if you like.'

Tosser started the song and soon the whole pub was arm in arm waving imaginary scarves.

'When you walk through a storm
Hold your head up high…'

There were a few tears and lumps in the throat but Tosser got a round of applause and just about salvaged the wreckage Matt had made.

'Sorry about my mate, that song was not really for mixed company. Massive Matt has had too much to drink,' Tosser said as he handed the mic over to Tony.

'Right, sorry about this boys and girls, it's last orders at the bar and then if you could leave the pub in an orderly manner. Thank you and what a great night we've had and hopefully we'll see you all again soon. Safe journey home, goodnight.'

Everyone rushed to the bar and some of the lads were going to have a go at Matt, but Eddie had got there first telling him in no uncertain terms what he thought of his act. This prompted Matt, who had got carried away with the moment to go and apologise to Tony and his staff. Tony said he thought it was quite funny but it seemed the rest of the crowd weren't impressed at all.

The pub slowly emptied and the lads all headed for the takeaway shops that dotted both sides of the road. Eddie was on to the job of ordering mini-cabs so that no one had to get one by themselves.

Most of them ended up in the KFC. Some got in the first cabs and went back to the hotel, mainly the old brigade who wouldn't eat 'that foreign muck' if you paid them. They thought they would get fish and chips back at the hotel or somewhere near. Tosser ordered a 'zinger' burger because he thought it sounded interesting but was soon realising what he'd actually done when his entire mouth began to burn. Tosser thought a korma was too hot let alone a zinger burger. Of course all the other lads were very sympathetic as Tosser was in agony, his eyes were streaming and so was his nose.

'Don't you want the rest of that?' asked Skip who had already eaten one and loved hot spicy food.

'No you can have it, you bastard, why did you let me buy one of them? You know I can't stand hot stuff,' protested Tosser.

'Shut up you big girl, I thought you knew it was red hot. Christ it's on the telly every five minutes asking you if you dare try one.'

'Well it's burnt me tongue, and all me face has gone bright red.'

With that the cab came for them and Tosser had to make do with nothing. He was moaning in the cab that he was hungry and that he was going to go to bed because he needed food.

'Mate just order a pizza at the hotel, if you spend over twenty quid they deliver free,' said the cab driver.

'There you are Toss, sorted, we'll order a pizza.'

The cab driver got them back to the hotel in one piece but only just, he hit a few kerbs and went through a few red lights, but none of the lads realised as they were half cut. They arrived at the hotel just as the students were arriving and they couldn't believe what they saw. The two Swedes that the students had picked up were real and not made up - and what's more they were absolutely stunning.

'Jesus Christ, how have you two pulled these?' Skip said opened-mouthed. The two boys smiled and introduced the girls. Tosser was still dribbling from the zinger and had to wipe his nose. Trev couldn't believe it and neither could Jonesy, all four of them just stared for what seemed an age at the two beauties.

'Well, have you seen enough?' asked Grant smugly.

'Not really, what the hell are these two doing with you two. I mean I've seen you in the showers Grant and to be honest was not impressed but you must have a big cock Mike if you've pulled these,' slurred Tosser.

'You've either got it or you haven't, and gentlemen you haven't. Do enjoy the rest of your evening,' scoffed Mike, knowing that they'd changed rooms.

The students then rushed the girls up into their new rooms before they could be followed. They even went the way they would go to their old room and then doubled back as to confuse Skip and his posse. Grant was young but he wasn't daft and he knew that Skip and the lads would try and spoil the night for them.

Skip, Tosser, Trev and Jonesy were still stood in the foyer area of the hotel still puzzled at what the girls saw in the two tits they'd brought on the trip.

'We'll have to fuck it up for 'em Skip?' said Tosser.

'Don't worry I've got their room number, give them half an hour to get settled then we'll get them, big style! Right, whose round is it?'

'I want some food,' said Tosser and he went into the bar to see if anyone else wanted any to save on delivery. He went to the reception and they ordered it for him and said it would be an hour. So it was back to the bar and more drinking and messing around.

'Hey you lot, we've just seen the students with their Swedish girlfriends,' Jonesy announced.

'What are they like? I bet they're two fat birds from round here and they've got blonde hair, that's the only thing that makes 'em Swedish,' laughed Thommo.

'No I tell you what, they are stunners, like page three girls but better,' Jonesy confirmed jealously.

'Get away, you must be pulling my pisser.'

'Tell you what, I'd give my right arm to be in that room now, they are hot,' Tosser confirmed.

'What, hotter than your tongue?' laughed Matt.

'Hotter than my tongue.'

'Give it half an hour and you will be in that room Tosser and we'll have a bit of fun,' said Skip

'Leave the lads alone Skip, you're only jealous,' Eddie interrupted.

'Too fucking right I am, but that Mike's gonna get it, did you hear what he said - you've either got it or you haven't - and they had it and we didn't. Little twat, he'll eat his words.'

'Well he's only telling the truth Skip,' Eddie laughed again, knowing the boys had switched rooms and the one Skip was going to bombard was empty. But what Eddie didn't know was that the hotel had put two new guests in the room, a pair of Japanese tourists who had booked in at the last minute.

The time was around one in the morning and Skip was going to get the key to the students' room. He was at the reception and told the guy who was on there his number and the fact that he'd left his key card in the room and could he have a duplicate. The receptionist was trying to impress his colleague and didn't ask Skip's surname, if he had done then Skip would have known that Grant and Mike weren't Japanese and neither of them had the surname Haruki. The receptionist gave him the card with no questions asked.

Then the pizzas arrived much earlier than anticipated, so Skip rushed back to the bar to tell the lads who'd ordered pizza that the guy was waiting for them to pay. Skip had a little laugh to himself and then told Tosser that the first stage of their plan was in place, they had means of access. All the ones who ordered food sat and ate it in the reception area and there was about six of them including Skip who nicked a bit of everyone's. Skip told them his plan and asked if they were in.

'Right then I've got the card to the students' room, we'll give them another half an hour while we prepare for the assault. We need to go to our rooms and get a towel each to put over our faces so we look like terrorists and we need an ice bucket to fill with ice from the ice machines. Get about three buckets of ice and one of water and the other two can get fire extinguishers. Are we all in?'

'Mmm, mmm,' they all mumbled and gave a thumbs-up as they carried on eating their food.

'Right then, one of us has to go straight for the bathroom so they can't make an escape into there and the other five can then blast them with ice, foam and water.'

'What does the bathroom boy do with his bucket?' asked Tosser.

'Good question Toss. He chucks his bucket first and then goes straight for the bathroom. Well you've either got it or you haven't and you two little bastards are going to get it big style,' Skip said with a hint of malice.

The six of them were quite excited by their mission. The Super six were Skip, Tosser, Jonno, Tom, Trev and Jonesy. They were going to ask Thommo and Daz but it might have got out of hand with Daz still being pissed off with them getting in the Hippodrome. Besides they didn't want everyone to know, Eddie would go berserk if he knew. But Eddie already knew they would be up to something that's why he pre-warned the students to move rooms.

The students were already having a good time and were quite shocked at the fact no one had tried to piss about, so the plan of moving rooms appeared to have worked. They had drank nearly all the mini-bar and were getting down to pairing off when the girls got on the same bed with the boys and they seemed to want them all to play together. The lads thought this was weird but in for a penny in for a pound, they were going to have their own mini orgy. The girls were used to this being free with your love, they were both bi-sexual and didn't mind who was touching, sucking or poking as long as it felt good.

Grant and Mike were a little more reserved, there was no way Grant wanted Mike stroking his arse, that was going over the line of acceptability. At one point Grant touched Mike's leg and nearly jumped off the bed as it was all hairy. It ended up with Grant giving Ulrika it from behind whilst she gave Mike a blowjob and Anna was sat on Mike's face while she was kissing Grant, a bit like an electrical circuit. Grant couldn't help but think how weird it was. He lived at home with his mother and father and had never been away without them before and now he was shagging two gorgeous Swedish women for the second night running. They carried on for a bit and then swapped about. They all ended up in the shower and then the girls carried on at each other while the two exhausted lads recovered a bit and then they started again until they all fell asleep.

But while all this was going on, Enid's daughter and her friend Ali had turned up looking for Matt and Daz. They went into the bar and Daz's face went red as he nudged Matt.

'Fucking hell, they've only turned up, what the fuck do we do now?' he whispered to Matt having forgotten all about them.

'Get them to the room after a couple of drinks but do it so no one notices.'

'Hiya, Daz this is Ali, Ali this is Daz and this is Massive Matt,' Karen introduced Ali to the two boys.

'Pleased to meet you Ali,' said Daz nudging Matt who wasn't impressed and fancied Karen more.

'Yeah, pleased to meet you, do you want a drink?' asked Matt.

'Go on then I'll have a lager and Ali will have a white wine please. Nice hotel isn't it?'

'Lovely,' said Matt as he went to the bar.

No one had noticed that the girls had made a beeline for Daz and Matt and just thought the girls were residents, apart from Eddie who saw all and knew who Karen was.

'So what's she doing here then Matt?' Eddie asked Matt at the bar.

'She said she was going to come and have a drink with us, and here she is. But I'm supposed to be with her mate but I prefer Daz's.'

'Well the way she looks at him you've no chance there Matt,' Eddie had observed.

'I know, well I'll shag her mate, I don't care, or a wank would be nice, save me doing it.'

'You two be careful, don't be going bareback, you might catch something,' warned Eddie.

'Yes dad, we will,' and Matt took the drinks back to the table they were sitting at.

Skip and the others were on manoeuvres and had got all the gear together for their mission. They all had their towel and all they had to do now was fill the ice buckets and get the fire extinguishers and they were ready. While all this was going on Matt and Daz were coming up with a plan to get the girls to their rooms without anyone noticing. The plan they came up with was that the girls pretend to go and get a taxi and then sneak back in after the lads have gone to their room and then they turn up at the room and no one would be any the wiser. This way they won't be disturbed by everyone trying to spoil it for them and therefore they will be left alone. The only person who knew what was going on was Eddie and he didn't care as the way he looked at it was this the less idiots running amok around the corridors of this 5 star hotel intent on causing havoc in the early hours the better as far as he was concerned.

Meanwhile tiptoeing along the corridors were the 'Super six' armed to the teeth with water and ice, they were reaching their destination and now the ice buckets were full to the top. It was decided that Trev would be the toilet boy and go in first. Skip had the card for the room and they were not far from touching base and so they had a little meeting. Just like five-year-olds playing war games. Skip got them in a huddle and began to whisper instructions.

'Right boys we know this is going to be tough but if we all commit 100% I believe that we will come through this with no casualties. We all know our roles so let's do this, good luck and I'll see you on the other side. Now hands in.' They all put their hands in and whilst pissing themselves laughing they whispered '1-2-3 go the Super six'.

They approached the corridor and put on their towels to cover their faces and then got to the room. There was no noise at all coming from the room, but Skip thought it must be because they were kissing of just getting down to it. Then he gave the signal, the green light shone as he entered the card into the slot on the door and pulled it out then quickly opened the door and Tom ran in and pulled the quilt off the bed and the rest of them pelted ice, water and foam at the general direction of the bed. Trev was in the toilet laughing as he heard the commotion thinking it was the students shouting when in fact it was two middle aged Japanese tourists who thought they were being hijacked and mugged for their belongings.

'You want money, take, take my money don't harm us,' pleaded the poor soaking wet Japanese man whose wife was crying and shaking. It was at that point when they put the lights on it dawned on Skip and the rest of them what had happened. They'd got the wrong room and how bad did this look. It was a police job unless someone acted pretty quickly. So Skip did what any normal bloke in the same situation dressed as a terrorist would have done, he ran away and the rest of the lads followed him, all except Trev who was blissfully unaware they had the wrong room. He was locked in the bathroom awaiting instructions that the mission had gone well. They were like shit off a stick as they flew through the corridors.

Back in the room Mr Haruki was ringing reception to ask what had happened and that the hotel was full of terrorists, when he dropped the phone as out of the bathroom came Trev all dressed up and shouting 'surprise'. Well it was Trev who got the surprise when he saw the two of them dripping wet with water and Mrs Haruki with foam all over her head. Trev decided the best course of action was to run, but he didn't get far as he stood on some ice and went flying across the floor and banged his head on the door. This didn't stop him, he got up and ran as fast as he could and he felt like he had done all those years ago when he'd been nicking apples from old Mrs Jones' garden and she came out and caught him.

They all regrouped in Skip's room and got their story together that they hadn't been anywhere near the room, but the receptionist knew what had happened and had already called Eddie over as soon as the phone-call came in from the room. Eddie then went to the room to apologise to the couple and when they found out it was meant to be a joke they took it in good faith and moved rooms and decided they wouldn't take it any further.

Trev had got back to his room to dispose of the towel and walked casually back to the bar passing Eddie and the manager on the way. Skip and the others had given it twenty minutes before they re-emerged from Skip's room and they thought they'd got away with it, until Eddie came in about twenty minutes later and went off his head at them.

'You bunch of bastards, this is the last trip I'm doing, you've gone too far this time,' Eddie fumed.

'Why what's wrong Eddie?' Tosser piped up innocently.

'Don't insult my intelligence Tosser. I know what you silly bastards have done. And it's lucky I've just paid for that poor Japanese man and his wife to go on an all expenses paid trip around the sights of London out of the spare kitty money to stop them calling the police.'

'How much was it?' asked Doug.

'About £100 I think, I've got to sort it out in the morning. Skip you are a prick.'

'Well, they gave me the room card. We were going to get the students for a laugh and they gave me the wrong card.'

'No they didn't Skip, I told the lads to change rooms, but I didn't expect them to hire it out so soon.'

'So it's your fault Eddie spoiling our fun,' Jonno joined in.

'No, I thought you'd pile in, see it was empty and piss off. Any way what did you do?'

'Threw water and ice and let off two fire extinguishers, that poor bloke when the lights went on, he was dancing and pulling the curtains and then we realised what had happened.'

'Yeah, and you left me in the fucking bathroom, when I came out his wife had a big white swirl on her head, she looked like Mr Whippy.'

Trev was very displeased.

Eddie started to laugh as did everyone else, even the manager had a smile on his face after he'd left the scene and got it sorted with the couple.

'He was saying don't harm us, take money, take money,' laughed Tosser.

'You rotten bastards you should and you will apologise in the morning,' Eddie insisted.

'Yes Eddie we will,' all the lads replied.

Matt and Daz winked at each other knowing that after that bollocking Skip and the others wouldn't dare try and do the same to them or it would be a police job. Everyone settled down to the last few drinks as the barman did as he had done the night before, closed the bar and left the shutters slightly open. He even said to them 'goodnight' as if to bring their attention to the fact he had finished for the night. In fact the hotel manager had told him to do as he did the night before, because when they checked the stock against the takings on the Saturday morning so much stock had gone missing. The barman was in deep trouble but luckily for him the manager was an old school friend who was trying his best to cover his back for him. Eddie noticed what had happened and quickly acted, telling all his party don't do what you did last night because after the Pearl Harbour revenge incident they could ill afford any more misdemeanours.

The word got around but not to the lads in the other party from Oldham, and this big fella got up and tested the pumps and then started taking orders for drinks. There was an immediate rush to the bar, but surprisingly none of the Hull lads joined the throng. They had done the right thing, as soon as the lads all sat down for their free drink the management came and caught the fella behind the bar. The manager looked at Eddie.

'Don't look at me, he's not on my trip, and none of my lads have been to the bar.'

'Well, I think unless you pay for those drinks you lot that's had them, then I'll have no alternative but to ring the police and report you for theft.'

Immediately the Oldham boys got up and paid.

'Is that it?' Eddie chirped up. 'Do yourself a favour mate lock your bar, what do you expect is going to happen with fifty-odd people left with an unattended bar?'

'Don't worry, the bar will be getting closed, won't it barman?' he then looked sternly at his mate as if to say you'd be looking for another job now if you weren't my mate.

'So before he shuts up can we get just one more round in?' Skip piped up looking at the manager.

'Go on then, the bar will stay open for another hour and then it will close.'

The whole bar cheered the manager, all except the barman.

'But I'm meeting someone in twenty minutes.'

'Tough shit, you're lucky you still fucking work here, get behind that bar and make some money while I think of a way to make up for the beer that was nicked last night.'

The barman did as he was told and they all ordered two drinks so that they could prolong the night.

'Cheers Eddie for speaking up for us,' said Trev.

'I had to because if he thought that we were responsible, then the police would have been called. Look you got away with it last night, just be grateful you did.'

'Why is it that they think everything that goes wrong is from our trip?' asked Jonesy.

'Because let's face it, 9 times out of 10 it is you silly twats pissing around, isn't it?' Eddie replied.

'I never thought of it like that before Eddie. Why do you do these trips Eddie? It can't be any fun for you.'

'You know what Jonesy, I don't know.'

'I do Jonesy,' interrupted Skip. 'He loves it, the silly old get. He loves hiding all the fire extinguishers and making sure we're all tucked up in bed, don't you Eddie?'

'I suppose I do enjoy it Skip, yes,' Eddie smiled and carried on with his drink...

Matt and Daz were still with the girls who had just finished their drinks.

'Isn't it about time you two got going?' asked Matt winking at the girls.

'Well I suppose so but we've just finished we might go in a minute, why, what's the rush? And why are you winking?' asked a puzzled Karen.

'You know the plan?'

'What plan?'

'The plan to get you back to our room?' Matt carried on while Daz, who hadn't mentioned anything of the sort to Karen, slid down his chair in embarrassment.

'And who said we're going to your room?' Karen demanded to know.

'No one but come on, you've come all this way, you must be here to have a shag.' Matt continued, then Daz stepped in.

'I think what my friend is trying to say is if you would like to come to our room for drinks then you can. But the plan he is referring to is the fact that if these lot see us all going to our room then it will be World War Three all night. I mean you wanted to see the view didn't you Karen?'

'Yeah that's what I meant. You know how much you wanted to see the view because it's spectacular.'

'So what's the plan then to get us to your room?' asked Ali.

'Well you pretend to go for a taxi and we take you to reception and then we come back here without you. Everyone thinks you've got a taxi, but you haven't, we've told you our room number and you've gone there instead and then you wait for us to come along,' Daz explained.

'How about you give us your room card and we get in and wait for you in the room?' Ali proposed. This threw the lads a bit as they hadn't really thought about it.

'Well I suppose so yeah, we could do that. So does that mean you're staying?' asked Daz a little too enthusiastically.

'Don't know yet, how much booze have you got?' asked Ali who was fairly fresh out and hadn't had a lot to drink.

'A few cans and that,' replied Matt thinking they could have what was left from the coach trip down. No way did he want to raid the mini bar.

'Well I need to powder my nose, are you coming Karen?' Ali gestured to Karen and the two girls went to the toilet.

'You fucking idiot Matt. Why didn't you just ask her if she fucked on first dates to save time.'

'What do you mean, I was being charming.'

'Fuck off Matt, if that's your idea of charming 'em, then I'd hate to see you when you're not. What about it, me and you darling, you can go on top if you like, you prick, if you fuck this up for me...'

'I won't, that Ali wants me big style mate, I can tell,' bragged Matt.

In the ladies toilets a very different conversation was going on between the two girls.

'Look, that Matt, he's a bit creepy and full of himself Karen, I want to go home,' said Ali.

'Look, let's go to the room and see what happens, have a few drinks and a bit of a laugh. He's not that bad really, he's funny and what he did for my mother was hilarious. Come on don't spoil it for me, I really like Daz,' pleaded Karen.

'Alright then but a couple of hours tops.'

'Okay, you tell me when you want to go,' confirmed Karen. Then the two girls left the toilet and rejoined the lads.

'We're off then, going to get a taxi,' announced Karen.

The rest of the lads who really hadn't taken much notice all said goodbye and carried on with their beers. They all went to the reception and Daz gave them the key to the room and went back to the bar. When Matt and Daz got back to the bar the rest of them started to take the piss.

'Blown out again you two, was it your patter or your ugly mugs that put them off?' Tosser started the barrage of abuse.

'A couple of gentlemen having a drink with a couple of ladies, all very civilised and you lot bring it down to the gutter,' Daz replied.

'So, if she'd have said shag me Daz, you would have declined then, is that what you're saying?' asked Skip.

Daz went quiet and that said it all.

'You've been blown out that's all there is to it. Granted you got further than we did tonight, but ultimately you got blown out,' scoffed Skip.

'Yeah you're right Skip, we got blown out,' Daz agreed, hoping to take away any suspicion that he'd actually scored, well nearly scored.

Then Matt suddenly had a thought that what if the girls were a couple of hustlers and they were in their room now nicking all their stuff.

'Daz, what if those two are in the room ripping us off. I mean we hardly know them do we?' Matt posed the question to Daz and Daz started to get paranoid.

'Drink up quick Matt and we better go,' Daz was thinking it was the classic sting, gain your trust and then bang, they've pissed off with all your belongings. In fact it had taken the girls a good ten minutes to find the room and they'd only been in it a couple of minutes when the lads decided to make their exit.

'Right lads, that's us, we're knackered. Goodnight.'

Daz yawned and said his goodbyes, as did Matt.

'Goodnight Massive Matt, you and diddy Daz go spoon each other, that's the only action you two'll get.'

'Ha, ha, ha, funny bastards,' Matt turned and shouted, knowing the girls were in the room, they hoped.

As soon as they were out of sight they began to run, convinced that Karen and Ali were a couple of East End hustlers who preyed on wannabe strippers from the north. They got to the room and rushed in to see the girls had helped themselves to a can each. Matt's face dropped as it wasn't one of the spares, it had come from the fridge, which was going to cost a fortune.

The lads sat down and there was an uncomfortable stand off between the girls and the boys until Karen invited Daz onto the bed to sit next to her. Daz sat down and Karen then started to kiss him. Matt didn't want to feel left out so he grabbed Ali and sat on the bed with her.

'We'll go on here, come on,' said Matt dragging a reluctant Ali onto the bed. She just sat and stared at the wall and when Matt tried to kiss her she turned away. She got up and turned the lights down as she didn't want to watch Karen at it, while she devoured Daz's face.

Matt tried again but to no avail, so he got up and turned the lights up and asked, 'Right, who wants a drink then?' This killed the moment stone dead as Daz and Karen got up blinking as their eyes got used to the bright lights again.

'So, you girls been here before then?' Matt said not realising the situation. All the other three knew that Ali was only there until Karen had finished with Daz and she wasn't interested in Matt in the slightest. The fact that Matt was oblivious to this didn't stop him.

'No we haven't, it's far too posh for us. Mind you it's far too posh for you by the looks of you,' Ali said with venom.

'Cheeky cow, I'm working class but I've got money,' said Matt defensively.

'Yeah but Matt you've got no class,' laughed Daz, which broke the tension between Ali and Matt.

'Look, let's turn the lights down and we'll have a drink near the window by the moonlight and these two can do whatever,' said Matt thinking that might get her in the mood.

So they sat at the small table near the window and finished their drinks while Karen and Daz got back on the bed and became two dark silhouettes making out in the moonlight.

Ali then got up and laid on the bed and Matt thought he was in, so he got up and tried to spoon Ali.

'Look, stay on the chair, I'm getting some kip on here while she's finished,' Ali said nudging Matt off the bed and wrapping the duvet around herself. So Matt went and sat on the chair and opened another can and pretended to not watch Daz and Karen at it. Daz had taken all Karen's clothes off and the two of them were naked as they got into the bed. Daz then began to kiss Karen all over eventually going down on her, which made her moan with excitement. She was wet and this turned Daz on as he slipped his tongue into her clit and worked it up and down. Matt was trying as hard as he could to make out what was going on. All he could hear was heavy breathing and moans of delight.

Then Daz got up and Matt could see his figure in the moonlight he was like the dancing girl from Roald Dahl's 'Tales Of The Unexpected' but with a rather impressive erection. Daz was looking for the condoms he'd bought in the toilet. He put on the bathroom light to look, which gave Matt a better look at him, the jammy get. Even Ali had to admire his erection as she took a sneaky peek. Daz found what he was looking for and then went back and fumbled around opening the packet and putting on the condom in the dark. He eventually got it on and carried on where he'd left off. There was more moaning and then Karen grabbed his penis and put it inside her and Daz had to use some self control as he didn't want to look like he wasn't experienced. He thought he was going to ejaculate as soon as he entered her he was that excited. Karen was getting into it and both of them forgot and really didn't care that two other people were in the room.

Now Matt was pretty pissed off as it appeared that Ali was asleep on his bed, but that was the least of his problems. He now wanted a piss and with the lay out of the room the toilet was about three feet away from Daz's bed on which he was at it with Karen. He tried to hold it in but couldn't and had to try and tiptoe across the room as to not disturb the two lovers and most of all not look like a perv trying to catch a look at them. So he set off on the small journey across the room guided only by the moonlight that shone through the window. He negotiated his own bed and crept past and just as he thought he'd made it, he tripped on what seemed like a huge elastic band, in fact it was Karen's bra strap. Matt fell forwards and landed on top of Daz who was by this point at top speed.

'What the fucking hell are you doing Matt?' Daz shouted as he was knocked down and nearly head butted Karen, who thought something was going on and that Matt was joining in.

'Hey no way, not two of you,' screamed Karen getting Daz off her.

'Sorry, I need a piss and I was trying to get there without disturbing you but I've just tripped on a bra strap, sorry you two, carry on,' Matt apologised.

Karen and Daz burst out laughing at this, it was like something out of a 'Carry On' film. Matt finished in the toilet and then came back out and went to sit on his chair and tried to get comfortable.

'Have you finished Matt?' asked Daz.

'Why have you?' Matt replied.

'No, so I shall carry on, if my knob hasn't broken in half.'

'You carry on, don't mind me, I just wish I had some popcorn.'

'Look, you can lay next to me but don't try anything alright,' said Ali whom everyone thought was asleep and had been until Matt did his acrobat's act. So Matt got on the bed fully-clothed. Ali was inside the quilt and Matt laid on top.

Daz and Karen carried on and this time they managed to have sex and then they both held each other and cuddled. They both fell asleep as did Matt and Ali. Daz felt no real guilt at committing adultery, as he was fairly inebriated, the guilt would hit him in the morning when he realised what he had done. Whereas Matt wouldn't have minded feeling guilty, instead of just feeling uncomfortable, lying on the edge of the bed with no covers to keep him warm.

The rest of the lads who had been left in the bar had all slowly made their way to bed. Some fell asleep fully clothed, others slept with nothing on, much to the amazement of their roommates and Gaz slept in the bath to get away from Thommo's snoring. Eddie waited until the last of them went to bed and then and only then was he convinced there would be no mischief. That was the only time that Eddie could relax and get some good sleep himself, that was if Greg wasn't too pissed. Eddie got back to the room and Greg was fast asleep and not making a sound. It was three in the morning and all was well…

In Blackpool Tag had woken up and lay there looking at Fay, feeling lucky he'd got a second chance and happy with the fact that he was going to be a dad. He dreamed of getting a son who would play rugby league for Great Britain and earn money doing something he enjoyed. If it was a girl then she would be beautiful and successful and have everything she desired. But he settled on the thing that most parents are happy for and that is that the child, boy or girl, is healthy. Tag slowly got out of bed and got ready and went downstairs to ask for breakfast so that he could treat Fay to breakfast in bed. The cook obliged and told him to bring the pots and plates back down with him when they'd finished. It was the same cook who had witnessed the events the day before and she was over the moon that Fay and Tag had kissed and made up.

Tag took the tray to the room and gently woke Fay who was delighted at the gesture and the effort Tag had made. She had always thought it the most uncomfortable way to eat breakfast in a bed but she thought it was sweet of Tag to do it for her, so she never mentioned it. They then planned what they would do for the next few hours as they had a bus to catch at 2pm.

When they got home they decided that they would go around and tell everyone the news. But then Fay thought she'd better see a doctor first and make sure that it was true that she really was pregnant. Tag eventually agreed but really he was so excited that he just wanted to tell the whole world...

CHAPTER 12
LATE AFTERNOON IN SUBURBIA

Back in London Ali had woken up and was ready to go. It was only 7 in the morning but she had fulfilled her side of the bargain and she went over to the bed where Karen was sleeping and she gently nudged her.

'Karen, Karen, come on I'm going, are you coming?'

Karen didn't respond, so Ali got a little bit louder.

'Are you coming Karen or are you staying here?' Ali then gave Karen one almighty shove which nearly knocked her out of bed as if to say you are coming with me like it or not.

'What's the matter Ali?' Karen said in a sleepy daze.

'We - me and you - are going, because if I have to lay next to that idiot one minute longer I'll swing for the bastard. That's what's wrong, now you had your fun so let's go.'

'Alright give me a minute.'

Karen then went to the toilet and discovered she had just started her period.

'Ali have you got any tampies or pads?'

'No, just stuff some bog paper down there for now and let's go.'

Ali couldn't wait to get out of the room. Then she had a wicked idea, in her hand bag she had some Immac hair remover. She looked at Matt snoring away. He had grabbed the quilt and was sleeping like a baby. She couldn't resist it. So she smeared his eyebrows with the Immac and left laughing, calling to Karen to hurry up. Karen wanted to say goodbye to Daz so she went over and nudged him and said what a great night she'd had and if he wanted to get in touch she'd left her number in the bathroom, if he didn't get in touch she'd understand. She wrote her number on a tissue in eyeliner pen and left along with Ali who couldn't wait to get out of the place. They went down to the reception and Ali insisted on getting breakfast and so they both checked into the dining area giving Matt and Daz's room number. There was no one in the breakfast area from the lads' party, they were all in bed as it was far too early for any of them, so the girls had a quiet breakfast and went on their way.

Eddie and the older crew were the first to emerge from the night's activities at around 8.30. They knew that none of the younger brigade would be down until later.

'Where are we going today then Eddie?' asked Doug.

'We'll go to Kings Cross, there's a couple of pubs around there where a lot of the Hull lot hang out, so we'll head for there, plus it's on the way out of London.'

'What time are we going?'

'Whenever all the lads and the driver are ready to go. They have to be out of the rooms by 11 o'clock so it shouldn't be long after that.'

They all finished their food and went for a walk to get a paper and have a look at the docks and the Wharf itself. It was a beautiful morning and was definitely t-shirt weather.

Back at the hotel, the first of the lads started to wake up and in Skip and Tosser's room they were feeling really rough. They had both fell asleep with all their clothes on for the second night and could have done to have spent the day in bed. Tosser looked over at the table where his change was and he could see Greg's teeth on Skip's bedside table looking at him and he had an idea. He would get a condom, blow it up and put the teeth in it and present Greg with it. Tosser thought this was a good idea although Skip couldn't quite hear him as he was being sick at the time that he was asked his opinion. They both then started to reflect on what had happened the night before and the fact dawned on them that they had to go and apologise to the Japanese fella and his wife for frightening the shit out of them. The students had enjoyed another great night and were having one last shag before breakfast. The two girls were sex mad and had been at it until the early hours and still wanted more. Grant and Mike couldn't believe how lucky they'd been and how impressed and proud they were of themselves for being able to stay the pace for two nights running. Their cocks were very sore but the way they looked at it they probably would go six months without a shag so they were getting it while it was available.

They finished off and the girls wanted breakfast, which the boys thought would be tricky, but it turned out there wasn't a problem. The guy on the entrance to the breakfast room was easily swayed by the fluttering eyelashes of the two Swedes. They arrived at the same time as Skip and Tosser who immediately asked the question they'd all been wondering.

'Where did you two get to last night?'

'We moved rooms knowing you twats would try to ambush us and spoil our night. But we were one step ahead Skip, up there for thinking and down there for dancing. Like we said you've either got it or you haven't,' Grant said pointing at his head and then his feet. Grant then ushered the girls away from Skip and Tosser and they settled down for breakfast.

'How the fuck did they pull those two Tosser?'

'No idea Skip, no idea. What a pair of lucky bastards that's all I can say. Come on let's get something to eat and then we can get back on it.'

Skip and Tosser got a full English and a loaf of toast to help them get ready for the day's drinking ahead. They both felt rough but knew that in a couple of hours they would be alright and on the final stretch of the weekend.

Back in Matt and Daz's room they were both waking up and Daz had wondered what had gone on. He felt knackered and strange and looked over to Matt who was still hanging on the edge of the bed, the only bit Ali had let him sleep on.

'What the fuck happened last night? I feel as rough as a badgers arse,' announced Daz.

'You my friend were shagging that Karen we met in the old George and I was sat watching for a bit until her growler of a mate let me lay on the bed for the worse night's kip I've ever had.'

'You are joking, I didn't shag her did I?' said a shocked Daz as the penny dropped and he got a flashback.

'You certainly did, she was all over you,' confirmed Matt as he got a wiff of the Immac.

'Can you smell something?' Matt enquired.

'No, not really, maybe your nose is too close to your arse.'

'No, it's like a bleachy smell. Anyway I'm going to have a piss and a shower and get breakfast.' Matt got up and went to the bathroom, where he discovered the note left by Karen.

'Hey Daz, there's a note with her number on it and an address. She says any time you're down this way give her a ring.'

'Fuck off, you must be joking, I feel dead guilty about Tracey, what the fuck am I going to tell her?'

'Nothing, you idiot, tell her nothing. Look you used protection so you won't have caught anything. Just forget it ever happened.'

'How can I? I feel shit now, how will I face her?'

'Look, silly bastard just forget it. It doesn't count, you were pissed, forget it, anyway I'm getting a shower now,' shouted Matt as he stepped into the refreshing spray.

Daz got up and went into the bathroom to go to the toilet but stopped dead and stared in horror as he got a glimpse of himself in the mirror. His face was covered in blood. He thought at first he'd been cut and he shouted out, 'What the fuck's happened to my face?' Matt heard this above the noise of the shower and looked out from behind the curtain to see Daz's face.

'Look at your pubes they've got blood on them. Did you go down on her?'

'How the fucking hell do I know, I can't even remember shagging her.'

Daz still hadn't twigged about what had happened until Matt with delight spelled it out for him.

'She must have been on her period and you have gone down on her, that's why you look like you've done fifteen rounds with Mike Tyson.'

Matt then pulled the curtain shut and got on with his shower. Daz was all over the place and got the shock of his life when he went to brush his teeth, they were covered in dried blood. He looked like a vampire who'd been to an all you can eat buffet. Matt carried on with his shower not realising he was washing away his eyebrows and seeing as he had dark hair he would look demented. As Matt got out of the shower laughing at Daz who was brushing his gums and teeth for the third time while being racked with guilt at being unfaithful for the first time. Matt was still laughing.

'At least you got a shag Daz, I got fuck all, just a bad back and the chance to watch you in action. I felt like David Attenborough watching animals mate. You made her moan and groan mate you must have been good, if that's any consolation for the fact you're covered in blood.'

Daz then took a look at Matt's face and couldn't quite work out what was wrong with him, he looked different but Daz couldn't put his finger on it. He didn't have to wait long as Matt knew what was wrong as soon as he clapped eyes on his reflection.

'My fucking eyebrows have gone, my fucking eyebrows have gone. Daz have you shaved them off you bastard?'

'How the hell have I done it I was drinking blood remember. Let's have a look. They haven't been shaved they've been burnt off with Immac or something like that.' The penny then dropped.

'That bitch Ali must have done it while I was asleep. I knew she didn't like me but this is a step too far.'

This time it was Daz who was laughing as he temporarily forgot about his red teeth and his sore gums.

'Don't fucking laugh, you can brush yours away. I can't grow new eyebrows before I get home and I look a twat. How am I going to explain this one away?'

'Easy just say one of the lads did it'

'Yeah but look at me, I look like someone on day realise, I'll have to paint some on, have you got anything I can use?'

'Oh yeah I'll just get my make up bag and get some eye liner out, silly twat what makes you think I'll have something. You'll have to go and buy some make up.' Daz was by now pissing himself at the thought of Matt in Boots going up to the counter and asking for an eyebrow pencil to match his hair. Daz went back into the room to get his stuff for a shower and looked at the bed it was covered in blood under the duvet and he thought how would he explain this if the maid came in and the room was rented out to two blokes. She'd think they were a couple of queers who'd been at it and one of them had bleed. He got in the shower and tried to forget it. Then the guilt of what he'd done hit him, and it didn't feel good he'd never been unfaithful before and didn't really remember being unfaithful at all because he must have been pissed. He felt sick to the stomach as he did remember flirting with Karen and inviting her back but that was just for show, he never in a million years expected her to turn up. But she did and they had sex, adulterous sex and now he had to live with it.

The two of them went down for breakfast as Matt had found a pair of shades in Daz's bag and put them on, that was the only way he would go down. He got a funny look from the staff as he entered the breakfast room and didn't take his sunglasses off, they thought he was a rock star. Skip saw him as he walked in and immediately was on the case.

'Now then lover boy and whose the Jackie Onnasis impersonator?'

'Piss off Skip, it's Matt and he's had an accident.'

'What kind of accident?' Skip probed further.

'Look we don't want to talk about it' and the two of them got their food and sat as far away from the crowd as possible.

'Be like that then, just because you got blown out.'

Matt and Daz ignored them although both were busting to tell the story of the night's event for different reasons. They had their food and tried to get back to their room but were hijacked on the way and dragged onto the chairs in reception where all the other lads had gathered, even Eddie and Dougie's lot were there.

'Come on why the glasses, so what went on then?' asked Tosser.

'Look we don't really want to say yet,' said Daz from the corner of his mouth trying not to show his teeth, as they still had a tinge of red about them.

'Come on, it can't be that bad, just tell us while we're all here. Why are you talking like Geoff Boycott Daz?' Daz looked at Matt who looked back blankly. Then Matt took his sunglasses off to reveal his eyebrow less face. Everyone fell about laughing.

'Is that it you shave his eyebrows off?' said Skip.

'No get a look at my teeth' and Daz smiled.

'Yeah and they look a bit red like he's brushed them too hard, so what's the story come on tell us.'

'Right we got those two birds back to our room, you know, the one whose mother was 64. Well she brought her friend for me. We got to the room and Daz and Karen got down to it and frigid Freda and me just sat there until she decided she would get in my bed and leave me with the chair near the window. Anyway King Kong over there gets down to it although he can't remember any of it, but by the sounds of it he was either good or she was very religious because she was shouting for God a lot. I then got pissed off and Ali her name was let me lay on the edge of the bed and try and get some kip. We both woke up this morning the girls had gone and Daz has a note thanking him for the night and if he's ever this way again he should ring her.' Everyone was cheering Daz who was deeply embarrassed at what he'd done in the cold light of day.

'So I gets in the shower and he goes for a piss, clocks his face in the mirror that's covered in blood, that's his face and not the mirror, and he screams out and then looks at his cock area and there's blood there as well. He's only gone down on her while she was on and all his teeth and gums are covered in dried blood and the bed is a right mess.'

'So what happened to your eyebrows?' asked Eddie.

'Well I think that Ali who didn't like me, I know what a shock everyone loves me, well I reckon she has put Immac on my eyebrows and I've got a shower and they've washed away.' People by this point were holding their stomachs in pain they had been laughing that much.

'You couldn't make this stuff up,' Eddie exclaimed.

'Look while we're all here, please keep this to yourselves I feel shit and I don't want Tracey to find out alright,' pleaded Daz.

'Look Daz what happens here stays here, when it's like that, but Matt what a twat you look,' Skip assured Daz.

'I'll go to the reception and see if the girls got any make up and we can paint you some on,' laughed Tosser.

Off he went and asked the female receptionist if she'd do them a favour and paint his eyebrows on. Tosser asked her to make him look stupid but she said no way. In fact Matt looked ridiculous and everyone could tell he'd had his eyebrows painted on. They all laughed as the receptionist did her best, but even she had to laugh because Matt looked like a bad female impersonator.

'Fucking hell Matt you look like Danny la Rue' shouted Doug as he held his sides laughing.

'One of your ex's Doug was she?' replied Matt but it was drowned out by the laughter.

'I can't believe that bitch did that. I even gave my fucking bed up for her. I tell you what Daz you owe me a big favour for this one.'

'How's that then? If your stinging chat up lines had worked, then you might still have your eyebrows.'

'What lines are these then Matt?' Eddie asked, never missing a trick.

'Er, do you come here often? What's your favourite colour? Do you want to see how many press-ups I can do? That kind of thing,'

Daz started to mock Matt.

'Piss off Dracula and go and brush your teeth for the hundreth time.'

'Now, now children it's time to ring Pete, we haven't told him what a great time he's missing for at least 12 hours, maybe longer. Who wants to ring him?' asked Skip. A whole host of hands went up and it was Thommo's turn as he hadn't yet had a go.

'For fuck sake don't mention us two with them birds,' begged Daz.

'Do you think I'm stupid? Right here goes,' and Thommo started to dial the number. Surprisingly Pete answered straight away.

'Hiya Pete it's Thommo, just ringing to tell you about the great time we've had. Me and Gaz got a massage and we were all shagging all night and the beer was free.....' Pete waited patiently while Thommo had finished and then politely asked if he had finished as he had some news to tell them all.

'If you've finished, well listen to this. Sally has just got back from the newsagents and she saw Steph and you know they all went looking for cock in Blackpool over the weekend. Well Tag only took his bird from work and was staying in the same hotel as the girls and Fay caught him out.'

'Fuck off you lying bastard, no way,' Thommo gasped.

'What, what's happened?' all the lads were trying to find out what had been said. Thommo handed the phone to Skip.

'Pete it's Skip here what's gone on?'

'Well Skip you know your lass and the other have been on a cock expedition in Blackpool. Well Tag took his bird from work there and was only staying in the same hotel as the girls and Fay who is now pregnant caught him red handed.'

'What happened after that?'

'Don't know, Fay and Tag are still in Blackpool sorting everything out.'

'The little twat he'll get it when her brothers find out. Anyway Pete hope you've had a good weekend, we have and now we're going to get stuck into some more birds and booze....,' Skip continued but Pete had rung off. Skip then explained to the baying pack what had happened.

'Tag got caught by Fay in bed with this bird he's knocking off from work. Guess what else he's only got Fay pregnant and now the two of them are in Blackpool sorting out who gets the house.'

'The jammy twat'll get out of it, he always does,' said Tosser with a tinge of jealousy.

'Well when her brothers find out he won't have any knackers left,' said Skip.

'Look if she's stayed there with him then he must have wormed his way around it,' Trev chipped in.

'Yeah, I suppose so the stupid little twat. What are the odds of that then pretending to go to London, but really going to Blackpool when your girlfriend is on a secret trip and staying in the same hotel,' posed Skip.

'I'd say about a million to one' Eddie answered before anyone could work it out.

'Right then is everyone ready to get going? The bus driver has gone for the bus and we have until 5 tonight and then we have to make our way home.' Eddie was trying to rally the troops to get away from the hotel before anything else could go wrong.

'All we need to do is get our bags from the rooms and check out and we're away. All except the students they haven't got back down yet,' said Skip.

'Alright I'll ring them and hurry them along and then we can get off' said Eddie who was ready to go and couldn't wait to get away from Greg who had done his head in from the minute they stepped into the room.

The students were in the room having a last shag and were saying goodbye to the girls as they were going onto France later that day and they needed to check out of their hotel and collect their stuff. Eventually after about ? of an hour the whole party was gathered in the foyer ready to go, they had all checked out and were waiting for the students to do the same as they waited outside with the girls for their taxi.

'Look at those two twats, they've been shagging those two for two nights and they couldn't get enough of them. I'll never understand women,' pondered Thommo.

'Look they're young aren't they and besides you'd have been shitting all Friday night so you'd have been no good,' laughed Daz.
Eventually the taxi came and the girls got in and left the two students with only memories and a couple of sore bell ends.

'Come on you two, let's have you checking out, now Abba's gone,' Eddie shouted over to the two of them. They then went to the reception and handed the key cards over and walked away, only for the receptionist to call them back.

'Excuse me sir, excuse me but you have a bar bill to pay of £110.' That news stopped Grant and Mike in their tracks.

'What? £110? That can't be right, I paid for all my drinks at the bar,' replied Grant in shock.

'No sir, it is for the mini bar, you drank all of the mini bar,' the receptionist informed them. Then it dawned on them, the two Swedes had got stuck into the drinks while they got stuck into the Swedes. Grant went pale and looked at Mike who went even paler. Then they both looked at Eddie who just smiled and calmly said, 'Well how much have you got between you?'

Grant and Mike turned out their pockets and between them they had £60. They looked at Eddie again for some comfort but Eddie was in a playful mood.

'What do you think lads, let these two work here for the day and pick them up later?'

'Why, what's happened?' enquired Thommo.

Eddie explained and the majority verdict was, 'Fuck 'em they had their fun and now it's time to pay.'

Grant and Mike looked like they were going to cry as the receptionist waited patiently until Eddie came to the rescue.

'Look, I'll lend you the money but I want it back next week alright, but you'll have to see these lot for a drink and some food, because I've got nothing left.'

'Cheers Eddie, you're a gent, and we will get the money back to you by Tuesday,' said a relieved Grant.

'Right then the bus is here so all aboard,' shouted Eddie as he marshalled the boys onto the bus. He then thanked the receptionist who had found the whole party quite refreshing from the normal day to day boring businessmen who stayed for a night and left with so much as a 'goodbye'. At least this lot had some life in them, even if they had left a bit of carnage behind.

Skip had told everyone to gather around the bus before they got on because he had a small presentation to make to someone. They all gathered around wondering what was going on. Eddie came out and asked what was happening. In fact only Tosser and Skip knew what was going on as Skip started his announcement.

'On Friday one of us lost something and I don't mean their virginity, students, or their arse, Thommo. The person I'm talking about is Greg who lost something which was very important to him. So now to present you with your teeth is Tosser.'

They all clapped as Tosser came forward with Greg's teeth inside a black condom that was tied at the end. Greg didn't know what to do, on the one hand he was pleased to get his teeth back but on the other hand he felt like flattening the two of them as he had been left to suck his food all weekend and had cut his gums.

'How did you get these?' asked Greg who still hadn't put them back in his mouth.

'I took my change out of my pocket Friday night and I had them in my change. They must have fell out when you had that fight with the coffee sign and I must have picked them up.'

'This condom hasn't been used has it?'

'Cheeky get. We cleaned the teeth for you, which was a job and a half and we had even more trouble with the wrapping. Put 'em in, they'll only taste of rubber for a bit.'

'Right then let's get going,' Eddie demanded as they had wasted enough time. Eddie then thanked Skip for keeping his teeth.

'Serves the twat right for keeping me awake and messing the room up all weekend,' said Eddie.

All the boys put their bags in the back and got on the bus. Eddie stood up at the front of the bus and told everyone the plans for the day. If they all agreed then they would proceed as follows. Pubs around Kings Cross and then at around 2pm they would head home and stop off at a small village the driver knew about, where they could have a piss stop and get something to eat. Then onwards and upwards back home for 10pm. Everyone agreed to go with whatever Eddie said. There were loads of cans and bottles still on the bus from the journey down and luckily the driver had taken the bin-come-toilet out and left it in the car park to give it an airing. They all got back on the bus and it slowly wormed its way down the road from the hotel. All the boys were quiet and a bit sombre at the realisation that the weekend was nearly over. They had packed their bags with as much shower gel and fancy soaps as they could. Gaz had had one hell of a job getting the Coca-Cola ice bucket in his bag but he managed in the end to get it in but then walked past reception as if he'd stolen a bed. His bag was bulging a bit, it looked like a snake that had just eaten a safe, but no one noticed it.

As per usual Skip was the one who started to talk first.

'Well we didn't get to go the Clipper for one last deal but we've got plenty on the bus and it's quite cold so come on you lot, get stuck in.' And he started to hand out cans to whoever wanted them. Some refused saying they would wait but the majority got stuck into the 'hair of the dog'. Pretty soon the banter was flying around again and was mainly aimed at the students.

'Well that was a dear shag boys, a 'prossy' would have been cheaper,' Thommo started.

'I know, schoolboy error there, mini bar got yer, you should have listened to us, no mini bar and no use of the phone,' Matt joined in, as the two students let the comments fly over their heads.

'I mean, was it worth it just to get your end away? I don't think so, you were all cocky and that paying through the nose to get into that nightclub and I bet them two birds fleeced you all night, what a couple of mugs,' Greg piped up. This caused a reaction like no other from Grant. He waited for the chatter to calm down, then he rose to his feet and turned to face the mob that had been baiting him and his friend. Everyone gave out a big 'Ooooh!' as if to say what's he going to do he's finally snapped. But Grant was far too intelligent and started to point out a few home truths.

'Right, let's start with you 'shitty arse' Thommo. You paid what was it? £30 and didn't even get a hand job, mate my knob is nearly hanging off. Then there's you Matt, couldn't even seal the deal with a bird that comes to your room, schoolboy error there mate. Me and Mike were shagging all night for two nights and they did the works. Now Greg, us a couple of mugs? - at least we've got our own teeth and if we didn't have, I'm sure we could keep the false ones in our mouths, go and have a fight with another coffee sign. You lot come out with all this shit about don't do this and don't do that and really you don't have a fucking clue about anything. I'm afraid this weekend the students have come out on top and the worldly wise men have looked like a bunch of fucking losers.'

Everyone cheered especially Eddie, but then Thommo pointed out a relevant point.

'We might be losers but at least we can afford a pint. You haven't got a pot to piss in.'

'Yeah, but we'll just sit on the bus with a couple of cans and remember the last two nights and catch up on some sleep, because believe me we've hardly had any,' Mike answered back in no uncertain terms.

'Look, let's calm down, I tell you what you could have had my mini bar for a pop at those two,' Skip said trying to keep the peace as it was getting quite heated.

'So then what were they like?' Skip asked as he sat next to Grant and Mike.

'Fucking hell Skip, we were at the bar and they came up and started talking and we just looked at each other. Then they asked us to dance, so we did. From there they invited us to go back to their room which was just around the corner. We couldn't believe it, we kept looking at each other as if to say is this a dream. Then they got a couple of bottles of vodka out and we just started to get it on. Then they swapped and then they started on each other,' said Grant.

'No way, lesbian act?' Skip blurted out.

'It was no act Skip, they were really into each other.'

At this point a crowd had gathered mainly when they heard the word lesbian and the students were laying it on thick. Mike continued the story.

'At one point, you won't believe this, one of us was getting sucked off and the other one was lapping her out while I shagged her from behind, it was unreal.'

'You jammy bastards, do you realise how fucking lucky you are. You could go through life and that would never happen to you let alone when you'd just come out of nappies.' Tosser was extremely jealous.

'I'm not finished yet, they came back here last night and we did it all over again, in the shower, on the floor, all over, then we all ended up in the same bed.'

'You two aren't going to confess now are you?' Skip asked.

'Fuck off! Although we had to be a bit careful not to get a handful of each other's bollocks,' joked Grant.

'No way man, not that you've just spoilt it for me,' said a disgusted Jonesy.

'Look, put it this way they didn't rip us off, they paid their way and we had a great time and we've got their number and if we like we can go to visit them in Sweden.'

'You do realise this isn't the norm don't you?' Daz said.

'Yeah, but what is the norm? Six months ago I couldn't get a sniff and now I've gone from the bingo queue to the model queue and all these women can't resist me.'

'And now you'll go on a drought of about two years,' scoffed Thommo.

'Well Thommo, it sounds like he's had more than two years action in two nights,' shouted Eddie putting Thommo in his place.
The journey continued and they carried on drinking until they reached Kings Cross. The driver dropped them off and went to park up and told them that they would be leaving at 2.30pm on the dot and going to a country pub for a bite to eat and some drinks.

The bus left them at the pub they usually frequented, but it had just opened and was empty so they didn't even bother getting a drink. They had taken all the cans off the bus and proceeded to the next pub, which had an advert outside saying, 'Exotic Dancer – Sunday - Free Entry'.

'This'll do, we'll go in here and watch the stripper. You lot take the cans to the back of the pub and a few of us will get a drink at the bar.'

Skip was in organising mode. So they went into the pub where there were about fifty blokes, all waiting for the stripper to come on. The lads all blended in and about three or four of them went to the bar to get the beers in. They ordered halves instead of pints so that they had some glasses and it wouldn't look like they were just drinking their own cans. Skip went to the bar and asked when the stripper was on and the barman said, 'In the next ten minutes'. While the barman was serving the lads with their drinks, Matt noticed there was a tin of cigars within reach from the bar, so he looked around and then quickly swiped them and went to the back of the pub. Matt then proceeded to hand out the cigars to all and sundry, even people that didn't smoke. Within about five minutes around fifty blokes were all puffing away at cigars doing Clint Eastwood and Jimmy Saville impressions. The bar had only taken about £20 even though it was full and everyone was smoking cigars and drinking glasses of beer. Ten minutes passed and still no stripper, so Tosser went to the bar and asked when she would be coming on.

'We've had a few problems but she'll be on in about five minutes,' said the barman who was a bit flustered as all the other punters were getting impatient and having a go at him.

'Can I have a cigar my friend?' Tosser asked. The barman went to where the cigars were supposed to be but there were none. He thought nothing of it and reached behind the till and produced another tin and put them where the others had been. He looked for Tosser who had disappeared, so he started to serve again. As soon as he turned his back Matt took the new batch of cigars as the barman was trying to serve punters and answer questions about whether the stripper actually existed. The fact of the matter was the manager who was trying to sort out the music had told his one and only barman to keep serving the drinkers and that way they would drink more because as soon as the stripper had been on they would probably leave. Everyone had another cigar and then the chanting started 'Why are we waiting? Why are we waiting?' The barman started to flap even more and went to find the manager who eventually introduced the dancer on stage.

'Here she is gentlemen, she's been worth the wait, so raise your glasses, you won't be disappointed, here she is - Talula'.

With that, this scrawny looking thing in suspenders came on stage to the song 'You ready for this?' Well, she was, the crowd was, but unfortunately the sound system wasn't. It got to the first few bars and packed up along with the stage lighting. Everyone started booing as the manager came back on stage and tried to explain that the electrics had gone and that he might not be able to fix them. The crowd booed even more and started shouting 'Conman, hustler....'

'Look can anyone sing? And she'll strip to that,' said the desperate bar manager as he looked at Talula for approval. She nodded as she wanted paying. Well her shifty looking boyfriend did, he was the one making her do it.

From the back of the room Jonno started to sing the only song he knew all the way through. It was the Hull F.C. song, 'Old faithful' and Talula started to slowly strip to the sound of fifty blokes singing about a cowboy and his horse. Eddie couldn't help but laugh at a sight that even he had never seen before. She'd only got half her gear off when they reached the end of the song, so Eddie started to sing the famous Hull K.R. song, 'When The Red, Red Robin'. She carried on stripping to that and eventually, after three renditions of each, she finally reached the end off her act. Now for the finale. All she wanted was for someone to take off the garter she had on. Skip immediately ran to the stage and announced that it was Greg's birthday and that he would do it. Greg protested that his birthday was in December but the whole crowd started singing 'Happy Birthday' and pushing him towards the stage. When he eventually got on stage the girl who had track marks all up her arm and was clearly a drug user whispered in his ear, 'Take it off with your teeth'. Greg stepped forward eagerly and with no thought for his teeth's safety, the same teeth he'd just got back a few hours earlier, he did as she said and the lads were shouting

'While you're down there' expecting Greg to kiss her fanny. She looked as if to say, I don't mind if that's what you want. Well Greg did, so he kissed her belly button and then vacated the stage as quick as he could to the howls of laughter that followed him.

'He kissed her belly button for fucks sake,' laughed Daz uncontrollably.

'Are you a bit queer Greg? You should have given her a good muffing, I would have done,' Tosser said knowing full well that he wouldn't have dared touch her.

'Well, why didn't you get up then?'

'Because it's not my birthday.'

'It isn't mine either, you twat.'

'Sorry Greg couldn't resist it, well look at it this way you can take your teeth out and give them a good bleach.'

The stripper then got off the stage and the manager came around with a bucket for a collection, which was a waste of time as no one put anything in. They'd had to provide the music and she was the worst stripper they'd ever seen.

'Come on lads, bit of spare change for the girl.'

'No chance pal, she was rubbish, we should charge you for the music,' said Thommo.

'She goes a bit further if you chip in and we get enough, she'll get someone up,' pleaded the manager who had the dancer's boyfriend eye-balling him from the other side of the bar and he wasn't pleased with the afternoon's event. He wanted paying a decent whack of cash for letting his bird strip in public.

'Jesus, we don't want to see her go any further, she's already gone too far. Where did you book her, dog's home?' Tosser said shaking his head.

'Anyway, we're off in about five minutes mate, so we won't be here, shame really,' said Skip being diplomatic as he signalled to Eddie to get everyone out. It was a bit of a dive and looked like a drug's den. They all left and some went to the café down the road for something to eat before the bus came. The others just drank the remaining cans.

Greg was the butt of everyone's jokes and they were all showing him their belly buttons and asking him if he was getting turned on. On the way Skip found a phone box and decided to ring Pete one last time. Sally answered and said that Pete was feeling much better and had gone to the local, meaning Shoey's pub, for a drink. Skip thanked Sally and hung up. He then grabbed Daz who virtually lived in

Shoey's pub and asked him the number, which of course he knew off by heart. He then rang the pub. Pete was in the bar relaxing thinking that no one would ring him here, he could have a nice quiet pint and read the paper. How wrong he was, as the barmaid shouted his name out.

'Pete Turner, telephone call for Pete Turner.'

Pete rushed to it thinking what could be wrong, was it Sally or had something happened at home? He rushed to the bar to answer the call. His heart was pounding, fearing the worse.

'Hello,' Pete said timidly.

'Hiya Pete, it's us, thought you could escape us didn't you? You're a little tinker aren't you but we've got spies all over the place working for us. Just rung to tell you we're setting off in about ten minutes and then we can tell you face to face what a great time we've had and all the stuff we've been up to.'

'Look Skip, fuck off,' and Pete hung up and told the barmaid that if any more calls came through for him, to tell them to stick it and he carried on with his pint and the sports pages.

The bus arrived bang on time and they all got on for the penultimate leg of the journey. They still had a few cans left but they were warm by now and only the most hardened drinkers wanted to finish them.

'How far is this pub then driver?' asked Gaz

'About an hour out of London and it's quite well to do,' the driver said trying to warn the lads of what to expect. This went completely over their heads as Thommo pointed out, 'We'll welcome them to the real world driver.' The driver just looked through his mirror as if to say have I made a big mistake here? Eddie was there to reassure him.

'Don't worry, I'll keep them in line, it's when they're spread all over the place I struggle to keep order.' Then Eddie collared Skip and told him to make sure the message got around that there was to be no pissing around in the pub.

The bus journey was a quiet affair due to the fact that no one had any energy and all wanted to fall asleep but no one dare for fear of the repercussions. There was however a bit more light-hearted piss taking with Greg about the belly button incident...

Back in Blackpool Tag and Fay had set off and were all 'loved up' on their way home, excited at the thought of telling everyone their good news. Luckily for them all the girls had kept relatively quiet about what had happened, even Shaz who had spent the afternoon in the company of Fay's brothers. She didn't utter a word. She never even let on that she'd been away with Fay for the weekend.

Meanwhile on the lads' trip, the bus had just pulled off the motorway and was making it's way through the leafy suburbs to their destination.

'Jesus driver this is posh, are you sure you want us on the rampage around here?' asked Gaz trying to wind him up.

'That'll do Gaz, come on the driver's been good enough to bring us here so let's behave and that goes for the rest of you as well, alright,' shouted Eddie, hoping they would all take notice.

'Yes dad, don't get your knickers in a twist,' came the collective reply. The bus came to a halt and parked outside a huge country house which was about fifty yards from the pub. The grounds could have fitted several football pitches on it. They had the short walk to the pub as the driver didn't want to block up the pub car park.

'Right then lads, you've got two hours here and then we've got to go. I'm getting my dinner here and believe me they do a mean roast,' announced the driver who stopped there quite often with coach parties and the manager gave him a free feed.

'Listen lads, when you get in Skip will ask what you want to drink and then I'll get it because I've got some money left from the kitty. It's not as much as I would have liked but then I didn't think any silly twats would soak and terrorise an elderly Japanese couple. So please behave for once, please,' pleaded Eddie.

They all trooped off the bus, went into the pub, which was packed and gave Skip their order.

The pub football team was in the bar and the lounge was full of locals and the dining area, a conservatory with tables, looked nice. The manager asked if anyone would be dining and a few decided that they would, as they hadn't fancied the 'greasy spoon' in London. The ones who had eaten were full and a bit pissed-off as the food looked top notch. The students had borrowed £20 each from Trev and Jonesy and were sat with them telling them more about the two Swedes. The others who were dining were Eddie, Skip, Tosser and Damo. The rest of the lads were just stood in the lounge as the beers just kept coming. In all Eddie had enough money for four rounds. Doug and the old brigade had gone into the bar as it was cheaper by 10 pence a pint in there and they could get sat down and away from the noise. The local village football teams were asking them where they'd been and what they'd been up to? The old guys liked telling them what a bunch of twats all the younger lads were and that this would be their last trip and the usual shit they loved to spout. In the lounge there was a piano and Matt decided he would have a go at playing it. So he sat down and limbered up, as if he knew what he was doing. He stretched his arms and started cracking his fingers as if he was about to play. Then the barman intervened by clapping his hands and announcing,

'Attention everyone, someone is going to play for us,' and all heads turned towards the piano and Matt.

Now Matt only knew 'Chopsticks' and half of 'When the Saints Go Marching In' but he thought fuck it, I'll never see these people again. So he started to play and the locals sat there open-mouthed, not believing what they were witnessing. He was halfway through 'When the Saints' when he suddenly stood up and took a bow. There was silence until the manager, not wanting to appear rude, began to clap and then a couple more joined in half-heartedly as Matt milked it for all it was worth.

The manager couldn't work out if he was simple and a sandwich short of a picnic or he taking the mickey, but he clapped anyway. Then Gaz sat at the piano and before the manager could say anything Gaz started playing away. Gaz was actually shit hot on the piano, he learnt it at school and also got to grade five and used to be in a band. He played a medley of the Beatles and the Stones and then some Elton John. When he stood up after about twenty minutes he got a round of applause but then he just went back to his beer. The barman handed over a free beer from the bar for the rich entertainment, which pissed off Matt who asked where his drink was. As quick as a flash the manager tossed him an ice cube, the people who saw it laughed and even Matt had to admire the manager's wit.

Matt then went to the dining area to be a bit of a pest. The food had just arrived and he was going up to each person and nicking potatoes off the plates of the lads who'd ordered food. He got a couple from the students and then went to get one from Eddie who had watched what was going on and had covered his with red-hot gravy. Eddie laughed as Matt quickly put the potato in his mouth and then suddenly realised it was too hot for him so he had to run to the toilet to spit it out. His eyes were streaming and his face was bright red.

'What's wrong with him?' asked Daz.

'He's a greedy twat who has just got what was coming to him, that's what's wrong with him,' replied Eddie. Matt was in the toilet and had burnt his mouth and his throat, and he emerged from the toilet looking the worse for wear.

'Want another one Matt?' Eddie scoffed.

'No thanks Eddie, I think I've had one too many,' Matt replied with a very croaky voice.

Trev and Jonesy were sat with Grant and Mike and the two couples sat on the next table were asking them where they'd been and what they were doing there.

'Well, we come down to London for the Rugby League Challenge Cup Final every year and we're just on our way home really,' Trev explained.

'Is that the game that was on the TV yesterday?' asked the taller of the two men on the other table.

'Yes, the one-sided game unfortunately. But we come for the atmosphere and a laugh with all the lads and that,' Jonesy chipped in.

'More of a rugger man myself,' replied the smaller man, and his girlfriend said she couldn't tell the difference, she thought they were the same.

'No love, they are totally different, league's a lot harder to play and faster. You need to be fitter as the ball is in play longer and you have to defend. Whereas in union there's a lot of kicking and stoppages in play,' Skip butted in from the table behind the couple.

'Well that's a matter of opinion old boy. I like union as it has a better social side to it, plus you boys play for money and we play for the love of the game.'

'I'll correct you there pal. We all play for nothing but the love of the game. A couple of these boys play for Great Britain and have toured around the South Seas and they had to pay their own way for the privilege,' Skip wouldn't let the guy have the last word.

'Anyway what have you been up to other than watching the game, anything exciting apart from drinking?'

'Well these two here they went on a sexual journey with two Swedish ladies and were at it all weekend. By the sounds of it that's exactly what they've been left with - week ends,' Skip blurted out as the two students turned crimson and told Skip to shut up.

'No come on chaps run us through it,' the guy carried on as Grant and Mike stared at their girlfriends as if to say in front of these two. The fella realised this and said 'Oh don't worry about the ladies, they like a bit of rumpy-pumpy like the rest of us don't you girls?' The girls nodded and sat up ready for the story to begin. Grant was very reluctant to say anything, but Skip knew how embarrassed he was and wouldn't let it go. 'Tell 'em about it go on right from the start, you know where you met them and what happened and how you fell madly in love.'

Grant was still not saying anything but then Mike started to tell the story and was well away. Grant was very embarrassed at first and then he started to look at the women on the next table they were getting excited and hanging on every word that Mike was saying. Grant started to join in and he could see the girls really getting into it. The two guys with them couldn't believe it they had never experienced anything like this and had only ever heard of this happening with prostitutes. Skip's little joke had backfired as after the coffees had come and gone the students Grant and Mike had created a buzz and the others thought they must be incredibly charismatic. The two girls got up to go to the toilet and left the men at the table.

'Thanks for that boys I think we'll be going in a minute as I think the girls are hot and sticky if you know what I mean.'

'Not a problem anyway I'm going to have to go to the toilet myself.' And Grant excused himself and made his way to the toilet area which was situated in a separate part of the pub and you had to go through a door and then down a corridor. Coming out of the ladies were the two girls and they grabbed Grant and took him into a cubicle and started to strip him off. Grant couldn't believe it and just went with the flow. The first girl started to undo his trousers and then started to give him a 'blow job'. While the other one was snogging him and grabbed his hand and put it up her skirt and to Grant's surprise she had no knickers on. He started to finger her well-groomed vagina and she was moaning in ecstasy. Then they swapped around and the girl giving him head stopped and got his other hand and put it up her skirt so now he was fingering both girls and they were tossing him off. They both had their tits out and he was taking it in turns to suck them. He couldn't believe it and eventually he came. The two girls had a proposition for him.

'When we go to toilet in the next half an hour you and your mate meet us in there and we'll get it on.'

'But what about your boyfriends?'

'Those two are fucking useless, you two really turn us on, so when we go again you two follow. Now you go out and we'll follow in five minutes.'

Grant did as he was told and although he was sheepish about going back to the table, he had only been gone for about 10 minutes and no one had noticed anything. He eventually paid for the food and got Mike on his own. Mike was wondering what was going on. The girls came back to join their partners as if nothing had happened. Then Grant told Mike what had happened.

'You'll never guess where I've been?'

'I know it's a shot in the dark but to the toilet for a dump.'

'Yeah the toilet but which one?'

'The pub one, the one on the bus doesn't exist.'

'No, no I've been to the ladies toilet.'

'Why?'

'I was going to the men's when those two women on the other table grabbed me and took me into their toilet and one started sucking my cock and the other one, I was fingering her. They think we are a couple of studs.'

'Fuck off, no way.'

'Yes, and listen to this, they want me and you, you and me to meet them the next time they go to the lav, can you believe it?'

'Well no because they are going now, the two blokes said the girls are hot and they are going to get it when they get home.'

'Well we'll see.' The two of them looked over to the table where the couples were to see if they were leaving, but there was no movement. In fact the girls had told the men to get another drink as they weren't ready to go yet. They continued to sit at the table and the two students continued to watch. The boys then stood nearer to the door that lead to the toilet so as not to raise suspicions. Time passed on and the pub was quite lively as the afternoon went on and then the girls told their boyfriends they were going to liven up and made their way to the toilets.

Grant and Mike gave it a couple of minutes and went through to the bar to have a word with the older guys and they casually left their drinks in the bar and went to the toilets. Thus this gave them an alibi if the shit hit the fan. They would have witnesses to say they were in the bar. The girls' boyfriends didn't have a clue, all they thought was that the girls were getting ready for an afternoon of rumpy-pumpy, which in many ways they were only not with them.

Grant and Mike entered the toilets but no one was in sight and then they heard a noise from two cubicles and Grant went in one and Mike in the other. They were shocked to find the girls had nothing on at all and they grabbed the two boys and quickly stripped them and got them aroused. Both of them were in a bit if a rush as although their boyfriends were stupid they weren't that stupid. In fact they could have taken their time as their boyfriend were deep in conversation with Skip and Tosser about which was the better game league or union and they both agreed that both beat football anyway 'bloody poofs game'. Back in the cubicles the girl who was with Grant was bent over the toilet and Grant was taking her from behind and she was backing onto him and loving it. She asked him to slap her backside while he was shagging her, which Grant was only too happy to do. In the other cubicle Mike was placed on the toilet seat and the girl straddled him while he sucked her ample breasts and she rode him like a Derby winner. The thought was going through Grant's mind that these two had done this before and he was right. They looked like butter wouldn't melt but they were a couple of high-class slappers. The whole affair lasted about fifteen minutes and the lads then went back to the bar to rejoin Doug and Bert telling them they'd been looking for a shop for some chewy. The girls got re-dressed and rejoined their boyfriends as if nothing had happened.

'Back are we? Well I think we'll be going chaps, got some business to attend to if you know what I mean?' The man then winked at Skip and Skip gave him the thumbs up thinking tossers what do those two see in you two pricks.

'Yeah you trot along mate and get the business done, looking forward to it girls?' Skip then gave the sign from the seventies that meant sex, the good old hand in the elbow and the 'phoarrh' signal. He did this hoping the girls would think they'd been talking about them, thus pissing them off and fucking up the afternoon for the two knob heads they'd had to listen to for the last hour. It actually happened the girls were far from happy that they'd been discussed.

'What in the hell was he talking about?' said the first girl very angrily.

'Nothing we were just saying we were going for some afternoon delight, after his friends story I could see how excited you were so we thought we could have some fun this afternoon. So come along and get into the car and we'll be off.'

The girls did as they were told as the guys were loaded and treated them well and half an hour of laying back and thinking of England was worth all the treats they got in return. But really they'd had their afternoon delight with two real men and would have loved some more. Grant and Mike had seen the girls leave and only when they saw the car pull out of the car park did they rejoined the rest of the lads in the lounge.

'Back are you? You've missed those two blokes they wanted to thank you for the story as it got their birds all moist and they've gone for an afternoon of shagging,' Skip informed them.

'Yeah, we know. Skip come here I want a word,' Grant said quietly.

'What is it?'

'What did those two fellas say while their girlfriends were away?'

'Nothing just talking rugby and how they were going to have a shag, why?'

'Well they've had a shag, both of 'em'

'What you mean, you shagged them?' the penny dropped with Skip the girls had been away for a long time.

'Just after the story they went to toilet remember?'

'I suppose so I wasn't taking much notice I had a bit of a hard on, you should write for them porn mags Grant you have a flair for it.'

'Anyway I went to toilet and they were coming out of the ladies and they grabbed me and we had a bit of an encounter. Then they said the next time they went to the toilet me and Mike had to go and meet them there. So we did and we ended up banging them in the cubicles in the ladies.'

'Fuck off no way.'

'Way why do you think we went into the bar to see Doug?'

'Come on you must be lying?'

'Ask Mike and I'll go over there.' So Grant left Skip and Skip then called Mike over who then confirmed that they had indeed had the two girls in the ladies. But as Mike pointed out don't broadcast it as their relatives might be in the pub and then it would kick off. Skip just stood there shaking his head. When he rejoined the rest of the lads Tosser asked what all the secrecy was all about and Skip just said they were asking about some money and not to mention it as they were embarrassed. Tosser accepted this and for once appreciated the need for a bit of discretion.

The driver had finished his meal and told Eddie that they would be going in an hour. Eddie told the lads they had about three-quarters of an hour left as they needed to get home as the bus was only booked for so long. In actual fact Eddie wanted to get home and had really had enough and wanted the stress of it all to end. Eddie never really relax when the lads were in a public place as he always felt some thing was around the corner. He wasn't far off the mark as Skip and the lads decided to treat the locals to a few songs, they started with 'Rhinestone cowboy' which went down well with everyone and then they sang 'Delilah' which was the club song after matches. The pub was loving this and the land lord had never had an atmosphere like it on a Sunday afternoon. Then the finale was 'The Cow Kicked Nelly'. This was of some interest to the locals as all the lads sat on the floor and some of the locals joined them. Skip explained the more verses, the louder it got and the higher the boys would jump. They got to verse ten and some of them were laughing that much they had to drop out. Trev went to the toilet and was stood next to one of the football team from the bar and by this time the noise was very loud and the lads had just started to jump around a bit. The noise was so loud you could hear it in the toilets.

'What's all this about then?' asked the footballer.

'It's just a song mate, with loads of verses all the same but the more verses the louder it gets and the more boisterous the lads get until they get to about verse 15 then they are as loud and as energetic as they can get. We're on verse 10 now so it will get louder and they'll get more excited.'

But surprisingly the noise stopped suddenly. Trev went back into the lounge and there was a deathly silence and frowns on all the locals faces. It was as if they were in a western and the local killer had entered the bar and the piano player stopped and everyone stared.

What had happened was Matt had got so excited he saw a brass plaque behind the bar and he thought it would be fun to try and hit it by flicking his trainer at it. Unfortunately he missed and smashed most of the optics that were behind the bar. They had gone from being good entertainment to being as welcome as a fart in an astronaut's suit.

'Get out you hooligans, get out,' shouted the landlord loudly, 'you are no longer welcome here.'

'I'm sorry…,' Eddie tried to make amends.

'Don't even try to justify this just leave and don't come back,' the landlord interrupted. Eddie then told all the lads to drink up, they were going. They all did out of embarrassment anyway and made their way out to what felt like the atmosphere the panto baddy must get night after night but instead of hissing and booing the locals were tutting and scowling at them. It was only one stupid act that turned the full mood of the place around. It was as if the locals were just waiting for something to happen so they could turn on the northerners for invading their sleepy hollow. The landlord had over reacted and was putting a bit of a show on for the locals. He even went into the bar to throw out Doug and the oldies saying they weren't welcome, to which he got a very stern reply. Doug was as quick as a flash with his answer.

'Well we've been welcome for the past two hours spending our money and we've done nothing wrong, so I suggest you get behind that bar and get me and my friends another round in. I don't know what has gone on in your lounge my friend but it has nothing to do with us. Bring the police in because we've done nowt wrong and we're not moving.'

'You're on the same trip aren't you? You're all the same, you lot, thugs.' Bert stood up to confront the landlord but Doug told him to sit down.

'It isn't worth it Bert. By the way who's all the same people from the north I presume you mean? Well let me tell you mate I'd rather be from where I'm from than some place where no one has got the time of day for anyone.'

'You come from your council estates and think because you spend a bit of money on a weekend you can do what you like.' The landlord had lost it by this time. Now Doug to look at him was an ordinary bloke who was a bit tight and liked a pint but to look at him you would never realise that he had been a very successful businessman in his time and had pots of cash. He never ever divulged what he had but he knew how to put people in their place when the need arose and the time had come to put this prick in his place.

'Tell you what you tin pot little Hitler, what's this shit hole of a pub worth? Half a million? well my friend I could buy this out of my small change.' Doug looked at the landlords face drop as he only leased the pub and could be replaced. Doug knew he'd won.

'Now then are we going to get those drinks or not because I'm thirsty?'

'Well I suppose you were in here all along and...'

'Look they've done nothing wrong, they've been good company and all your worried about is the twats in there who buy a couple of gin and tonics a week. If you don't serve them then we'll stop coming in.' The captain of the football team piped up in defence of Doug and the old brigade. The landlord started to pull the beers as he knew that the football team did spend a lot of time in the pub and he could ill afford to piss them off. He did like lording it up with the

Toffs but he knew which side his bread was buttered on.

'Cheers lads we'd get you a drink but we've spent up nearly. Is he always like this then ?' asked Bert.

'He's been here for about 6 months and thinks he's hit the big time, he came from a shit hole in London and this is like the Hilton compared to that. Most of the regulars in here are alright, but the Sunday brigade who dine here want him to bend over backwards, which he does the grovelling twat. That's why we're in here can't stand listening to them boring bastards through there talking about money and what car they drive.'

'So do they spend a lot in here then?'

'No we spend most of our time in here, we all play for the darts team as well. That's why he served you lot so quickly if we piss off he's had it. You'll find the people who have money around here don't come in. Most people around here are just ordinary people and don't think they're better than everyone else. Are you really loaded then?'

'Yeah! I suppose I am now I sold my business and retired. But these lot aren't we've been mates for years, all played rugby together and have been mates for forty years. Money is never mentioned. If one of these is in the shit they know I'll help them out and do you know not one of them ever asks for anything.'

The landlord had sorted out the order.

'There you go gentlemen your drinks and may I apologise for my outburst, I was out of order.'

'Not a problem. Can I ask you are you from a council estate son?' asked Bert.

'Yes actually I am' answered the landlord.

'Thought so, nothing wrong with living on a council estate son we all come from somewhere. It's where we end up and how we conduct ourselves that counts not the house we live in or the car we drive. Some of the finest people I know haven't got a pot to piss in but they're great human beings. Tell me what happened next door?'

'One of your party threw his shoe at my optics and smashed them.'

'Well what you should have done was thrown that person out and not the rest of the lads. You took their money all afternoon and then treat them like that. If you played your cards right we would recommend this place as a stop over and you'd be packed when people came. Think next time son because we spend money and your posh twats don't. If you've got a till full of money and a few broken glasses is it worth putting up with? I think you'll find the answer is yes.'

'Thanks for the advice maybe I should have just asked the guy to leave, but he was out of order, I suppose I was a bit short with the older one in charge.'

'His name is Eddie and he keeps them all in line, but he can't help it if some idiot does something silly. Now if I know Eddie he would have offered to pay for the damage am I right?'

'Well he never got the chance I was that shocked by the incident I just flipped.' With that the door opened and in walked Eddie sheepishly to see where the old guys were. Eddie got a shock when the landlord asked if he wanted a drink to say sorry for flying off the handle at him and he realised it wasn't his fault.

Eddie declined the drink but accepted the apology and said that all the lads were sorry for what had happened and then offered to pay for the damage. The landlord declined the offer, then thanked Eddie for his custom and said they would be welcome whenever they were passing. Eddie asked the oldies to hurry up as the driver wanted to get away and all the lads were on the bus. Doug, Bert and the coffin dodgers all finished their drinks and forced themselves to go to the toilet as they couldn't face the bin on the bus.

'By the way here's £10 tell the poor barmaid to get herself a drink or some new knickers, I think she shit the ones she had on dodging that shoe,' said Eddie handing over a tenner, he then shook the landlords hand and went on his way.

On the bus Matt was being slagged off in some quarters and in others they were laughing about it.

'I can still see that barman's face as your trainer missed his head and hit the whiskey,' laughed Jonesy.

'That was the only bell's he was going to be ringing,' added Trev.

'Look lads I'm sorry for that I don't know what came over me. I just thought it would be a laugh,' Matt said with some regret.

'Look don't worry about it Matt we'll just have to add it to the list of places we'll never be welcome again,' said Skip. Then it went silent as Eddie and the old brigade got on the bus. The silence lasted about 30 seconds until Matt broke it.

'How much do we owe then for the damage? Don't worry I'll foot it, I mean it was my fault, so come on Eddie how much?'

'£350' came the reply.

'Fuck off no chance it was only one bottle of whiskey.'

'Yes but it was a vintage bottle 60 years old whiskey and it was £20 a shot, we're in a different part of the world now Matt this is the stockbroker belt and you know things cost a hell of a lot more. The finer things in life cost money..' Eddie went on loving the fact that Matt was sinking further and further into his seat and he could see him thinking how the fuck am I going to be able to get £350 together, I've barely got £3.50 left. Then Eddie put him out of his misery.

'It costs nothing in fact you can thank Doug and Bert I think they gave him a bollocking. Get this we are all welcome to come back whenever we are passing as long as we take our shoes off before we enter.'

'You bastard Eddie you had me going there for a minute,' Matt smiled with a huge sigh of relief.

'So then come on Doug, Bert what did you say?' asked Daz. Doug came half way down the bus and explained.

'He came into the bar and tried to turf us out. So I said fuck off we haven't caused you any trouble, we've been filling your till all afternoon and then some prick throws his shoe at you or whatever and you think you can throw us all out. I told him we wanted another drink.'

'What did he say to that?'

'He went on about us being northern thugs and from council estates and not knowing how to behave and that and that was when I pointed out I could buy his pub with my small change. Plus the football lads who drink there all the time told him if he didn't serve me they would all fuck off to another pub to drink.'

'What happened then?'

'He got us our drinks and Bert gave him some pearls of wisdom and said he'd acted too hastily and should have only chucked out dickhead over there, pointing at Matt. The landlord agreed and then offered to serve Eddie with a free drink. That's it really.'

'So he didn't want any money then?'

'No but I gave him a tenner and told him to get the barmaid a drink, so you owe me that Matt,' Eddie chipped in.

'Cheers fellas for that I really appreciate it' shouted Matt putting his thumbs up.

'Look Matt I like you and that but you've got to start controlling what you do, I mean you could have knocked that poor girl out or had her eye out,' Doug pleaded with Matt.

'Cheers, Doug I really am sorry.'
Matt bowed his head.

'Right then driver, we're all here let's go,' shouted Eddie and the bus finally pulled out of the village and onto the road and onto the last leg of a most memorable journey...

CHAPTER 13
WILL IT
WORK OUT?

Tag and Fay arrived back in Hull and got in a taxi and made their way home to the house they shared. They were a lot happier than they had been before they left it two days earlier. They seemed to know now where they were going and it appeared they were going together on a journey both of them wanted. Fay had told Tag that she would go to doctors the next day to get the pregnancy confirmed and then tell the family. But by the time they'd got home and she rang her mother she couldn't help herself and she just had to tell her the good news.

Fay's mother was the only one in Fay's family who actually had a soft spot for Tag. Her brothers hated him and her dad wasn't bothered either way, he just wanted a quiet life and found himself agreeing with whoever was speaking. If his sons were slagging Tag off then he would agree and the same the other way, if his wife or Fay was praising Tag he agreed, anything for a quiet life. On this occasion he actually expressed an opinion and asked if Tag was going to make an honest woman of her. Fay assured him Tag had already asked to marry her but she had held back as she didn't know what she wanted. Fay's dad then got hold of the phone.

'Look, a child needs a mother and a father Fay and I might be old fashioned here but what's the baby's surname going to be?'

'We haven't thought about that one,' replied Fay.

'Now then you see the child won't know whether it's coming or going, it'll have a different surname to you or Tag. Do the right thing and get married. I mean you already live together what's stopping you?'

'Nothing I suppose, but we'll decide when we will get married and no one else.'

'Well then ask him if the offer is still on the table and grab it,' continued her dad.

'I'll see dad, I'll see.'

Fay wasn't going to divulge the reason she was hesitating was that she had just found out Tag was trying to have a relationship behind her back and that if she hadn't caught him red handed he would have gone through with it. Fay got off the phone and told them not to tell anyone as she wanted to get it confirmed by the doctor the next day. Then it was Tag's turn to tell his parents and they said pretty much the same 'are you getting married?'

Tag explained that they didn't know and got pretty much the same reply about the modern generation and what would the child's surname be? Eventually after an hour on the phone they sat and looked at each other with relief as if to say we're glad that's over. Fay had seen a marked change in Tag in the last 24 hours and she was seriously thinking about what her dad had said. Fay then turned to Tag and asked him.

'You know what you asked me in Blackpool? Well the answer is yes.' Tag looked puzzled and took a couple of minutes to click about what Fay was saying.

'Yes to what?'

'Yes, I will marry you if the offer is still there.'

Tag was taken aback and then a big smile came across his face and he jumped up and started dancing around the room.

'Let's ring everyone,' said an excited Tag.

'No it's too late and I've had enough excitement for one weekend. We'll wait until tomorrow and tell them all face to face.'

'Kill joy'

'You might be right there Tag but I'm pregnant and tired, I haven't had much sleep and it's hardly been a normal weekend has it.'

'I suppose you're right, so what do you want to do?'

'Well get a bath and go to bed.'

'Right I'll go and run you a bath and make a sandwich or some toast, which one will it be?' asked a rather enthusiastic Tag which shocked Fay as he'd never made a sandwich in his life.

'What sandwich are you going to make?' Fay was calling his bluff, thinking he'll never manage it.

'Err! Don't really know I thought toast would be good. I just about know how to make toast.'

'Toast will be good then, make it after you've run the bath, I'll eat it in there.'

Fay chuckled to herself as Tag rushed off to run the bath like a schoolboy trying to impress his teacher who he had a crush on. Fay thought this won't last as he'll explode but it would be nice while it lasted.

Tag returned about five minutes later and told Fay that the bath was ready. He helped her up from the chair and walked behind her as she went up the stairs. She stopped half way and Tag was concerned.

'What's wrong is it the baby?'

'No it's you, I can walk up the stairs by myself, I know you're being caring but for Christ sake Tag, I can walk. So go and make that toast and you can make a hot chocolate while you're at it, there's some in the back of the cupboard.'

So Tag rushed downstairs to the kitchen and Fay went to get her bath. The sight that greeted her as she walked into the bathroom was one of horror it looked like an 18-30 club foam party or something from 'It's a knockout'. There was about two feet of foam coming out of the bath. Fay shouted down to Tag.

'Did you put any bath foam in?'

'Yeah why?'

'Oh, I would never have guessed, must have dropped the bloody bottle in,' Fay said the last bit under her breath as she prepared to enter the foam castle. Tag seemed to be gone for ages and Fay was worried. She eventually shouted down to him, as it was very quiet.

'Are you alright?'

'Yeah but this grill is taking a long time, the oven bit is hot but it isn't making the bread toasty.'

'Have you got it on the oven setting?'

'I don't know what you mean. I just turned it on and put it under the grill bit.'

'Look at the big knob, no not the one on your head, the one on the front of the oven.'

'Yeah I can see it, it's on pointing at the boxy thing.'

'Well it should be pointing at the other boxy thing that looks like it's got a saw on it, can you see that one?'

'Yep, got that one, so what do I do now?'

'Turn the knob to that setting and the toast will grill, that's the grill setting. Give it a couple of minutes and then the bread should start to toast. When it's toasted turn the bread over and toast the other side.'

Fay then lay back in the water and tried to have a soak without getting covered in foam all over her head and ending up looking like Father Christmas. Low and behold five minutes later Tag appeared at the door with the toast. Fay looked at his proud face as that was the first 'meal' he'd ever made Fay. But his bubble was soon burst when Fay asked where the hot chocolate was.

'Shit I knew there was something else, I tell you what this cooking is all go isn't it?' Tag said as he ran downstairs.

'You've only made toast Tag, next job will be making your 'packing-up' on Tuesday.'

'I'll go to the café with the lads,' shouted Tag.

'Well that'll have to stop now, we've got a baby on the way, café costs three times as much as packing-up yourself.'

Fay was doing it on purpose to try and make Tag crack but so far he'd passed the test with flying colours. She figured if she was really unreasonable and he didn't bat an eyelid then he was serious about marriage. Tag had to grow up and realise that he had been living a charmed life as far as things went. He was doing as he pleased, well that had to stop. Not only was he getting away with murder as far as going out and birding it, but he never did anything to help Fay around the house and she worked full time as well. It was pitiful he had never used the grill to make toast, if he wanted toast he went to his mother's or the café. He didn't know how to work the hoover or the washing machine. He had never been shopping in a supermarket before. This was all going to change and Fay thought why not start as I mean to go on and put him through his paces.

Tag eventually found the hot chocolate and had to read the instructions on the back, he put the required spoonfuls in the Cup and waited for the kettle to boil. He waited and waited but the kettle didn't even start to boil. So he felt it, it was stone cold. So he flicked the switch on but still nothing happened. It was only after about five minutes when he realised the kettle wasn't switched on at the mains. After about twenty minutes he made the chocolate and presented it to Fay who was ready to come out of the bath.

'Here is your hot chocolate Fay, hand prepared by myself' and Tag handed the cup over feeling rather proud of himself and looking for Fay's approval.

'What are you looking at?'

'Well what do you think?'

'What about?'

'The chocolate, how is it? Was the toast good?' Tag was bursting at the seams with pride.

'Look Tag the toast was toast and this is a cup of hot chocolate. Look I know you want to please me but you don't want me to assess everything you do surely, we'd both be driven round the bend by the end of the week. Look it may surprise you to know this but toast and hot chocolate are easy to make, wait while you make tea tomorrow night. By the way get your bag emptied, we'll need to put a wash on.'

'I'll do it Fay I'll get your stuff and put it in.' Tag rushed out of the bathroom and downstairs to get the bags.

'No, no you won't.'

Fay leapt out of the bath and ran after Tag with just a small towel around her. Tag was trying to find her bag and had just located it when Fay grabbed it from him. She was panting and Tag told her to sit down.

'Tag listen, we'll take one step at a time, now I think putting a wash load on is a bit much at this stage for you, so you jump in the foam bath and I'll do the washing and then the next time I put a wash on I'll show you what to do. Now I'll get a sticker for you for your chart I'm going to buy you and you can put it on the chart to say you can now make toast and hot chocolate.'

Fay looked at Tag to see if he had caught onto the fact she was taking the piss out of him, but Tag just trotted off to get a bath. Fay put the washing on and went upstairs to the bedroom to get dressed. Suddenly she heard Tag saying to himself, 'Cheeky cow' as the penny dropped and then he shouted out to Fay.

'Cheeky cow, you were taking the mickey out of me weren't you?'

'Who, me Tag? Never, how could I possibly do that,' Fay replied innocently.

Tag was laughing in the bath at how useless he was and how life would never be the same again.

'Do you think you'll cope with a baby Fay?' asked Tag.

'I will, I've had good practice living with you Tag. A baby would be a piece of cake compared to you,' Fay was as sharp as a tack with her answer.

'I think I preferred the old you, not so witty and mouthy.'

'Well mate forget her, she's long gone and never to return.' And she stuck two fingers up behind the bathroom door. Tag had his bath and then made himself some toast and a drink and they both went to bed and cuddled each other and fell fast asleep...

The bus had been quiet since they'd left the village mainly because everyone was knackered. They started to talk about how the atmosphere had changed in the pub from one of being hospitable to one of being hostile.

'How much do you reckon we spent in that last boozer Eddie?' asked Skip.

'With food I would say about £400. The price of a beer was dear but then you only had to look at the people in there, they were earning some cash, did you see the motors in the car park?'

'How much was it in the bar Doug?'

'It was exactly 35 pence cheaper per pint, I reckon that they put 20 pence on a pint because it's Sunday and none of those people drink in there midweek. They only go in for Sunday lunch, the football team told us. You go in there on a Saturday night the place is totally different with different people in.'

'Well, do you know those two posh birds with those rah rah twats?' Skip posed the question.

'Yes they were very nice young ladies and you lot shouldn't have been talking the way you were in front of them,' Eddie answered in disgust.

'Well Eddie my old chum, listen to this. Grant come over here with your little friend Mike.'

'What for, we're talking?' protested Grant.

'Come on, tell these lot about the two ladies from the pub,' Skip urged Grant to come over.

'What do you want to know?' asked Grant.

'Eddie said you shouldn't have been talking in front of the ladies about sex and that. What would you say to that young Grant?'

'Well Eddie they were a couple of slags believe me,' Grant informed Eddie.

'How do you know that then Grant?' asked Eddie.

'Well me and Mike shagged them in the toilets just before they left.'

'You did what?' shouted Jonesy at top of his voice, attracting the attention of everyone and waking most of them up.

'We shagged those two birds, the hot totty from the pub and they loved it.'

'Bullshit.' Thommo joined in the ranks of non-believers.

'Don't believe us then, I don't care but I went to toilet after they were powdering their noses and they grabbed me and took me into the ladies and sucked my dick. Then they told me to get Mike and meet them when they went to the ladies again. They went to the ladies, we followed and shagged them and then went back to the bar so as not to look suspicious. That's it believe it or not, I don't really care. Can we go now?' and Grant and Mike walked back and sat down where they had been trying to quietly get some sleep as they hadn't had much in the last 48 hours.

'Do you know what, I believe them. Those birds were getting really excited when they were telling the story of the Swedes,' said Tosser.

'How the fucking hell can those two pricks get their end away everywhere we go, I mean look at 'em, they're like two school kids.'

Thommo still couldn't get over the Friday night that had passed him by. It's a good job he didn't know it was them that supplied Trev with the laxatives to ruin his Friday and give him a sore arse all weekend. The subject soon changed as one of Skip's spotters who told him someone had broken the rules was telling him that someone was breaking the rules right now and just had to be punished.

It was Eddie who informed him that Greg had fallen asleep near the front of the bus. Skip came down with his bag of tricks and decided that Greg was going to have his head sprayed green. Slowly someone touched Greg's eyebrows to see if he moved, but there was no movement. So, very slowly and carefully Tosser began to spray Greg's head green and Greg didn't moved a muscle. The whole bus came to have a look at the 'poor man's incredible hulk'. When they'd finished Tosser stroked his eyebrows until he eventually woke up with a start.

'Piss off you lot, I wasn't asleep, I was kidding, you have to get up early to catch me out you bastards,' Greg moaned sleepily.

'You're right there Greg like fucking lightening you are,' Skip shouted trying not to laugh as Greg's head was all green - his hair, his ears and part of his face.

'What you lot laughing at?' shouted Greg.

'You and your belly button fetish,' Thommo shouted out. And all the lads at the back of the bus pulled up their shirts to reveal their belly buttons.

'Are we turning you on Greg?' said Daz as he fingered his belly button.

'Piss off, none of you would have done any different. Anyway it wasn't even my birthday and she was well dodgy. You wouldn't have touched her.'

'Well I wouldn't have kissed her belly button that's for sure,' replied Skip biting his lip at the sight of Greg's head and face.

'Are we going for a drink when we get back?' enquired Greg and it wasn't long before he got an answer.

'I fancy 'Green Man' or 'Green Bricks', how about you Eddie?' quipped Gaz, keeping a straight face.

'I think 'Land of Green Ginger' that sounds alright,' Thommo joined in.

'I think I'll go home for my tea, our lass has done me steak and chips with that sweetcorn what do they call it?' said Trev.

'Green giant,' answered Greg.

'Yeah that's the one Greg, Green giant - ho, ho, ho Green giant.'

Greg didn't have a clue about his face and soon there was to be another victim, this time it was just someone who worked with Eddie on the docks. He had come with his friend who had alerted Skip to the fact his mate was asleep. Usually the ones who weren't players or part of the club got away with falling asleep but on this occasion his mate spragged him and begged Skip to make him a victim. Skip came down with his bag of tricks to see what he could do to his victim. Was it going to be green head the second? Or could it be an eyebrow sacrifice? These seemed too extreme as they didn't even know the bloke's name, which happened to be Nigel.

Then, while rooting around in his bag, he noticed a roll of sellotape. Now what could he do with that? Now Nigel had fallen asleep with his head side on to the head rest and was facing in looking at the window, that's how his mate noticed him sleeping. So after the usual tests to see how asleep he really was - and he was in a deep sleep - Skip slowly and methodically sellotaped Nigel's head to the head rest so that it looked like a giant spider had got him in its web. His mate was crying with laughter and then Tosser brought the camera to take a photo for the album. Once the deed was done and Nigel's head was firmly stuck and everyone had been down for a look at him, they thought it would be funny to wake him up. So his mate Dave decided he wanted to do it. Dave was trying to calm himself down but after five minutes he bent down and shouted in Nige's ear.

'Fire! fire! quick Nige the bus is on fire.'

Poor Nige struggled unsuccessfully to get free and wondered what the hell was going on with his head. At first he thought he was dreaming and then through the sellotape that was half stopping him from speaking but not from breathing came the muffled sounds of 'Help me! Help me!' He sounded like a ventriloquist's dummy stuck in a box. He couldn't see there was about 20 people around him and all he could hear was laughter and the only thing he could see was a flashing light now and again, which was Tosser with his camera.

He finally twigged that they'd stuck his head to the headrest and eventually, once everyone had poked fun at him, Skip got some scissors and cut him free. Whilst he was doing so he was explaining that he had been hired by Dave his mate to do the job and it was in no way his idea. Nige took it in good faith and was eventually freed to a round of applause and cheers and cries of 'Speech, speech'. To everyone's surprise he got to his feet and faced the back of the bus, but no one knew what to expect as no one really knew him. The bus was deadly silent.

'I would just like to thank you all for a cracking weekend, it's been brilliant and you lads have let us tag along with you and you don't even know us really. Me and Dave have had the best time and you boys take some beating and we will be coming next year. By the way I will be suing for the trauma just caused by the sellotape. I was dreaming I was in a fire and then when Dave shouted 'Fire' I thought oh shit and then when I couldn't move my head I thought I was still dreaming. One last thing, could I have a copy of the photo please whoever took it, cheers,' and Nige sat down.

The lads all clapped him and took the piss but deep down they were really rather humbled by the fact that they had given someone a great weekend without even trying. Then it was back to showing Greg their belly buttons and asking him if he was turned on. Greg told them all to piss off and that none of them would have touched her, as she was definitely a junkie as they could see the track marks up her arm and the boyfriend sat at the bar was shifty too.

The boys were a bit more lively and had got a second wind and were now looking for mischief, then as the bus was approaching the Peterborough area, Matt had an idea.

'Skip have you got any sellotape left?'

'Yeah ! Two rolls. I used to be a boyscout, always come prepared. Why what mental thing have you got in mind?'

'A record attempt,' announced Matt.

'What record?' asked Jonesy.

'Well from Leicester to Hull, Daz here rode the bus naked and that's the record. And I think someone should try and break it.'

'And why do you need the sellotape?'

'I just thought we could sellotape up the person for a laugh.'

So Matt stood up and asked who would like to break a world record and travel from where they were to Hull, naked, and beat the previous record of Leicester to Hull?' Matt didn't mention the sellotape bit.

'I'll do it,' shouted Damo with great enthusiasm.

'Come to the back of the bus to the record panel then,' Skip told Damo and then gave instructions to grab him as soon as he had his gear off and get the tape on him. Damo was bounding to the back of the bus and started to take his gear off.

'Don't show Greg your belly button, he'll get a hard on' said Matt.

'Fuck off Matt, you aren't funny,' snapped Greg but as he turned around about ten blokes all started to finger their belly buttons and Greg just turned his green head around to face the front. They then grabbed Damo who hardly put up a struggle and began to tape his hairy body. This was all well and good until Daz came up with the bizarre idea to tape up his knackers.

'Not the cream crackers, please!' Damo pleaded but to no avail, it had already been done as they wound the tape all around his body. He looked like he was covered in cling film.

'I bet you're green with envy Greg aren't you about not being able to grab his button?'

Matt was pushing it now. Greg just looked and Matt got the message and shut up. Damo was still slightly pissed and was in a bit of pain so God knows what he'd be like when the tape had to come off. At first Damo thought it was funny until it dawned on him he would be having a couple of hours of it. It wasn't long before the bus then pulled off the motorway for a toilet stop and some food for those who hadn't eaten at the pub.

'Damo, do you want anything from the shop?' asked Trev who was the only one who was left on the bus as the rest piled off leaving Damo sellotaped up.

'Can you go in my pocket and get a fiver out and get me a KFC with a coke please Trev. Oh and can you hold my cock while I have a piss?' Trev just looked as though his jaw was going to drop off and before he could tell Damo to fuck off, Damo stopped him by saying he was joking.

'Only joking mate I only want a KFC, but you can still hold my cock if you like.' And Damo winked as Trev just smiled back. In the service station the lads were tired and weary and still had a couple of hours left before they reached home. They had nearly spent up and were just trying to stay awake, actually some of them were getting some shut eye on the seats at the KFC.

It was at this point that a rather lively Doug started to sing at the top of his voice. He had been drinking from a bottle of whiskey he'd found in his bag that he'd forgotten he had. He stood on a chair and everyone just ignored him at first, then he called for everyone's attention.

'Listen everyone, I have a song to sing and it goes like this,' and Doug started singing his song to a captivated audience. It went like this...

'Rambling Rose, Rambling Rose
Drop your knickers, Touch your toes
Part your sweet lips, Heaven knows
Here's my big dick, My rambling Rose'

Doug then fell off the chair and rolled over and then got straight back up again and walked back to the bus, leaving everyone stunned at what they'd just witnessed. All the lads started laughing and wondered what all that was about. The few people who were in the services looked as bemused as the lads.

'What the hell's he been on?' Skip asked Eddie.

'Whiskey I think but I'll get it off him or he'll be a fucking nightmare when we get back to Hull.'

'Right lads let's go, last leg,' Eddie called all the lads to get back on the bus. He rounded all the strays up and off they went for the final leg of the journey back home and ultimately the end of the 1992 London Wembley trip...

Everyone was back on the bus and as Eddie had successfully got Doug's whiskey from him, it seemed the final hours would be quiet ones, until Skip came up with one final game.

'Right from now on and for the next half hour it's got to be Kenneth Williams impressions.'

'Who's Kenneth Williams?' asked Grant.

'Don't you students know anything? He's from the 'Carry On' films. He's the one who says, 'Oh matron,' now do you know him?' asked Jonesy. Grant just nodded but decided to keep quiet as he wasn't sure who the hell they were on about.

Damo was at the back eating his chicken and it finally dawned on him how much pain he was going to be in when he took the tape off.

'Here - I'm in bloody agony - how the hell did anyone sit with this tape all over them when they set the record?' asked Damo.

'They never,' replied Matt.

'Well what's the record then?' asked a puzzled Damo.

'Daz travelled naked, not naked with his body in tape, just naked,' explained Matt.

'So you mean to tell me I can take the tape off?'

'If you like, we were wondering why you had left it on so long. That's going to hurt when it comes off though, rather you than me,' laughed Matt.

'You pommie bastards, you've had me haven't you?'

'Looks like it, yeah. Now then, for calling us pommie bastards I reckon we de-tape him lads, what do ya think?' asked Skip, to which everyone agreed, apart from Damo of course but he was in no position to argue.

'Right, we'll have a vote, raise your hands if you don't want to take the tape off Damo?'

Damo tried to put his hand up.

'Now all those in favour of us taking the tape off raise your hands.' Everyone raised their hands.

'Well Damo, sorry mate but we live in a democratic society and the people have spoken. We shall de-tape Damo.'

They all started to pull at the tape and within five minutes it had all come off, some of it with parts of his skin still attached. Damo screamed blue murder when his genitals had been tugged at and the pubic hair was slowly removed. In the end he stopped struggling and let them get on with it. He looked like a sheep that had been sheared by a blind shearer. He had patches of hair poking out and chunks of hair missing. Damo was pretty sore as he took his seat at the back.

'Give in Damo?' asked Daz who still held the record.

'No fucking way after all that I've been through,' came the cry from a defiant Damo sat at the back of the bus, his body throbbing with pain.

'I don't know what he's doing it for, the idiot, he's going to get nothing out of it,' Daz whispered to Matt.

'I know, I think he imagines he's going into the world record books but Norris McWhirter isn't here.'

The Kenneth Williams' half-hour was up and so for the last few miles Frankie Howard took over 'oh yes' he did. Again Grant asked who he was and this time Skip just looked at him as if to say, you are a stupid boy.

'Look, how are we supposed to talk like him if we don't know who he is?' asked Mike.

'Well he used to talk like this and say stuff like 'Oh yes missus, no missus, Up Pompeii and all that. Oh well I never,' explained Skip in a rather weak impersonation, which was the idea of it for a bit of fun.

'Sounds hilarious, not!' said a sarcastic Grant.

'Alright then from now on it can be either Frankie Howard, Frank Spencer, Eddie Waring or Sean Connery. There you are you two must at least know one of them?'

'Is Eddie Waring the 'up and under' fella?' asked Grant.

'Look you're only a bit younger than me and I know all those people, don't you have a telly in your house? Right Eddie Waring 'up and under', Frank Spencer 'um Betty, the cats done a whoopsy on the carpet' and Sean Connery is James Bond 'shaken not stirred', got it?' ranted Thommo. The two lads just nodded and thought silence was the best policy.

At first there was a flurry of sound as everyone got their impressions going and then there was a lull as they nearly reached home. The signs were 'counting down' the miles to Hull and they were around 15 miles away. Then came that wonderful sight that greets anyone from the area who wants to get home, The Humber Bridge, all lit up and looking fantastic.

'Nearly there boys, who's for last orders?' asked Tosser.

Only a few mumbled that they would go for one last drink. The realisation of the fact that it was the end of the trip had dawned on them and all they wanted to do was go home, they'd had enough.

At least Eddie could relax for the first time in three days. He had loved every minute of it and agreed to have a drink with the boys. They could stay out a bit as it was the Bank holiday the next day and they didn't have to go to work, and they could reminisce about what had happened in the last 72 hours.

Eddie went around with the hat for the driver, the lads were pretty generous as always, and the driver thanked them for a great weekend. In fact, it was always a great weekend for the driver as although they hired him for the weekend, they never used him. He was supposed to take then to Wembley on the day of the game but they all got the tube and he was supposed to drive them all over but the lads just told him not to bother. So the driver got a weekend in London on pay but did no work, so therefore he loved it as he could have a drink and 'join' the trip.

The bus drove through the City centre and then onto Holderness Road and dropped-off the lads who wanted dropping off - which was most of them - at Shoey's pub. It then carried on to the Willows Club where the whole trip had started three days earlier.

Shoey was behind the bar serving himself as they had just got back and for a brief moment it was like the old George. All the lads went in for a drink except Trev, Jonno and Tom. They went home as they had had enough and wanted to get home to see wives and family. The two students only went in because Skip lent them a couple of quid to get a drink. When they told their tale a few freebees came their way, as no one could believe it. However, it was confirmed by everyone that they had pulled two stunners in London and another two birds in a country pub. As it happened, word got around and Shaz and Charlie were in and they told the story of Tag and Fay, which had everyone transfixed. But they soon got off the story as they wanted to get to know the two 'studs' better. Two weeks before hand Grant was trying to chat up Shaz at the club but she told him he was just a spotty twat of a student, but now the boot was on the other foot.

'Would you like a drink Grant?' asked Shaz.

'Go on then I mean I'm only a spotty twat of a student but I do like a drink, go on I'll have a lager and Mike what do you want?'

Grant could see Shaz's face, thinking cheeky bastard I only asked you. But he figured that two beers could cover the spotty student slur. Shaz was barking up the wrong tree, as Grant didn't like her one bit after she slagged him off and humiliated him. He wasn't stupid and he knew that if he did take her home then it would be all over town. Mike was getting on well with Charlie though and they seemed to be hitting it off.

One by one the party of 'Wembley Warriors' fell away and went home. Greg fell asleep in the corner at a table looking like a shagged-out, incredible hulk. Skip and Tosser as ever inseparable, went for a take away and a taxi and Eddie bid everyone a fond farewell as his other half turned up to give him a lift home.

Grant and Mike didn't end up shagging Shaz and Charlie, although Mike did arrange a date with Charlie for later in the week. Shaz was hoping that Grant was going to make it a foursome but he wasn't so forthcoming.

They all eventually got home and met back up with families and told the tales of a legendary trip, one that would go down in the folklore of the club...

The dust had settled and as they met at training on the Tuesday. They relived the events of the weekend and all the things they'd done. Pete was pissed off as he had missed it all.

Grant was given a new respect from his fellow players and was loving the attention, he had gone from being a twat of a student to the hunk of the team and his confidence soared. Women were looking at him in a different way at Uni and it seemed every girl he asked out said 'yes'.

Tag was at training and got the third degree about what had gone on. The main view was that he was a jammy get and should cherish this chance to make something of a life with Fay. At work he had seen Suki clearing her desk out as she was leaving and he took the time to apologise profoundly about what a tosser he'd been. She accepted this and they left on speaking terms, with a few tears from Suki.

Greg eventually got the green out of his hair but had a hell of a job getting it off his face. His wife went berserk when she saw him as they were due to go to the coast on the Monday but Greg couldn't go because of his green head.

Damo got his clothes back and was still sore for days after his botched waxing. He still holds the record though and probably will do for a long time. That all-important record of travelling naked for the longest amount of time, I mean they're hardly queuing up to break that record are they?

All the others got back to normality by the end of the week as the alcohol had knocked them for six up until about Thursday. On the Thursday Eddie came around for the subscriptions and asked who wanted to pay a deposit for the following year's trip.

They all paid their deposits a few weeks later to go the final again in 11 months time. They didn't know which two teams would compete in it, but they didn't care, and neither did the other thousands of rugby league people. All they cared about was upholding the tradition of the packed house at Wembley. All they wanted was to be there. Their grandfathers and fathers had gone on the trips for years and now they would keep the tradition alive and who knows their team might get there.

They only really cared about the trip because it was always something very special. For three days they were kids again having fun with their mates. The trip did wonders for the team, they won the league and two cups in the following month and that was partly down to the team spirit the trip brought out.

Within a month of them returning home, the next trip was fully booked and they were excited about what would happen on that one, at least this time Pete wouldn't get chicken pox. And as soon as Eddie had all the deposits in, he booked the next trip, this time promising the lads a toilet on the bus.

Thommo never found out who gave him the laxatives and still thinks it was something he ate.

The curtain had come down on another season and as they went into the summer break and although they had won loads of trophies, it was the trip that was still the main talking point.

What an adventure they had...

Would you like to be a Wembley Warrior?

Do you think you've got what it takes?

Get yourself down to a pub or club that runs a trip and book yourself on it.

You won't regret it.

SEE YOU NEXT YEAR...